Praise for the futuristic fantasy of
Robin D. Owens

Heart Change

"The story accelerates as new dangers to Avellana crop up, and the relationship between Signet and Cratag develops, making for a satisfying read."
—*Booklist*

"Each story is as fresh and new as the first one was. I am always delighted when a new Heart book is published!"
—*Fresh Fiction*

"A satisfying return to an intriguing world. Cratag and Signet will leave you wanting more."
—*The Romance Reader*

Heart Fate

"A superb romantic fantasy filled with heart."
—*Midwest Book Review*

"A touching tale of learning to trust again . . . Even for readers unfamiliar with the Heart world, Owens makes it easily accessible and full of delightful conceits."
—*Publishers Weekly*

"A true delight to read, and it should garner new fans for this unique and enjoyable series."
—*Booklist*

"[This] emotionally rich tale blends paranormal abilities, family dynamics, and politics; adds a serious dash of violence; and dusts it all with humor and whimsy . . . Intriguing."
—*Library Journal*

Heart Dance

"The latest Heart fantasy is one of the best of this superior series . . . retaining the freshness of its heartfelt predecessors."
—*The Best Reviews*

continued . . .

"I look forward to my yearly holiday in Celta, always a dangerous and fascinating trip."
—*Fresh Fiction*

"Sensual, riveting, and filled with the wonderful cast of characters from previous books, as well as some new ones, *Heart Dance* is exquisite in its presentation."
—*Romance Reviews Today*

Heart Choice

"The romance is passionate, the characters engaging, and the society and setting exquisitely crafted."
—*Booklist*

"Maintaining the 'world building' for science fiction and character driven plot for romance is near impossible. Owens does it brilliantly."
—*Romance Reader Connection*

"Well written, humor-laced, intellectually and emotionally involving story, which explores the true meaning of family and love."
—*Library Journal*

Heart Duel

"[A] sexy story . . . Readers will enjoy revisiting this fantasy-like world filled with paranormal talents."
—*Booklist*

"An exhilarating love story . . . The delightful story line is cleverly executed . . . Owen proves once again that she is among the top rung of fantasy romance authors with this fantastic tale."
—*Midwest Book Review*

"With engaging characters, Robin D. Owens takes readers back to the magical world of Celta . . . The characters are engaging, drawing the reader into the story and into their lives."
—*Romance Reviews Today*

Heart Thief

"I loved *Heart Thief*! This is what futuristic romance is all about. Robin D. Owens writes the kind of futuristic romance we've all been waiting to read; certainly the kind that I've been waiting for. She provides a wonderful, gripping mix of passion, exotic futuristic settings, and edgy suspense. If you've been waiting for someone to do futuristic romance right, you're in luck, Robin D. Owens is the author for you."
—Jayne Castle

HeartMate

Winner of the 2002 RITA Award
for Best Paranormal Romance
by the Romance Writers of America

Titles by Robin D. Owens

HEARTMATE
HEART THIEF
HEART DUEL
HEART CHOICE
HEART QUEST
HEART DANCE
HEART FATE
HEART CHANGE
HEART JOURNEY
HEART SEARCH

Anthologies

WHAT DREAMS MAY COME
(with Sherrilyn Kenyon and Rebecca York)

Heart Search

Robin D. Owens

B

BERKLEY SENSATION, NEW YORK

THE BERKLEY PUBLISHING GROUP
Published by the Penguin Group
Penguin Group (USA) Inc.
375 Hudson Street, New York, New York 10014, USA
Penguin Group (Canada), 90 Eglinton Avenue East, Suite 700, Toronto, Ontario M4P 2Y3, Canada
(a division of Pearson Penguin Canada Inc.)
Penguin Books Ltd., 80 Strand, London WC2R 0RL, England
Penguin Group Ireland, 25 St. Stephen's Green, Dublin 2, Ireland (a division of Penguin Books Ltd.)
Penguin Group (Australia), 250 Camberwell Road, Camberwell, Victoria 3124, Australia
(a division of Pearson Australia Group Pty. Ltd.)
Penguin Books India Pvt. Ltd., 11 Community Centre, Panchsheel Park, New Delhi—110 017, India
Penguin Group (NZ), 67 Apollo Drive, Rosedale, Auckland 0632, New Zealand
(a division of Pearson New Zealand Ltd.)
Penguin Books (South Africa) (Pty.) Ltd., 24 Sturdee Avenue, Rosebank, Johannesburg 2196,
South Africa

Penguin Books Ltd., Registered Offices: 80 Strand, London WC2R 0RL, England

This book is an original publication of The Berkley Publishing Group.

PRINTING HISTORY
Berkley Sensation trade paperback edition / August 2011

Library of Congress Cataloging-in-Publication Data

Owens, Robin D.
    Heart search / Robin D. Owens.—Berkley Sensation trade pbk. ed.
       p. cm.
    ISBN 978-0-425-24138-7 (trade pbk.)
    I. Title.
    PS3615.W478H47 2011
    813'.6—dc22   2011014835

PRINTED IN THE UNITED STATES OF AMERICA

10   9   8   7   6   5   4   3   2   1

To Cindy and Deidre.
Thank you.

Characters

Calendula (Signet) D'Marigold: The last of the GrandHouse of the Marigolds, Signet has great but unknown Flair.

The Hawthorns:

GreatLord Huathe (Laev) T'Hawthorn: Head of the Hawthorns, a widower who made a bad mistake in wedding a woman who he thought was his HeartMate.

Nivea Sunflower Hawthorn: Laev's late wife.

Brazos: Laev's Familiar companion, a young long-haired black cat. Son of Black Pierre, once the companion to Laev's FatherSire (Grandfather), but now the cook's cat.

Cratag Maytree T'Marigold: Distant kin of the Hawthorns, like an elder brother to Laev, now married to Signet D'Marigold. (*Heart Change*)

Cal Marigold: Cratag and Signet's four-year-old son, who has interesting memories.

Alma Hawthorn: Housekeeper of the great intelligent house, T'Hawthorn Residence.

Camellia Darjeeling, Her Family and Friends:

Camellia Darjeeling: Owner of Darjeeling's Teahouse and Darjeeling's HouseHeart. As a girl of thirteen, she spoke up during a legal case regarding a shipwreck and requested the salvager look for a priceless fifty-piece tea set. The set was discovered and Camellia sold one piece to finance her businesses.

Mica: Camellia's young calico FamCat.

Senchal Darjeeling: Camellia's brother.

Guri T'Darjeeling: Camellia's father.

Takvar Darjeeling: Camellia's uncle.

Glyssa Licorice: One of Camellia's two best friends. Glyssa is the daughter of the Licorices who run the PublicLibrary system, and is endlessly curious and an excellent researcher. She has a secret regarding her HeartMate.

Tiana Mugwort: Camellia's other best friend. Tiana is studying to become a priestess and has a secret regarding her home.

Artemisia (Mugwort) Ginseng: Tiana's sister, a Healer, four years older than Camellia, Glyssa, and Tiana. She was a girlhood friend of Laev's late wife, Nivea Sunflower, whom Nivea dropped when she married well.

Others:

Jasmine Ash: Daughter of GreatLord T'Ash, journeywoman student to Laev.

GreatLord Rand T'Ash: Jeweler/blacksmith, T'Ash has the premier testing stones to discover a person's Flair. (*HeartMate*)

GreatLady Danith Mallow D'Ash: HeartMate of T'Ash, Danith is an animal Healer and the person who usually matches intelligent animal companions, Fams, with people. (*HeartMate*)

Garrett Primross: A private investigator hired by Laev to find missing Hawthorn treasures.

SupremeJudge Ailim Elder: The highest judge in the land and wed to Ruis Elder, the Captain of the grounded starship, *Nuada's Sword*. (*Heart Thief*)

Dani Eve Elder: Daughter of Ruis and Ailim Elder, a Null, a person who suppresses psi abilities, or Flair.

Tinne Holly: Younger son of the GreatLord, he owns and operates the Green Knight Fencing and Fighting Salon.

GreatLord Nuin T'Vine (Vinni): The prophet of Celta.

GreatLord Heather: The retired premier Healer of Celta.

GraceLord Cymb Lemongrass: Camellia's sparring partner.

Aquilaria: Manager of Darjeeling's Teahouse.

Acacia Bluegum: Former Druidan guardswoman, she's set up her own sparring salon and wants to expand it to a social club.

241 RANGE

GREAT WASHINGTON
BOGHOLE

DRUIDA

HARD ROCK MTNS

GAEL CITY

GREAT
PLATTE
OCEAN

DEEP
BLUE SEA

BRITTANY

CELTA

One

Laev Hawthorn, GreatLord T'Hawthorn, didn't think the intelligent house he lived in had forgiven him for marrying the wrong woman. The Residence was cool to him, both physically and emotionally. Tough to blame the house, though, when Laev was still cleaning up the resulting mess of the mistake he'd made when he was seventeen.

He was thirty-one now, and new evidence of Nivea's selfishness had been revealed when Laev's FatherSire had died three months ago.

She'd stolen Family heirlooms. More, she'd hidden or given away the HeartGift Laev had offered her when they'd first wed. Since she'd been dead for two years, he couldn't ask her what she'd done with the items. His FatherSire had been protecting him from the knowledge of how low his wife had stooped. Now Laev could only continue to fix the problems resulting from his marriage.

Yes, the room was cooler than he cared for. His grief was deeper than he'd have ever imagined. The Residence and the Family were caught in a rut, running on tradition.

Perhaps when he retrieved the heirlooms, that act being his first real contribution to the Family as the GreatLord, he could shake everyone out of the torpor.

The Residence sent the echo of a banging door. An exuberant breeze seemed to rush toward Laev. He smiled. Or perhaps he could just encourage his journeywoman to chip away at the present stasis.

His student, who was like the younger sister he'd always wanted, had arrived for her morning lesson in finance and estate building. It took real effort to slam a door in the Residence, but Jasmine Ash always managed. And it always amused him. She'd stop at the kitchens for a treat and to stroke Black Pierre, the old Familiar companion cat who'd survived Laev's FatherSire's death.

No time now for Laev to send his psi power, his Flair, out to search for his HeartGift. He was glad to abandon the futile exercise.

On to the standard workday. He authorized an anonymous donation to the Saille House of Orphans, then moved the holosphere detailing a current project to the center of his desk.

The door to his den slammed open and Jasmine rushed into the room, small and fine boned and fifteen, with a scowl on her face. Her short dark brown hair was windblown, her blue gaze sharp. "Brood, brood, brood." She shook a finger at him. "You know I come from a household that has forbidden brooding."

It always surprised Laev that this exuberant girl was the daughter of taciturn T'Ash and quiet Danith D'Ash.

"You need to forget that *flitch* of a wife and get on with living."

"Stop right there." He cared nothing for Nivea or her memory, but cared a great deal about his honor and she'd been his wife.

He and Jasmine locked gazes. Hers dropped. He modulated his tone. "Easier said than done." Laev felt a thousand years older than her. "And why have you brought up the subject?"

"It's Nuin," she said, referring to her older brother. "He's going through his Second Passage, fever dreams that free his magic. Like you were when you made that unfortunate decision to marry the fl—Nivea."

"Jasmine," Laev warned.

His student huffed. "Nuin's acting weird and I can see how it happened, which I couldn't before, but, really, it's been two years since your wife died." She stopped and swallowed. The sickness that had swept through Druida City had taken the old and the young and Jasmine had lost grovestudy friends. Laev had lost Nivea, but they'd been estranged, living in separate suites.

Unknown to all, the sickness had weakened his FatherSire's heart.

Before Jasmine could continue, Laev said, "What of your assignments?" He tried to make it an easy question. He could still recall being a young child and standing stiffly in front of his father and FatherSire reporting on the activities of his day.

Jasmine sniffed and set a holosphere on his desk, flung herself into the winged chair embroidered with the dragonflies she preferred, and grinned. "The new bio-liquid technique for saffron farming that I researched was good. My investment quadrupled!"

He lifted a brow. "Our investment."

She sat up straight. "You put money in, too?"

"Of course. You convinced me months ago that the deal was sound."

"Then you got the funds today and already knew." She sounded deflated.

"Yes, but hearing you tell me was the best part of the morning. Excellent job, Jasmine."

With one last wiggle, she settled into the chair and nodded to the folder on his desk. "The first quarter of this year I have made more than the amount I'll receive as NobleGilt from the Council when I come of age in two years."

"You're well on your way to succeeding in your personal goals. I think it's time I speak with your father about allotting some of the Ash Family funds to you to invest."

"Really!" Her voice rose to a high squeak, her blue eyes sparkled.

"Yes."

She began hyperventilating and put her head between her knees, her voice came muffled. "Thank you, *so* much. Father doesn't like handling the Family finances, and the sooner I can take that over, the better. He's very conservative."

"I'll ask your father to give you a quarter of his funds," Laev said.

Face flushed, Jasmine bobbed back up. "A third."

"A quarter. I'll give him a report of your last two years' investments and my personal opinion on your progress as a financial estate manager." Laev slanted her a look. "You will write the report. Include graphs. Don't manipulate the figures, I'll know if you do. Make sure it's thorough." He waved. "Again, excellent job. You're dismissed for the morning."

She nodded and went to the door of a small office off his den. So she planned on working here instead of at home. He admitted he'd like the company.

He activated a holosphere about an airship venture he was considering. All in all, Jasmine was more conservative than himself. But she'd been brought up by T'Ash and D'Ash, both very aware of the value of gilt, and with the ingrained idea that the Family fortune must be preserved and grow and must not be put at risk. Gilt was important to them, but the bedrock of that Family was love.

He'd been raised by his father and FatherSire who weren't averse to wagering a great deal to win a great deal, always knowing that their Family fortune was secure. Plans for increasing their wealth and influence had always been paramount for the Hawthorns. The men had been demanding guardians, always pushing for success, with little affection between them. He wouldn't be like them in that.

"You should get married again. Consult with a matchmaker to find your HeartMate," Jasmine said.

She'd caught him off guard and inwardly he flinched. Everyone knew his mistake, that he'd disappointed his Family. Tendrils of past guilt and shame snapped like lashes. He quashed them as always. "Over the line, Jasmine."

Jasmine wrapped her arms around herself and shivered. "Brrrr," she said. "You can really freeze someone with that gaze. You look just like your FatherSire when he was displeased, like when you took me on as an apprentice."

"Long time ago and I'm waiting for an apology."

Her head dropped. "Sorry." She shifted from foot to foot and he knew her outburst wasn't just about him. He gestured her back to the chair.

"What's the problem?"

Blinking rapidly she took the seat, whipped a softleaf from her sleeve pocket, and mopped her eyes. "It's Nuin. His Passage fugues to free his Flair, his magic, are so big and intense and scary." She shuddered.

Laev rose from his own seat, went to the no-time drink storage, and pulled out steaming hot cocoa with a swirl of white mousse. He handed the mug to Jasmine, weighing his words. He'd always been honest with her. "The greater the Flair, the stronger Passage is."

She sipped, nodded, and looked up at him from under spiky lashes. "Dad and Mom are taking turns being with Nuin, but they have a Healer and a couple of fire mages, too," Jasmine whispered. "Nuin's always had fire psi. They've stripped his bedroom of nearly everything. No one's died in Passage for a long time, right?"

"I haven't heard of anyone." Laev infused confidence into his voice. Families would usually keep such an occurrence a secret.

Again she drank her cocoa, slurping a little. "Mother and Father are HeartMates. Second Passage is when you first link with a Heart-Mate, right? In sexy dreams?"

Laev supposed Jasmine needed reassurance that common knowledge was true. He took his chair, kept his manner cool and voice matter-of-fact. "That's right. If there is a woman or man out there that you can bond with emotionally, physically, spiritually—one made for you, Second Passage is important. That's when your mind and emotions spiral out to connect with your mate."

Jasmine shifted again, this time in her chair. "And you make a HeartGift." She stared at him. Everyone knew Laev had made a HeartGift—and given it to the wrong woman.

"How does that work?" Jasmine asked.

"I'm sure your parents told you," Laev said.

"Well, yes, before Nuin's Passage, but I wasn't paying attention, and now they're concerned and I don't want to bother them."

He was never supposed to have to talk about sex with Jasmine. That was a deal he'd made with her parents. Too bad she trusted him for answers.

He tapped his fingers together, one of his FatherSire's mannerisms, which would age him even more in her eyes. Just an older brother-figure. For a moment he thought of her real older brother, Nuin, felt the echoes of his own hot passion for his HeartMate during Second Passage. No. All his problems stemmed from that mistake when he was seventeen.

"I don't recall exactly making the HeartGift during my Passage." Just the connection, the lust, the need to imprint a sculpture with all that he was, pour all his Flair and energy into it. It reflected his deepest self at the time. And it was gone.

"Laev?"

He jerked his mind back to the girl in front of him. She'd bounced back already, sure her brother would be fine, years from her own Second Passage. Still wanting answers.

"Most people don't recall making a HeartGift." He knew that for a truth. "You have just enough knowledge and control not to hurt yourself during the fever dream. There's an urgency to make the gift."

Jasmine grimaced. "Well, Nuin is a glass artist. Dad cleared out most of Nuin's sitting room and set up a workshop for him instead, for him to make his HeartGift."

"Your father's a wise and pragmatic man."

The girl rolled a shoulder, then leaned back and drank her cocoa in silence. After a minute, she nodded, hopped to her feet, and translocated the mug to the cleanser. When she smiled at him, it was brilliant. "Everything will be fine."

"I'm sure it will."

"And everyone thinks Nuin has a HeartMate. And being a HeartMate is wonderful." Enthusiasm laced her voice.

"So they say," he replied drily.

She lifted her chin. "I *know*. I see it every day with Mother and Father. You just need—"

"Jasmine—" he warned.

"—companionship. If you don't want to look for your Heart-Mate right now, why don't I ask my mother to find you a Familiar animal companion?"

"I have a Fam, Black Pierre," Laev said. He would never want another wife, a HeartMate supposedly made for him or not.

"He was your FatherSire's Fam. He's old and sleeps in the kitchen all day. I think he's the chef's Fam now."

She was right. That realization had pain splintering through Laev. Nothing he'd show her. His throat tightened and he scraped words from it. "The morning is going downhill."

Jasmine winced. "I'm sorry, but you're too lonely, and I love you as much as my own dad."

"I'm considerably younger and I don't need companions." He felt his gaze frost again. "There are fifty Hawthorns working in this Residence."

"Which of them are you really close to?" she asked softly. When he didn't answer, and the silence became strained, she looked at the door to her office, then at him. She inhaled deeply and marched back to his desk. Picking up a card from the "invitation" basket that Laev emptied every week, she flipped it in front of him. "You should go to this party tonight."

He glanced at the card that was an odd shade of gray and had artistically ragged edges. "The Salvage Ball." He grunted. "What is this?"

"It's more of a party than a ball, I hear. We Ashes are not invited. We did not have any investments or property in the merchant ship that went down centuries ago and was salvaged in '07."

Laev stiffened. He didn't care to be reminded of the trial regarding that ship. That had been the day he'd first seen—and fallen for—Nivea. But he recalled that Nivea had gone to the Salvage Ball though he never had.

Jasmine said, "And be sure to take an ugly item from your storage rooms. Everyone does. That's what makes the party unique."

"Ah." He glanced at the holosphere he'd been studying.

"Life isn't just about business," Jasmine said. "It's about love and Family, too."

"I have enough Family." And he didn't believe in love.

Jasmine stared at him from under lowered brows but said

nothing to refute that. He figured her Family had sayings about love as much as brooding, and he didn't want to hear them.

But again she tapped the Salvage Ball card. "And you should go to this one because more than just FirstFamily nobles will be there. This one could be fun. Go. Act like Laev instead of GreatLord T'Hawthorn." She offered him a sunny smile. "I know you can do it." Then she said, "I'll work on that report now." She actually went into her office and shut the door behind her.

He rubbed the cheap papyrus of the card. At the party there would be items a household didn't want . . .

Could Nivea have taken Hawthorn property there? She might have, to hurt him and the Hawthorns. Just give away their heirlooms.

She might have hated him enough to do that by the time she'd died. That hurt, but it was his own fault that he hadn't worked at his marriage after the first few years. He cared for Jasmine—as a younger sister or a daughter—more than he had for Nivea after his infatuation had worn off.

His chest was tight. The girl made him feel. More, she made him understand his current circumstances. He *was* lonely. But he didn't want a Fam. And he didn't trust his judgement in choosing another woman to be his wife again.

Even if he ever found his HeartMate.

*C*amellia Darjeeling stood behind the counter of her tearoom, surveying it for perfection, and grinned. Finally, finally, the dream she'd striven for was coming true. This was her *second* teahouse. A tearoom, shop, and gathering place.

It was only one cozy room, but it was full of customers. The atmosphere was almost hushed, the three servers unhurried.

She moved into the room, walked toward a table to talk to patrons—a woman and a man who were often at her first place, Darjeeling's Teahouse. From their expressions she was sure they liked her new tearoom, and some tension eased. "Welcome to Dar-jeeling's HouseHeart. I'm glad you came."

"Different than the teahouse, but nice," the man said.

"Serene," the upper-middle-class woman agreed.

"Thank you. I wanted serene." Business was great, if it only stayed that way once the novelty wore off. Darjeeling's HouseHeart had opened at the beginning of the week.

"I think you have another hit," he said.

Camellia let out a quiet breath. "That's good to hear."

"You really modeled this place after a HouseHeart?" asked the woman.

"Yes. I did a lot of research," Camellia said. Since only the old-est of the houses on Celta—usually FirstFamily Residences who were sentient beings—had HouseHearts, her tearoom drew in every-one who wanted to know what a HouseHeart looked like, or experience the ambience of the innermost ritual space of a house.

The walls were windowless—a detriment to the space that Camellia had turned into an advantage—and of various shades of brown, roughly plastered and cavelike. Everyone knew House-Hearts were hidden under the Residences, so cavelike made sense.

Inserts in the corners rounded the room. Light was just low enough to be flattering, provided by several spell-lights glowing like miniature suns. High in the north wall was a ventilating shaft with an ornate grill that also let in natural sunlight.

"I like how you included the four elements," the woman said.

"Everyone knows a HouseHeart has all the elements," said the man. "I like the fireplace in the south wall." The fireplace was fash-ioned to look rough and worn into the rock, natural rather than man-made. On this warm late spring day, the flames were small.

The woman laughed. "I prefer the round pool in the middle. That copper lily fountain is fabulous." She gave a little cough. "I wouldn't have thought to have floating copper flowers. The sound when they bump against each other is lovely, just lovely. I like the water sound, too. I have this entryway . . . Might I ask the artist?"

"Enea of Yerba Lane."

The man raised a brow at the woman, who was fussing with her napkin. He glanced up at Camellia. "Good of you to give your sources."

Camellia chuckled. "Everything Enea does is unique."

"Thank you." The woman gazed around again, her forehead creased. "Lovely place, wonderful atmosphere." She breathed in and her nose twitched and her lips pushed in and out as she studied the sculpted greeniron tubs on either side of the door that held lush plants. The greenery climbed toward the ceiling on trellises in the same pattern as the ventilation shaft above the plant life.

"Very, very lovely," the woman said. She eyed the long shelves lined with jars of tea. Behind the counter was a note of color from canisters, tiles to set teapots on, and teapots themselves. All wares Camellia sold. "You have different products here than at Darjeeling's Teahouse."

"More suited to this place," Camellia said.

"I like that brown teapot," the woman said.

"I can set it aside for you."

"Yes, please do."

At that moment the server arrived with their food. Camellia kept the menu very simple, foods a person would have during rituals: cheese and crackers, fruits, breads both salty and sweet, some sandwiches, flatsweets, whatever would complement her teas. The teas themselves were more robust here than at her other place, strong and hearty.

"Enjoy."

"Mmmm." The man nodded as he chewed a sandwich.

Camellia welcomed other patrons—some she didn't recognize. All seemed pleased.

Then she went to the east wall where sconces held statues—one of the Lord and one of the Lady. Before them stood tall urns with many-holed tops for the subtly fragranced incense sticks that patrons could light. One odor-free but sparkling-smoke-producing stick always burnt in each of the urns—the element of air. A stick had finished and she needed to replace it.

When she was done, she examined the room again, making sure it matched the image she'd had in her head for so long. Yes, she was sure her concept would work. All in all, it seemed like a House-Heart to her.

Not that she knew of a HouseHeart personally, but she'd done her research—hard not to when one of her best friends was Glyssa Licorice, the Heir to the PublicLibrary Family. So Camellia had seen records describing HouseHearts in general, and even some private records and record spheres of an unnamed HouseHeart or three. Since the destruction of the HouseHeart would kill the Residence, information on them was stingy.

Her friends were the best. At thirteen they'd had a grovestudy research assignment on a sunken ship that had been discovered and was being salvaged. Camellia, her mother, and brother had been living in her Family house at the time. Camellia had recalled a story of losing their fortune in a shipwreck. Her friends and she had searched the few Family documents and found a letter and the invoice for a tea set from a famous Chinju artist.

Camellia had interrupted the hearing on a lawsuit about salvaging the ship at JudgementGrove and was awarded the tea set—if GrandLady Kelp could find it in the ocean. The woman had; the fifty-piece tea set had not only survived but increased in value astronomically. Camellia had sold the largest item, a huge urn, and had enough gilt to found her business.

She owed everything to her friends, to the women who had helped her.

A server came to Camellia and discreetly gestured to a table where two women sat. Camellia knew the smaller one with brown hair, GreatLady Danith D'Ash. She'd married into one of the twelve GreatHouses, the crème de la crème of Celtan society. Danith liked tea, and Camellia had concocted a special blend for the woman. The GreatLady often patronized Darjeeling's Teahouse.

Camellia didn't know D'Ash's companion, a boldly voluptuous woman with flaming hair and cream-colored complexion, but since her clothes were in the latest fashion and of the most expensive fabrics, she must be another high-status Noblewoman.

"D'Blackthorn wishes to speak with you, Camellia," the server said, identifying the other woman.

"Take the counter for a moment, please," Camellia replied. But as she walked toward the table, her pride in the HouseHeart trickled out, replaced by a stream of anxiety. Of course both of the ladies knew what real HouseHearts looked like.

D'Blackthorn was *the* interior designer of Druida. If she said the design of the HouseHeart was poor and uninspired, she could ruin Camellia.

Two

Danith D'Ash stood and offered her hands along with a smile, and the knot in Camellia's stomach loosened. "Greetyou, Camellia."

"Greetyou, GreatLady D'Ash." She took D'Ash's hands and accepted a little squeeze before withdrawing her fingers.

D'Ash sniffed. "Haven't I asked you to call me Danith?" She turned to the redhead. "This is my friend, Mitchella Clover D'Blackthorn."

Current fashion had slits running up Camellia's tunic with little material to grab and curtsey, though she managed a quick, discreet wipe of her palms on the cloth as she bobbed. "I'm pleased to meet you."

D'Blackthorn smiled, did a scan of the room. "You've done something quite unique here."

Camellia's stomach squeezed again. *Unique* was one of those words that could mean a lot of things.

Though she thought she was keeping a pleasant expression, D'Blackthorn must have noted something because the woman laughed. She held up a hand as if to stop any of Camellia's racing thoughts of disaster. "A very unique and special place."

That wasn't much better.

"I'll enjoy coming here. The food is wonderful."

Relief filtered through Camellia. "Thank you."

D'Blackthorn slanted a look at Danith D'Ash. "Danith was trying, again, to convert me to tea." GrandLady D'Blackthorn shook

her head. "But I'm a caff person and will remain a caff person."
Another look at her friend. "Though I did like that smoky tea enough
to buy a few ounces."

Camellia featured several "smoky" teas. She'd have to ask the
server which one D'Blackthorn ordered. "Thank you," Camellia
repeated.

After pursing her lips, D'Blackthorn said, "Yes, you did very
well here. A little mysterious, but comfortable. I don't doubt that
you'll have continuing business. Definitely appeals to commoners
and lower nobles as a place to aspire to, and would give comfort to
anyone. Well done."

Huge praise. Now Camellia felt shivery with elation. "Thanks
again."

With a considering look in her eyes, D'Blackthorn said, "I've
meant to drop by Darjeeling's Teahouse but haven't done so. I'll
have to put that at the top of my outings list."

"I've always told you you'd like it," Danith D'Ash said smugly.

"And sometimes you're right," D'Blackthorn replied with the
easy teasing of longtime friends. One more glance around, and then
D'Blackthorn picked up her pursenal and moved to the payment
counter.

D'Ash remained by the table, studying Camellia. The GreatLady
dipped her hand in her opposite sleeve pocket and drew out a card.
"Come see me at MidAfternoonBell. I have a young FamCat who
just came in who I think will suit you." She followed her friend.

Camellia stared at the business card. A Fam! She was torn. She'd
love to have an intelligent animal companion, but she also had wonderful, delicate items in her house. She could imagine the tears, the
crashes.

But would she ever get another chance at a Fam if Camellia
turned D'Ash down? You didn't say no to the FirstFamilies. Not
even friendly and generous ladies.

Absently, Camellia did a brief cleaning spell of the table, sending
the china back to the kitchen to be washed.

Neither she nor her servers could do such spells often during the day, but energy from her delight with D'Blackthorn's compliments ran high in Camellia.

At the counter D'Ash asked for several types of tea, one of them "smoky," which was probably what D'Blackthorn had had. D'Blackthorn gestured to the prettiest and most expensive teapot Camellia carried. Selling that item had just made her operating expenses for the day.

The two ladies took their purchases and, chatting, sauntered from the teahouse.

Camellia refrained from skipping as she passed the counter and went into the kitchen for a quick check. All was fine.

All was fabulous.

"You handled that very well," said a familiar voice and Camellia turned to see one of her best friends, Glyssa Licorice.

Camellia's breath whooshed from her. "Thanks."

"So *the* designer for the nobility approved of Darjeeling's House-Heart?" Glyssa asked. Glyssa's Family valued intelligence over status, information more than gilt.

"Yes, she did." Camellia chuckled, another bit of relief. "Both seemed to think the HouseHeart was as it should be. Thank you for your help."

Glyssa tucked her hands in her opposite sleeves and made a noncommittal noise.

Camellia raised her hand, palm out. "Don't criticize. They were both born commoners, lower in rank than we, and were very gracious. A few mentions from D'Blackthorn and this place will pull in more folk—from the nobility because she's one of them, and from the commoners who'll think that this truly *is* like a HouseHeart."

"I am corrected and rightly so," Glyssa said. "But I believe you think too much of business."

Camellia was always thinking of business, but *she* didn't believe that was a fault. Business was exciting. Glyssa's comment was an old one, and Camellia dismissed it as usual. The Licorice Family was wealthy and Glyssa had never been poor. They just weren't interested in appearances.

Then Glyssa's smile broke out and made her serious and thin-featured face beautiful. "But I came to say that *Nuada's Sword* wants to see you and me and Tiana again."

Another summons—from the last starship.

Camellia waved the card D'Ash had given her. "Can't today."

"What's that?" Glyssa asked.

"Appointment with D'Ash to get a FamCat today. MidAfter-noonBell."

Glyssa's brown eyes rounded with pleasure . . . and, as always, curiosity. "Then tonight . . ."

"This evening is the Salvage Ball."

"Oh. Right." Another attraction for Glyssa since one never knew what people would bring—anything from jewelry that just might be valuable to grotesquely ugly knickknacks. Camellia admitted she enjoyed going for that reason, too.

"I'll scry *Nuada's Sword* and tell it that we are busy," Glyssa said.

"For the next couple of days."

Glyssa scowled.

"Really. I am. Still getting this place running smoothly, and I need to cat-proof my house."

"That's for sure."

"You didn't already tell Tiana to meet us at the starship?" Camellia asked. Tiana Mugwort was the third friend in their triad.

"No, she's busy at the Temple."

"That's all right then." The stiffness in her shoulders eased.

"Can I come with you to D'Ash's?" Glyssa asked.

As far as Camellia knew, Glyssa had never been to the animal Healer's office . . . which was located in a Residence, a sentient house. Glyssa seemed to throb with inquisitiveness. "Maybe I can get on the list for a Fam," Glyssa said, then grumbled, "D'Ash gave Fams to the PublicLibrary, but not to our Family."

Camellia would be the first of their group to get an animal companion. Another benefit of taking D'Ash up on her offer of a cat.

"Of course you can come." D'Ash's offices were open to all who needed an animal Healer.

Glyssa pulled her hands from her sleeves to rub them. "An afternoon at D'Ash's and the Salvage Ball tonight." She grinned. "Life is good."

For the moment. Camellia wouldn't be able to get out of visiting the starship for long. She and Glyssa disagreed on this, too. Glyssa loved visiting the Ship.

At first, Camellia had been thrilled. She and the Ship had discussed growing a tea crop and experimented with some ancient strains. Camellia's Flair—psi power—was for blending tea, and she'd chosen species that could be adapted for Celtan tastes. So now some of the teas served and for sale in her places were grown in the starship's great greensward. A good selling point.

But lately Camellia sensed that someday *Nuada's Sword* would realize she kept secrets it wanted.

She didn't know what she'd do then, but at least that day wouldn't be today.

*L*aev had just returned to his desk after a solitary lunch in the formal dining room when a yowl jolted him from his work. He stared at the FamCat, Black Pierre, progressing toward him with a very young cat—maybe seven months—walking behind him, staring at the room.

Jasmine erupted from her office, nearly stumbled over the cats, and hopped back. Black Pierre hissed. "Sorry," she said, choking a laugh.

They both watched as the old cat trod across the thick carpet until he—and the sleek cat—circled Laev's desk to his feet.

Your Fam, Black Pierre said telepathically.

The cat tilted its head to stare up at Laev coolly. Its slinky tail twitched. *He will do.*

With a flick of a paw, Black Pierre knocked its head. *Quiet, you. This is GreatLord T'Hawthorn. You should be honored.*

The youngling moved to pounce on its elder, but Jasmine, used to animals, caught it and brought it up to rub against her face. "Aren't you pretty," she cooed. The animal calmed.

I am, it said.

Black Pierre sniffed. *My son. Not as beautiful as I was at that age.*

Laev was almost afraid to ask, "Where did you get him?"

Turning his back and walking toward the door, tail high, the older cat said, *My get.*

Laev choked. "Yours? You're ol—" he stopped before he insulted the cat.

I am not as old as your FatherSire when he died in the bed of his lady.

Jasmine snickered. Laev rubbed his temples with thumb and forefinger. Another scandal that he'd had to live down, how he'd come into his title three months before. The back of his neck heated.

You are too alone, Black Pierre said. *But you do not deserve such a wonderful Fam as I.*

"Uh-huh," Laev said.

But you can have him. An indiscretion. The cat gave a tiny cough. *And you may name him. Now I return to My FamMan, the chef.*

Sure showed where Laev ranked in the cat's priorities. Black Pierre teleported to the kitchen.

Jasmine stroked the cat she held along his back. His purr filled the room.

"Maybe you should take him home—" Laev began.

"Did you forget who you're talking to?" Jasmine arched her brows. "I am not allowed to bring home Fams for my mother to place. Father's rules, and I don't want to alienate him before you speak to him and a quarter of my Family's funds are in my hands." Jasmine placed the cat on Laev's desk, where he deigned to bat a crumpled piece of papyrus, sending sheets to the floor. Turning around, he knocked over the basket of invitations.

He hadn't quite come into his full growth, but he looked to be a good hunter. His fur was long and black. When Laev reached out to pet him between the ears, the cat bit his fingers. "Ouch!" Laev shook his hand. Droplets of blood welled from tiny holes. "Keep

that up and you're gone to the gardening shed. Have you been vet-
ted by D'Ash?" he asked the tom.

The cat lifted its nose, sat like a proud cat statue *No. But I will
be pleased to see D'Ash. She will recognize My worth.*

"Of course she will," Jasmine said cheerfully. "Mother loves all
cats."

The tom inclined his head and his tail gave another swish.

"I'll scry her now." Jasmine went to the wall and touched the
screen. "The cat needs a name."

Laev and the cat stared at each other. The young tom's eyes were
a light green. Nice.

The cat glanced aside, lifted a forepaw, and licked it. *You have
nice eyes, too.*

Laev figured the compliment was progress. Maybe he could live
with it.

Maybe I *can live with* you, the tom replied.

All right, the cat was very telepathic.

The tom stood and stretched, his back arching in that sinuous
way that amazed. *Being telepathic is one of My best qualities.*

Laev shielded his thoughts. The cat narrowed his eyes, hissed,
batted another piece of papyrus off the desk, followed it down to
pounce on it and shred it. *I think I will like living here.*

"I think the garden shed would suit you better," Laev said.
"I don't want a biting cat."

The cat looked around and smiled ingratiatingly. *No biting.*

"Mother says you should bring—" Jasmine hinted heavily.

"Brazos," Laev said.

Brazos. I like that name. The cat gave the papyrus one last slice
of claws, sat proudly.

"—you should bring Brazos around MidAfternoonBell. She will
be squeezing you in as it is."

For a moment Laev's pride was ruffled. He was T'Hawthorn!

Brazos sneezed.

"We'll be there," Laev said.

Jasmine relayed that to her mother and the scry screen went

dark. The girl beamed at them, nodded. "Great. You can meet with my father before the appointment and convince him to give me gilt to invest. I'll get my report right to you." She hurried back to her office and closed the door.

The tom stalked through the room, tail switching. *There is a smell I do not like.* He reached a bookcase, stretched tall to insert paws in the dimness of a shelf and yank something from the shadows to fall on the floor. The glass bottle rolled awkwardly and the stopper came off, decanting a puddle of perfume.

A thick, musky odor filled the room. Nivea's scent. Laev's pulse pounded and a headache exploded. He rubbed his temples, staring at the tom, whose eyes were wide.

Laev and the tom stared at each other before choking. Jasmine bulleted into the room. "What a stink. Smells like that disgusting scent that your wife liked." She stopped for breath and began coughing.

"Win—windows *open*!" Laev snapped.

The glass of the windows thinned and a brisk spring breeze wafted around the room. Laev circled his desk to stare at the pool that was staining the rug he loved. Brazos shot to a far corner of the room, hissing. *Don't like, don't like, don't LIKE.*

"Uh-oh," Jasmine said thickly, holding her nose.

"Residence?"

"Yes, T'Hawthorn."

"Please send the housekeeper here to clean up this mess with the proper spells."

"Yes, T'Hawthorn. She is on her way."

Breathing shallowly, Laev said, "I didn't know that bottle was there." He hated the stench, too. The odor of the past, of failure. He'd moved beyond that, but here it was again, clinging like the perfume, reminding him of past mistakes.

He'd—they'd—ritually cleansed the Residence after Nivea's death, annually since then. There should have been no more scent of her.

But he knew in his bones that she must have left other reminders of herself throughout the house. She didn't like him, but she wouldn't let herself be forgotten—even if her soul was long gone to circle on the wheel of stars until her next life.

He gritted his teeth. He wouldn't let her haunt him.

*C*amellia shifted from foot to foot in a pretty little pastel vet examination room with a high counter that held a bedsponge. The odor of animals pervaded the office suite. She was alone in the room.

Danith D'Ash had appeared briefly to welcome them, laughing at the curious gleam in Glyssa's eyes. But before D'Ash brought out the cat who was supposed to be Camellia's Fam, a horrible emergency alarm pulsed and D'Ash ran.

Glyssa had stayed in the room for about three minutes, then mentioned something about "taking a peek around, maybe at D'Ash's famous Fam Adoption Room" and slipped out the door.

Camellia glanced at her timer, wondered whether she should wait, but she didn't want to alienate a FirstFamily lady. Nor did she want to return another time.

When she couldn't stand it any longer, she opened the door, glancing down the short hallway for Glyssa. She didn't see her friend and tentatively walked to the mainspace. The room was empty. Apparently the teenaged boy who'd been at the desk was helping his mother. A reddish light still pulsed in an alcove that held the huge teleportation pad. The indicator showed it was in use. Camellia touched the button to clear the pad in case it was needed for another emergency.

There were four large doors. Which one would Glyssa have gone through?

Camellia opened one and passed through. Her feet sank into thick carpet. An atmosphere of wealth and luxury—peace—enveloped her. Her nose wrinkled. The air *smelled* rich. Furniture oils and unique incense or perfume—maybe even spells. Expensive spells that would cost the amount she'd make in a month.

Or maybe it was just the knowledge that she was in a true,

intelligent Residence, a FirstFamily home, even if it had been rebuilt—or the aura of such a being. Camellia shivered and turned back.

A door opened a long way toward her right. "Thank you for your kind words about my daughter," T'Ash's deep voice rumbled.

Another man answered, "Not kind, though you should be proud. I'm factual. Give her the gilt to work with, T'Ash, she'll double or triple it, I assure you."

Something about that man's voice hit her like a blow, disorienting her. Wrenched something open inside her that she never wanted open, had suppressed until she'd forgotten about it.

She knew that voice.

No, she didn't! Remembering that voice would be hurtful to her heart. Threaten her present life with one she couldn't have. No.

She turned and ran, stumbling, back to the examination room, shut that door.

Dizzying darkness pressed on her and she folded over, bracing her hands against her legs, panting, forcing back unconsciousness. Her skin was clammy.

No. She wouldn't let a past realization emerge that would shatter the life she'd crafted.

No.

The door opened and D'Ash and Glyssa were there. The lady was splattered with blood. The men stopped outside the door.

Camellia's breathing hadn't steadied before Glyssa and D'Ash entered together.

"That was just amazing!" Glyssa enthused. "You saved that horse's life."

Camellia stared. The emergency had been a horse?

"Thank you." D'Ash was beaming. She shook her head and went to a hook to pull down a pale blue over-tunic. Sickness washed over Camellia as she saw D'Ash's pastel green sleeves showed streaks of the deep and gleaming red of blood.

Turning her head, she sagged against the counter with the bedsponge, heard small noises as the GreatLady stripped away the old over-tunic and donned the new.

"Uh-oh." Glyssa was there, putting an arm around Camellia, stroking her back, helping her to a bench. "It's all right. The horse is fine." Then Glyssa tsked. "She doesn't do well with blood."

Yes, that had to be the reason Camellia felt so bad. Not the shadows of the men near the door. One of the men.

She would ignore them. Had to.

Camellia dropped her face in her hands, hiding from the sight. Hiding from her friend and the GreatLady, hiding from the men.

Hiding from herself.

"Give us a few minutes," D'Ash said to the men.

"We'll wait right here," her husband said.

The lady shut the door gently. Camellia lifted her arm and wiped her forehead with her sleeve.

D'Ash gestured and a spell whisked through the small room, leaving the scent of fresh and soothing herbs, banishing the faint tang of blood that had layered on Camellia's tongue.

"Cat," Camellia said.

"Yes, of course. Your Fam will be quite helpful in calming you, Camellia," D'Ash said.

Maybe, maybe not. Camellia just wanted everything done and to be out of here.

Three

❦

Long time and I have been VERY good, came a small mental voice.

D'Ash said, "Yes, you've been a very good FamCat." D'Ash went into a back room and came back with a little calico cat who had large splotches of orange and black, not much white except on her belly.

"Oooooh!" Glyssa leaned over the exam table. "Pretty."

"Yes. Isn't she, Camellia?"

"Beautiful." Her hands itched to hold the cat, young, charming, with the last hint of baby fat. Camellia rose and went to the table.

The FamCat tilted her head, opened her mouth, and used that extra sense cats had. *My FamWoman is beautiful, too. Smells-tastes verrry interesting.*

"Thank you," Camellia reached out.

The cat leapt from D'Ash's loose hold to land in Camellia's arms.

"There!" D'Ash put her hands on her rounded hips. "A very good job."

"D'Ash . . ." Glyssa sent the GreatLady an appeal.

"I think you'd bond best with a fox kit," D'Ash said. "The next one I get with good intelligence is yours."

"Thank you." Glyssa shook her head, pulled at a rusty-colored lock of hair that had fallen from the knot at the back of her head. "We'll match in coloring."

The door opened. "It's been a few minutes. T'Hawthorn is here to have his new cat checked," T'Ash said.

Camellia didn't want the men to come in. Too bad, they'd already crowded into the room, as well as a long-haired black cat. She didn't look at the younger man who was as tall as T'Ash and moved with a prowling grace. Instead she smoothed out her frown, cuddled her cat closer; the soft rumble of her Fam's purr vibrated against her arms.

She felt better holding her FamCat, a symbol of the life she had now, not teenaged dreams that she refused to remember.

It's Black! Camellia's cat squealed. Wriggling away, she jumped onto the bedsponge and hopped a couple of times. *Greetyou, Black!*

A young black tom stretched before Camellia in a long leap, landed several centimeters before her smaller calico.

Camellia made a noise of protest.

But the larger cat didn't pounce, just gathered himself into an upright sitting position, leaned over, and bumped noses with the calico—who squeaked and jumped high, alighting on Camellia's shoulder, which was just big enough for the kit to balance on. *You smell. Smell, smell, smell. AWFUL.*

Now that the little cat mentioned it, a new odor had entered the room.

Camellia found herself stiffening, met Glyssa's eyes. They recognized the perfume the late Nivea Hawthorn preferred—their old acquaintance, Nivea Sunflower. Who'd scorned them all. That hurt, too. This whole visit was impossible now.

Did T'Hawthorn need to have a reminder of his dead wife always close? Camellia wouldn't have thought it, the way that woman had treated him, but men were strange. She found herself breathing too quickly and evened it out.

"The smell is a problem," T'Hawthorn said, smoothing a stroke along his cat's back. More heavy fragrance puffed into the air. "My office has been cleaned, and I took a waterfall and tried to—ah—banish the odor from Brazos, but it didn't quite work." His smile was charming. "We need an expert."

The calico cat burrowed into Camellia's shoulder-length hair. *Black has a name, now?*

I am a FirstFamily Cat. My name is Brazos.

The calico licked Camilla's neck. *I need a name, too.*

Unlike most Families on Celta, Darjeeling wasn't a botanically based name but some sort of ancient Earthan place-name. Camellia had run through several ideas. "Mica."

That is a very good name. The little cat sniffed, sneezed. *Bad smell tickles my nose. And Mica is prettier than Brazos.*

Glyssa chuckled but moved around the table toward the open door. She bobbed a brief curtsey. "Greetyou, GreatLord T'Ash, GreatLord T'Hawthorn. Excuse us, we must be on our way." She waved a hand. "Business, you know."

The men bowed.

Camellia curtsied, too. "Greetyou and farewell." She turned to D'Ash. "Thank you for Mica. Let me know how much—"

"Mica is a gift," D'Ash said firmly. "Since I don't know her heritage. She just strolled into the adoption room last week." The GreatLady handed Camellia a rolled papyrus.

I was ready for FamWoman, Mica said. *Knew Black-Brazos on the street. Told him to go to his Sire. Now we have FamPeople.*

Now I am Brazos Hawthorn, a great noble, the black cat projected.

Mica's tail flicked. *See you later, when you are unstunk.*

Aiming a false smile at the lords and sliding past them, Camellia was out of D'Ash's office and into fresh air in two minutes.

Mica tumbled down Camellia's front, snagging the cloth of her tunic on the way. Good thing it was only a work tunic, but it was a *nice* work tunic. Camellia looked at the slubs and shook her head.

Glyssa held up a small, round sphere. "Instructions from D'Ash. Spells on how to attach your cat to your shoulder in a "safe" and "stay" spell. How to mend cloth and, um, other things."

Camellia thought of all the china in her house—cups, porcelain boxes, delicate figurines.

Who are you? Mica muttered. Her gaze fixed on Glyssa.

"She's one of my best friends, GrandMistrys Glyssa Licorice, Heir to the PublicLibrary Licorices."

"And we're going to a round temple so you can meet our other best friend," Glyssa said, waving her arm toward the end of a small parking area. A big, old, red-black Family glider moved toward them. "Her name is Tiana Mugwort and she is a priestess of the Lady and Lord. I think you should meet her before we do anything else, because you are now another best friend."

Mica preened. *I am a FamCat friend.*

"Yes," Camellia said.

Does Tiana have a Fam?

"No," Camellia and Glyssa said together.

Good, then I am First. Glyssa will get a FamFox kit, but I will always be First. She rubbed against Camellia and smiled sweetly.

Camellia laughed with Glyssa and let the disturbing memory of meeting T'Hawthorn dissipate. She felt better and would continue to do so. She would not think of T'Hawthorn, had managed to suppress thoughts of him for a long time. With a little spell, she banished him from her mind.

*D*anith D'Ash eliminated the perfume clinging to Brazos in under a minute. She spent another ten praising the tom and getting his particulars for her lineage of Fams, then assuring Laev that his FamCat was in excellent health.

At the same time, T'Ash casually leaned against the examination counter and consulted his HeartMate about his decision to give their daughter a quarter of their capital to invest. After a few cogent questions and a promise to read Laev's report, D'Ash agreed, humming with pride.

Laev had asked about Jasmine's brother, Nuin, and was told with beaming smiles that he'd weathered the last fever fugue of Second Passage. Laev didn't ask whether Nuin had linked with his HeartMate.

In fact, Laev began to feel uncomfortable. When he'd entered the room with the two women a few years younger than he, something about their attitude ruffled his Flair. They certainly left as soon as they could, with as minimal a greeting as he'd ever received. Now the strong and loving bond between T'Ash and D'Ash stirred envy inside him.

He'd wanted that loving bond, had married a woman thinking he'd gotten it. Even when he'd discovered Nivea wasn't his Heart-Mate, he'd done his best to work at a good marriage. He'd always treated her with the courtesy his wife deserved. Never broke his marriage vows, even after they were estranged.

Lord and Lady knew the sexual attraction between them had been great, and the first couple of years of marriage had been . . . good. Until Nivea wanted to move back to the capital city of Druida and take over as mistress of Laev's FatherSire's household. Everything deteriorated after that.

T'Ash was holding his wife's hand and Brazos was looking on with approval. Laev cleared his throat. "What do I owe you?"

Breaking the kiss, a flushed D'Ash leaned back in her husband's encircling arms and chuckled. "I think Brazos has already authorized payment."

Laev looked at the bedsponge where the young tom had been a couple of seconds ago. Now he was on a different counter in front of a scry panel that showed T'Hawthorn ResidenceDen. His black paw patted the screen. *DONE!* Lifting his chin, he smiled gleefully at Laev. *Residence likes Me. I like it, too.*

"I didn't know cats could use scry panels," Laev said.

"Oh, yes, all the younger generation," D'Ash said indulgently.

T'Ash snorted. "Not only the younger generation. My FamCat, Zanth, can. I'd advise you to set limits on the gilt authorization amounts that your Fam has with your Residence." He sounded as if he learned from experience. D'Ash giggled.

"T'Hawthorn Residence?" Laev projected his voice toward the panel.

"Yes, T'Hawthorn?" the Residence said.

"Please note that except for medical emergencies, Brazos has an authorization limit of . . ." Laev had no idea.

"Fams don't order their own collars," D'Ash said loudly. "A collar is a gift from their FamPerson."

Good point. But what was reasonable? What else would Brazos want that the Residence couldn't provide?

T'Ash was muttering, "Pillows, thickly carpeted perches for every room in the Residence, Earthan catnip grown on the starship *Nuada's Sword*, specially prepared cocoa mousse bigger than his head . . ."

Sounded like T'Ash's FamCat had really done a run on T'Ash's gilt. That was amusing until Laev recalled how Nivea liked to shop. His smile faded. "Residence, except for medical emergencies, Brazos has an authorization limit of a hundred gilt a month to be given him in weekly installments upon good behavior."

There was no protest from Brazos, though he tapped the scry screen with his paw and ordered, *End scry to T'Hawthorn Residence.*

"Good thing you got a feral Fam," T'Ash said. "He doesn't know everything that he wants."

"Yes," Laev said. "The last thing I need is another—" He stopped himself before he said something less than complimentary about Nivea. He was thinking about her too damn much. That was the *past*. The future was what mattered.

D'Ash handed him a loudly purring Brazos. "I'm glad you got a Fam." Her eyes were full of pity as she slid an arm around her HeartMate's waist and leaned against him.

Laev jerked a nod. Everyone knew of his mistake, and he'd learned to live with that. One last mess to clean up—find his Family's heirlooms and his HeartGift. Then he'd be done with wife problems forever.

*C*amellia's day had been one of ups and downs: the compliment from D'Blackthorn that would boost Darjeeling's HouseHeart's popularity, the invitation from the starship, the strange experience at the Ashes, getting a Fam, the pleasure of her friends with Mica. Intense emotions that were all very wearing. A few minutes relaxing in her home before the Salvage party would be welcome.

Yet her steps dragged as she walked to the door of her small bungalow.

Is this it? Is this My new home? It looks pretty. Ooh, flowers! Mica purred in Camellia's ear.

"This is it." The small house was of faded redbrick with a large round front window. Colorful summer flowers danced in the breeze, in the beds around the small grassyard. Camellia thought of warning the cat not to squash the blooms but figured that would be a waste of breath and just irritate them both. Of *course* a cat so young would pounce on the flowers and shred the petals. Find a good spot to lay on them and smash them.

Camellia sighed.

Why did you make that sad noise? Mica asked.

"I don't know. I'm feeling—" She noticed her door was cracked open and she hurried up the porch, into her mainspace.

"Darlin' girl!" a voice boomed. She was crushed in a hug, meaty fingers clenching her ribs too tight, the scent of hated clove smothered her nostrils like the chest she was against. And she knew *something*, some Flair, some instinct had warned her.

She struggled away from the big man, turning her head. Hadn't this day been emotionally difficult enough? Tears stung hard against the backs of her eyes. "What are you doing here?"

"Is that any way to greet your beloved father after nearly two years?" He stepped back, looking far too large in the small room, too clumsy, too dramatic. His face was still square and florid, just beginning to show the excesses of drink and the lines of selfishness. Just as his waist was starting to thicken with belly fat. As always, his eyes were small and sly—and the same gray as her own.

She calculated how much gilt she might have had in the house, whether he would have found it. He might not have, but she sensed her uncle here, and he would have taken it. "What do you want?"

"Just to see my darlin'."

"Don't lie to me."

He put on a hurt expression, raised his hands palms out. He still wore blousy sleeves cuffed tight at his wrists but that didn't mean much. The material would be just stretchy enough to slide paper money under, the sleeves large enough to hide it. "I'm not lying."

"How much?"

"How can you treat me like this?" He flung himself into her favorite cushioned chair, which creaked under the sudden onslaught of his weight. His hurt face morphed into false disappointment. Camellia glanced around the room, didn't notice any small valuables missing.

This is the Sire of My FamWoman? Mica's perky mind-voice projected.

A gleam came to Camellia's father's—T'Darjeeling's—eyes. He stood and glided forward, reaching a hand large enough to encompass the cat's head, and stroked her with a thick finger. "A Fam, a real Fam. You found a Fam?" His voice was nearly as smooth as the young cat's purr.

I am from D'Ash, Mica said.

"Oh." T'Darjeeling dropped his hand.

"Yes. She *is* valuable. But you can't steal her because she is in D'Ash's records."

His brows lifted, his lips curved in an easy smile, but his gaze had hardened. He set a hand on Camellia's shoulder. He could squeeze there and bring her to her knees, from force and pain and the bludgeoning of his Flair against her.

She wrapped her own hands around his wrist. "You just do that. I've been practicing. I'm strong enough to 'port us to the local guard station." She cast her mind toward the nearest guardhouse, the emergency teleportation pad was busy, so was the next, but the third in the network she'd studied was free . . .

His fingers clenched tight, pain bit. She inhaled and he released her, flicked his wrist hard, and broke her grip. "I don't think so."

But he'd shown her the trick he might use in the future. Information gathered. She lifted her chin. "I will. I'll take you to the guards and report assault. I'm a responsible adult."

His gaze veiled, his smile grew lopsided. "A responsible adult." There was an almost mocking lilt in his tones. "A successful businesswoman." Scorn.

He didn't think much of people who worked for a living. One of his brows rose as he looked around her mainspace at the pretty knickknacks. "Nice place. I'm sure you can spare a couple hundred gilt for your father."

She took a step back from him but kept her voice level. "I could report you for extortion, too."

"Your own father." He paced forward, crowded her. "You try—"

"Now, now, Guri, don't pester the girl," another genial voice said as a man as large as her father strolled into the room.

Camellia flinched. "Uncle Takvar." She glanced at him. His gray eyes were worse than her father's: cold and flat and deadly, despite the handsomeness of his face. His smile was an incipient threat.

He half lowered his eyelids, raised a languid hand. "But four hundred gilt should keep the wolves from the door."

It would be worth it to get them to go away. No. Bad thinking, *old* thinking. "No." She moved back to a corner marked on the rug for teleportation. "I'm leaving, and if I find that you have broken *one* object, I'll report you to the guards."

Her father's hand swept out and knocked a china mug from her table with such force that it hit the wall and shattered. He smiled. "Oops."

Mica, we 'port on three. Just hold on. One, Mica cat, two . . .

Her uncle had linked arms with her father, pulled. "You don't need to go, Cammi-girl. We'll leave."

"Same old song." Her father's lip curled, he set his voice at falsetto. "You broke my cup. Boo-hoo." As they strolled to the door, he glanced over his shoulder, now all fake affability gone from him. "You're pitiful."

"I wonder that you bother to visit, then," Camellia said thickly as fear-tears coated her throat. She didn't think they'd heard her as they left, slamming her front door. Her knees weakened and she tottered to the sofa and fell onto it.

Mica revved her purr. *I did not like them.*

Camellia curved over herself, panting, nearly trembling with reaction, holding her arms close around her middle.

I didn't like them, Mica repeated, hopping down from Camellia's shoulder, walking along her thigh, and nudging her elbow. *Want on lap, now.*

With a gasp, Camellia straightened and Mica set her claws in Camellia's trous and climbed up. *They were not NICE.* Mica sounded shocked as if she couldn't imagine someone being "not nice" to her or her FamWoman. Staring up at her with wide yellow eyes, Mica put a paw on Camellia's breast. *They were Not NICE.*

"No." Camellia stroked the kitten. "They weren't. They were mean. They've always been mean."

Mean. Mica lashed her tail. *I know that word. Now I know "mean."*

"Oh." It was a small break of the heart that Mica's first hours with Camellia had taught the kitten the definition of mean. "Oh." Tears trickled down Camellia's cheeks. She stroked Mica and began to settle until she recalled that she'd left her diamond bracelet in her antique puzzle box. She jolted to her feet, tucked Mica under her arm, and sped to her bedroom.

Four

The wooden box lay in shards on her bed, broken open. Her bracelet was gone. So were a few pieces of costume jewelry that would give her uncle a pittance from someone dealing in stolen objects.

Her stomach squeezed nausea up her throat. She'd purchased the bracelet the first year Darjeeling's Teahouse showed a good profit, to celebrate. She'd worn it like a talisman at the opening of Darjeeling's HouseHeart earlier in the week. Left the bracelet in the box in her wall safe instead of taking the time to return the diamonds to her private box at the bank.

The door of the safe was wide open and empty. No gilt paper or coins. There hadn't been much there.

She looked at her second safe, the hidden one. Her uncle, obviously in a hurry, had vanquished the spellshields and punched the wall instead of trying to finesse other physical levers and combinations. His Flair for finding gilt and valuables, no matter how secret, was still strong.

Hadn't been much in there, either, but they'd gotten more than four hundred gilt from her.

Camellia sank down on the bed, put her head in her hands while Mica played with pieces of the pretty antique puzzle box. Her uncle hadn't needed to break that. He could have worked it in seconds. He simply enjoyed breaking things, maybe her things in particular. She rubbed at her face, went to the waterfall room to splash water on her cheeks, hot with anger and despair. No matter what she tried to do, this never ended.

After she patted her face dry, she donned a mild expression and went to the new wall scry panel and called her brother.

He answered on his perscry, his small personal scry pebble, and the angle and movement was odd enough to make her stomach lurch again.

"Greetyou, Senchal," she said.

His thin shoulders wiggled and he shifted as if uneasy. "Hey."

"Senchal, did father and uncle visit you?"

His gaze slid away. "No."

So they had.

"Did you give them any gilt?"

"I'm an artist and always broke, what do you think?"

She thought he had.

"Senchal, they are bad men. We have to file a Family action against them, declaring them a danger to us and the community."

His pale face turned mulish and she knew she'd already lost. "They aren't that bad," he said.

She didn't think their father had ever hit him. Ever stolen anything important from him. Probably had even given him a few gilt now and then . . . and affection. A person would do a lot for affection from someone they loved.

"Look," she said, trying again. "The authorities won't do anything against them until they've investigated our claims, but meanwhile it will keep them away from us."

But Senchal was shaking his head. "No. Can't. Gotta go."

He cut the scry with a quick flat-handed gesture . . . before she said something stupid like *he* wouldn't be getting any more monthly "loans," either. The words had been ready to spurt from her mouth. Mean words. Like those her father would say. She loathed that most of all.

She gathered up Mica, the cat's soft fur caressing her palms. "You want to see another new place?"

Mica opened sleepy eyes, yawned wide, showing tiny, pointy teeth and red tongue. *Where?*

"Horsetail Park Guardhouse."

Fun, the little cat said, but she was asleep when Camellia attached her to her shoulder with the safety spell.

A guardswoman commiserated with Camellia as she filed the complaint, and praised Mica. Camellia let out a long, slow breath. Here *she* was believed. As she'd told her father, she was a respected member of the community, and he was shady.

The guard shook her head as she consulted papyrus. "He and your uncle are on our watch list. I have a note that they just boarded a luxury airship to Gael City."

Gilt from Camellia's bracelet had bought those tickets. She unclenched her jaw to thank the woman.

A male guard came in, glanced at the complaint, and jerked a bit. "Filing a report on your *father*? A noble lord?"

"Shut up, Reptan," the guardswoman said, "and if you want to know what happened instead of reacting like a stup, read the report."

Without answering, Camellia went to the teleportation pad and left.

Men. They were no good.

A woman had found the lost ship and Camellia's tea set, which was the foundation of her career. A woman judge had ruled the set was hers. A woman had bought the large urn from the tea set for a more-than-fair price. Those three women, nearly strangers, had helped her escape her house and found her business, her life.

She loved and valued her friends, Glyssa and Tiana, who were more like sisters. She could count on them if no one else. Men had only hurt her.

*S*he'd scried her fighting trainer for an appointment and was cleaning up the mess when two feminine voices called, "Camellia!"

"You left your door open," Glyssa scolded.

Camellia had opened her front door so her father's and uncle's odor would be whisked away by the wind and the fragrance of her flowers would infuse her home.

Glyssa stopped on the threshold of the bedroom as she saw the pieces of the jewelry box.

"You've been crying," Tiana said, coming over to put her arms around Camellia.

"That man has been here. That bastard of a father of yours." Glyssa's hiss was hard. She put her arms around Camellia and Tiana and they had a threesome hug. "Your uncle, too?"

"Yes," Camellia hiccupped. The damn tears were starting again.

"What did they get?" Glyssa asked.

"They destroyed her beautiful puzzle box!" Tiana said.

"My diamond bracelet. I wore it to the opening of Darjeeling's HouseHeart. My fault, I didn't take it back to the bank."

"It is *not* your fault that you have to hide valuables," Tiana said.

"No, it's not your fault. Tell me you 'ported the fligger to the guardhouse," Glyssa said.

"I was going to. He broke my hold." Camellia lifted her face, accepted the softleaf Glyssa held out to her. "I'll have to practice more. I've already called my teacher for a lesson."

"Did you file a complaint?" Glyssa pressed.

"Yes. For entering *my* house without permission and theft of the bracelet. Against both of them."

"Good girl."

With one last hug, Tiana and Glyssa stepped away. Tiana's gaze went to the bedroom wall. "I see your uncle found the 'secret' safe we put in." She shook her head. "You told me he would, but . . ."

Camellia shrugged a shoulder, blew her nose into Glyssa's softleaf, and dropped the linen square into the cleanser. Going to a dresser drawer, she pulled out two softleaves with little teapots embroidered in the corners, handed one to Glyssa, and put the other on top of her dresser. "I haven't dressed. I'm running a little late." She eyed her friends. Costumes for the party fell into several categories. There was the ragged, "salvage" look that Glyssa wore, no trous under a tunic—this was a tattered-hemmed skirt scandalously above her naked ankles and feet. It was shades of green and appeared like seaweed to Camellia. Mica hopped from the bedsponge to play with a trailing end.

"Hmm," Camellia said, staring.

Glyssa turned around, modeling the complete costume. The sleeves were barely substantial enough to be pointed pockets. Most tunics had rectangular pockets built into the sleeves.

"I like it," Camellia said.

"Homage to the sunken ship," Glyssa said.

"Um-hmm," Camellia said.

"I think it's a little much," Tiana said.

"That's because you're turning into a staid priestess," Glyssa retorted.

Tiana herself wore formal wear, a robe of deep blue with a twinkling spell of white, blue, yellow, and red "stars." Celtan night. She, too, twirled for Camellia. The robe was cut full and circular so it belled wide and beautiful.

"Lovely," Camellia said.

"All right. You've seen ours, and you've been secretive about yours. What are you wearing?"

"I considered going as an ocean diver."

"Oooh," both her friends said.

"But decided against."

As Camellia turned to the closet, her smile died and her insides clenched again. What if her uncle or father had found the gown? What if they'd destroyed it? They knew exquisite-quality fabric and embroidery when they saw it. Not that they could have sold it . . . she didn't think. Maybe . . .

Glyssa saw her face. "I'll look for you."

"We'll take care of it if something happened to your outfit," Tiana added. "You won't have to see it, and we'll make sure it's mended."

"You . . . you can't. It's heavy silk. Embroidered by D'Thyme."

"That means it's artwork," Glyssa said matter-of-factly, opening the closet door as Tiana put her arm around Camellia's shoulders and angled her gently away.

"Doesn't appear like any of your clothes have been touched," Glyssa said. She sniffed, then said, "Mica, come here and tell me if you smell the—"

Mean men. Mica trotted over to the dark opening of the closet. She lifted her nose. *Only a trace smell. Like someone looked but didn't touch.*

"Excellent," Glyssa said. "And what am *I* looking for?"

"A celadon green silk robe—"

"With exquisite embroidery," Tiana added.

"It's shot with silver," Camellia added.

"Ah, here it is," Glyssa said.

Tiana kept her grip on Camellia so she couldn't see.

There was an intake of breath from Glyssa. Camellia flinched.

"So gorgeous," Glyssa said. "Artwork, indeed. It almost makes me want something like it."

Tiana released Camellia and they turned at the same time to look at the robe. It was a formal gown with a built-in breastband and a low heart-shaped neckline. The sleeves were long and had rectangular pockets. The dress was lined with a cream-colored silk.

But what captured the gaze was the sheen of the fabric and the shades of pale green, cream-colored, and white embroidery that made the subtle floral pattern appear woven into the cloth.

"Lady and Lord!" Tiana gasped. She turned to stare, open-mouthed, at Camellia. "How could you afford that? It must have cost—" She snapped her mouth shut.

Glyssa continued, "—a year's worth of both my and Tiana's salaries and your business profit."

"I stood in line outside D'Thyme's home all night Halloween and the morning of New Year's Day, Samhain, a year ago. You remember."

It was a tradition that the first hundred people who arrived at a noble's door on Samhain received the services of the noble for free—or rather subsidized by the NobleCouncils as part of their yearly NobleGilt.

"I thought you were crazy," Glyssa said. She angled the hanger so the silk and thread caught the light. "It was below freezing."

"I wanted the gown."

"And you do tend to be determined," Glyssa admitted.

With hesitant fingers, Tiana touched the pale petal of a flower. "Beautiful, and it's your pattern, isn't it? On your tea set."

"Yes."

Glyssa shook her head in admiration. "You did fabulously well. As usual." She handed the dress to Camellia.

"It could be a bridal gown," Tiana said.

"No!" The word was too violent, but Camellia couldn't help it. "No husband."

"No HeartMate, you mean. You have one." Tiana lifted her chin.

Camellia laid her dress on a chair. Sweat had sprung on her palms. "I thought we'd decided we wouldn't discuss that."

"You have a HeartMate, not everyone does. That's rare," Tiana continued.

Camellia's mind buzzed and a haze of hurt and anger seemed to separate her from her friend. Tiana wasn't the confrontational sort. Her numb mouth formed slow words. "Why are you talking about that *now*?"

Glyssa stepped next to her and flung her arm around Camellia's shoulders in a hug, facing Tiana. "Yes, why *now*? Hasn't Camellia had enough problems today without you poking at her?"

Tiana's face scrunched, and she mumbled, "We discussed Heart-Mates at temple today. How fate will bring HeartMates together."

"Now is *not* the time, Tiana." Glyssa's voice held a note of arrogance that Camellia had never been able to master. "We all have our sore points, *and our secrets*. Maybe you'd like to tell us—"

Camellia shook all the stupid emotions aside. Her friends needed her. Of them all, when Tiana and Glyssa argued, the friendship came closest to shattering. "No. Stop. We know she can't tell us about her home."

"I swore an Oath, swore a Vow of Honor, I'm bound to say *nothing*," Tiana said miserably, backing away from Glyssa and beginning to tidy the room.

Nudging Glyssa with her elbow, Camellia collected her shredded emotions and tried to mend them together. She knew that if they were shaped into a garment they'd look nothing like her gown. Not now. "Glyssa, you know there are great consequences to breaking a Vow of Honor, and you wouldn't expect her to." Camellia whistled out a breath. "Yes. I have sore spots." She had to pant through the next sentence. "And secrets, and I don't ever like to think of my HeartMate. I don't intend to claim him." Her jaw flexed and she stared at Tiana, who had her calm-and-serene-but-I-will-get-back-to-the-subject-so-you-will-release-your-problems-and-change-for-the-better expression on.

"We'll thrash this out later." Camellia's mouth pulled up in an ironic smile. "Tiana, you want to help us work through our problems and grow, that's why you became a priestess, to help. But not tonight." Rough anger clawed through her, erupted in acid scorn. "Not after I've seen those wonderful examples of manhood, my thieving father, my deadly uncle, and my gormless brother. I'm taking a waterfall." She scooped up her gown, tried to moderate her feelings. "Since we're running late, I'll need some of your combined spells to make me presentable." She swept from the room but heard Glyssa say, "Way to ruin a party."

"All right. I spoke out of turn. Let's forget about it," Tiana said.

"That's optimism for you," Glyssa said.

I am going, too! Mica said loudly. *I want to party! My first party!* "Rrrmm." *I love My FamWoman.*

Camellia's shoulders relaxed and she smiled at Mica's comment, the sounds of her zooming around the bedroom. It had been a horrible day . . . except it appeared Darjeeling's HouseHeart would be doing well, and she now had a companion. Not a HeartMate but a Fam, and that was quite enough.

*L*aev darkened the last investment holosphere, ending his business day, and turned his mind to the Salvage Ball. He was grimly certain that the odd party was just the sort of venue that Nivea would have used to dispose of his Family property. He'd go. "Residence, what's proper dress for the Salvage Ball?"

There was a slight hum in the air. "We approve that you will attend the Salvage Ball. We have clothing from the era that the sunken ship set sail."

Of course they did.

"The clothes are stored in a no-time storage wardrobe in the northwest tower attic," the Residence prompted.

"Fine." As he climbed the stone stairs, the Residence said that it was glad that another Fam had joined the household, someone young and lively. Which, of course, made Laev wonder if the sentient house was hinting that it was time for Laev to marry. He'd have to, of course. But this time, he'd wait. Decades.

Five

Laev didn't consider it much of a party. The gathering was held in a warehouse, dimly lit with a murky tint of green. There was no music—an insult in their culture—the liquor was bad punch, and the punch was red.

His new FamCat, Brazos, thought it was wonderful. *So many people!* His whiskers twitched. *So many smells! So many admirers of Me.*

Laev didn't think so. In the shadows, Brazos could barely be seen and slunk around, pouncing upon unsuspecting feet. Laev had remonstrated, but of course the cat hadn't listened.

With all his senses extended, Laev had roamed the room, searching for anything that felt like a Hawthorn object. He'd found nothing after two rounds. His previous hunch that Nivea might have discarded Hawthorn Family property here sometime in the past stuck with him. She'd have liked bringing a treasure to the ball, carelessly leaving it on the table for anyone to pick up.

Now he stood on the side of the room and observed people. He shifted and his trousers clung to his ass, then loosened. No, he didn't like this style. For as long as he could remember, trous were full. He felt nearly naked in straight-legged trous with little excess material in the legs. The cloth was heavy, too, and much less able to hold spells than modern fabric. He was dressed in black, with a leather vest that had been cut close to his ancestor's chest and was also too small. The shirt size had been hopeless, but the Residence stated that shirtless was acceptable at the Salvage Ball.

If he hadn't seen other men dressed like him when he'd entered, he'd have left.

There was a woman's muffled cry, Brazos cackled with telepathic laughter, and Laev dropped his drink into the deconstructor. He'd take a quick survey of the items on the counters that ringed the room, then nab his Fam and go.

He'd asked the Residence for an object to discard at the ball. Apparently there was a meter-tall china vase that had bothered the Residence for years in one of the rarely used parlors. The house was eager to see the piece go.

Paws ran over his feet and Laev was fast enough to scoop up the cat—and found himself looking down at a sweet calico face.

Greetyou, the little cat said in a female voice, then yawned in his face.

"Mica?" It was a hushed call.

"Over here," he said.

With a swish of silk, a woman hurried to him. Her cat rolled over, presenting a white belly, and revved her purr. He liked the vibration against his arm. "Pretty cat," he said to the younger woman, then remembered that she and her friend had been cool to him. Pity. She was tall and willowy, but with an underlying flexible strength. Her features were even and attractive, her mouth wide. Her very dark brown hair held more than a hint of auburn and was styled close to her head to fall to her shoulders. He couldn't make out the exact color of her eyes, but he thought they were an unusual deep gray with a hint of blue. He tried a smile. "Merry meet."

The pretty woman hesitated. "Thank you for catching Mica." She reached up to take the cat and Laev noticed her gown and stepped back.

"Lovely dress," he said. He knew exactly how much a gown embroidered by D'Thyme cost. Nivea had ruined several. "You don't want Mica to harm it."

"Look at her claws," the woman said, holding out her arms for her Fam.

Laev did. The tips of Mica's claws were deep red as if they'd been dipped in blood.

"Claw caps, an easy spell. She chose the color."

For tonight only! Mica shifted to perch on his arm. *Because the dress is ir-re-place-able. Very important. Not as important as Me, but I am not allowed to touch.*

He wouldn't think so. "Ah," he said and handed the young cat over. He bowed and his trous caught tight around his ass and groin and he decided against doing that again.

"Did you find her?" The gingery-haired woman he'd also met at D'Ash's office walked up. "Oh." With nearly insulting slowness, she curtsied to him, not that she had much skirt to spread. A green raggedy thing.

Why were these two nearly impolite?

Then the host of the party, Feam Kelp, a soft-looking man his own age, was there, bowing, dressed like a pirate—and holding a purring Brazos. "T'Hawthorn, we so rarely see you here, though your lovely wife attended, of course. You honor us." He chuckled and scratched Brazos under the chin. "As does your Fam."

"Greetyou," he said.

Kelp sent a charming smile around the group, raised his brows. "Ah. I was sure you all knew each other." Amusement lurked in his voice.

"There you are! And Mica, too." Another woman drew close, saw him, hesitated, but lifted her chin and kept on coming. When she reached them, she curtsied and said, "Greetyou, GreatLord T'Hawthorn." Not quite as disapproving as her friends. Something about her coloring snagged his recollection—dark, curly hair and green eyes. Old images flashed of a girl who must have been a relative. Artemisia Mugwort, who'd been a friend of Nivea's.

Then the wave of memory crashed.

The day he'd met Nivea, she'd been walking with a group of

girls. These girls. Nivea and Artemisia had been older at seventeen, these three women had been young teens.

Their names slipped into his mind. No use for it, he'd have to bow again. If he just inclined his head, the women would be further insulted. He had no doubt that they'd heard a lot about him—and nothing good—from Nivea, until she'd dropped Artemisia for higher-ranked friends.

Yes, Nivea would have gossiped about him. Did they think she'd have gossiped about *them* to *him*? That felt right. Why they were cool. Nivea had tainted so many things.

With gritted teeth as his trous bound his crotch, he made a sweeping bow that included them all. He thought he saw Kelp smirk, as if he'd experienced tight pants, too.

"Ladies. Forgive me for not recognizing you, GraceMistrys Darjeeling, GrandMistrys Licorice, GraceMistrys Mugwort."

"It's quite understandable that you didn't know us. We don't move in the same circles as you," Tiana Mugwort, Artemisia's sister, said.

"And Tiana isn't a GraceMistrys. She's a priestess," said GrandMistrys Licorice.

"Ah, my apologies."

High instrumental shrieks pierced the air.

"Finally, the band has arrived, please excuse me," Kelp said. He dumped Brazos in Laev's arms. The cat sprang to the floor and began prowling, lost in the shadows.

Kelp rushed toward the corner that held a platform framed in seaweed.

GrandMistrys Licorice looked down at her cup and made a face. "Kelp doesn't have the style of his late mother or his elder sister. This party is going downhill. Maybe we should skip it next year." She turned her gaze on Laev, and he saw gleaming, insatiable curiosity in her eyes. "Did you bring something from T'Hawthorn Residence?"

Darjeeling answered, "Yes, he did." She set her wiggling FamCat down. The calico followed Brazos. "T'Hawthorn brought a large china vase. It was snapped up in under three minutes."

Priestess Mugwort chuckled. "Leave it to you to notice any china."

"If you will excuse us?" Licorice said, and all three of the women curtsied again.

"Merry meet." Laev gave the first line of the farewell blessing.

"And merry part," the ladies chorused.

"And merry meet again," he said, not meaning it, and knowing their nods were polite falsities, too. They faded away gracefully and he took a few paces back. Once they were across the room, Glyssa pointed to something and they converged on the counter and became animated.

Laev discreetly rubbed his temples. The band was loud and the music off-key. Looked like everyone who was coming was here, so he made one more circuit of the room. Again nothing resonated of Family, so he said his good-byes to Kelp and called Brazos mentally.

The black cat appeared just as Laev was about to step onto the teleportation pad and leave him. He had layers of dust graying his fur. His mouth was slightly open as he held something in it. *I have found something that smells of Our Residence and Us!*

Laev swept the cat up into his arms and stepped onto the teleportation pad. A moment later he was home in the MasterSuite bedroom and the spell-lights made the rich colors in the chamber glow.

"What is it?" he demanded.

Brazos pranced along the top of the bedsponge, set in an antique platform instead of on the floor.

"Brazos!"

With a sniff, the cat came over to Laev, opened his mouth, and spit out a miniature golden acorn. Laev's mouth dried and his heart pounded. The acorn had been attached to the base of his HeartGift sculpture of the Lady and Lord dancing.

No one other than himself would have noticed it. Not Nivea, to whom his HeartGift was a minor thing, meaning little after she'd wed him and accomplished her goals. No one would have considered the acorn something to put on the exchange table. "Where did you get this?"

Brazos sneezed. *Not easy to find. I am a Very Intelligent Cat.*

Laev stroked his hand down Brazos's back, uncaring of the dust that clung to his fingers. "Yes, you are."

It was in a corner.

Easily overlooked. "Was anything else there?"

Dead bug, crumbled when I touched. Piece of ribbon, slip of papyrus—

"Oh." Well, he hadn't truly expected to find his HeartGift there. Would have been appalled if he had. *Was* appalled that Nivea might have taken it to the Salvage Ball from anger or spite or malice . . . or all three.

But he'd made the HeartGift during his Passage, and he'd followed his instincts, even during the fever sweats and the working-in-a-dream. He'd shielded his sculpture so that only he or his HeartMate could see it well, sense what it was. If Nivea had left it on the Salvage table, it would have been overlooked.

He'd been informed when he'd teleported into the party with the vase that if no one took his Salvage away, he must keep it. Those were the rules.

Nivea only followed others' rules when she wanted.

Had she really taken his HeartGift to the party? Had she left it there or had someone sensed something about it and taken it? Now that he seemed to be coming closer and closer to actually finding it, he yearned to know.

What had happened to his HeartGift?

*C*amellia *was aware when T'Hawthorn left. She couldn't have missed it since Mica, who she cradled in her arms, yelled telepathically, My friend Brazos is going home now. His FamMan is very pleased with him. Brazos found a treasure.*

Camellia shared a glance with Tiana; they were both sure there was nothing in the room that could be called a treasure to T'Hawthorn.

Glyssa snorted, stroked the cat's head with a couple of fingers. "Not much here of interest."

I liked the stuffed fish.

"No," Camellia said. "We are not having a stuffed fish on the walls. It's revolting." She thought it was a real fish, but the whole thing was a nasty shade of pink. The eyes had been creepy, like they were real and dead and bespelled, not glass. She avoided looking in that direction.

"There wasn't any interesting china here for Camellia," Tiana said.

"Or interesting books, ledgers, memoryspheres, et cetera, for Glyssa," Camellia said.

"Or pretty jewelry for Tiana." Glyssa stared again at the nearest table full of sad trinkets.

"We didn't do well tonight, and the crowd seems, ah, scruffier." Tiana turned a slow circle.

"It's changed," Camellia said.

"It's probably been changing all this time and we didn't notice," Tiana said.

"It has changed since Feam Kelp has taken charge." Glyssa squinted as if prodding her memory. "How long has that been?"

"Not sure," Camellia said. "But there wasn't anything worth a second glance on the tables tonight. No wonder that vase T'Hawthorn brought was snatched up."

"Was it incredible?" asked Glyssa.

"I didn't see the pattern close up, but it didn't impress me. It appeared to be expensive, though."

"Of course it would be," Glyssa said. "Let's go. There's nothing here for us anymore." There was a hint of mourning in her voice.

"It used to be fun." Tiana sighed.

They strolled toward the teleportation pad in the corner.

Wait! Mica rolled from Camellia's grasp and landed on her paws. *Since no one is getting a gift, may I?* Her tail flicked back and forth in excitement.

"You found something you liked?" Glyssa said with indulgent amusement.

Mica lifted her nose. *Gifts for all My new friends.*

Camellia looked at Tiana and Glyssa. They all shrugged together.

Better for hands to take instead of paws. Mica trotted off and the women followed. She stopped. *No Fams here tonight, except Brazos.*

"Also true," Tiana murmured.

Mica leapt onto a table and tapped a grimy object that looked no more than a smoothly rounded rock. *Smells right for Fam-Woman. For FamWoman from Me,* she said with pride. Slowly, Camellia reached out and took the hand-sized stone. Dirt slid under her fingers. She kept her smile curved. "Thank you." She held it, wasn't about to drop it into the cream-colored lined pocket of her expensive gown.

"What is it?" asked Glyssa.

Is a sculpture of a Cat. Looks a little like Brazos. Mica sniffed.

Tiana peered at it. *I'm sure it will be lovely when we clean it up.*

"Yesssss," vocalized Mica.

Tiana held out her hand and Camellia gave her the stone. With two crisp Words from Tiana, sparkles surrounded the item, a wave of her hand and she held a black rock. There were simple, fluid indentations that showed a curled cat with closed eyes and smug expression.

"A little crude," Glyssa said.

Mica sniffed. *Kit made it.*

"A cat? I don't think so." Glyssa frowned.

Tiana snorted. "A young sculptor carved it, a boy or a girl. Obviously, but I think it shows talent."

Smells and feelings and Flair from it mostly gone.

Tiana frowned, tilted her head as if she probed the item with her Flair. "You're right. I don't feel much of anything. I wonder why."

Mica inhaled lustily. *Being in pig stopped smell and other stuff.*

"A pig! Like the animal?" Glyssa asked.

"Yesssss," Mica said.

They all stared at her. Camellia pondered how Mica knew what the inside of a pig smelled like and decided not to ask.

"How do you know how the inside of a pig smells like?" Glyssa asked.

Love porcine. Plenty of pigs and pig guts on noble estates. As if to punctuate, Mica burped. None of the women had eaten the buffet food, but that obviously hadn't stopped the cat.

"Ugh," Tiana said, took Camellia's hand, and dumped the small sculpture into it.

Camellia rubbed a spot that looked like the remnants of an upright ear, studied it, hefted its weight. Mica was wrong, a slight tingle emanated from the raw sculpture. She smiled, let her fingers close over the piece, cradle it. "It's charming."

I did good. Mica purred and leapt gracefully from the counter to trot to another table. When the women joined her, she was clawing at the top of a ragged grayish piece of papyrus rolled as a scroll and tilted against the wall.

"I'll get that," Glyssa said.

Mica batted her hand away. *Is for Tiana. Smells good for* her. Mica wrinkled her nose. *Incense, maybe.*

"Me?" Tiana asked.

"Yesss," Mica said.

Brows raised, Tiana took the scroll and touched the knot of the grimy string. It fell into her hand and she put it in her pocket. As she unrolled the piece of papyrus, Camellia drew one of the bobbing spell-lights over so they could see better.

"It's an architectural drawing," Tiana said blankly. She tilted her head. "Interesting."

"Hmm," Glyssa said. "The lines are good, the drawing shows promise, but this one isn't the work of a master. Maybe a journeyman."

Unroll all! Mica demanded.

Propping the scroll on the table, Tiana did.

Mica tapped a legend in fancy writing that was shakier than the lines.

"The Turquoise House!" Glyssa said. "A diagram of the layout of the Turquoise House, the House that's recently become sentient!"

She reached avidly for the scroll. Tiana lifted it and the papyrus rerolled; Tiana held it to her chest. "This is mine."

"You don't understand," Glyssa said. "I don't think the Public-Library has any plans of the Turquoise House and it has been very protective of its privacy."

"Very exclusive," Camellia agreed.

"Secretive," Tiana said, lifting her chin. "And I like protecting a house's secrets. This is mine and I'm keeping it."

"At least let me make a copy for the Library."

"No."

"It won't even go into the public areas. We'll archive it."

"No. Mine."

Look, look! Mica hopped up and down, pointing her red-tipped claws at the scroll.

They looked. The papyrus had changed, appearing to be heavier and with the tiniest hint of gold along its edges.

Tiana unrolled it and the drawing was now in multicolored inks. "Oooh. This is pretty, worth framing and hanging on my bedroom wall."

"Ti-an-a!" Glyssa shifted from foot to foot, her shoulders hunched. "Please let me—"

"No." Tiana rolled the papyrus tight and tapped the middle, fastening it together with a spellword. Then she dropped it into her sleeve pocket.

Now for Glyssa! Mica said and trotted along the table.

"How is she *doing* this?" Glyssa asked. "Finding stuff we didn't?"

"I saw the sculpture," Tiana said, "but it looked like a stone and I didn't pick it up."

"I didn't see the scroll," Glyssa grumbled. "I missed it."

"Me, too," Camellia said. If she'd seen it—if any of them had—they would have studied it or given it to Glyssa.

"It's rather the same gray as the shadows against the walls," Tiana agreed.

"Cat noses and smells," Glyssa muttered. She walked quickly to where Mica sat, looking like a realistic art object herself. Camellia smiled, *her* FamCat.

Mica had her paw on a grungy velveteen pouch. The embroidery stating the brand of liquor it had once held was broken. The strings of the dirty tassels had unraveled.

"For me?" Glyssa said.

"Yesss," Mica replied.

No one protested at the condition of the gift.

Smells like you. Adventure. Something from the southern continent.

Glyssa's hand hesitated, her shoulders tensed, then she rolled them and lifted the edge with her fingertips and gingerly pulled open the string around the top of the pouch, glanced inside, and exclaimed. Plunging her hand in the bag, she grabbed what was in there and dropped the pouch. A slight crackle came as she opened the folded papyrus—to reveal nothing on the sheet, but that it was wrapped around a lovely tooled leather wallet of dark red, embossed with gold.

"My," Glyssa said, her smile wide as she stroked the fine leather, traced a finger over an elegant curlicue. "So lovely."

Mica preened before the small clump of people who had gathered. She groomed a few strands of orange fur on her shoulder, lifted her head in graceful pride. *Good gifts for My new friends.*

Camellia petted her Fam, knowing her smile had gone soft and foolish. "That's right."

So now you can give Me the gift of the stuffed fish.

Tiana and Glyssa laughed.

Mica turned her head toward them and offered as innocent and virtuous a smile as a cat can manage. *And you can tell My Fam-Woman how wonderful the fish is. How nice it will look in My closet.*

"Closet! You think you get a closet?" Camellia asked.

Brazos says He gets a whole room. An image came to Camellia's mind of a small room she thought might be a dressing room attached to a great Residence MasterSuite.

I want a room, too. But you don't have many. So until We find a new house, I will take a closet.

Camellia reeled back against the table. "I don't want a new house. I like my house."

Mica lifted her nose. *We need a house that the mean men can't come in.*

"A fortress more like," Camellia muttered.

Yes, a Residence would be fine.

There weren't many intelligent houses and most of them belonged to the highest nobles. The women laughed.

Scooping up Mica, Camellia settled her along her folded arm. "No Residences for us. And I've never seen a house that my uncle can't get into." She took off toward the teleportation pad.

My fish! Mica wailed, both telepathically and aloud.

Tiana altered course and swept up the fish, cleansed it with one of her excellent housekeeping spells as they walked to the pad. "It's really not too bad," Tiana said.

"Revolting," Camellia repeated.

"At least it's small," Glyssa said. "And you're hanging it in a closet."

*T*he dream that was a memory began well. It always did.

He was seventeen and the future was a road he owned. He was Laev T'Hawthorn, and someday he'd be T'Hawthorn, a GreatLord, maybe even the Captain of All Councils.

His Flair was strong inside him, rising through him like a tide, being released by his Passage. Sure, the dreamquests had been rough—especially when he relived the worst day of his life, at thirteen. He'd nearly killed and been killed.

In the dream-memory, he rose from the blanket he'd shared with friends at JudgementGrove, and his legs felt wobbly. Couldn't show weakness, though, so he stiffened them and pretended nothing was wrong, that he wasn't dizzy. That another occurrence of his psi magic wasn't wildly spiking. Passage threatened. He should get home.

But he smelled something wonderful that hit him straight in the groin. His HeartMate was here! The power of his own Flair and Passage—a whiff of her Flair, too—told him that. He turned to follow his nose and there *she* was. His HeartMate! The one who would match his soul, as he matched hers. She was walking in a group of girls.

His heart thumped hard in his chest, rushed so his pulse drowned out the words of everyone around him. His Flair flashed and the atmosphere pressed on him and he knew he had to have her. He walked toward the group, his gaze fixed on the golden girl—golden hair, amber eyes, skin as if it held the glow of the sun itself.

STOP! His older sleeping-self became aware, as ever, of what would happen, had happened. Dreaded the consequences of this one fall into senseless infatuation.

But his younger-self was drawn by Flair and scent and sheer lust toward Nivea. She filled his vision.

Not . . . quite.

For the first time in ages, the image of Nivea blurred and the other girls beyond Nivea sharpened.

Six

His dream changed from the way the real event had occurred. He saw the girls. The shy, round-faced girl with long, curly black hair and beautiful emerald eyes—his age, seventeen—Artemisia Mugwort.

Then there were the three younger girls in their early teens. One was obviously Artemisia's sister, though she had a sharper chin. Another stared at him with penetrating eyes and the gingery hair that marked the Licorice Family who ran the PublicLibrary.

The third girl, Camellia Darjeeling, had just had the guts to interrupt the case in JudgementGrove and request the ship salvager look for a fifty-piece tea set—and claim that set.

Her aura throbbed Flaired delight, she wrapped her arms around the other two girls her age and grinned. Laev felt a pull . . .

And Nivea, the golden girl, put her hand on his arm and he focused back on her.

Mistake! his older dream-self shouted. He tried to pull back, change what had happened, and couldn't.

The atmosphere around Laev thickened, like misty clouds shrouding past mistakes. Then the light took on a green cast, as in the Salvage Ball. This time it *was* a ball and he had a supple woman in his arms and the music wasn't fast and raucous but a smooth ancient waltz. They danced and he didn't look too hard at the woman. Her scent was light and spicy, and included an undertone of female arousal.

Every step had their bodies brushing and lust fired. Vaguely he remembered sex dreams like this . . . maybe even this woman. A little taller than Nivea, more slender. Nice ass, though; his hands were on it. And then they were in his bedroom, in his bed and skin to skin, and her skin was so smooth and hot and her body was hot and wet and he was moaning and plunging and releasing all his cares into the sweet, sweet woman.

Camellia woke as an orgasm rolled through her. She shuddered, panted, then settled back in the bedsponge. She'd been making love with—No! No one she knew.

She would not admit that the door in her mind had exploded open. She shut it and refused to acknowledge that it remained open a crack.

The night was dark, warm, she was safe and happy . . . go back to sleep. Back . . . to . . . sleep.

One last shudder and she pulled the darkness around her and instructed herself not to dream.

A purr rumbled at the edge of her mind as she let herself sink back into unconsciousness.

Laev rose, took a waterfall, and let water pound on the base of his neck, slide down his back. He'd changed the sheets of his bed, embarrassed that he'd lost control of his body. He'd liked the sex dream, though, and it had been more satisfying than his last couple of affairs.

He wasn't in the market for a real woman. Maybe he should welcome such dreams instead of pushing them away as he'd always done before. He stopped the hot herbal shower with a wave of his hand, stepped from the small stone room onto tile, dried.

Now that the sex was over, he wouldn't be able to sleep. Memories would loop in his brain.

Gently he sent his mind searching through the night . . . and

found that his older friend-like-a-brother, Cratag Maytree T'Marigold, was awake and walking the halls of his own Residence. Laev
ignored the writhing envy that Cratag had a HeartMate and two
beautiful children, and sent Cratag a clear mental call. *You up for a
fighting bout?*

Surprise and pleasure flowed to him from Cratag. *Always. Here.
Training room one.*

I'll be there in ten minutes.

Whip your ass, Cratag responded. Even with Family he didn't
speak well telepathically.

Laev was already drawing on fighting clothes. *You hope, old
man,* he said but knew the taunt was a lie. Cratag had made his living fighting, still hired out as a bodyguard. Laev himself had missed
his weekly training sessions at the Green Knight Fencing and Fighting Salon for a few months. Something he must start again, especially if he wanted to keep his current fighter ranking.

Yeah, Laev'd get pounded into the mat, but he'd spend time with
his friend, and that was worth it.

Camellia's morning was productive, as usual. She rearranged her
knickknack shelves, removing some. Both Glyssa and Tiana would
approve of that. They'd always believed her house was too cluttered.
But they hadn't lived with her father and uncle. Those two men
always took anything nice in the house to sell if they needed any
money. Most of her life, Camellia had lived with a bedsponge, a
rickety table, and four chairs.

Her father would smash things if he felt like it.

The luckiest time in her life came when her father and uncle had
abandoned her, her mother, and her brother when she was twelve.
Her mother hadn't had much life in her then, and even less hope,
but she'd worked to support them and had helped Camellia find a
job mixing potions for an herbalist.

Camellia scanned her modified home. The house was pristine,
shelves with valuables too high and narrow for Mica to reach, the

paisley fabric of the chairs had an odd sheen with the no-scratch, no-pee repellent on them.

She'd put away the matching plate to the cup that her father had destroyed.

House arranging done? asked Mica. She'd been sitting on the rounded top of the furrabeast-leather chair—that had already had a few pinpricks of claws in it—"supervising."

"Yes." Still a little too bare for Camellia, but her life had changed again with the advent of Mica. Someday the young cat would settle down and Camellia would be able to display more of her art objects.

What do we do now?

"I'm hungry, how about you?"

"Yesss."

"Let's go to Darjeeling's Teahouse and I'll introduce you to the staff." She hoped they liked Fams. She'd also have to look into mastering—or paying for—premium spells to keep any Fam residue from contaminating her restaurants. There was a section on that in the instruction sphere D'Ash had given her.

More gilt to spend.

Mica brushed across the full legs of Camellia's trous, purring loudly.

Gilt had been a primary motivator in Camellia's life, sometimes secondary to love—the love of her friends—but not now. She didn't have quite enough to feel financially secure, but she had her health and her drive and the resource of her tea set if disaster struck.

Now she had Mica, and the little cat had already made a place in her heart. Gilt would get tighter, but they'd make it. She'd just have to work harder.

*O*nce again *Laev was behind his desk. This time he was staring at* the private investigator, Garrett Primross, in the scry panel. Laev had hired the man to find his Family treasures. Primross, of Prime Investigations, was a master of his craft and several years older than Laev. The detective had a craggy face and impassive manner.

Laev had received an invoice from the private eye for the entire cost of the case and wanted a full report.

"Ah, the report. You should have received a record sphere, also."

"I did, but I prefer to speak with you personally."

"Facial and body cues are important," Primross agreed. He stared down at sheets of papyrus on his own battered desk. "I've retrieved seven objects for you that were Hawthorn Family treasures, which your late wife . . . distributed."

"You never told me where you found them."

"Three I obtained from the Sunflowers, your late wife's Family, to whom she'd given them as gifts—one to her father, one to her mother, and one to her next younger sister."

Laev gritted his teeth, he'd been afraid of that. At the time of his marriage, he'd given the Sunflowers a large dowry for Nivea, from funds that his MotherDam—the mother of his mother—had bequeathed him. He knew that Nivea had also made "loans" from her allowance to her Family. Anger cruised through him that he'd paid them once more.

He cleared his throat, rough with renewed irritation, and dipped his head to Primross. "Thanks for dealing with them." The Sunflowers had never cared for him—his status and money and what he might do for them, but not him. They'd been completely chilly to him after Nivea's death.

"'Welcome. Glad to be finished, though. They have assured me that they have no other pieces that have Hawthorn Family markings."

"You believe them."

"If they could make you pay more, they would." Primross's gaze met Laev's, went beyond him. "Your wife died during the sickness?"

"You know that, why ask?"

"There seemed to be some feeling that she might have been neglected."

Fury buzzed in his brain. Laev set his palms on his desk, rose, leaned forward, glaring at the man. "Nivea and I were estranged, but she lived here, in a sentient GreatHouse that monitors all the life signs of its inhabitants. She received the best of care." He made a flat cutting motion. "The sickness killed a lot of people. She was one of them."

"So I believe." Primross held his stare steady.

Laev inclined his head and sat. When he spoke, it was with the cold tones he'd learned from his FatherSire. "The Sunflowers don't care for me. If they thought Nivea was neglected during her sickness, they would have sued. No doubt about that."

"Agreed. Now you know what they feel and might be saying."

Shrugging, Laev said, "They have never praised me. People know that." A corner of his mouth twisted. "The newssheets enjoyed reporting Nivea's excesses." Another reason why he wanted to keep this investigation quiet. "She was not gentle with their reporters." He wasn't the only one his wife disaffected. A fleeting vision of the three women he'd met the night before rose. Nivea had dumped them as friends.

His FatherSire and Laev himself had had to mend alliances that Nivea had tested.

Laev missed the first part of Primross's reply.

". . . true. Your reputation is more sterling than hers," Primross said.

Brazos leapt from his velvet-cushioned chair to the desk, hissed, and arched at Primross. *WE ARE NOT MEAN. SHE WAS MEAN.* His tail thrashed. *I HAVE HEARD THIS. SHE KICKED FAMS.* He ended as if that said it all. Brazos sat, curled his tail around his paws.

"I see," Primross said.

"You heard my Fam?" asked Laev.

"Oh, yeah." His eyes narrowed. "She kicked Fams?"

So WE can prove. Brazos lifted a forepaw, extended and retracted his claws, seemed to see a hair out of line, and licked it.

Primross nodded and continued, "Of the other four items I retrieved for you, T'Hawthorn, two were from collectors and two were in separate antiquities stores. You'll find the exact shops named on my invoice." The detective paused, then asked, "How many other pieces were lost?"

"At least two." There had been a red-gold desk set—and his HeartGift. Feeling as if his face had gone grim and brittle, Laev continued with new information for Primross, "I am not sure when my late wife began removing Family items from the Residence. Neither my FatherSire nor the Residence itself informed me of the matter. My FatherSire left few notations in his journal." He drank from a cup of caff that had cooled. "The items were not pieces my Father-Sire considered valuable or important to the Family."

"But you do," Primross said.

"Yes. I do." That Laev had brought a woman into the Family who had stolen lacerated his feelings. He wanted *everything* she'd taken back. "There's no record of the exact objects Nivea took."

"Your wife, as the lady of the Residence, didn't keep an accounting journal?" Primross's tones were even.

"No. I wish to speak to you about something of a more personal nature. Are you available for an appointment tomorrow at Mid-MorningBell?"

Primross's eyes flickered as if he internally consulted his own schedule. "No."

"I would like to speak as soon as possible." Laev knew damn well that he was the highest-ranking—and paying—client Primross had. If the man wanted his business to grow, he'd give Laev what he wanted.

The private eye stared at him, finally muttered, "I can be at your place in about a septhour and a half."

"Fine. I can send a glider—"

"I'll teleport to your front gate," Primross said gruffly, words Laev had hoped to hear. He didn't have a glider without the Family arms tinted on the side, something he was considering remedying right now.

"I'll meet you there."

Primross nodded. "Merry meet," he said formally.

"Merry part," Laev returned.

"And merry meet again." Primross ended the scry.

Laev scrutinized the invoice. All had little logos beside the entries—the Sunflower's Family arms, business logos of the shops. He'd seen one of those logos last night, embroidered on shirt cuffs. The man who'd pounced on his vase. No doubt Primross had already winnowed everything there was to know from that source, but . . .

"Nivea went to the Salvage Ball more than once."

Brazos stopped licking the pads of his paw. *Took your best gift there.*

Laev's HeartGift. "Probably. The women we met last night attended that party for years, too. They seemed sharp." Between the three of them, they might have memories of objects left on the tables. A few of the missing items showed the Hawthorn arms.

Mica said they talked a lot about the party, what was there and what wasn't. Mica is a smart Cat, too.

"Residence, scry the Temple directory and ask for Tiana Mugwort."

A couple of minutes later, the Residence said, "She is unavailable today."

Laev recalled the avid curiosity of Glyssa Licorice.

Brazos leapt onto his lap, looked up at him, and purred loudly as he kneaded Laev's thighs. *Mica and her FamWoman are at Darjeeling's HouseHeart.*

"What?" He hadn't thought GraceHouse Darjeeling had an intelligent Residence.

The TEAHOUSE.

Teahouse. Yes, he'd heard of Darjeeling's Teahouse. The connection between a rare tea set and the teahouse snapped together.

Brazos leapt from Laev's lap and strolled over to the teleportation pad. *Follow Me. I know the coordinates.*

Laev stared at the cat. Did he really want to put his life in a cat's paws? He stood. "You fail and I die and you won't be welcome here in the Residence."

"No, he will not be welcome," the Residence boomed.

Laev figured it was only upset because he didn't have an heir yet. But since that was the first sentence the Residence had offered independently since the previous T'Hawthorn died, Laev decided he was making progress. He stepped up on the teleportation pad and picked up Brazos.

He'd thought the cat would send him an image, but the animal teleported them both. They fell a few inches to a rug covering a firm pad, and Laev instinctively sucked in a breath.

He was rewarded with the scent of tea and spices and a whiff of calming incense.

For a few blinks he let his eyes adjust to the dim light as he let the concept of restaurant-as-HouseHeart roll in his mind. All the HouseHearts he knew were secreted in the depths of sentient Residences, closely guarded with the greatest Flair. Usually the Residences belonged to the FirstFamilies—or the FirstFamilies belonged to them. But in the last decade or so, some GrandHouse noble houses had begun to become intelligent.

The place didn't much appear like T'Hawthorn Residence's HouseHeart. That reminded him that he hadn't spent the appropriate amount of hours there this month and irritated him.

Brazos shot from his arms, through tables, and leapt over the counter and through the door to the kitchen.

All the tables were full, so it was doing a good business.

Mica says FamWoman will come see you soon, Brazos said.

A young woman dressed in a brightly colored work tunic and trous and a brown bib apron approached Laev.

"Welcome to Darjeeling's HouseHeart. Please follow me."

"I'm here for GraceMistrys Darjeeling." He should have set up an appointment.

"Ah. She'll be right with you. I'll show you to the office." There was a slight hesitation in the server's voice that made Laev think she was mentally communicating with Darjeeling. Then she turned and led Laev around a pretty fountain, across the room, and behind the counter to an office that looked like it had been converted from a closet. Inside was a small desk with a chair behind it, and another chair jammed between the desk and the wall, with enough room for the arc of the door.

Camellia Darjeeling stood staring down at two cats who lapped from a bowl of milk. She looked up and he caught a smile on her face and something inside him twinged. Pretty woman.

But when she turned fully toward him, her hands were in her opposite sleeves and her smile had faded to one of pure politeness. More, she'd gone pale. "How can I help you, GreatLord T'Hawthorn?"

"Are you all right?"

Her jaw flexed. "A little headache."

"I'll be brief." But he'd wished he'd planned out the meeting. This was beginning to feel like a mistake. Why hadn't he just scried Primross to handle this? Because the women already had a poor opinion of him and he didn't trust Primross to overcome that?

"I'd like to ask you some questions about the Salvage Ball."

"Last night?"

"Can we be private?"

She gestured to the door and it began to slowly swing shut. There was a loud belch and the cats jumped. Both of them hit her shoulders, used them as springboards to leap over Laev and through the door before it closed.

Camellia toppled.

Laev caught her.

Seven

Shrieks of cat glee and the sound of racing paws came from beyond the office door and the odor of spilt spiced milk swirled around Laev and Camellia.

There wasn't much room to move. He held Camellia, noticing that she felt really good in his arms. Womanly supple. Smooth skin over firm muscles.

He liked being close to her. There was a quality about her that soothed . . . or maybe it was just the place, because she pulled away and adjusted the sleeves of her gown. Her lips tightened as she glanced at the milk-soggy carpet.

She bent and righted the bowl, and Laev appreciated how her tunic showed the shape of her ass. Her hips appeared a bit larger than her bustline . . . not a perfect figure, just endearing. Nice and full. He had to curl his fingers to stop himself from squeezing her butt—something that hadn't happened for a long time. Still he liked the buzz of attraction.

Too bad she was obviously a very serious woman who'd take sex seriously, also.

With a muttered couplet and a flick of her fingers, she cleaned the carpet. He noted that it was a standard pattern favored by the middle class, like most of the furnishings in the teahouse—the menu tables and cushioned chairs. The statues of the Lord and Lady in their individual niches were sold by temples, only the fountain was unique—a very wise choice.

She moved gracefully around the desk and sat on the chair, her expression once again one of courteous inquiry. "The Salvage Ball, you said?"

"Yes." This was going to be difficult, he wished the priestess had been available. He tried his most sincere smile, spread his hands.

Camellia frowned.

Not good. "I was wondering if you or your friends might have recognized any T'Hawthorn items in previous years."

"Nivea took things from your home?" Camellia's voice was sharp.

Laev straightened in his chair. "I realize that I am a relative stranger, and that you and your friends probably have little good-will toward me and mine—"

"Nivea didn't believe that goodwill was important. Beauty and status were more—" Camellia snapped her mouth shut. "I beg your pardon."

"Granted."

"She was difficult to become close to."

Laev nodded but was mentally considering statues in his work-shop that he might offer as compensation. An instant later, he trans-located a forty-five-centimeter-high statue of the Lord to Camellia's desk. "I am prepared to trade for information," he said easily.

Camellia's eyes had widened, deepened to dark gray, her mouth opened a little.

"It's much like the one you have in front." Something he'd sculpted as a young man, copying from a standard statue, practic-ing his technique.

She slid her hand down the brownish marble. Laev tensed, he hoped it was smooth, he hadn't looked at that particular piece for years.

"It's wonderful. And a better color than the stock white," she said.

"An appropriate trade for information."

She smiled and it appeared almost easy, some strain that had been in her since he'd arrived—*since they'd met*—eased.

"Yes, indeed," she said.

Good. He liked her better when she relaxed. He was pleased his gift hadn't offended, been more than she'd expect for information. No need for her to know that he'd carved it.

Camellia turned the statue slowly around. Her lashes were lowered and her face impassive as she said, "There was a T'Hawthorn desk set some years ago. Red gold."

His heart jumped. "Yes? Did you notice what happened to it?"

Her gaze met his briefly, then slid away. "It was the cause of a quarrel—the final quarrel between us and GreatMistrys Hawthorn." Camellia's cheeks tinted with color. "We—my friends and I—have strong feelings about objects going missing from homes. Glyssa Licorice was of the opinion that GreatMistrys Hawthorn shouldn't have brought the desk set—especially since it had a spray of hawthorn leaves in the corners of the blotter and engraved on the writestick and stand."

An emotional blow. He kept his face immobile.

Again Camellia's glance flickered on his face, then went beyond him. "Tiana Mugwort remonstrated with Niv—GreatMistrys Hawthorn, who wasn't pleased at the slight. And since Hawthorn was the highest-ranked person at the Salvage Ball that year, she made it hard on the rest of us and we left early. We didn't see what became of the desk set."

"When was that?"

Camellia leaned back and her old comfortchair jerked. Laev's fingers twitched. He could fix the chair spell for her. But he had to make sure that she felt they were on an equal footing.

After a minute, she said, "It was about six years ago."

Another jolt. He hadn't thought Nivea was that angry at him so long ago. And it was too long ago to believe that he could find the set.

He stood and inclined his torso. There wasn't enough space for a full bow. "Thank you. Could you ask your friends about any memories they might have?"

Camellia stared at him for a moment, her face serious, mystery lurking in her eyes. A corner of her mouth lifted in a wry smile. Again she trailed fingers down the statue. Laev's body clenched.

"I'll do that." Reaching into her left sleeve pocket, she pulled out a perscry—a personal scry that was a drop of water encased in glass—and addressed it. "Message to Tiana and Glyssa's scrycaches, come to dinner at my place, half septhour after EveningBell."

Glyssa Licorice's face formed in the small sphere. "Dinner at your house. Will you be cooking?"

"Yeah—yes, I will," Camellia said.

The gleam sharpened in Glyssa's eyes. "Good. You're the best cook of us all."

"Should be, I did all the cooking at the teahouse until I could hire it done. Later." Camellia rubbed a thumb over the glass and it returned to dark opaque green. She rose from her chair.

"I must compliment you on Darjeeling's HouseHeart, a well-conceived and well-run business," Laev said.

Her smile was slow. She ducked her head. "Thank you. A pleasure doing business with you"

"My pleasure."

She glanced at a wall timer. "I have an appointment."

"I do, too."

A knock came on the door and it opened to show Tiana Mugwort, dressed in the in the pale blue of a ThirdLevel Priestess. Behind her stood a priest and priestess, both in darker blue—second level.

"I wanted to show my mentors Darjeeling's HouseHeart," Tiana said.

Another half bow to the newcomers. "Excuse me. I have an appointment, and my apologies for my abrupt departure." For some reason—the serenity of the place, the energy of Darjeeling or the priestesses and priest, or all three—energy hummed around him, boosting his own natural Flair. "Merry meet," he said.

"And merry part," everyone replied.

"And merry meet again." He glanced at pretty Camellia, her coloring and body type so different from his hurtful ex-wife's, and realized he was pleasurably anticipating meeting her again. Then he thought of his den and teleported away.

*C*amellia's trainer, *Acacia Bluegum, seemed unsurprised when Mica* accompanied her for the lesson. The ex–Druida City guardswoman gestured to a Fam play center that would keep the young cat interested during the lesson. The woman also casually mentioned that there were mice in the alley behind the gym.

Mica watched as Camellia stretched, practiced her fighting patterns, and managed to draw her instructor to a tie in the first light bout.

My FamWoman is sooo skilled, Mica said mentally, purring.

Camellia saw the corners of her teacher's lips twitch. Acacia could use Camellia to polish the wooden floor if she wanted.

As soon as Mica got bored and headed to the play center, Camellia informed her teacher of the confrontation with her father and the trick he had used to break her grip.

For the next three-quarters of a septhour they practiced holds and releases, grappling, then they did a full-out fight. Once again adrenaline raced through Camellia and she held her own.

After the bout, Camellia lay panting on the mat. Renewed confidence sizzled through her. Next time her father came, she'd be ready. If he dared break the tiniest cup of a miniature tea set, she'd haul his ass to the guard station.

"I would like to recommend you to the Green Knight Fencing and Fighting Salon," Acacia said.

"No!"

Camellia received a flat and steady look. "You need to train with men. That will help you in several ways. You will become accustomed to men's strength, weight, mass." Acacia's smile came and went on her face, leaving a brief impression of white teeth ready to bite. "You can pick out one of the patrons there who is close in build to your father, practice with him."

With a skeptical glance at her teacher, Camellia rolled to her feet. "The Green Knight Fencing and Fighting Salon has older men running to fat?"

A snort. "Not the teachers or the higher levels of patrons. But it is also considered a fashionable social club." The former guards-woman walked over to a wall panel, slipped it aside, and touched a couple of buttons. Camellia winced as a full-sized hologram of her father appeared.

"I believe we last updated this profile several years ago. Is it still accurate?" her teacher asked.

Swallowing hard, Camellia rolled to her feet and walked around the thing. "He's put on weight around the middle. And he never was a fighter, never very fit that I know of. Always depended upon his charm." He was still a big man, with more brute strength than Camellia could summon.

"So you informed me," her trainer said, holding down a button. "Say when."

To Camellia's delight, she saw her father's paunch thicken. "When . . . no, I lie, a little less." She sighed. Since the colonists arrived on Celta, the birthrate had lessened, sickness took more of a toll . . . but the compensation was that people lived much longer than they had on their home planet. Her father would be stronger than she for years . . . unless she worked harder than he on her training. Became better physically, more clever in a fight.

She didn't want to concentrate on physical training. She wanted to spend time honing her businesses until they were exactly as she'd envisioned . . . then laying ground for her next teahouse, a small place, catering to the ultra-feminine crowd.

Currently both Darjeeling's Teahouse and Darjeeling's House-Heart were decorated to be comfortable for both men and women, but Camellia had old pics and holos of Earthan places that were obviously targeted at women. It was an idea that had spun in the back of her mind . . . when she thought she'd be able to afford a third place. She frowned. To get the detail she wanted, she'd have to consult with the starship, *Nuada's Sword*. Would that be worth the risk that it would uncover her own secrets?

". . . you need to feel a man's hands on you."

Camellia reeled, luckily the wall was there to brace her shoulder against. "What?"

"I thought that would bring your mind back to me and to training." Her teacher's smile was wide with real amusement. "I can tell when you're thinking of your career and businesses. Excellent job at Darjeeling's HouseHeart, by the way. Like it a lot."

"Thank you." Camellia sucked in a deep breath. Under her tutor's eyes she held it for a few counts, released it slowly.

"You need to feel a man's hands on you—in a variety of ways. Just the impersonal touch of an instructor. Hard when fighting . . ."

Camellia had liked Laev T'Hawthorn's hands on her . . . when they'd stood together, she hadn't panicked. She was pleased with herself.

"When was the last time you had sex?" asked Acacia.

A croak stuck in Camellia's throat. She flushed, mostly from the recollection of the sexual dream last night, but some from anger that she had to deal with this issue again.

Acacia continued, "Sexual frustration can be used in a fight, but it's not the best energy. Like any emotion, it can cloud your fighting, especially for an amateur."

Another deep breath . . . and . . . hold . . . and . . . release. "I don't think I'll have a problem interacting with men in a training salon."

"No, I don't, either. But your best friends are female and you spend most of your time with them. When did you last have a *social* interaction with a man?"

She wouldn't talk about Laev T'Hawthorn. "I was at the Salvage Ball this year," Camellia defended.

"Did you dance? Touch men's hands and waists and arms as you went up and down the lines, made the patterns?"

"Ah. No. The music was bad." And she and Glyssa and Tiana had left before the dancing started.

"Camellia. You need to spend some time with men, learn that they aren't all like your male relatives." Acacia flicked her finger, saving Camellia's father's bio profile.

"It will be good for you to experience a mostly male atmosphere. Despite that they've integrated the classes, most of those who frequent the Green Knight are predominantly men. Some of the evenings are social. Which reminds me." Acacia rubbed her hands. "Maybe you can help me set up a women's fighting-fitness club here? I'd like to bring more social events here. Maybe have drinks and food in the building next door. That space is finally for rent. We can do a trade."

"Maybe," Camellia said, seeing more of her time swirl down a sucking drain. "But if you want me to go to the Green Knight instead . . ."

"Let me work some comp time out with the owner, Tinne Holly."

"It occurs to me that the fee for sparring at the Green Knight is probably considerably higher than here. So my 'trade' will not go as far."

"That's right. But I can get you in, which I don't think you'd be able to do on your own. We're talking the highest class of nobles. Think of the business you might do, the connections you might make, the information you might gather . . . at the very least, you'll be able to study how they think. Noblemen and -women of the highest class."

Camellia narrowed her eyes. "You're a member?"

"Yes. But you won't be working with me. My level and sessions are strictly for professional fighters."

"Oh. Maybe. I'll think about it—"

"You'll outclass your father in this, too," Acacia said.

"Done," Camellia said.

Her teacher slung an arm around Camellia's shoulders, squeezed. "Let's head for the waterfalls."

Loosening her muscles as she walked, feeling twinges as she stripped in a small cubicle and went into one of the sectioned-off stalls, Camellia called to Acacia, "You know one of my best friends is a priestess, right? I've been getting advice from her, too."

Steam rose from another waterfall. "Then you should listen to both of us."

Camellia sighed. "She's on the topic of HeartMates lately."

There was a pause and Camellia felt a pulse of surprise from Acacia. "I'd forgotten. You have a HeartMate, don't you? All the more reason you need to spend time with men." Acacia's tones hardened. "You're lucky to have a HeartMate. I don't. Most don't. By the Cave of the Dark Goddess, why aren't you looking for him?"

"It's complicated." Camellia was more defensive than when she'd been fighting.

"Oh. And is opening a business and making it successful simple?" Acacia asked.

"No!"

"None of the best things in life are."

*T*he *Residence informed Laev that Primross had arrived to discuss* business. Laev walked down to meet the man and waved the great greeniron gates open. Brazos gamboled at his side, making forays into the bushes and trees that lined the gliderway.

Laev also keyed the security spellshield to allow Primross access to the estate during the day. The private investigator stared at Laev from under heavy brows and grunted his thanks.

They circled the castle, walking over a smooth green lawn that had been tended for centuries, until they reached one of the sacred groves on the estate. This was a small, private place that Laev had claimed when he was a teen—a mere circle of tall birches with a lichened stone bench in the middle. The grass here was not mown but grew wild in the tiny glade. Spring flowers were revealed as spots of color when the breeze moved.

Laev gestured for Primross to sit, then took a seat himself, looking toward the south and hints of rolling hills instead of toward the great Residence, the city, or the ocean.

"Nice place." The words seemed dragged from Primross.

"Thank you."

"Must be some big reason that you don't want to talk even in the Residence."

Laev slanted him an ironic look. "My staff is large, and like most FirstFamilies, they are all relatives. Many are older than I and believe they know my affairs better than I do."

Another grunt from Primross.

"Not to mention the Residence," Laev continued.

"What about it?" Truculence laced Primross's tones, but when he turned his head to look at the castle, his gaze was admiring . . . and with a hint of envy.

"The Residence is the oldest being in the Family," Laev said drily. "It will *always* be the oldest member of the Family. It has centuries of perspective." He stretched out his legs. "And it has disapproved of me since I was seventeen."

"Ah."

"There are drawbacks to being from the FirstFamilies," Laev said.

Primross stiffened beside him, and Laev knew the man's prejudices were as strong as ever.

Laev focused on the unfurling birch leaves and said, "Now for business—"

"I can guess that, too. The late GreatMistrys Hawthorn stole your HeartGift."

Eight

Emotions wrenched through Laev at the words no one had ever spoken aloud. His head went light even as he shuddered at flashing scenes of the past laden with emotion—his Passage at seventeen, sensing the girl he thought was his HeartMate, wooing her, giving her his HeartGift, claiming her, wedding her . . . then the awful discovery that she wasn't the one for him. That she'd lied and deceived him.

His scalp prickled with sweat.

"Tough situation," Primross said, still staring at the hills in the distance, and Laev knew the man had followed his history just as he himself had. Everyone knew he'd thought Nivea was his HeartMate when he'd wed her.

"My wife and I were estranged for the last seven years of her life," Laev said.

"Separate suites?"

"Yes."

"The Residence didn't like her, I guess. That must have been hard on her, too."

"Yes," Laev said. He pulled in a deep breath, let it cleanse the depths of his lungs. The past was gone. He'd say what was necessary to Primross, then leave it to collect dust again. "I didn't discover Nivea was disposing of Hawthorn items until I read my FatherSire's Family journal after his death."

"A shock," Primross said.

"Yes," Laev said.

"Tell me of this HeartGift."

"As usual, I made it during my Second Passage at seventeen. I sculpt."

"Sculpt?"

"My HeartGift is a sculpture of the Lady and Lord embracing."

Primross's brows went up. "The Lady and Lord embracing."

Laev slanted him a look. "Not intimately. Arms around each other's waists. Both with one foot stepping forward as if ready to dance." He smiled. "Both clothed."

"What material is the statue made of?"

"Marble. A very unique chunk." Laev vaguely recalled creating it through the haze of the Passage fever dreams. "Part was brownish with brown veins, the other more pinkish."

"Ah. The Lord a different color than the Lady?"

"Yes. That's what the piece of marble felt like in my hands. That's what I saw in my mind when I picked the stone up for the first time." He pulled out the tiny gold acorn and handed it to the private investigator. "I carved a pedestal under the couple and edged it in gold—acorns for my Oak heritage, Hawthorn blossoms, and leaves for my Grove ancestry. This is one of the acorns."

"Where did you find it?" asked Primross, setting the small bit on his palm and angling his hand so it wobbled back and forth. The way his nostrils widened and his mouth opened slightly, Laev thought that the man was using all his Flair to sense the essence of the piece. Which was, of course, mostly Laev's essence at seventeen— and whatever smudges from others it had picked up in the years since.

Laev had given his HeartGift to Nivea to claim her as was Celtan law, before they'd married. Before they'd had sex—well, he'd been making love and she'd been having sex.

I found the acorn! Brazos surged out of the high grass and pounced on Primross's boots. *I found it.*

Primross lifted his brows at the cat. "Young and sturdy tomcat."

"Yes."

"All black," Primross said.

"A blessed cat," Laev said.

I am BRAZOS HAWTHORN.

"Loud, too." A smile lurked on Primross's mouth. He jiggled his feet a bit and the Fam followed the movement and continued the attack. Now Primross smiled, easily, sincerely. "A real warrior."

"Yessss," Brazos hissed.

"Yes," Laev said at the same time. "I am lucky to have him."

Primross's expression soured. "FirstFamilies lords and ladies often get Fams."

"This one arrived as a present from my FatherSire's old Fam. An indiscretion." Laev shuffled his feet and Brazos pounced again, trying to sink a tooth into the smooth and expensive leather. "He has no pedigree." He laughed.

Primross's gaze slid toward Laev. The detective tossed the small gleaming acorn in the air, caught it with the flourish of a stage magician, held it a moment, opened his fingers, and the bit of gold had disappeared. He'd used sleight of hand instead of Flair to do the trick. Primross cocked a dark eyebrow at Laev. "Where was the acorn found?"

"At the Salvage Ball. Very dusty."

With a dead bug, added Brazos.

"That event was at one of the Kelps' minor warehouses," Primross said. He stood, and Laev rose, too. Brazos abandoned their boots for a brightly colored flutterby.

"Yes. I'd never been before, though Nivea had attended." He couldn't help it, his voice cooled and tightened along his throat.

Primross took a step back, nostrils pinched. "She was only a GraceLord's daughter."

With deliberation, Laev turned toward the investigator, let his annoyance show. "I wouldn't have cared if she was a Downwind beggar. She was beautiful, dazzling. I thought she was my Heart-Mate, and she—" He bit off the sentence, shrugged.

The detective's face had softened slightly. Guess the man liked it better when Laev showed all his flaws—though his pride had been savaged enough by circumstances that he usually covered any weaknesses with thick shields.

Slightly inclining his body, not enough to be called a bow, Primross said, "I've seen holos and vids, pics and the portrait that the great T'Apple did of your lady wife, T'Hawthorn. She was pretty." Primross tilted his head. "Attractive and it appeared as if she had a touch of charisma and charm. But I believe you were the one man who was drawn to her the most."

Laev tapped his temples. "As the ancient saying goes, to see her beauty you had to look from my eyes."

"Exactly," Primross agreed. "And she used and betrayed you."

Laev's teeth gritted, then he said, "You've been very successful in tracking the missing items." He moved so he could see the edge of the ocean. It appeared gray. "Can you find my HeartGift?" His voice came out as low and as rough as the rumble of the distant surf.

The acorn appeared in Primross's fingers again and he rubbed a thumb over it as his amber eyes deepened with thoughtfulness. "What kind of spellshield does it have?"

"The usual. Hard for anyone except my HeartMate or me to sense."

The detective nodded, looked down at the acorn. "So it has considerable HeartMate-Passage-illusion-type Flair shrouding it." His nose twitched as if he might even be able to scent such Flair. "I intend to find it." He slid his glance away, then back, and Laev steeled himself for the comments or questions that he'd been dodging for two years since his wife died.

"Your HeartMate could sense your HeartGift. Do you know . . ." For once the man wasn't pressing.

Laev continued to stare at the far white line of the surf. "No, I don't know who my HeartMate is. That was one issue I buried during my marriage. I would never get a divorce." He looked at Primross. "Family pressure is considerable. I behaved the way my FatherSire, the Residence, and the rest of the Family believed to be honorable. The way I believe is honorable." He'd endured an estranged and angry woman living in his home. He'd used spells to banish his sex drive.

Primross appeared inscrutable. Laev wasn't accustomed to explaining himself. Though the man didn't seem to need explanation, there was a certain relief for Laev in putting his reasons and actions—inactions—into words. "I have no intention of looking for my HeartMate. I'm not interested in another wife."

Primross grunted. "Women can be troublesome . . . but Heart-Mates . . ."

"Claiming a HeartMate is not always easy. If anyone is an example of that, I am." Laev figured his face was as grim as his voice.

"Um-hmm." The detective moved with a fighter's panache to stand beside Laev and look toward the sea. "HeartMates."

"Do you have one?" Laev asked.

The investigator was so silent Laev figured he wasn't going to answer. Finally he said, "Yeah."

"You're not HeartBound or married?" Laev looked at the guy's wrists, no marriage bands. His own arms felt light and free.

"No," Primross said.

Laev liked the man. He was trusting the detective, someone he hadn't known all his life, and it felt good. Maybe it was easier to trust someone who hadn't known him for many years.

His calendarsphere popped into existence. "Appointment with your lawyer in half a septhour."

"You're a busy man," Primross said mildly.

The investigator was different than Laev's noble friends. "You are, too. Glad you're on the job."

Primross nodded. "I'll get your HeartGift."

"I expect you will."

*M*any evenings Camellia and her friends would eat very casually, but tonight she wanted a bit more . . . ritual. Indications that the evening was important. Revealing secrets usually was, and she was finally ready to talk of her most personal one.

So she'd set up her small ritual room for food. All that work on Darjeeling's HouseHeart was reflected here. In keeping with most of their gatherings, there were no chairs and tables but large, soft pillows to lean against. The room wasn't large, about three and a half meters square, fine for an intimate gathering of her friends.

Mica had pounced on each pillow, rubbed herself against each, and kneaded them all, settling for the new, smallest one. Camellia had bought it that morning, cannily choosing a muted orange ginger to match the calico's fur, making sure the seams were piped in bright gold. The tassels were thicker than mice and were designed to withstand kitty claws . . . or unravel in a satisfactory way.

She'd bought the pillow in a shop that catered to Fam companions, Lady and Lord help her. A whole shop that sold nothing but objects for Fams, with brushes for everything from housefluffs to foxes to horses. And now Mica knew where it was, though she had no gilt of her own.

Mica pranced around the room, purring loudly. *Brazos has no room like this. He does not even have his own pillow.*

Yet, Camellia thought.

Yet, Mica said. She circled, setting claws in her pillow. She gazed approvingly around the chamber until her gaze lit on the upright slab of green black granite in the corner and the water streaming down it into a basin and cycling up to fall again. Mica got off her pillow and pushed it closer to the small fireplace in the opposite corner. Though the days had been nice for spring, the nights had been unseasonably cool.

Camellia's friends arrived right on time . . . with Tiana bringing a mixed vegetable salad and Glyssa a dessert to complement Camellia's finfish casserole.

"Nice," Glyssa said, before putting the pastry box in the tiny food storage no-time in the altar. She took her favorite plump pillow of a rusty red and gold pattern. Tiana sank down onto the blue green paisley, and Camellia sat on the silver and gold one.

The women made happy anticipatory eating noises as they settled around the long, low table.

Glyssa opened the wine and poured them all a full glass. "What's the occasion?"

"Secrets," Camellia said bluntly. "We're *sharing* tonight."

Tiana wiggled her butt deep into her pillow, grinned. "Good."

"That means you, too." Camellia lowered her brows at her. "One statement. That's all we want. About homes or HeartMates."

"One statement won't satisfy Glyssa." Tiana filled her mouth with casserole.

"We'll discuss it or not as much as needs be," said Glyssa.

Camellia let the taste of the spices sit on her tongue before swallowing another bite. This was one good dish. She kept an eye on Mica, who was eating from her own plate filled with shredded furrabeast bites. Not begging. That was good. A stray thought passed through Camellia's head that she didn't think T'Hawthorn would be as strict with Brazos as she was with Mica.

As if Tiana had picked the image of the man from her mind, her friend said, "You looked very cozy with GreatLord T'Hawthorn today."

Food fell off Glyssa's fork and onto her plate as she jerked. Her head swiveled toward Camellia. "Laev T'Hawthorn? Where? What did he want?"

"Two people in my office at Darjeeling's HouseHeart always looks cozy." Camellia chewed. Yes, she loved the food. "And he wanted to know if Nivea had ever left Hawthorn items at the Salvage Ball."

"She *stole* from the *Hawthorns*!" Glyssa and Tiana exclaimed together. Camellia reflected that they'd all been friends a very long time.

"Petty thievery is not only limited to villains like my father and uncle."

"Nivea was always low," Glyssa said.

Tiana hesitated, then offered womanfully, "We don't know what she was feeling. She must have had a very unhappy marriage."

"That she brought completely on herself," Glyssa pointed out ruthlessly. "She pretended to be Laev's HeartMate and snagged one of the highest nobles in the land—against his Family's wishes. Unhappy marriage or not, I guarantee you that she enjoyed her status." Glyssa stabbed at a chunk of finfish and noodles.

Mica trotted back to her pillow and circled a couple of times before lying down and draping her tail around herself and yawning. *Talking about mean woman bad for stomach.*

"That's right," Camellia said. "I told him about the desk set."

That surprised a soft snort from Tiana, no doubt recalling her argument with Nivea. Camellia knew Tiana hadn't been so much personally hurt by Nivea as protective of Artemisia Mugwort. Nivea *had* been spiteful to Tiana's older sister.

They ate in silence, Tiana's gaze dreamy and unfocused, her face turned toward the windows; Glyssa frowning in thought as she probed her prodigious memory, eating absently. She loved a problem like this, enjoyed all riddles.

Camellia closed her eyes and drew in a deep breath, concentrating on the now, the simplicity of the moment of being with good friends.

After a couple of minutes, Glyssa let her fork clink against her plate. Mouth still tight, she shook her head. "I don't recall anything other than the desk set. I *think* there was something else, but the recollection is foggy." Her shoulders shifted, uncomfortable with such an admission. "I can't even remember the year of that one."

Camellia recalled the year and the object clearly. She'd had to stay across the room from it. She wasn't about to say so.

"I don't believe I noticed everything Nivea brought; she came to the Salvage Ball for years, since she and Laev Hawthorn returned to Druida from Gael City." Glyssa's upper lip lifted. "I *do* remember that the first three years she brought some tawdry trinket. I'd guess that wasn't from T'Hawthorn Residence. What about you, Tiana?"

Tiana started. She blinked. "No. I don't have your memory, and I got sidetracked."

"Thanks," Camellia said. She gathered Mica's and her friends' plates—clean like her own—and the casserole and walked to the kitchen. The plates and silverware went into the cleanser, the casserole into a no-time.

"Beautiful sunset tonight," Tiana said. She stood at the threshold of the galley kitchen, really only comfortable for one, and looked out the large mainspace windows. She moved into the mainspace and Glyssa and Camellia joined her.

Camellia's home was in a refurbished upper-middle-class, lower-noble area to the south of CityCenter. She only had a glimpse of the southern end of the starship *Nuada's Sword*, the artifact-being that dominated the western Celtan skyline. Just a few kilometers away was the ocean—not quite close enough for her to hear the sweep of the tide. The trees swayed. No longer were the branches skeletal black. New leaves were outlined against the color-shot sky of pink and gold splendor.

As they watched, white clouds faded to lavender, then to gray, the last of Bel's rays flashed silver, and day became twilight.

Tiana flattened her hands to her breasts, spoke in a hushed tone. "Such a lovely hurt. And I love you both, and my sister and my Family, but I want my HeartMate. I want to share such sunsets with him, and loving afterward."

"Or loving in a sacred grove as Bel sets," Glyssa added.

Yearning swelled so in Camellia that it stopped any words from escaping. Yearning and fear . . . and, underneath it all, old anger and embarrassment—all that she'd soon spill to Tiana and Glyssa.

Dessert now, Mica said, walking back and forth across Camellia's feet.

Tiana sighed and Glyssa turned away from the window. Camellia rhymed a couplet and soft spellglobes lit in the mainspace and along the short hallway back to the ritual chamber and the room itself.

This time when they entered, Camellia shut the door behind her, encasing them in privacy.

"Girl talk," Tiana said.

I am female, said Mica.

"So you are," Glyssa said.

And I want dessert. White mousse inside puffs. I do not want the puffs, though.

"All right," Glyssa said. "I want dessert, too. We need more plates."

Tiana was closest to the altar and opened one of the two cabinets in its base, pulled out a set of three plates with cheerful-tinted spring flowers scattered casually around the rim, set them on the table.

Mica meowed. *Where is My plate?*

"I'll have to get you one," Camellia said. She translocated a sturdy blue Fam plate from the cleanser to the bricked hearth of the fire.

"Is our floral pattern still available?" asked Tiana, dishing out the dessert.

"Yes," Camellia said.

"You always know," Glyssa said.

"We all have our little obsessions," Camellia said. She took the mousse-in-puff and bit into it, nearly moaned as the taste of vanilla and white cocoa filled her mouth.

"Mmmm," all of them hummed appreciation, including Mica.

"Luscious," Tiana said. She'd finished hers first, and licked her fingers before rising from her pillow and moving to the fountain in the corner and washing her hands.

"Speaking of luscious," Glyssa said, white teeth snapping up another bite. "T'Hawthorn seems to be showing up in your life on a regular basis, Camellia."

Camellia had eaten half of her mousse puff and set the other half aside to savor for later—if she could. She took a big breath and said, "That's because he's my HeartMate."

Nine

*G*lyssa *choked.*

Mica squealed and tore around the room, leaping over the foun-tain basin. *We knew it. We knew it. Me and Brazos.* Camellia decided that feeding the cat sugar was not a good idea.

"So how long have you known?" asked Tiana.

"Since my Second Passage to free my Flair at seventeen."

Glyssa grimaced. "Ouch."

"I bespelled myself to forget."

"You'd have to, he was married to Nivea," Glyssa said.

"Yes." Camellia's teeth hurt, she was clenching them so. She rose and went to the fountain, let the cold water run over her hands. It helped calm her so she could stand to turn back to her friends' stares.

"It was that hurtful?" Glyssa asked.

"Do you have any idea how it feels to link sexually with your HeartMate during the Passage fever dreams and know he is turning to his wife to slake his own lust?"

Tiana jerked. Blinked. "Oh. That's why you've been avoiding—"

"Yes."

Glyssa got up and came to hug Camellia. "I'm sorry for pushing. I didn't think."

"I didn't think, either," Tiana said, completing the group hug. "Forgive me."

It was *good* to feel her friends on both sides of her, with hugs just the outer expression of their emotional support. Tiana was softer of body and shorter. Glyssa was almost her own height and wiry. She broke away first and prowled with Mica.

"That day. That first day in JudgementGrove when you won your china, when we were with Nivea. That upsurge of HeartMate Flair."

"Yeah," Camellia said, sitting down and looking at the wine bottle. She'd have preferred tea. "I've thought a lot about that day. I was flying high emotionally because I'd presented our findings to the SupremeJudge and she listened to me and awarded me the tea set, if it could be found in the shipwreck."

"And Laev T'Hawthorn was going through his own Second Passage at the time. Everyone knew that," Tiana said. She spread her hands. "The energies of HeartMate love spiked and spiraled through JudgementGrove."

Glyssa snorted. "And the stup of the boy saw the beautiful Nivea and decided right then that she was his HeartMate, not you."

"He barely saw us, we were too young, thirteen," Tiana said.

"And Nivea, being Nivea and a Sunflower with an eye on wealth and status . . ." Glyssa shrugged. They'd already been over that ground. Her brows dipped. "Must have been a shock to him on his wedding night when he tried to HeartBond with her and couldn't."

"Yes, poor Laev," Tiana said.

Camellia didn't think there was anything "poor" about Laev. He might look noble and elegant, but he was a lot tougher under that surface than people believed. She'd have thought her friends would realize this—but, like she had, they'd given little consideration to Laev Hawthorn—far above them in status.

"Poor Nivea," Tiana said more perfunctorily.

Glyssa made a disgusted noise.

Camellia looked straight at Tiana. "I was . . . glad . . . when Nivea died." Again her jaw hurt.

"Unsurprising," Tiana said, but her hands were in her opposite sleeve pockets. She'd be thinking just as hard as Glyssa, feeling more. Camellia sensed the waves of empathy coming from them.

"He's free now," Glyssa said. "You could claim him. You made a HeartGift during your Second Passage, didn't you?"

"No," Camellia said.

Her friends stared at her. "No!" Glyssa said.

Camellia certainly didn't want to explain that she'd spent most of her Second Passage in bed, thrashing with sex dreams, hating herself for connecting with a man who gave another woman fulfillment. "Why should I? I knew he was wed. I knew he was a man that would always honor his marriage vows despite anything."

"Of course he would," Tiana agreed.

"I'm not ready to claim him," Camellia said.

"So he's a man who's hurt you, too." Tiana spoke softly.

"Huh," Glyssa said and plopped down onto her pillow, shaking her head. "You haven't had any kind of luck, have you?"

"I've had bad luck with men," Camellia said, lifted her chin. "But I've had good luck in business."

Glyssa sent a pulse of comfort down their link and Camellia found it easy to smile after all. "And I've been blessed in my friends."

"Uh-huh," Glyssa said.

"I still think you should see a counselor about your issues with men," Tiana said.

Glyssa shot her a disgruntled look. "I'm usually the one who pushes too hard and too far. Let Camellia go at her own pace. Her father and uncle are—"

Mean men! Mica said.

"Right," Glyssa said. "Her brother—"

I have not met this littermate, Mica said.

"Not worth meeting," Glyssa said. "He's weak. And Laev T'Hawthorn, the stup, still doesn't realize you're his HeartMate, does he?"

"I doubt it."

Brazos and I will HELP! Mica bounced up and down.

"Please don't," Camellia said, but noted that Tiana had turned a considering gaze toward the little cat. Then her friend met Camellia's eyes, her own warm. Her head tilted. "I would say that if Nivea wasn't ultimately pleased with her marriage, Laev T'Hawthorn wasn't, either."

"With a woman who led him on, married him for his gilt and his title, betrayed him with other men? Who would be happy with such a marriage?" Glyssa added.

"So he's probably not eager to find and claim his HeartMate," Tiana ended. But there was a note in her voice, a light in her eyes, a studied nonexpression on her face that Camellia had learned meant that she would be watching Laev, too.

"She's going to meddle," Glyssa told Camellia. "She can't help but meddle. Her nature and why she became a priestess. Has to try to fix things. Wine." Glyssa topped off their wineglasses.

We will help! Mica shouted again.

"Just as you can't help but be curious about everything and ask questions all the time," Tiana defended.

Camellia took her plate with the rest of her treat, sat down on her pillow. She'd revealed all and her appetite had come back. Mica crawled into her lap. Camellia smiled at Tiana. "And so I've told a secret."

"*One* of your secrets," Glyssa said, nose twitching, changing her focus to Camellia.

"All that I'm going to talk about tonight. So it's Tiana's turn. I told you, one statement regarding your secret."

"I am bound by a Vow of Honor not to reveal my secret," Tiana said stiffly, as she always did.

"Or what happens?" Glyssa pressed.

"I can't say," Tiana said.

"You won't say," Glyssa said.

"I won't say," Tiana agreed.

"But I think you'd lose your home." Camellia let the last of the vanilla white mousse melt on her tongue. "You never invite us to your home. We don't know exactly where you live. You told me,

generally, of HouseHearts, so it must be an old house, a Residence."
She drank more wine.

"I won't say," Tiana said, but a faint smile curved her lips.

Glyssa lifted her glass and Camellia thought she was studying
the flames of the fire as seen through her wine. A few heartbeats
later she sipped, then angled her glass toward Tiana as if in a toast,
shifted as if to settle more comfortably, met Camellia's eyes, and
gave her a sincere smile. "But we've talked about this, Camellia and
I. There are legends you know. Of First Grove, the original Healing
Grove of the colonists. Of the lost estate of BalmHeal, which only
opens to those in desperate need."

"I can't say anything. I swore a Vow of Honor." The sentence
left Tiana on a sigh. She stared at Glyssa. "What's your secret?"

"One of them," Camellia added.

Glyssa's body braced. "I think, I'm *sure*, my HeartMate and I
had a flaming affair for four days, five years ago, while he was passing through Druida. I didn't realize who he was, what he was to me
until later." She flushed red that didn't go with her hair. "I finally
understood how much lust and Flair, singly and mingled together,
can blind people."

Camellia thought her mouth hadn't fallen open as wide as Tiana's. She snapped it shut, still staring at Glyssa as her brain buzzed.

Glyssa took advantage of their stunned immobility to fill their
wineglasses. She lifted hers in a toast. "To HeartMates."

"You both know yours," Tiana said wistfully but chimed her
glass as Camellia and Glyssa did.

Glyssa drank deeply. There was a wild hurt in her eyes that made
Camellia share a look with Tiana. The two of them shook their
heads. They wouldn't press Glyssa now.

Camellia was all too aware of the hurt a HeartMate could
cause. Since she'd let that door inside her swing wide, had admitted
Laev Hawthorn was hers, she'd experienced again all the pain and
despair and anger. She couldn't bear yet to talk to her friends about
Laev, so she wouldn't press Glyssa. Instead Camellia drank her
wine.

"I've set up an appointment for the three of us with the starship *Nuada's Sword*, MidMorningBell tomorrow," Tiana said.

"You sent me a cache message. That time's good for me." Glyssa drank some more, but her body slumped a little as if tension had seeped from her muscles.

"Fine," Camellia lied.

Tiana's gaze went to the window, which showed a black night and pinpricks of stars. "I know I have a HeartMate. I want him." She nearly slurred her words, snuggled into her pillow, then fell asleep.

"So." Glyssa wiggled a little more, sipped her drink. Her eyes were shiny, her voice a little clogged. "I suppose I can say that Laev T'Hawthorn is one good-looking man. Tell me all about those Passage sex dreams."

*I*t must have been the short—very short—conversation Camellia had had with Glyssa about Passage sex that had primed Camellia. Or the fact that she'd finally admitted, out loud and to more than just herself, that Laev T'Hawthorn was her HeartMate. But after her guests had left and she'd checked the house security and fallen into bed and asleep, Camellia found her mind reaching for Laev's.

He, too, was asleep—and aroused. His lust flowed easily to her, without any emotional or rational-thinking barriers.

She found it difficult to keep up the shields she'd built between them. Before last night, it had been so long since they'd connected sexually . . . four years since her own last Passage . . . and only two or three times since. Until her spell affected her dreams, too.

The rare mental sex they'd shared—when he hadn't turned to Nivea—had spoilt her for any other man. Camellia had gone ahead with occasional sex dates, and minor affairs focused on the physical, but hadn't opened up emotionally with any of her short-time lovers.

She didn't intend to open up to Laev. But now it was safe to love him . . . no, have telepathic sex with him. He wasn't married. He couldn't hurt her by making love with his wife. He might not even recognize her, since he never had before.

And the warm sensuality wrapping around her felt so good. She could give in to it.

She could revel in it.

The next moment she was in the large bed with him, pressing her body to his . . . just *feeling* him, his size, the texture of his skin. Her breath came fast. Maybe she wasn't ready for this.

It had been too long and last night too brief . . . but she'd touched him in real life now, been pressed against him . . . and now feeling him naked and front to front was so much different. Her hands trailed over the strong slope of his shoulders. She dared to touch the nape of his neck, feel the silkiness of his hair fall across her fingers.

His hands clamped on her butt, kneaded, brought her close to his erection. In another minute . . .

No! Not ready, not ready, not ready.

With a gasp she jerked away and awake. What had she been doing!

Enjoying herself. Enjoying Laev. Laev, her HeartMate, whom she was free to love now. Whom she was afraid to love now.

Rolling off the bedsponge, she rose and headed for the waterfall room. Even as she stood under a tepid plunge of water, she swore. There would be no going back now, she understood that. Her libido would not be stuffed back into a box. Not when every day brought some reminder of Laev, or chance meetings, and destiny was determined to bring them together.

Lady and Lord, she hurt from unfulfilled need, from her body wanting her HeartMate and her mind and emotions shying away from him.

I don't think you should do that, Mica said. She sat just outside the sill marking the waterfall area, protected from the wet by a Flair shield across the open doorway.

Avoid Laev T'Hawthorn? Camellia replied blankly.

Not that, either! Mica emphasized that with a short yowl that pierced Camellia's brain. *See, you don't make sense. All that water on your head can't be good for you.*

Camellia huffed, stopped the waterfall, and dropped the shield.

Mica hopped back, hissed at the few droplets that evaporated before they reached her.

Big baby, Camellia said. She dried herself under a quick heat lamp, contemplated sleep again, and decided to drink a soothing tea with a spell that would narrow the link between her and Laev. She'd concocted the recipe and made the tea herself. Some was in the kitchen no-time.

A few minutes later she was asleep and dreaming of searching for something in a cavelike HouseHeart.

The sexual climax rolled through Laev, leaving him shuddering with satisfaction and waking him. The best dream sex he'd had in years—well, since last night. The best sex he'd had since even before Nivea had died. They hadn't had much sex in the last years of their marriage—only when Nivea decided it was time to try for an heir to the Hawthorn line again.

The pounding of his heart eased from ragged after-orgasm and edged toward the rapid beat of caution. His HeartMate had been with him. He didn't know her. Didn't want to know her. They'd only come together because people, beings, had been pestering him about her lately, that was all.

But he'd enjoyed the sex, even though she'd left him to experience release alone. Thinking about the brief encounter, he understood that the bond between them had been strictly physical. Nothing more than a tiny filament connected them otherwise.

So she didn't want to acknowledge him, either. His first stung pride gave way to amusement that he'd been irritated.

HeartMate sex, without emotional trauma-drama. He liked that idea. And that was all he could accept now, perhaps all she could, too. Fine with him.

He rose and headed to the waterfall room. Earlier he'd chanted a complicated spell on his sheets to keep them clean, and now the fragrance of herbs wafted from his bedroom.

Glancing at the wall timer, he saw it was close to TransitionBell, that time of deep night when many souls passed to the next world. Energy still hummed along his nerves.

Like the night before, he reached mentally for Cratag. The man was asleep. The Green Knight Fencing and Fighting Salon wasn't open. With a roll of his shoulders, Laev passed through his suite to the sparring room on the end. There he stretched, then began a fighting pattern. It was more work than he'd anticipated. He'd lost his edge, but he'd get it back.

"T'Hawthorn?" the Residence asked.

Laev kicked high and grinned. The Residence had initiated a conversation! Ha! "Yes, Residence?"

There was a quiet soughing through the house. "It is the time for the annual visit with Captain Ruis Elder of *Nuada's Sword* to check on our investments with him and the starship."

Grunting, Laev finished the second pattern and bent over, hands on thighs, until his breath was even. "Is Captain Elder available?"

"No, the Elders keep Celtan time, not Ship or Earthan time. Ship, of course, is available."

"Of course." Occasionally he'd gone with his FatherSire to the meetings, but Ruis Elder was older than he. And Ruis was a Null, suppressing all Flair, having an odd effect on everyone. Yet his Father-Sire had enjoyed those meetings. Laev ran through his schedule for the next day. "I can meet Captain Elder at MidMorningBell. Ask Ship if that is acceptable for them."

Laev had moved smoothly through the third drill before the Residence said, "Captain Elder can give you his undivided attention at MidMorningBell, and Ship states that it can 'multitask.'"

"Fine." One more pattern and he should be weary enough to sleep. "Fill my bathing pool, please."

"Done."

A few minutes later he sank into the pool, letting the water soothe his muscles. He wasn't sure what herbs went into the bath and swirled around him in scent, but they meant comfort and home.

"You have only been in the HouseHeart once this month," the Residence said.

Laev opened one eye. He was beginning to think that the Residence keeping silent for the last six months had been a boon.

"I will go when I am ready."

"T'Hawthorn should spend twenty-eight septhours in the House-Heart every month."

Laev stretched his senses. The Residence was full of Flair, all spells were funded, everyone in the castle was healthy. "All the spells are fine, both in the HouseHeart and here."

"T'Hawthorn—"

"That's right. I am T'Hawthorn. I will go when I am ready. Good night, Residence." He rose from the bath and headed to bed.

He hoped for more sex, but he didn't expect it, and she didn't grace his dreams. Instead he capered in a meadow like a damned fool—a lord dancing without his lady. Joyful but not complete. He tried not to care.

*T*he day was bright and beautiful with no wind, and the last thing Camellia wanted to do was enter the huge six-kilometer, twenty-five-story-high metallic starship *Nuada's Sword*. Most of the people in Druida were descended from the multigenerational crew. The First-Families were descended from those who'd had psi powers on Earth and had funded the trip.

Her ancestors had not traveled on *Nuada's Sword* and that was a remaining secret.

Mica was hopping through the high grass of Landing Park. The cat surprised moths and chased them, then rushed back to Camellia and her friends. The cat was excited, hoping to be initiated into the

FamCats who visited the Ship to watch the *History of Cats*—and maybe even get a ride on Samba cat's flying saucer.

They walked through the park to the Ship and up a ramp. The iris door of the bay opened. They were greeted by Dani Eve Elder, a petite eighteen-year-old with a heart-shaped face, auburn hair, and brown eyes. She was a Null—a person who suppressed Flair—like her father.

"Welcome, ladies!" She curtsied, and Camellia and her friends curtsied in return.

Like most people, Camellia didn't care for losing her Flair—it was like losing her eyesight or hearing—and like everyone who dealt with Ruis and Dani Eve, Camellia gritted her teeth and accepted it when her psi power vanished. As she spent more time on the Ship, she'd become accustomed to the lack.

"Glad to see you," Camellia said.

Mica mewed, scowling. No one could communicate telepathically in Dani Eve's presence.

Dani Eve chuckled, reached down to pet the young cat. Camellia held her breath.

"Who's this?" Dani Eve asked.

"My FamCat, Mica," Camellia answered. She glanced at Tiana. Shouldn't her friend have notified the Elders and the Ship that Mica would be there?

Tiana bit her lip. "I forgot to tell them."

"Mica has only been with me a few days," Camellia said. "She wanted to visit to see *History of Cats*."

"Ah, *History of Cats*, of course." Dani Eve rolled her eyes. "Our bestselling holo."

Mica meowed. Loudly.

Male voices echoed off the sides of the metal corridors and Laev Hawthorn appeared alone, obviously talking to the Ship.

Camellia froze, then memories of the night before, the incomplete sex, flooded her with warmth. The pressure of her teeth clenched together pained her jaw as she used irritation to vanquish the recollection. Was she fated to see Laev T'Hawthorn walking toward her wherever she went?

She glanced at her friends, who were both staring at her, Glyssa with a look of surprise, Tiana with a hint of smugness that destiny seemed to be working on Camellia's behalf.

Ten

$\mathcal{L}$*aev joined them and greetings were made all around.*

Mica's yowl pierced the air, drawing all attention back to her.

Dani Eve laughed. "As I was saying, we sell *History of Cats*."

"I'll take one," Camellia said.

"The two-, six-, or twelve-septhour version?" Dani Eve asked, her mouth twitching.

"Rrrrrowwwrrr!" Mica said, began tapping her paw.

Camellia ignored the twelve taps. "We'll go with the two-septhour one for now."

With a wicked grin, Dani Eve turned to Laev. "Your Brazos is watching *History of Cats* now."

His lashes lowered for a moment, then opened to show his lovely lavender eyes. Camellia slid her own gaze away but caught her friends' smiles.

"I'll take the twelve-septhour one," Laev said. "Anything to keep the cat occupied."

Camellia hadn't thought of it that way. Maybe it would be worth the gilt . . . "How much is the twelve-septhour—"

Laev lifted a hand. "Don't bother, GraceMistrys Darjeeling. Our cats will no doubt share."

That was the truth, but Camellia was torn. She'd like to pretend that gilt was no object to buying a gift for her FamCat, but of course it was.

Her smile at him felt frozen. "Thank you, no doubt." She turned to Dani Eve. "The two-septhour one is fine for us."

"I'll have Ship send them to your home caches," Dani Eve said.

"Thank you," Camellia said, her words matched with Laev's.

A whooshing noise got louder and louder.

"Here's Samba," Dani Eve said.

The Captain's FamCat zoomed down the corridor on a flying saucer. The calico cat seemed leaner since Camellia had last seen her, but was still plump. Her colors were darker and she had more orange in her fur than Mica.

"Wheee!" cried Samba.

Laev T'Hawthorn jumped out of the way with nimble grace.

Samba stopped the saucer close to them, tipped it upside down, and stared at Mica, then flipped it back over and lowered it to the floor. Mica stared at the older cat, looked at the saucer, then Camellia.

As much as Camellia didn't want to explain in front of Laev, she did, speaking to Mica, "I'm sure you and Samba don't want to clean up vomit on the way to her quarters, so she probably won't do any acrobatics." She met Samba's gaze, ignored her white twitching whiskers, the heat that flushed her own cheeks. "Mica ate grass on the way in."

Dani Eve frowned at Samba. "You be nice to Mica."

Samba purred.

"Go ahead," Camellia urged her cat, still feeling red under Laev's amused eyes. "All you talked about was Samba and her saucer on the way over."

Samba's purr increased in volume.

Mica hopped onto the saucer. It tipped, righted itself, then slid slowly through the air back the way it had come.

"I'll see you in a couple of septhours!" Camellia called. Their trips to *Nuada's Sword* were never shorter than a septhour and a half. Surely Laev would be leaving. But he just lounged against the nearest wall, watching them.

"How's the training going, Dani Eve?" Tiana asked. Dani Eve, like Tiana, was still in the midst of her studies.

An impish grin that showed dimples in both cheeks creased Dani Eve's face. "I've been promoted by the Ship to Commander."

"That's wonderful," Tiana enthused, though Camellia thought she had no more idea of the word and status it brought than Camellia did or Glyssa.

"What's that mean?" Glyssa asked.

Dani Eve laughed. "It means I am formally the second in command of the Ship." They began walking down the hallway to the omnivator, heading to the great greensward where they kept gardens. Laev ambled with them.

"Second in command." Glyssa rolled the words out of her mouth with a hint of envy.

Camellia blessed her luck in having been able to create her own business and control her own life.

Dani Eve lowered her voice, though they all knew that Ship itself was monitoring them. "I have most of the security codes, and, and . . ." Her voice thrilled with excitement.

"And?" Camellia and her friends prompted at the same time.

"And I am working on refurbishing a dagger ship."

"A dagger ship?" asked Camellia.

"A small spaceship that can be launched by Ship into orbit, then to cruise nearby space."

Camellia stopped. Her mouth fell open as horror filled her. Get off the ground? Off Celta? She heard ragged breathing and was glad she wasn't the only one sucking and puffing air.

"Sounds wonderful," Glyssa said faintly.

"I'll want to bless your ship before you try any such thing," Tiana said.

Dani Eve grimaced. "Mother is not much for the adventure, either. But we'll do quadruple fail-safes before we launch." She emitted a tiny sigh. "It doesn't appear as if this will happen anytime soon." Her bottom lip poked out. "Maybe not even in this decade."

The omnivator door opened, they all got in. Laev stood close enough to Camellia that his male scent wafted to her nose—he smelled rich. Simply rich. Like all the best materials and spells and cleansers and any other thing that had a scent, with only a hint of his own masculine odor.

The omnivator zoomed them to the greensward that comprised a third of the Ship.

"Did you hear the news?" the Ship boomed in its multivoice as they left the vator.

"What news!" Glyssa bit, as always.

"It's about the other starship, *Lugh's Spear*!" the Ship caroled in harmony.

Camellia stiffened. None of the women noticed her reaction, but Laev T'Hawthorn cocked an eyebrow at her.

"I saw nothing in the newssheets, heard nothing at the Public-Library this morning," Glyssa persisted.

"I haven't heard anything, either," Tiana said.

"The discovery team has finished marking the boundary around the location of the starship, the excavation will begin next week."

"Wonderful!" Glyssa whirled. "How exciting. This whole thing has been fascinating, finding the lost starship and now confirming its location!"

"Oh, yes!" Tiana enthused.

"Yes," Camellia whispered.

Laev's gaze was on her face. She tried to keep her expression impassive, her own gaze shuttered, her body still, but thought he noticed everything.

"We are loaning earth-moving equipment," Dani Eve said. "But father is worried about casualties in such a major venture."

Tiana sighed. "Yes, there usually are deaths in something as risky as that. Blessings upon all engaged in the *Lugh's Spear* expeditions!" She traced a pentacle in the air.

"Blessings!" everyone repeated.

Decisions loomed before Camellia. Options she couldn't think about right now, in front of so many people. Tough choices.

Like other events in her life demanding decisions, it crashed down on her with weight settling on her shoulders. She wasn't ready.

"All those Families who are descended from *Lugh's Spear* must be fascinated," Glyssa said.

"We don't have a good roster or genealogical history," the Ship said with disapproval. "We only know those Families who have come forward and those listed in the diary that the Cherrys gave us. I am not allowed to do genetic scans of my visitors anymore," Ship grumbled.

Thank the Lady and Lord. Camellia said a silent prayer. Her lips must have moved because Laev's penetrating glance intensified.

Would he say anything?

He was still nearly a stranger to them all. Surely he wouldn't.

She swallowed. "A good thing Ship isn't allowed to scan. Invasion of privacy."

"That's right," Dani Eve agreed. She blinked and frowned. "One of the gardening robots is making a weird noise. I'd better take it into my workshop." She flipped a hand. "See you later. Have lunch with us. You, too, T'Hawthorn."

"Yes, honored," Glyssa said, as she always did.

"We would like to share with you the updated maps of the discovery site of the starship *Lugh's Spear*," Ship said. "We receive regular reports from the site. We can compare the maps to my own from when we orbited, and those vids we received from the other two ships, *Lugh's Spear* and *Arianrhod's Wheel*, as they landed."

"Honored," Tiana said.

Laev waited a beat. Expecting Camellia to respond. Still staring at her, he said, "Perhaps."

They separated to their gardens. Camellia supervised tea crops: black, green, and herbal. Glyssa checked on original Earthan seedlings that were being slowly reintroduced to Celta after they'd died out, and Tiana had a plot of Earthan-Celtan hybrids she nurtured.

Laev walked beside Camellia.

"What are you doing here?" she asked.

His brows went up. "Checking on Hawthorn's Earthan cinnamon crop that we grow here. Profits fully shared with the Ship and the Elder Family."

"Of course." She was turning as red as cinnamon. Laev's father and FatherSire had introduced cinnamon to Celtan tastes, and the spice had been an instant hit. They must have made another fortune.

And of course his Family would have a premium Earthan source grown on the Ship. Just as she had teas that came from the Ship and not the plantations of the southern continent.

"The Elders and *Nuada's Sword* do a great deal of business," she said.

"As the only complete and sentient starship left, *Nuada's Sword* has expensive maintenance programs," Laev said.

"I do," Ship affirmed.

Camellia was walking down a steeply tiered hillside, damp ground underfoot, checking the plants. Laev continued to stroll with her. She liked his company but wondered what he was thinking.

Ship said, "Darjeeling isn't a Celtan-culture name. It is an Earth place-name."

"We've had this conversation before," Camellia said.

"We never scanned you as a child," the Ship said.

"Thank you," Camellia said.

"But as Captain Elder and his Family have helped us come to our full senses and memories, we recall two boys who visited us decades ago. They, too, were Darjeelings."

The Ship had learned from Samba, it was playing cat to Camellia's mouse. She waited for it to corner her and pounce. Laev was watching her again. How expressive *was* she? Probably too much.

Ship continued, "Those boys visited with a school group—what you would call grovestudy."

Time to go on the attack. "Ship, we've been on this planet for over four centuries. You're on Celta, you should use our terminology, otherwise you seem"—Camellia paused to add emphasis to the insult—"*antique,* of no use to modern Celtans."

"We are *not* antique. We have an incredible amount to contribute to Celta. We still have all the Earth DNA and databases."

Her strategy to distract Ship was working. She continued to

prod. "I was told that you transferred all your databases to the PublicLibrary as backup, even let a few FirstFamily Residences have some specific information." And hadn't that last irritated Glyssa and her Family.

Laev said, "I believe my FatherSire, as Captain of All Councils, received several databases. Certainly anything that dealt with our ultimate forebears."

He was helping her! Did he know that? From the gleam in his eyes, she thought he did.

She pressed on with the distraction. "As for the DNA, Ship, aren't you in negotiations with Primary HealingHall about cloning some for their storage? Flaired no-time storage where the specimen remains as it was placed in the unit. Something you don't even have now. Ship, you must move with the times." She paused, continued gently, "Your glory days aren't all in the past, Ship. You need to remember that."

"We can contribute to Celta." There were hisses and pops in the background of its layered voice.

"I agree. But consider yourself a citizen of Celta, not Earth."

"A citizen of Celta." Ship lilted the words.

"Perhaps the *first* citizen of Celta," Camellia said.

"T'Hawthorn, would you contact the FirstFamilies Council and All Councils about this?" Ship asked.

"I would be honored to do so." Laev angled his body and bowed. Camellia never had figured out where the Ship's cameras were, but apparently Laev didn't have that problem.

"Good idea," a woman's voice said, and SupremeJudge Ailim Elder, wife of the Captain, walked from behind a screen of greenery.

Laev smiled at the judge, stepped forward. She offered her hand and he bowed over it, murmuring, "I think between you, me, and the Captain, we can push through a proclamation that *Nuada's Sword* be made a citizen, maybe even the first citizen."

The SupremeJudge's lips curved.

"What are you doing here?" The question spurted from Camellia, again, and rude. Again. She'd been distracted, too. Just by the presence of Laev. "My pardon."

"MidDayBell rang some time ago," the SupremeJudge said mildly.

Camellia glanced at her wrist timer and didn't have to pretend to be aghast. "Lunch. I'm missing the lunch crowd at Darjeeling's HouseHeart! I've got to go."

"You don't need to be there every minute," Glyssa said as she and Tiana walked up to them.

"No, but I do need to supervise this first week. It's vital, and I have to go home first to change my clothes. Not the right image for the HouseHeart." She shook out her business tunic. It was an old tunic and trous suit of uninspired brown. A fleeting thought that Laev had seen her in it and not something more flattering writhed through her mind. "The crop looks good." That was all she needed to check on right now. "Can you take care of Mica for me?"

"Of course," Glyssa said. She slid her gaze to Laev and back to Camellia. "We'll have dinner at your place again."

Camellia wasn't prepared for that, either, but the press of unspoken questions—about her HeartMate, her background—enveloped her and she wanted to get away fast. "Fine."

She hugged Glyssa and Tiana, then curtsied deeply to the Supreme-Judge. "Merry meet."

"And merry part," the judge said.

A thought tugged at Camellia, something she could do to make up for her rudeness. "Why don't I send you and your Family dinner over from Darjeeling's Teahouse or Darjeeling's HouseHeart?" She waved a hand. "Ship can access the menus from my newssheets ads." Another curtsey bob. "Family of four, two males, two females. My thanks, my thanks to Ship, and merry meet again." She half turned to Laev. "Ah, good seeing you again, T'Hawthorn."

"Always," he said and she wondered if that were true.

She ran to Landing Park then teleported to her bedroom in front of her closet. Bumped into someone. She screamed.

Eleven

Rough hands shoved Camellia away hard, she landed on the bedsponge and bounced.

"Fliggering fligger, what do you think you're doing!" yelled her uncle Takvar. "If you'd have 'ported into me, we'd have both died!"

Camellia wrapped her arms around herself, equally shaken. She wouldn't let it show in her voice. "I was teleporting into my own bedroom, in my own house." She hopped up and jutted her chin, headed back to the closet. Takvar grabbed her arm and squeezed. "Where's that custom-made gown you have from D'Thyme?"

"In T'Reed Residence's no-time storage." She yanked away, but not before he bruised her. Relief welled inside her that she'd put the garment in a safe place, though inward shivers rippled through her that Takvar had heard of the expensive gown. She slid the folding doors to her closet wider, saw a nice long robe of gold silkeen, old but still elegant, and flung it over her casual tunic and trous, leaving the bloused sleeves unbuttoned. As she turned around, she saw her safes open again. Her nerves quivered.

She pivoted to stare at her uncle. Takvar didn't bother to hide his smirk. His eyes were the flat gray of thick winter ice coating a lake. She didn't quite dare take his arm to teleport him to a guard station. As far as she knew, he hadn't gotten anything.

"Are you finished?" she asked.

He slowly tucked his fingers into his trous pockets, his nostrils widened, and his upper lip lifted. "You have nothing of value here."

"Why should I?"

"Where's the cat?"

Now she smiled. "With SupremeJudge Ailim Elder. You want me to teleport you to JudgementGrove?"

Something lurked in the depths of his gaze like a monster under the ice. He snapped his fingers and the one cup from her antique tea set appeared in his hands. He smiled as she jolted. Lifted the delicate cup above her reaching hands, a malicious sneer twisting his features. "A teacup fashioned by the famous Zisha. From the famous salvage of the famous sunken ship. The only object from the set not owned by Camellia Darjeeling. It should go for a nice amount of gilt."

"You can't! No one would buy—"

"Of course I can. The whole set should have belonged to me, or your father. Ours by right."

"You weren't here to claim the set. Didn't even know the china existed. Wouldn't have had the brains to ask the Kelps to look for the set."

He swiped at her and she ducked but was off balance and fell against the closet doors.

A creaky laugh came from Takvar, then he flicked a finger against the delicate china and a sweet note chimed. "You got the set. You have it . . . for now." He turned his back and strolled from the bedroom, through the short hall to the mainspace, and out the front door.

Seething, Camellia went to reset the front spellshield. Her uncle was already out of sight, teleported somewhere else. Good riddance. As she pulled the door shut, an outline in the shadows across the street formed into a man.

Watching her? Or her uncle?

He vanished between one blink and the next, teleporting away to some area he knew well.

She shut the door quietly, layered an additional spellshield on the lock. That would keep everyone out but her uncle. She pulled off the robe, stripped from her other clothes and put them in the cleanser, dressed again, smoothed her hair with a simple spell. All in a measured, controlled pattern that soothed her with its everyday sameness.

Her mainspace wall scry panel sounded with the trickling noise Camellia had programmed—tea pouring from a pot. The flicker of Darjeeling's Teahouse logo pulsed from it. "Here," she answered.

The tight face of her trusted manager, Aquilaria, showed in the panel. "Greetyou, GraceMistrys Darjeeling," she said with unaccustomed formality. "Your father, GraceLord Darjeeling, is here with an authorization from you for gilt from our intake today. Unfortunately we don't have as much gilt as he anticipated." From Aquilaria's words and manner, Camellia guessed that her father was just out of sight of the scry—and Aquilaria was lying. She was a friend, not as close as Tiana and Glyssa, but close enough that Aquilaria knew that Camellia would never willingly give gilt to her father. Aquilaria was protecting her.

And Camellia had an emotional link with Aquilaria, so she used it now for mental communication. *I will be there transnow. Give him nothing unless he threatens you or begins to make a scene. If my uncle arrives, give them anything they want.* Aloud, Camellia said, "I just got home from the bank, let me check . . ." Without cutting the connection, hoping her father would stay there, wondering if *she* had the guts to cause a scene in the teahouse, Camellia hurried over to the teleportation area, checked the private pad in the small teahouse office, and 'ported. Aquilaria and her father stood just outside the designated area.

"Aquilaria, thank you for helping me in this matter. Can you check the front?" Camellia asked. Her manager whisked from the room.

"Dear father." Camellia smiled brightly, stepped off the teleportation pad. "You shouldn't have visited here, especially while I was away. My staff have instructions not to give any gilt to you or Uncle." Camellia rubbed her hands, reached for him. "Now we have an appointment with a guardhouse about my diamond bracelet."

He grew red. He sputtered. Finally he shouted, "Curse you, you Sheela Na Gig!"

Camellia was shocked at the insult to a sacred goddess. "I wouldn't take a goddess's name in vain if I were you," she gasped. Swallowed. "Not many do that."

He grunted another infuriated bellow, leapt to the teleportation pad, flung his head up as if checking a distant public pad for availability, and disappeared. A lot of men were doing that in her life today. With her father and uncle, it was nothing new and she was glad to see them go.

Camellia tottered a couple of steps to her comfortchair behind her desk, sank into it, and rubbed her temples. Aquilaria slipped sideways through the doorway. "Did he actually say what I thought he did?" she asked.

Wincing, Camellia wondered how many people in the three dining rooms of Darjeeling's Teahouse had heard him. Now that she *listened*, sounds were muted.

Like everyone else in her culture, Camellia had been brought up to revere the goddess of fertility, the Sheela Na Gig.

Aquilaria followed her thought. "For a man to have such contempt for a goddess . . . he has no respect for women." It seemed like an alien thought to Aquilaria.

"That's more common than you know," Camellia said. "Our culture is based on the Lady and Lord, equals and partners. But Earthan society was patriarchal for a long, long time. And some men don't respect anyone or anything that is weaker than themselves. Think of those weaker as prey."

"Warped men," snapped Aquilaria, coming over to give Camellia a hug.

"I think so, too."

"Well, it's no wonder you don't like men."

Camellia winced again. "It's that obvious?"

"Yes, though you're good with male employees. No problem there."

"That's something, I guess."

Slowly Aquilaria turned and sniffed the room. "There's a smell in here."

Camellia hadn't noticed. Aquilaria was frowning, staring at the spot where Camellia's father had been. The manager's shoulders wiggled. "Something about that curse—"

Two cats bulleted into the room. The black one stopped before he ran into Aquilaria, but the little plump calico—Mica—tumbled over him, bounced off Aquilaria's calves, then lit on a circular spot on the carpet that seemed slightly scorched. Mica yowled. *Bad, bad, bad. Bad smell. Bad spot. Bad place!* She leapt onto Camellia's desk, then onto Camellia's lap, tucking her head in Camellia's armpit.

Brazos lifted his upper lip to show sharp incisors and growled. *Do NOT want to stay here.*

"I think that makes it unanimous," Aquilaria said. "The energy in this room has mutated, Camellia."

Camellia frowned. "I don't feel anything wrong."

"Maybe because you've been used to your father's awful energy for a long time," Aquilaria said.

"Excuse me," said Laev T'Hawthorn from the doorway.

Camellia bit back a groan. Just what she needed—a man she was unwillingly attracted to overhearing her humiliating problems with her father. She lifted Mica and stood. "Can I help you, T'Hawthorn?"

"Simply following my Fam. I'm sorry to intrude." That sounded obligatory. Again his eyes gleamed with interest. She sure was giving him some good raw material to think about today—much as she didn't want to.

This spot SMELLS! Brazos said.

One side of Laev's mouth lifted. Dammit, she was thinking of him as *Laev.*

When she shouldn't be thinking of him at all. When she shouldn't be feeling a nice little tingle rush through her as she thought of him. When she shouldn't have to force the image of him as sympathetic from her mind.

No man was sympathetic unless he wanted something.

She said, "I don't smell anything, Brazos. Certainly nothing as bad as you smelled a couple of days ago."

Brazos hopped onto the desk and began grooming his whiskers. *That was fake flower smell and nasty. THIS is curse bad stuff.*

Brows dipping, Laev's smile vanished. "Curse?" He sniffed, his nostrils opening elegantly. He made no sound.

Contrasting with both Mica and Brazos, who seemed to be having a sniffing war—to see how loud and long each could do it. Heat crept up Camellia's neck and she figured it painted her cheeks, too, since they were hot. The room had gotten very small.

Aquilaria glanced at the cats, pressed her lips together hard, drifted toward the doorway. "Excuse . . . me."

Camellia glared at her, knowing she wanted to laugh at the predicament of the sniffing cats. How to really impress an attractive GreatLord.

Laev hesitated, then stepped into the room so Aquilaria could glide out in a nicely professional manner.

"Oh, GraceMistrys Darjeeling, I think you should have your friend, the priestess, check out this office . . . perhaps your person, too. It's no small thing to be in a place where a goddess was insulted," Aquilaria said.

Interrupting Mica midsniff, Camellia set her down on the desk. The small cat sighed and bumped noses with Brazos.

"Which goddess?" Laev asked sharply, scooping up his Familiar as if he was in danger.

"Sheela Na Gig," Camellia muttered.

His eyes widened. He met her gaze and looked away. All images of the goddess emphasized her sex. "Ah." Then he took a step back. "*That* goddess was insulted here? By whom?" Outrage emanated from him, his whole body had tightened again into strict noble posture.

"GraceLord Darjeeling," Camellia said drily, folding her hands, meeting his gaze steadily. "Actually he was cursing me." She angled her chin daring Laev to comment. Their gazes met, locked, mingled, and once again he seemed sympathetic. Which made her cheeks heat more. She was a blushing fool lately.

Mentally she called Tiana. *Ti, I need you. At my office. Curse!* A short, emphatic blast so Tiana knew it was urgent, but not an emergency.

Before Camellia turned toward the teleportation pad, she heard a slight displacement of air and scented Tiana, who smelled of Temple incense.

"What's wrong?" Tiana asked.

The cats sniffed in unison, long and lustily.

"What—" Tiana began, then she stilled, and instead of moving her head, she slid her gaze around the room as if not wanting to attract attention. "Listen to me," she said quietly, barely moving her lips. "GreatLord T'Hawthorn, I want you to step carefully over to Camellia and teleport her away when I count to three. Cats, you need to go also, with your FamPeople or by yourselves."

"Is the teahouse in danger?" Camellia whispered.

Tiana's forehead creased. "I . . . don't . . . think . . . so. Just this office, and I'm sure we can contain the curse . . . or at least send it to follow the one who invoked it, so it rebounds on *him* and not you."

"My father," Camellia said flatly, a little too intensely, because Tiana grimaced at her.

"I'm going to call in a couple of my mentors—a FirstLevel Priestess and Priest."

Treading quietly, athletically, Laev T'Hawthorn moved closer to Camellia. Brazos leapt to her shoulder and stretched out his paws as if he wanted to lay on both of them. With a little burble, Mica jumped up and Laev caught her.

Get close, Mica ordered.

Another step and Laev slid his arm around Camellia's waist. Her heart began to thud strong and fast. His grip was tight so he could take them all when he teleported to a location he knew.

"Where?" she breathed out.

"To my ResidenceDen," he murmured.

They were all so quiet that Camellia noticed that the cheerful conversations had picked up in the dining rooms of the teahouse. She shut her eyes and prayed to the Lady and Lord that her clients would be safe—as well as the business that was the livelihood of her and her staff. When she opened her eyes, she found that she was within a hairbreadth of leaning against Laev's shoulder.

The rustling of robes announced the arrival of the priestess and priest. Their Flair swirled through the room.

The priest made a disgusted noise. Bushy silver and black brows lowered over rich brown eyes set in a thin, lined face. "We'll take care of this." His voice was hard. "We'll make sure the insult and curse is removed from here, attached to the one who profaned. He will pay for the hatred that is his life."

"When?" asked Tiana.

Bending a stern look on her, the priest said, "You were right to call us, and you may work with us, but only the Lady and the Lord and the offended Sheela Na Gig will determine when the curse activates. Go." He turned his head to stare at Laev. "If you please, GreatLord T'Hawthorn. This is no place for you."

"Will the patrons of the dining rooms be safe?" asked Camellia again, watching the priestess as she sprinkled a powder on the rug that revealed a black and oily spot.

"Yes," the priest said. "Only this space will be affected, and we will cleanse it thoroughly when we are done. Go!"

"Thank you, T'Sandalwood," Laev said. Of course he would know the priest; T'Sandalwood was only one step lower in status than the FirstFamilies. Camellia stared at the man who was the highest priest on Celta. She'd never seen him up close before.

"On three," Laev said. "Let me do the teleporting." Well, of course, she couldn't visualize his ResidenceDen.

His arm drew Camellia close until their bodies touched along the side. Her head whirled with the scent of him.

"One, Mica cat. Two, Brazos cat, *three*!"

Camellia's Flair seemed to merge with Laev's . . . and she felt his strong psi power. Magic that had been bred into his blood and bones for centuries—even before his ancestors had landed on Celta. For a moment she felt caught and was pirouetting through a spiral of darkness with bright multicolored pinpoints of flickering light. Then there was an instant's sensation of falling and Camellia found her feet on a thick rectangular carpet that obviously served as a teleportation area for the elegant room.

A room that smelled like Laev, only more so. Generations of Hawthorns. A room that looked like him, intelligent, sophisticated, *noble*. Another deep breath and Camellia realized the odd atmosphere in the room was because the house—the FirstFamily Residence—was a sentient being itself.

She stared around her, at the bookshelves that lined the walls around the windows, the thick, darkly patterned rugs of an incredible knot count.

This is My house. It is FUN. Come with Me, Mica! Brazos shouted excitedly.

"Wait!" Laev commanded. "I don't want you running all over the Residence, distracting or upsetting people. You are to stay in the ResidenceDen." His arm dropped from Camellia's waist and she let her breath out in a whoosh. The place—the man—was overwhelming. She wouldn't move from the teleportation corner chamber.

With every scan of her gaze, she lusted more for a room like this—and the reason it was so wonderful was because it was nearly four centuries old. She could spend a massive amount of gilt replicating the room with antiques the same age, furniture—that incredible burled desk—everything else, and her room still wouldn't be the same. No, she didn't move as Laev spoke to the cats.

Brazos was throwing a fit, thrashing around, black hair flying from him in his stress. *This is MY home and I WANT to SHOW it to MY FRIEND. Especially MY ROOM.*

There was a click. "I have physically locked the door," said a quiet cultured voice.

Camellia jumped, looked around, felt foolish when she realized the Residence itself spoke.

"Thank you, Residence," Laev said.

Clearing her throat, Camellia said, "Mica, come back to me. This was an emergency teleportation. We weren't invited here."

Laev's back and shoulders stiffened. He moved to face her, his expression blank. "You *are* invited. I would not have brought you here if I did not want you here." He sounded courteous, but it was clear to Camellia that she'd insulted him. Of course he had the Flair to teleport anywhere with two cats and a stranger.

"Thank you." She stretched her arms out for her FamCat. "Mica!"

The calico ignored her. Sucking in a breath, Camellia translocated the cat from near the door into her arms, held her Fam tight. *Behave or you will not get furrabeast steak like the rest of us for dinner.*

Mica subsided.

"Thank you very much for your help, T'Hawthorn." She dipped a curtsey. "I did want to tell you that I spoke to my friends about the Salvage Ball. Neither of them recall any other items that Nivea brought to the party." Camellia would never tell him about the strange item she'd sensed. Didn't want to think about it herself.

She dragged in a breath. "I'm sure you understand that I'm concerned about my business. I need to monitor what's going on from my other location. If you will excuse me—"

"You don't take tea with us?" asked the Residence.

Camellia jumped again.

Twelve

T'Hawthorn Residence continued, "Our housekeeper has retrieved some tea made by a D'Hawthorn two centuries ago, for your delectation and experienced palate," the Residence said, almost silkily.

Camellia hadn't realized that a Residence could express itself so well. She didn't say so. In fact, she couldn't seem to think of anything to say. "Ah, hmm."

The door clicked and swung open. Brazos shot through it. Mica leapt from Camellia's arms and bolted from the room after Brazos. A woman dodged them but chuckled tolerantly, saying, "Tea and sandwiches from the hands of GreatLady Huathe Blanca D'Hawthorn. Made in the year 219. The best cook the Family has seen." The housekeeper beamed. She pushed a tray through the air that contained a complete tea for two—teapot, fragile cups and saucers, cream and sweet pots. There was a tiered tray that held tiny, crustless sandwiches.

Laev was staring at the setup as much as Camellia.

"That isn't the same pattern as the vase you took to the Salvage Ball," Camellia said and wished she'd kept quiet. Then her mouth dropped as a fully set table appeared next to one of the windows and nearby chairs moved themselves in front of the place settings. She heard Laev mutter under his breath, "Lord and Lady."

"No, the china is not the same," the housekeeper answered Camellia. "The vase was the last of a set that an ancestor brought with him when he wed one of our GreatLadies. Residence never liked it. *This* set is GreatLady Huathe Blanca's herself. Tea and sandwiches and all." Camellia wasn't sure about drinking and eating food that was a couple of hundred years old, no-time or not. She kept her mouth shut.

Housekeeper and tray had positioned themselves close to the table. "Laev, escort GraceMistrys Darjeeling," the housekeeper ordered, obviously a Family member with strong Flair.

"Of course," Laev said. He angled himself toward Camellia, bowed formally to her as if she were a GreatLady herself, offering his hand.

Another thing she stared at . . . his long, elegant fingers. More than a few heartbeats passed before she gathered her wits enough to take the couple of steps toward him and put her hand in his.

A surge of lust with a hint of *more*, of intense possibilities. Camellia's mouth dried, and she yearned for the tea. The fragrance steaming from the spout of the teapot was something she'd never scented before.

They were both silent as he seated her and sat himself. The chairs moved closer to the table and Camellia pretended that she was used to that, even as she wondered whether the spell was on the chairs, the table, the rug, or something the housekeeper or Laev did. She considered how much it would cost for her teahouses.

She recalled what was going on in Darjeeling's Teahouse and desperately wanted to be back there but didn't dare contact Tiana in case the priestess was in the middle of a ritual.

"May I pour?" asked the housekeeper. Both she and Laev were looking at Camellia.

"Please." She tried her best smile. "Forgive my distraction. There is a touchy situation occurring at my business."

The housekeeper clicked her tongue as her hand tipped the teapot, pouring golden brown liquid with a little fragrance of bergamot into the teacups. Camellia knew that black and bergamot tea had been very popular on Earth at one time, but wasn't currently a taste that Celtans liked.

"You think too much of work." The housekeeper gave Laev a frown, too.

Camellia took a dainty silver spoon with a bowl in the shape of a scalloped seashell and sprinkled some sweet in her tea, tasted. "Lovely," she said truthfully.

Laev drank, too. His jaw bunched. "Good," he said, but Camellia knew he lied.

The housekeeper sighed and went to a corner cabinet that Camellia recognized as no-time dedicated to drinks only. A minute later the older woman returned with a coffee carafe in a subdued masculine-looking pattern. She removed Laev's teacup and saucer and they vanished from her hand to be replaced by a sturdy mug that she filled with strong caff that overwhelmed the fragrance of the tea.

"Here you go, Laev." Her tone was indulgent and Camellia stilled, observing. There seemed to be a pattern going on . . . both the housekeeper and Residence outwardly deferred to Laev as GreatLord T'Hawthorn but seemed to speak to him like a youngster. Not her problem, but . . .

"T'Hawthorn has been very kind to me today. And to *Nuada's Sword*." Camellia lowered her lashes and lifted her cup to inhale the fragrance again. She'd mix some bergamot into her teas and try them on her friends. "I know the SupremeJudge appreciated T'Hawthorn's help."

Laev angled a glance her way. His brows rose ironically. She understood then that he was very aware of the attitudes of his Residence and Family, and for whatever reason, he was letting them ride. The Hawthorns were a patient Family.

Diversion had worked earlier with the Ship, maybe she could use it now, too. She grinned up at the housekeeper. "If you ever need a job, you have one at either Darjeeling's Teahouse or Darjeeling's HouseHeart, in any capacity." Camellia looked at Laev.

"I am honored to introduce my cuz, Alma Hawthorn, to you, GraceMistrys Darjeeling," he said. He drank down some caff and his exhalation was soft and a smile curved his lips.

"I'm also honored," Camellia said.

The woman flushed. "So kind of you to offer, GraceMistrys. I'm sure I wouldn't know what to do if I left T'Hawthorn Residence."

Camellia figured the woman would do just fine anywhere. "My loss," she said. "And I am most honored that T'Hawthorn helped me." She cautiously picked up a bite-sized sandwich and popped it into her mouth. Terrible, just terrible. And the ingredients were definitely fresh. Celtan tastes must have changed. Of course she wanted to spit it out and couldn't.

She chewed and swallowed as soon as possible. "Quite unique." Her gaze slid to Laev, and though his face was impassive, his eyes glinted with humor. She noted then that he hadn't touched the food. Wise man.

Alma nodded. "I'll leave you two." She exited the room.

"Thank you for asking your friends about the Salvage Ball, and telling me," Laev said.

Camellia choked a little before replying, "'Welcome."

"Too bad you already ate the sandwich," Laev said.

"Yes." Camellia gulped down some more very good tea. "I noticed you didn't touch it."

"Once is enough for most of Huathe Blanca's exotic food, though she really was a good basic cook. It shouldn't harm you any."

"Thanks."

He rose and took the plate of sandwiches, dumped them on a piece of papyrus, tapped the sheet. "Farm pigs," he said, and the whole thing disappeared.

"That's handy," Camellia said.

"Yes, though I haven't done it much since I was a child." He joined her again, picked up his cup, and stretched his legs out. This time his smile was lopsided and genuine and affected Camellia much more. Not good. How would she ever be able to put the man out of her thoughts if he smiled at her like that?

"Beautiful room."

He glanced around. "Yes, thank you." Another quirky smile. "I haven't put much of a mark on it. The room remains much like it was when my FatherSire was alive. And I think he didn't change it from his father or FatherSire."

Camellia savored the last of the tea in her cup. "So your Family hasn't been led by a D'Hawthorn, a GreatLady, for a while?" She placed the cup in its saucer, found her Flair had extended to test the atmosphere. Overwhelmingly male. Recalled that the Residence had spoken in a male voice.

Laev was frowning, as if tabulating the past Heads of Households in his mind. "You're right, it's been some time. At least a century and a half. And I'm the fifth T'Hawthorn in a row." He grimaced. "We haven't been as long-lived as some of the other Families."

"But powerful," Camellia said. "Your FatherSire was Captain of the FirstFamilies Council, which made him the head of all the councils."

Laev's lips curved deeper, but his eyes took on a hint of tension. She should leave, not want to ease that strain, to help the man who seemed now to have vulnerabilities she'd never have guessed. Despite the essential male feeling—and with no bitter tang of anger or hatred for those less noble—the room was comfortable. She poured herself another cup of tea and met Laev's eyes steadily. "I think you've added more to this room than you believe."

He blinked as if coming back from a past vision. "I haven't."

She pursed her lips. "Maybe not in the furnishings, but in the . . . quality of the Flair." The more she felt the psi power around her, the more it sank into her skin; she experienced its undertones, like a perfume, or the taste of a complex tea.

"I've only been GreatLord for three months," he said.

"But you worked in this area for a long time before, yes?"

"The ResidenceDen has two offices off it." His smile turned tight. "For the usual two children of the Family. I am an only child, as my father was, and FatherSire. I had an office here."

"You miss your FatherSire?" There had been affection in the tone.

"Yes." He looked at the impressive desk. "He was . . . tough . . . when I was a child, but he mellowed in his later years."

Not from what Camellia had heard, but no one saw the real inner workings of a Family. "He was an impressive man."

"Yes." A touch of red showed on Laev's cheeks, and she finally recalled how the last T'Hawthorn had died. She couldn't help it, she laughed.

Laev closed his eyes.

"Don't you think it's wonderful?" she said.

"Why? Because despite his public service, the fact that he made cinnamon a common spice, what most people recall most is that he died in a lady's bed?"

Camellia wasn't sure of the *public service* bit, either, but she saw that the manner of his FatherSire's death bothered Laev. She reached out and put her fingers over his clenched fist, met his turbulent eyes, the color of a deep lavender that she used in some brews. "Isn't that the way most men want to die? During sex? Hell, I wouldn't mind it, either." She shouldn't have mentioned sex. Warm tremblings began stirring in her lower body.

He turned his hand over but didn't link fingers with her . . . yet the touch of palm on palm went straight to her core. His hand was strong, not soft. She rushed into speech.

"What would he have thought?"

"He'd have been mortified."

"Are you sure? Maybe his proud. . . um . . . business and professional persona. But the man?"

Laev opened his eyes wide and grinned at her. Grabbed her fingers and squeezed, withdrew his hand. "You're right. As a man . . . well, it was pretty evident that he'd satisfied the lady, at least, and he'd have cared about that."

Camellia choked and leaned back into her own space. "Ah, yes. How was his sense of humor?"

"Deeply buried," Laev said. He stood and prowled the room, and Camellia could almost see the paths along the rugs that he— and his forebears—used when they considered important matters. Laev looked up and his smile was easy, like a boy's. The boy he might have been before Nivea. "You're right, though. He might

have been amused." Laev looked away, murmured, "The situation
has been difficult to deal with, though."

"Ah." Camellia cleared her throat. "Well, he was human, and
every human makes mistakes." She knew at once she'd made one as
soon as the words left her mouth and Laev's smile vanished.

Nivea. She always stood between them.

He pulled on his impassive mask. "Yes," he said coolly.

She rose and kept her chin lifted and her eyes steady. "Everyone
makes mistakes, T'Hawthorn." Her mouth turned down. "I have."
Because she couldn't walk away from the hurt that filled him, she
walked toward him, stopped close enough that she had to tilt her
head back a bit to meet his gaze, spoke bluntly.

"You aren't the only one to make a life-changing mistake."

"A bad mistake for my Family."

Narrowing her eyes, she said, "Your mistake was very public.
Don't you think that every single FirstFamily has recovered from
bad mistakes? They may be less well known, so they are private
Family secrets." Her shoulders shifted. "Better that all is known."
The urge to reveal some of herself could not be fought. "That's
what I tell myself when *my* father humiliates me. When I know
someday he will land in gaol." She breathed heavily through her
nose, cheeks continuing to flame. "But there's no room for black-
mail there, like other Family secrets might draw."

He watched her with an inscrutable face. Why had she bothered
to tell him such? Making a cutting gesture with her hand, she
walked back to the rug in the corner of the room that was his teleportation pad, then faced him. "You weren't the only one to be
deceived by Nivea and the Sunflowers."

"Others knew I was making a mistake and I didn't listen to
them."

She snorted. "Lady and Lord, who does at seventeen? Mica, I
am leaving; 'port to me now!"

Her Fam appeared on the rug, back arched and hissing. *Don't
want to go! Like it here!*

"I am your FamWoman, and I am leaving."

"And Brazos will answer to me for disobeying," Laev said loudly, as if he knew the Fam would hear his words, either mentally or relayed by the Residence. "No special pillow he requested."

With a growl, Mica jumped into Camellia's arms and turned her head to look at Brazos, who appeared on Laev's desk, whipping his tail.

Camellia sent a tendril of her mind questing in Tiana's direction. She was in GreatCircle Temple. A check on Darjeeling's Teahouse found Camellia's office teleportation pad available. Breath pushed from her lungs. "Appears like everything's fine at my business." She looked at Laev, who was as urbane as always, GreatLord T'Hawthorn, rich, noble, powerfully Flaired.

"Thank you for your graciousness. I do appreciate it." She looked at the beautiful china on the lovely antique table. "Thanks for the tea, also." Then she squeezed Mica.

Had good time, Brazos, the cat sulked.

"You're welcome," Laev said.

Camellia 'ported before he said anything else.

When she arrived at her office to the sweet scent of prime spiritual cleansers and a new rug—Aquilaria must have authorized that—and the babble of conversation from the dining rooms, a sigh bubbled from her. All was right in this portion of her world. "Scry Darjeeling's HouseHeart."

The wall scry panel lit and connected with Darjeeling's House-Heart. Camellia's manager answered immediately, smiling. "There has been no problem here, Camellia."

"Thanks."

"Your brother dropped by, but that was all."

Camellia's gut tightened and she really regretted eating that sandwich. The taste seemed to coat the back of her throat again.

"He was favorably impressed, I think," the manager said, beaming. She had a soft spot for Senchal. She raised her brows. "And he paid."

"That's good." Camellia heard a noise and saw Aquilaria standing in the doorway, hands tucked in the opposite sleeves of her tunic. Camellia said, "I'll be by tomorrow."

The manager nodded. "See you then."

"End scry," Camellia muttered, then spoke to Aquilaria. "How much did the ritual and the new rug cost?"

Aquilaria stared at Mica, who was checking out the rug with punctuating sniffs. Aquilaria laughed.

"Yes?" Camellia asked.

"FirstLevel Priest T'Sandalwood sent an invoice to the Noble-Council and the Guildhall, to be charged against T'Darjeeling's NobleGilt account."

"As far as I know, my father hasn't fulfilled his annual Noble-Gilt salary for years . . . decades, maybe," Camellia said. "Great-Circle Temple won't ever see that payment."

Aquilaria shrugged. "And the priest and priestess considered filing charges of blasphemy."

"Blasphemy!" Another unusual occurrence.

"But decided that your father would be punished enough when the curse catches up with him."

"Huh." Camellia hoped so but didn't think that would happen. Her father always slid out of situations.

"Everything is fine here, Camellia. You don't need to stay."

"I'll tour the dining rooms," Camellia decided. It would soothe her nerves to know everyone was having a good experience.

At the end of a septhour, she was satisfied that the happenings in the office had minimally affected her patrons. The teahouse itself was doing well, and several customers said that they'd been to the House-Heart to compare. Occasionally some stated that they had a preference for one over the other. That tested Camellia's hostess smile; she'd have liked them to love both, but tastes were definitely subjective.

Mica had pranced along beside her and accepted many pets, faded away if the patrons didn't care to see her. All in all, Camellia was satisfied with her Fam, too. The little cat hadn't sulked for very long.

Camellia, with a purring Mica attached to her shoulder, congratulated Aquilaria on a good job, then went to the teleportation pad in her office and 'ported home. She landed on the small, inexpensive rug in her mainspace and stood a bit, looking around her home. It was *hers*, reflected herself, and was comfortable enough. She shouldn't compare it to Laev's ResidenceDen. Her house wasn't even a century old, not to mention nearly four.

But she really liked the ambience of T'Hawthorn Residence. Like the man, it throbbed with possibilities. Had Laev *listened* to her? She didn't think so. Men didn't. For a while she'd treated him as if he was a friend and wasn't sure why. It must have been the charm of the place . . . or the nice way they'd all treated her, including Laev. Respectfully.

She walked through her home, decided that she should do a little ritual cleansing here, too. She hadn't taken the time since her father and uncle had first invaded her space a few days ago, and they'd definitely left smudges in her atmosphere. Camellia didn't want her friends to be besmirched by any of her relations' negative emotions . . . or her equally negative reactions to them.

So she lit special incense sticks and placed them in every room, then went to the no-time to pull out the expensive steaks she'd bought for the next time she wanted to pamper herself and her friends . . . and stared at the empty space where six thick furrabeast steaks should have been. Where they'd been that morning.

Gone.

Thirteen

❤

$\mathcal{M}$ica stretched to stare into the no-time raw meat storage compartment. *There is no furrabeast.*

"I know," Camellia said through gritted teeth. Frustration spewed through her, stinging the back of her eyes with angry tears. She swallowed bile, looked down at Mica. "I think my uncle took our steaks."

The little cat gasped in shock. *No!*

"Yes."

The mean man took MY food!

"That's right."

I will scratch him, again and again! Bite him!

"Can you smell any trace of the steaks?"

Nose elevated, Mica trotted from the small galley kitchen to Camellia's bedroom, back to the front door. *Went like this.*

"That's what I thought." Pressing her lips together, Camellia closed the door of the no-time. She wanted steak.

You said I could have furrabeast steak, Mica whined.

"We'll pick it up on the way back from the guard station. Come along."

Mica hopped to her shoulder.

This time it was the male guard who was available to take her complaint. He was cool. "Come to swear out a complaint against your father again?"

"Mostly it's against my uncle." She showed her teeth in an unfriendly smile as the guardsman lazily handed over a small holosphere for her to record.

"Can't believe that," he muttered.

Camellia gave her name, her uncle's name, and that she'd found him in her bedroom and the time, and noted that she was missing "Six prime furrabeast steaks at thirty gilt apiece."

The guard straightened swiftly. "Steaks! Your uncle stole steaks!"

"That's right." She finished the complaint, and when she handed the sphere back to the guard, his face was hard.

"That was really low, stealing a person's steaks."

"Nothing is too low for my uncle," she said, then nodded to the guard. "No doubt I'll see you again. Now I want to cleanse my home before my friends come to dinner."

"Blessed be," the guard said.

"Thank you, I like all the blessings I can get. And blessed be to you."

She took Mica and headed for the meat shop.

As soon as they arrived back home, Camellia picked Mica up and stared into her eyes. "I don't want you teleporting to anything but the pad here until my father and uncle are gone."

Bad men. Mica's gaze fired, her tail lashed.

"That's right."

Bad men should not be able to come and go in Our house when they want.

A sour taste infused Camellia's mouth. She drew Mica close and held her, rocked a little. "No, they shouldn't. But that's my reality, FamCat. Promise me, now."

Oh, all right, Mica grumbled. *I won't let Brazos come except on pad, either.*

"Good idea."

Mica slid a sly gaze at Camellia and she waited for what her Fam would say next.

Would be very nice to have catnip sprinkled on the pad.

"I don't think so, then you would lay around on the pad and maybe not remember to do the signal for free or in use."

Mica mewed pitifully.

"So I will put a pillow in the opposite corner of the mainspace. Big enough for you and Brazos, and catnip on it."

Butting her head against Camellia, Mica purred loudly. *You are the BEST FamWoman.*

"Yes, I am. Don't forget it, and be a good FamCat."

Mica said nothing to that.

The evening went well. Camellia and her friends didn't speak of *Nuada's Sword* which was a relief, because Camellia wasn't ready to talk about her ancestry. Or the only man she knew in the Family who'd been good. Since Tiana had been involved in the office curse incident and Glyssa was irritated that she'd missed the excitement, she wanted information. "Tell all. I heard that fligger of a father of yours went *too far* and someday will get a tough lesson." She chewed and swallowed and a mean smile curved her lips. Camellia echoed the smile. Tiana arched her brows in slight professional-priestess disapproval at negative emotions like glee at someone else's misfortune. Of course, Tiana didn't have a smile like that in her repertoire.

"I just hope it's soon. He and my uncle are hanging around Druida more than I care for."

"The more they're here, the more they'll bother you." Glyssa nodded.

Mica burped and walked away from her clean plate. *Mean men.*

"That's right," Camellia said. "And you know what you need to do if you are alone and see them . . ."

Teleport to D'Ash's office.

"That's right."

Or to Brazos at T'Hawthorn's. Mean men can't get into Residences.

"I would prefer you go to D'Ash's. I've already apprised her of the situation."

"Lots of other Fams at D'Ash's," Glyssa added.

"Tiana, do you know what kind of form the curse on my father might take?"

Tiana shrugged. "No. But she's the goddess of fertility." Her smile was bright and overly sweet, and Camellia thought it might just match her own and Glyssa's mean ones. "It might rot his cock right off."

Mica fell down on the floor and rolled, laughing. *Mean man likes his cock as much as Brazos?*

"Oh, I'm sure," Tiana said. "Males are alike in that."

"And Father won't anticipate it," Camellia said. "He'd never think that his own hatred would come back to haunt him."

Will the goddess come visit and say hello and admire Me? asked Mica

"Ah. Goddesses aren't really . . ." Glyssa stopped.

Tiana took up an explanation. "Energies are always around us—for good and for ill. And we add to such energies and forces with our own Flair and beliefs, but it is not wise to ruffle a benevolent energy stream . . ."

The whole spiritual thing escaped Camellia. She was happy just praying to the Lady and Lord, or, very occasionally, the Lord and the Lady, and considering them as mostly benevolent and distant parents. *Good* parents . . . like Glyssa's or Tiana's.

"Now you should tell us what happened at T'Hawthorn Residence. And what a GreatLord's ResidenceDen looks like," Glyssa said.

"Ah, that story includes T'Hawthorn and his housekeeper and a GreatLady D'Hawthorn a couple of centuries ago . . ."

Glyssa and Tiana ate, listening to Camellia's story.

"He actually sent his ancestress's food to *pigs*!" Glyssa sounded shocked, but she would try anything. Might have even eaten more than one of the ancient sandwiches.

"Yes."

"What was in the sandwiches?" Glyssa asked.

"I've given it some thought. I think it was mashed bean curd with some rather odd spices."

"Oh," Tiana and Glyssa said at the same time.

Tiana added, "Do you want to say anything more about T'Hawthorn?"

"Not right now. It's been a very long day—long week." Camellia flopped back on her pillow. "Just a few days ago I was in total denial."

"You're doing well," Tiana said.

"Thank you," Camellia said.

Later, after she put on her nightshirt for bed, she caressed the small sculpture of a sleeping cat that she'd picked up at the Salvage Ball.

Laev had carved it, she knew. She'd known he'd sculpted, even before he'd given her the statue of the Lord—one she'd placed in Darjeeling's HouseHeart yesterday.

She wasn't sure how the cat had sensed Laev's sculpture at the party, but Mica had said that Brazos had told her the piece hadn't been there when he and Laev had first arrived.

So someone had added the sculpture to the tables after Laev had come. Brazos hadn't sensed it belonging to Laev because of the pig smell. The black cat still turned his nose up at it because it was more like his Sire, Black Pierre, than himself, and the ear was broken off.

Camellia figured Laev must have pulled that trick of sending an item to the farm pigs with Nivea. Camellia had no problem envisioning Nivea taking the cat from wherever Laev had stored it—or maybe it had actually been a gift—and sending it to the pigs.

The sculpture was Camellia's now, and thinking of Laev and Nivea together would just hurt her—and Nivea had caused enough hurt in this lifetime.

One last rub of the small sculpture and Camellia doused the spellglobe. Night gathered in the room and Mica snored softly.

But as soon as Camellia slid between the linens, she thought of the previous nights, the sensuality of telepathic sex with Laev.

She'd admitted he was her HeartMate, and for the first time ever, she'd spent some time with him. Liked the time she'd spent with him.

Her body wanted him, wanted the sex that he could offer. And here, in bed, in the dark, she could rationalize that mental sex with him was acceptable. No strings . . . he probably wouldn't even recognize her. She continued to believe that he didn't want a relationship with all the boggy pitfalls any more than she did. Dared she *reach* for him mentally?

No. But she could relax. If she relaxed, her mind might drift toward his again. She shifted in bed. Mica snuffled and snored louder.

And Camellia closed her eyes, thought of Laev.

He was abed, too—and waiting for her.

His strong hands grasped her shoulders. *Lady,* he whispered, arousal ladening his mental voice.

She hesitated, then responded. *Lover.*

Tension ebbed from his fingers. No, he didn't want to acknowledge her as his HeartMate.

Then she was naked in his arms, her breasts rubbing against his chest, sending tingles straight to her sex. Wanting him. More, needing him.

His hands slid under her, stroking down her back, rounding over her butt, squeezing her, feeling her own muscle. She shimmied a little, wanting his fingers to slide somewhere more sensitive than her bottom, and he laughed. The very sound sent shivers ruffling her nerves. Here was her HeartMate—no, her *true lover*—finally in her arms, sharing sex with *her.* She arched up, rubbing her body against his muscular flesh, running her own hands down his biceps, intimately discovering the lines of her lover, the breadth of his shoulders, the weight of his body on hers. Finally, finally.

She rubbed his backside, and he groaned and arched and his sex slid into her. For a moment they both stilled. She realized he was braced, tensed for her to leave as she usually did if she came awake at this point. When she could move the breath from the back of her throat, puff it through her lips, she whispered, "Lover," and sent it mentally in a chant. She arched again, and let pleasure shimmer through her in waves of anticipation. "Lover."

That set him off; he surged and she circled her hips to increase their delight, wind the sensations higher and higher, faster and faster. His skin grew slick under her hands. Their uneven panting breaths came in unison like the pounding of their hearts, the rhythm of loving. They moved together, climbing, searching for the release they'd find together. Then all whirled away and explosive stars streaked through the night, through her mind, through her body, and she screamed, and his long, low groan made her heart burst with ecstasy that he was with her, in her.

She lay gasping, and he rolled and their limbs were entwined and she shifted with him. More sparks of pleasure danced before her eyes as her body contracted around him. He fit her so very well.

Still in his arms, she slept, and as she did so, she floated away from him and back into her home.

When she awoke, it was to new hope that the day would be better. She considered the sex with Laev, decided it was fine right now, no need to change. Thinking more on the topic when she bathed, she realized that once the sex dream had ended, his dreams had not continued to blend with hers. He had withdrawn, mentally, emotionally, back to his own place.

Maybe, just maybe, they would get through this without savaging each other with their own problems.

The scrybowl pulsed a bright yellow and made the pouring tea sound. Her teacher, Acacia Bluegum.

"Here," Camellia said.

"I set up an appointment with Tinne Holly, the owner of the Green Knight Fencing and Fighting Salon, to test you for membership."

Camellia's stomach dropped. "Oh? When?"

"This afternoon right after WorkEndBell. The testing won't take long, and you'll do great!" Acacia grinned cheerfully.

"You're sure about that?"

Mica hopped onto the marble-topped dressing table that held the old-fashioned scrybowl and stared at Acacia's image hovering over it in the mist. *I have not been to this Green Knight place.* She moved her fixed gaze from Acacia to Camellia. *Brazos has been. I want to go!*

"Of course you do," Camellia said.

"What's the cat say?" asked Acacia.

"She has a male friend who has gone to the Green Knight."

Acacia laughed, winked. "And does this male cat have a male owner?"

"Yes."

"Do go." Then Acacia's face dropped into serious lines. "This is the best thing for you, Camellia. I promise. Learning to fight a man your father's size, training with male fighters, getting—"

"Men's hands on me, yes, I know." She tried not to think of the telepathic sex bouts.

"If you need me to be there . . ." Acacia offered.

Camellia sucked in a deep breath. "No, I'm fine."

"You certainly are. Later." The scrybowl went dark.

Mica widened her eyes. *What are we doing today?*

Smiling wryly, Camellia said, "I'm hoping to finally show you our usual routine—we'll go to both the restaurants."

Good food!

"For sure, and let's start with breakfast."

*F*or *Laev, the day was crammed full of intense investment negotiations* with several fledgling companies that should lead to another nice fortune for the Family in another decade. He'd let Jasmine watch the proceedings, and Brazos had popped in and out, until finally WorkEndBell had rung and he darkened the scry panel.

You have been behind that desk all day long! Brazos accused.

"That's right." Laev grinned at him. "Making gilt . . . enough so that in a year I could boost my Fam's allowance."

Brazos purred loudly, cocked his head. *Muscles stiff.*

Surprised that the cat noticed, Laev said, "Yes."

We should go to the Green Knight.

Now the cat mentioned it, Laev liked the idea. He stretched.

Brazos followed suit, flexing his young muscles. *Maybe other Cats there for play. I am large and strong and will be alpha.*

"Holm HollyHeir and his HeartMate have cats who play there." Laev rolled his shoulders, anticipating action that would wring the stress from them. "And you aren't larger or stronger than Tinne Holly's hunting cat."

We will see. I will have a bit of shredded clucker before we leave.

Laev thought he'd have broth. He considered cats and violent activity after eating. "I'm not cleaning up your vomit. You have to do that yourself."

I won't regurgitate my food.

Laev figured those were famous last words.

You are holding me too tightly! Mica said but didn't wriggle or hop from Camellia's arms as they headed to the Green Knight Fencing and Fighting Salon for her testing. Camellia loosened her grip, uncaring that the cat's claws were ripping holes in her loose fighting tunic. Her clothes were grayish and frayed. She hadn't noticed until she'd scanned the three sets. Finally she just put on the best.

Down, please, Mica said. *Are we near the training place?*

They'd teleported to the closest pad that Camellia knew. Pushing her shoulders back, she said, "Right down the street, see the big sign?"

Mica sniffed. *I smell other Cats!*

"Probably, I think the Hollys have cats." Camellia lagged a little behind her Fam. She'd added a cloak over her clothes. Soon she was entering the door, and her nose was hit by the scent of men.

She stopped. Breathed shallowly. How often had she smelled the sweat of her father or uncle? Not often, not much; they didn't work or play that hard. They preferred scamming through life. She could do this.

The lobby of the salon was wide and had a teleportation pad to her right, double swinging doors ahead of her with small glass panes, and a lecternlike thing with a silver appointment sphere spinning in the middle.

Camellia swallowed, walked up to the lectern. Shouts and yells came from beyond the doors, then they swung open and Tinne Holly walked out, a muscular man in his prime. A man who was from the highest of Families. A horrible feeling of being in the wrong place dropped over her like a blanket. She didn't think she could move.

He offered a charming smile and a bow . . . a fighter's bow. A few seconds passed before her muscles jerked a response. Her lips felt numb. Too many men.

"Greetyou," Tinne said, smiling with real charm.

"I . . . think this may be a mistake."

His platinum brows rose. "No. You're just nervous. Are you going to let your nerves . . . whatever caused them, win?"

She sensed that Acacia had told him more than Camellia was comfortable with, but he had a point. Her spine stiffened. "I'm here to test."

"And so we shall. There are some private rooms through that door." He gestured to a sturdy wooden door in the left corner.

"Thank you for seeing me." Gathering her courage, Camellia walked to the door and opened it.

Mica mewed.

Tinne Holly squatted easily, holding out his hand. "Who are you?" He scratched her under her chin.

I am Mica Darjeeling. I am a friend of Brazos Hawthorn.

"Ah, I know Brazos." Tinne rose. "You, Fam, are welcome here as long as you keep to the sides of all the rooms. If you are ever on a mat, you will be banned from ever coming back."

Mica gasped. *Ever!*

"That's right. I've found it best to lay out firm rules for Fams." Tinne winked at Camellia. She knew he was trying to relax her, but with every minute, her muscles strung into tight strands. He motioned for Camellia to step into a narrow hallway lined with several more doors that must lead to private sparring rooms.

Camellia heard Mica squeal behind her, but the cat didn't enter the hallway.

The next few minutes passed in a blur. Camellia knew she was stiff, slow, fearful. Somehow she couldn't get past that, knew her moves were lackluster.

Then Tinne shouted, and the door burst open and a large, dark shape shot toward her. Father! Run! No, stand! Stand and fight!

Her breath came short, true fear now, he'd hurt her if he could. She whirled and kicked, caught him in the gut, he folded in a grunt, she continued with her move, set up the next, took him down with another kick, jumped to place her foot on his neck, and stared into protuberant blue eyes of a red-faced and sweating man.

Not her father. He caught her foot and it was her turn to go flying, then they rose and circled . . . and she got a good workout. They were down on the mat and wrestling when Tinne shouted, "Stop!"

Camellia came to herself, rose, and bowed to her opponent, turned to Tinne, hesitated as she saw Laev T'Hawthorn, Brazos, and Mica with the Holly.

Fourteen

Camellia bowed to Tinne.

He nodded to her and to her opponent. "I believe you are well matched. I'll put you down for sparring practice . . ." Tinne stared at the man's thickened middle. "Three nights a week for a septhour and a half, and a septhour before NoonBell on Koad so I can check on you both."

My FamWoman is very good, Mica purred, sitting proudly by Brazos.

Tinne's lips twitched, then he clapped Laev on his shoulder. "As for you, my friend, let's see what we can do in sparring room three."

Sweaty hair hanging in her eyes—she'd have to get that cut or put it up better—Camellia offered Laev a weak smile. All she could think of was that she must look terrible, hair tangled and sweaty, face flushed. Her shabby fighting clothes showing patches of sweat.

My FamMan is even better, Brazos said. He looked at Mica, then Camellia, and sent a strong telepathic sentence. *You should come watch.*

The last thing she wanted to do was see Laev's muscles move in exertion that might remind her—and him—of midnight sex. "Thanks, not this time. I must set up our appointments."

Her opponent was wheezing and on the mat. She went over and offered her hand. He took it gratefully, rocked to his feet with her help, and was close and in her space and smelling—not like her father. Citrusy. His hand was plumper than her father's and he was scowling, but it held no threat. He aimed his frown at Tinne Holly. "Least you could do, boy, is introduce us properly."

Laev strolled forward. His lashes were low over his eyes and his mouth curved in a half smile. Camellia felt every droplet of sweat on her body. Damn, she must look terrible. She tried to discreetly sniff and find out her scent, but her partner's was too strong.

Laev bowed to him, a fighting bow to an equal.

The man snorted and dropped Camellia's hand. "I ain't your equal here, T'Hawthorn. Surprise you remember me."

"I remember everyone in my clubs," Laev said simply, and Camellia knew it was true. He would, because he was trained that way. He gestured from the man—surely a lord—to Camellia. "Grace-Lord Cymb Lemongrass, may I present GraceMistrys Camellia Darjeeling."

"Good meetin' you," said the man who was rather shaped like her father, but so obviously unlike Guri in any other respect.

"A pleasure." Camellia bowed as a lesser to him. They were close to equal in fighting experience, but whatever edge she might have in that area was lost in the outer-world's social status.

Now Tinne Holly joined them, buffeted Camellia on her shoulder, enough to unbalance her if she hadn't been strong in her fighter's stance. "Good," he said. "I accept you into the mid-level program, and we don't follow outside rank here, only fighting levels count." He nodded at them both. "Three nights a week." Jerked a head to Laev. "And you're rusty, so let's go remedy that."

Laev nodded to Lemongrass, turned, and smiled at her. "Grace-Mistrys."

She cleared her throat, but her words still came out a squeak. "T'Hawthorn." She watched the men leave . . . all right, she watched two very fine backsides leave, Brazos and Mica following. When she turned back to her opponent, he was at the side of the room, drying sweat from his neck and face with a towel. She winced, reminded once again how bad she must look.

"Let's set this up," Lemongrass said. He sounded irritated. Not angry, but the waves of annoyance kept her feet in the same spot, not crossing over to him. He caught her look, expanded his explanation. "Dammit, I wanted to be better than I am."

A chuckle escaped Camellia. "So do I."

He puffed a breath. "Suppose that means that we have to practice."

"I suppose so."

Grunting, he called up his calendarsphere. "Three nights a week," he grumbled.

Camellia sighed, walked a little forward so her calendarsphere could interface with his. "Yes."

They synchronized and chose their nights, and Lemongrass watched her with a considering look but said nothing more, and Camellia was glad. Did he know why he was specifically chosen as a partner for her? Her face heated, but her teeth gritted. She *would* do this.

Tinne Holly didn't bother to hide his grin as he ushered Laev and the cats into sparring room three. "Glad to have Darjeeling here. She was a little nervous and stiff at testing, but will do better." He rubbed his hands. "She was recommended by Acacia Bluegum. We can make Darjeeling into a real fighter, once she gets over her issues with men."

"What issues?" tore from Laev.

Tinne's brows went up. "You saw her father yesterday, didn't you?"

"No."

"All the noble circles are talking about his blasphemy."

Left very nasty smell in office, Mica added. *I have met the mean men.*

"What mean men?"

Sire and Sire's littermate, Brazos projected matter-of-factly, then went to sit on a carpeted wall shelf made for Fams.

"Yes, Darjeeling will make a fighter," Tinne said, then ran through a drill so fast he blurred. Laev winced. He was going to be a floor mop. Tinne would emphasize that he was out of practice. Well, he'd go down—literally—fighting.

Tinne bowed to him. "And she's a very attractive girl."

The back of Laev's neck heated and he was glad he wore a groin guard and his trous were loose. He'd just caught a glimpse of her as he'd walked up to the threshold of the doorway and his body had hardened. The woman had looked like sex. Her breasts round, lifting and falling rapidly under her tunic, tendrils of dark brown-red hair curling damply at her temples, the sheen of perspiration revealed by the V of her tunic.

"Bow, Laev," Tinne said.

Laev yanked his mind back to the present. No thought of the sexy Darjeeling or her past or her problems must distract him.

Too late.

*C*amellia left the private sparring room and found Mica in the entry chamber. The cat sat near a pile of clothing and a bag, tail around paws and a toothy smile.

"What's this?" But Camellia knew, one of her better tunic and trous sets. She snatched the pale gold clothing up, shook out the few wrinkles that had gathered.

We should stay here.

"Why?"

You should watch people in big room. First big fight coming up.

The cat must mean there was a general free-for-all melee instead of any classes.

And Mica might have a point. Camellia would like to watch others—maybe even some of the good, even great, fighters. At least see who was here.

You didn't bring other clothes, so Brazos and I went home and got these for you! Mica's smile widened into a scary cat grin.

"Thanks."

The little cat relaxed a little and the smile went away.

You go to waterfall room through big room, Mica informed her.

"I see you've explored."

"Yesss," Mica vocalized. *And I have been very good, always close to the walls.*

"Wonderful."

Yes, I am. Mica stood and flicked her tail and waited for Camellia to open the door. Fighters stood silently on all four sides of the room, behind the sparring line, and she realized that a melee was about to start. She hurried into the ladies' section before too many people noticed her since she still looked awful.

There were no other women in the large, tiled common female waterfall room, and Camellia was both glad and sad. Glad she had it to herself because she was used to privacy, but sad that once again she felt the lone female. But from the glance she'd had of the main room, she thought there were women taking part in the general melee. Tilting her head, she heard female fighting cries.

She hurried through her waterfall, stepped through the drying field, and dressed, stuffed her training robes into a bag. Then she took an extra minute or two to make sure her hair looked good. Would Laev Hawthorn still be here? Would he stay to watch the melee?

But once she reached the small enclosed area between the entrances to the men's and women's private areas and the large fighting chamber, she lingered, fastening her bag, smoothing her tunic. She couldn't gauge her own emotions, whether she wanted to see Laev or not. Didn't know how she'd react—mentally or physically.

As she was standing there, a large man with a scarred face came out of the men's area. He wore the highest-level belt. "I'm Cratag T'Marigold." The man offered his hand to Camellia. A small frown line twisted between his brows. "You look familiar."

She put her hand in his. It was hard with fighting calluses. "Camellia Darjeeling."

He jerked a nod. "I was in JudgementGrove on the day you claimed your tea set. Good to see you again."

Of course he'd been there. And everyone knew he was. *Cratag T'Marigold*. He who had been Cratag Maytree. The chief guard of the Hawthorns. Considered to be like Laev's older brother. The man had been the only one of Laev's Family at his wedding to Nivea.

"Greetyou." She bowed to him as a lowly trainee to a master. He was one of the top four fighters in the world.

"Good to meet you," he said politely, then held open the door for her.

So she had to go out, and as she did, she noted that the melee was winding down. "Oh, I'm sorry I missed observing that."

T'Marigold smiled. "It was only the warm-up. There are two more."

"Oh." She shrugged deprecatingly. "It's my first night. I was just admitted to the salon."

"Congratulations."

"Thanks." To her relief, she saw Tinne Holly close by, standing near his private office door. She wasn't sure what to say to Cratag T'Marigold. She thought he was still close to Laev, but couldn't dredge up any gossip. "Ah, GreatSir Holly." She dipped a curtsey. "I thank you for allowing me to join your salon." She *wasn't* going to think of the cost of it.

"Glad to have you here," Tinne replied. "I'd like you to work on—"

Cratag cleared his throat. "My deepest apologies." He bowed to Camellia. "If I might speak to Tinne for one moment—"

Get between two of the best fighters on the planet? In a place where they ruled? No. She curtsied twice. "Of course."

She had started to back away when a small piping voice said behind her, "I wemember you, too."

She stopped, pivoted warily. Looked down to see a boy of about four.

Both T'Marigold and Holly went extremely still, radiating intensity.

"You were little when you were in JudgementGrove. Older than me now, but littler."

Camellia swallowed. The boy spoke with authority and enunciated each word well. She'd been thirteen. This boy hadn't been born.

"This is my son, Cal," Cratag said, his tones thick. But he stared at Tinne.

The boy bowed to her.

She bowed back.

"You're going to start him on fighting." She tried to infuse a little lightness into the conversation.

"He's a natural," Cratag said. "We've been training at home, but he needs this place." There was pride in his tone, but still an odd intensity. "Cal, please wait for me on the east side of the room," Cratag said.

Cal nodded and walked away with a little roll to his gait. Both Cratag and Tinne focused on the boy's small legs.

"He's walked like that from the beginning," Cratag said hoarsely. "I've been thinking . . . but I didn't want to say anything. Especially not to your Family if I wasn't sure. It isn't often someone remembers . . ."

Reincarnation. That's what this was all about. It was a tenet of their culture and, of course, Camellia believed in that, in the main religion of their planet. It made sense to her. But a chill rippled through her and she wanted desperately to be somewhere else. Her feet seemed stuck to the ground.

"Lady and Lord, Lord and Lady." Tinne Holly wiped a hand across his eyes. His voice was thick. "If anyone would, he would. We've missed G'Uncle Tab so much."

Yes. She must go, now. Camellia took a step back, fingers tightening on the straps of her bag.

Tinne Holly said to her, "We can talk some other time. Please stay as long as you wish to watch the sparring. We have another open melee for exercise and the first one for salon ranking this week."

"Of course." She smiled and began to walk to the opposite side of the room, where there were rolled-up mats against the wall for seating.

Watching the fighters line up again, she noted there were about half a dozen women interspersed with a dozen men. She felt better about her training robes. Some of the ones here were downright tattered. Everyone was her level or better. All the women looked like they'd been sparring here for years. Some of the younger men weren't quite as good as Camellia considered herself to be, so that was also reassuring.

She went over to the mat and sat, found it didn't accommodate the length of her legs well, and wiggled back on the fat roll to sit cross-legged. She set down her bag beside her.

A bell rang sharply and people leapt into the fighting area and began to spar. She studied them, the milling and mixing of the free-form melee. There were one-on-ones, groups, three-on-twos, all sorts of combinations—male and female, and it didn't seem as anyone noticed or gave any quarter according to gender. That was good, but she wasn't used to it and would feel self-conscious for a while.

Then a movement caught her eye and she saw the child, Cal Marigold, studying the fighters with far-too-old eyes. Yes, this was a child shadowed with a dusty, unraveled spiderweb, memories of his past life. Only one?

Not a question she wanted answered. Not something she even wanted to think about.

To her amazement, Cal came up to her and climbed the mat roll to sit on her lap. Instinctively her arm came around him. He gazed up at her, a dimple in his cheek. "I like you."

"I like you, too."

"I will be T'Mawigold dis time. Dat's my name now, Cal Mawigold." He glanced at Tinne Holly and Cratag Marigold, who continued to stare at them, snuggled again, looked up at her. "I like being a Mawigold. De Residence is very pwetty. I like pwetty. You are pwetty."

"Thank you." Considering the fact that reincarnation tweaked and twanged her nerves, she hoped that didn't show.

"I will be de Head of a Household," he said with great satisfaction.

Camellia wasn't sure what she should do. Tiana should be here to handle this. Camellia would damn well babble about the whole experience to Tiana, and soon. "It's good to be the Head of a Household," she said, supposing it was true.

"Yes, and dis time I will have a HeartMate, dat's better." He leaned against her, snuffled a little, and fell asleep. All Camellia could do was hold him closely . . . and think of fate. Feelings swirled inside her. She hadn't felt a small body in her lap . . . maybe never. She'd been focused on her career. So had her closest friends. She didn't know children.

And despite what Cal said, she didn't know this one. But she liked holding him very much. Her brain settled with a *thunk* inside her skull. She wanted children.

She wanted a man, a husband, a HeartMate, too.

Looking up, she saw Laev T'Hawthorn enter the room from the men's private area.

Fifteen

Everything about the moment sharpened to near pain. The light brightened, the scent of sweat, male and female, coated the inside of her nose, thuds and groans and grunts pounded at her ears. The heightening of all her senses affected her emotions. Too extreme. Her heart seemed to pull in her chest, as if it wanted to arrow to Laev. Lady and Lord!

He looked wonderful. Now she noted he wore a fighting tunic and trous that had obviously been tailored for him though they were loose for training. He didn't have the same muscular grace as Tinne Holly or Cratag T'Marigold, but he held himself with an essential self-confidence that proclaimed he'd fit here, sparring, or in a business meeting . . . or sitting behind the long, ornate table of the FirstFamilies Council.

Camellia swallowed. Her life was kinking and twisting so much, so fast, that she wasn't sure what path she was on, or whether it was good or bad. Only daunting.

She'd managed not to tense up enough to wake the boy, but knew she couldn't stay.

Slowly, gently, she slipped her bag straps over her arm, stretched her legs. Cradling the child, she rose slowly so as not to joggle the sleeping boy. With an outsized sense of relief, she saw that Cratag T'Marigold was closer to her than Laev.

Easy, then, to give Cal back to his father, nod in passing at Laev, and move on toward the door and teleportation pad in the entry-way. Discreetly, she sucked in a breath, kept the child still as she walked to Cratag.

He held out his arms and she passed the youngster to him. The boy murmured in his sleep, then turned his head into his father's large chest, curled his fingers around the edge of the V of Cratag's tunic.

Without warning a tender smile curved Camellia's lips, and she couldn't prevent sifting her fingers through the boy's soft blond hair. "He's tired," she whispered.

"It's been an emotional event," Cratag allowed, nodding at her. "My thanks for keeping him safe." The man angled his head in the direction of the main area, where people still fought and were tossed and fell and rolled.

"I don't think there was any danger to him," she said. "Not here." She figured any one of the people on the floor—including the men—would have flung themselves away from the child.

"A wise man once told me . . ." Laev Hawthorn began.

He was there, giving Cratag a one-armed hug, staring down at Cal! She hadn't noticed him draw near, though now she thought about it, her nerves were midshiver.

". . . that accidents happen in a fight, a foot might slip in a deadly duel." He glanced at the sparring. "A fall might go wrong."

Cal stirred in Cratag's arms, opened his eyes, blinked sleepily. "Gweetyou, Laev," he grumbled. He thrashed a little, but Cratag kept a good hold on him, and the boy looked at the sparring. "Nice to be back here."

Laev appeared startled.

"Sure it is," Cratag said. "But now we're going home."

The child blinked faster. "We awe? Not spawwing here?"

"No. Back home to your mother, and *dancing*."

Camellia had heard that the Marigolds were dancers.

"Dancing. I *love* dancing," the boy said, and his smile was purely a child's smile.

Camellia thought all of them exhaled with relief. The shadows of a former life behind the child's eyes had disappeared.

She curtsied to Cratag, to Laev. "Must go. I haven't eaten dinner."

She walked with Cratag T'Marigold and Cal through the doors to the entry room and the teleportation pad, all too aware of Laev. He watched them, and Camellia didn't know who he'd focused on. Had he realized who she was from the intimate contact last night? But he followed Cratag and Cal and her.

Then Cratag and Cal were gone from the teleportation pad and she stepped onto it.

"Rrrrowwwrrr!" Mica bulleted into the room, chased by Brazos, hopped onto the teleportation pad. *You did not wait for Me!*

Camellia cringed. She *had* forgotten her Fam.

Mica leapt to Camellia's shoulder, dug in her claws, and Camellia winced and accepted the pain as punishment. The small cat tapped her paw on Camellia's cheek. *We are FAMS now.*

"That's right." She settled into her balance, stared into the big yellow cat eyes close to her face. "And I didn't see you at all in the training space. Nor did you spend much time with me when you visited Brazos yesterday." She looked down at the large, long-furred black cat. "He is a very beautiful cat," she said. Actually more beautiful than Mica.

Brazos preened.

"But I am your FamWoman. I like your company, too."

Mica grumbled, looked down at Brazos herself. *We are going home now.*

He sat and lifted a forepaw to lick. *We stay to fight with other males, then I will go home to My room.*

Mica's twitching whiskers tickled Camellia's face. *But I will have furrabeast steak with special spices. My FamWoman makes excellent food.* Her tongue came out to swipe her muzzle. *Let's go home.*

Keeping a laugh in her throat, Camellia smiled at everyone and 'ported to her house. Her last sight was Laev swallowing a laugh, too.

She was still smiling when she landed on her home teleportation pad.

There was a whoosh of air and she was shoved hard into the corner. Her head hit the wall. Mica screeched and leapt off her shoulder.

"Fligger!" Just from the one word, she knew her uncle was back. "Filthy beast!"

"Mica teleport to D'Ash's."

No, BITE MEAN MAN.

Camellia couldn't see. Her uncle backhanded her, a blow to her cheek. "That's for the cup not being unique. Some flitch owns an urn." Camellia lunged toward his voice, caught him a glancing blow with her body, tucked and rolled to her feet, turned . . . and heard the soft whoosh of air indicating he'd teleported.

"Lights on!" They blazed and Camellia shook her head as her eyes adjusted, then saw Mica bristled and arched atop the back of the leather chair. "Are you all right?"

She growled. *Only scratched him a little.* She turned wheeling eyes on Camellia. *He HURT you.*

"Oh, yeah. Come on, let's report this to the guards, then we'll stop off at AllClass HealingHall on the way back." Her NobleGilt included medical benefits so there was no cost. "We can teleport to the guard station, but will have to take the public carrier to the HealingHall and home."

I will tell the guards all about how I scratched mean man.

That made Camellia smile. Painfully, she licked blood from her lip. "Sounds good."

*L*aev felt itchy under his skin as he watched Camellia Darjeeling teleport away. His gaze had been glued to her firm ass when she walked away. Tinne Holly was right, she moved well, had fighter training, and he hadn't noticed.

He should be considering the other information that had just been flung at him—little Cal's reactions to the salon, Cratag's and Tinne's sharp stares on the boy. Something was going on, and if he could stop thinking about the woman, he could figure it out.

"She interests you, Laev. Another good reason to accept Grace-Mistrys Darjeeling here," Tinne said. He hesitated a beat, then added, "Acacia Bluegum says she needs to spar with men. Have men's hands on her."

Laev jolted and Tinne smiled.

The soft buzz of an alarm sounded.

"Two minutes until melee ends," Tinne said, clapping Laev on the shoulder. He stretched in a fluid movement. "Let's go in and clean up those standing, clear the room." He sounded cheerful at the thought of fighting, as always, and strode into the main room.

Laev loosened his body and hurried after Tinne. Remaining standing at the last would be a challenge for *him*, but he couldn't back down. He already had bruises from their previous session, wondered how badly he'd get pummeled.

*C*amellia scried Tiana as soon as she and Mica had gotten home and eaten. She'd reported briefly about her uncle's attack, said that both she and Mica had responded, and Tiana soothed. Camellia was just glad that Glyssa was in a family meeting and not part of the scry. Camellia didn't want to talk anymore about the men in her Family.

So she mentioned the scene in the Green Knight Fencing and Fighting Salon with Cratag Marigold, his son, Cal, and Tinne Holly.

Tiana's face went sober, but wonder touched her green eyes. "Yes, we've already heard about that—last month."

"The kid's remembering."

"Yes," Tiana said.

"Well, who is he? I mean, who *was* he?"

"You couldn't guess?"

Camellia frowned . . . she thought she'd heard a name, but didn't recall it. She ran a finger over her middle toe. The weather was heating up and soon she could wear sandals. She was tinting her toenails a nice peachy color. "No. I don't move in those circles." She glanced up at her friend on the panel, and, sure enough, saw raised brows, and continued, "You will, Tiana, because you'll be a First-Level Priestess, perhaps *the* priestess . . . the priestess of GreatCircle Temple."

Tiana didn't deny that was her ambition, but said, "And you will be in that circle because your HeartMate is Laev T'Hawthorn."

"No, and no, and no." She changed the subject and went back to her toes. "Who was Cal Marigold in his past life?" She strained her ears to hear Tiana's answer. Neither Tiana nor Camellia ever left a question unanswered—they'd learned that Glyssa would pester them for days if they didn't provide information.

"The current FirstLevel Priest and Priestess believe that Cal Marigold was formerly Tab Holly."

"Yes, that was the name." She scraped her mind for information. "He was the previous owner of the Green Knight Fencing and Fighting Salon?"

"That's right."

"Wow."

Tiana wiggled her butt in her plush chair, settling in for a lecture, Camellia figured, but that was all right, because she was interested in this . . . especially if she was going to see the child when she went to train . . . or in the far, far future when she was part of the Hawthorn Family, along with Cratag and Cal. All those noble bonds slithering here and there, beginning to wrap around her.

"Doctrine is divided as to whether it is better for a child to forget his past lives or remember details. And in this particular situation, with regard to the very close Holly FirstFamily, the Temple's been abuzz with speculation and opinion."

Camellia flexed her toes. The nails looked good. She'd like a hint of gold on them—perhaps a sweep of glitter? "From what I saw today, I think the boy can handle both past and present . . ." She frowned at the thought. "But I think he'll let the past slide for the present."

"Living in the moment and this life fully." Tiana nodded. "From what I understand, that was Tab Holly's philosophy, too."

With a glance up, Camellia caught her friend's gaze. "Startled me a little when he said he was in JudgementGrove that day. The boy's four." She frowned. "And I don't think that Laev knew about all this until today. Don't know what he knows now."

"The old feuding Families, Hawthorns and Hollys, linked together by Lark Hawthorn Holly and her children and now by this child's life. It's a good thing," Tiana said.

Trickling tea sounded. "Incoming call," Camellia said. Tiana's image flashed dark, then a lavender screen with a coat of arms Camellia was coming to know all too well. Her finger jerked and zapped her toes, coating the ends with gold. "Eeek!"

Mica, who'd been watching the process and examining her own claws, snickered.

"Who is it?" asked Tiana.

"Laev," Camellia said, stunned. "Laev T'Hawthorn. It's his sigil."

Tiana smirked. "Answer it. I'm signing off to scry Glyssa. Her Family meeting should be over now. Thanks for reporting your conversation with Cal. It will help us aid all concerned. Love you."

"Love you, too."

Tiana's image vanished and Laev's replaced it, and once again she wasn't looking at all attractive. Her hair was caught up haphazardly in a comb, ends sticking out at odd angles. Mouth open. Hunched over. Old robe.

Gold toes.

Laev's eyes widened, but he didn't comment. "Greetyou, Grace-Mistrys Darjeeling."

No use pretending she wasn't a mess. She gave up her toes as a bad job she'd fix later, stood up from the floor, and moved to a chair. Mica hopped onto her lap, sat straight.

GREETYOU, T'HAWTHORN. WHERE IS BRAZOS? the cat yelled mentally, as if being loud would diminish the kilometers between Camellia's house and T'Hawthorn Residence.

But Laev nodded. "Greetyou, Fam Mica. Brazos"—he glanced aside—"is sleeping on a twoseat."

HE GETS TO SLEEP ON THE FURNITURE!

Camellia winced. "I'll put a fluffy sweater on the small café chair for you." The llamawool one that had a hole in it.

Mica sniffed, turned her head, and ostentatiously groomed her shoulder, ignoring Camellia.

"Oops," Laev said.

Camellia's turn to stare. She'd never have expected a word like that to fall from his lips—lips that were curving in a deprecating smile. "I admit the Residence and the household and I are spoiling Brazos."

"This competition for luxuries between our Fams is getting out of hand. They're manipulating us," Camellia said.

"Tell me about it," Laev said, his smile fading, running a hand through his thick black hair. Camellia tried not to recall touching that silky hair herself.

"One of the reasons I am scrying is because Brazos, and my chef, and my chef's Fam, Black Pierre, all want that recipe for furrabeast steak bites with spices."

Camellia blinked. Black Pierre was almost as legendary a Fam as T'Ash's Zanth. And he was *the chef's* Fam now instead of Laev's? Had that hurt?

"GraceMistrys?" Laev asked.

"Ah. Um. Sorry, busy day. Furrabeast steak bites with spices. It's a marinade."

"So we supposed."

Standing and dumping Mica on the floor, Camellia walked over to her antique drop-front desk and opened it, took out the file of her special recipes. She liked to keep papyrus copies so she could write notes instead of dictating them to a recording sphere. Papyrus notes were less likely to be destroyed by certain members of her family than recording spheres. She pulled out a pink-tinted slip, bent over to put it on a piece of blank papyrus, swept a thumb over the original, and made a copy of the contents.

After putting it all away, she turned to see that Laev had continued to watch her from the panel. Like her friends, she'd positioned the panel to show the whole room. That might have been a mistake.

She held up the larger piece of papyrus. "I'll transfer this to T'Hawthorn Residence's cache." With a whisk of her hands, she did so.

Laev nodded. He appeared more cheerful. "Thank you."

"We use the marinade for a dish we serve in Darjeeling's House-Heart," she said austerely.

"I enjoyed the food there," he said.

I would like My sweater on My chair now, please, Mica said.

Camellia's lips tightened as she stared at her Fam, who radiated an innocence that Camellia no longer believed.

You promised, Mica said.

Laev coughed and covered his mouth.

"One moment." Camellia excused herself.

"Of course," Laev murmured.

She stalked into the bedroom and took out the sweater, returned. Mica sat beside the café chair near the desk. It had a round seat and pillow. At least Camellia had limited Mica's piece of furniture to the smallest in the house. She bent and arranged the sweater so it added decorative interest instead of just looking as if it was there to protect the chair from the cat.

Mica immediately jumped up and began kneading.

When Camellia focused her attention back on Laev, she noted the gleam in his eyes had deepened and his smile was broader. His gaze rose from a lower level to meet hers, and she understood that he'd been watching her butt. The robe was long, but thin. Had it tightened over her backside?

Yes. She flushed and pretended she wasn't. Well, she'd been watching his, so she guessed they were even.

This chair is adequate for now, Mica sent telepathically through their private bond. *You need to wed with your HeartMate now so We can move into T'Hawthorn Residence.*

"T'Hawthorn, you said there was more than one reason you scried? How can I help you?" Camellia said a little stiffly. She could ignore her Fam.

His expression folded into an admirable businessman's face.

"I was hoping you could shed some light on the scene at the Green Knight that I walked into." He hesitated. "I'm very close to Cratag and I don't want to upset him by prodding a touchy subject."

"I think Cratag Marigold can take anything life dishes out," Camellia said.

Laev had been sitting casually, now his body drew tense. "I've hurt him in the past. I won't do so in the future."

"Why do you think I can help you?" The more she thought about FirstFamily stuff, the more she didn't want to be entangled in it.

His brows rose and his nostrils pinched. "Perhaps because you were holding my sleeping nephew in your arms."

So he considered Cratag like a brother. No use for it, the sticky strands of relationships were enveloping her. She'd enjoyed her independence so long that she would still struggle against them. "He's a nice boy," she said.

"Yes, he is."

So she took her seat again, kept her spine straight, and breathed deeply and saw Laev prepare for the news she'd deliver. "And it also seems as if he is the reincarnation of Tab Holly."

Goggle eyes and open mouth didn't look nearly as bad on Laev as it did on her. His breathing picked up. With the rise and fall of his chest, she noted the quality of his white shirt. Very nice. More importantly, his chest was nicely broad.

Laev choked. His hand flicked, and suddenly there was a heavy crystal glass three-quarters full of amber liquid in the curve of his fingers. He tossed back several swallows. Breathed even heavier after the drink. Shook his head. Cleared his throat, stared at her, shook his head again. "Tab Holly?" he croaked.

"That's right." Probably wrong of her, but Camellia was beginning to enjoy herself, liked seeing Laev startled out of his cool manner. Laev the man.

No, she didn't want to think of Laev the man.

Another sip of the alcohol, his lovely purplish gaze locked on hers. She couldn't look away from those eyes. The color was so beautiful. A few Families had lavender or purplish eyes, but the tint of the Hawthorns' . . . exquisite.

"Tab Holly," he repeated, setting the glass aside, leaning his head back onto his chair, eyelids lowering.

"Yes," Camellia said.

"The Hawthorn-Holly feud is long past," Laev said. But the darkness of old pain shaded his expression. "It is good that Tab Holly is . . . now . . . Cal Marigold. Another link between our Families. But I am not prepared for this." More than a shadow of pain glinted in Laev's eyes. Rawness of tortured memory. "I thank you for telling me, GraceMistrys." Another flick of his fingers and the scry panel went blank.

He'd called her GraceMistrys, and she was thinking of him as Laev. Time to pull back a bit more.

Sixteen

He'd been rude in ending the call with Grace Mistrys Darjeeling . . .
Camellia . . . so abruptly, but the past had overwhelmed him.

Cal, the boy he considered his nephew, a reincarnation of Tab
Holly!

Laev pressed fingers to his temples. It wasn't often that he was
confronted with a tenet of his culture made real.

He'd known and respected Tab Holly, the man had been his
teacher at the Green Knight Fencing and Fighting Salon for years.

And Laev loved Cal.

Reincarnation.

There was no escaping the past. He could handle this. He must
handle it. The present and the future were always based on the past.

His mind switched from Cal to women. Camellia Darjeeling's
face had faded and mind's eye images had flashed through his
head—mostly of Nivea. She'd always been beautiful to him, always
had been perfectly groomed.

Even in bed, she hadn't ever seemed to have lost herself in him.
Something he'd denied for a long time, hating to realize it, feeling
diminished as a man.

And Nivea had had an ideal of what a prospective FirstFamily
GreatLady should look like, how she should dress and act, and had
molded herself into that shape. She'd been the title and not the
woman.

Camellia Darjeeling seemed all woman, and he couldn't imagine her setting aside any aspects of her own character to fit into some title. He couldn't quite imagine her with a title at all, though he thought she was in line for it. At the Salvage Ball, she'd been gorgeous in a formal robe, but still approachable, making the robe a part of her statement as to who she was, instead of living up to how an expensive, unique robe would define her.

The next time he'd seen her, in her office, she'd seemed an intelligent, sharp businesswoman, dressed well in a professional tunic and trous. When he'd had her to tea, she'd been pale, dealing with an emotional blow, but in control.

And she'd fit well in his ResidenceDen—as both the Residence itself and his housekeeper had made a point of mentioning to him.

At the salon this evening, she'd been all woman, again. More female than any woman he'd seen for a long while. Tender, caring, soft of face and body while cradling a child.

Tonight she'd looked so adorable and silly and female and emotions had clashed in his chest with the thought of reincarnation and the past.

By the end of their scry conversation, he'd known she was dangerous. Ruffling and riling emotions of the past. It seemed like the past was haunting him more—because he was finally trying to deal with it instead of stuff it away?

It had always been difficult for him to deal with his nearly fatal childhood mistake. He'd almost killed D'Holly with a blade, lost his head when he was in a street fight, didn't even know he was stabbing and slashing at a woman. D'Holly was a HeartMate. If she'd died, her husband, the greatest fighter of Celta at the time, would have died, too.

He'd almost killed two people. He'd seen D'Holly dying in the HealingHall, people surrounding her, draining themselves of energy to save her. That vivid memory was one he'd never forget.

His mistake with D'Holly. His mistake with Nivea.

He didn't dare make a mistake with Camellia Darjeeling. A third mistake with a woman could shatter the self he'd managed to glue together after the first two disasters. Even if no one else saw the cracks in his being, he knew they were there.

But she'd been beautiful, hair showing strands of light and dark, deep pink lips, shining eyes more blue than gray.

And, infinitely charming, the tips of her toes had been gold.

Over the next couple of weeks, Camellia met Laev T'Hawthorn unexpectedly several times. Their schedules at the Green Knight Fencing and Fighting Salon dovetailed. The one evening she'd been invited to the general melee, she'd seen him there and had watched, not taken part. She'd made sure their contact was brief and in passing.

And despite the fact that she'd intended to keep her distance from him, she and Laev shared wild sex dreams.

Her friends took an avid interest. Glyssa, disappointed that she couldn't be admitted to the Green Knight to watch events unfold, began training with Acacia Bluegum. Tiana was closemouthed about Temple stuff but smug that fate was bringing Camellia and Laev together. Camellia figured that fate was getting a push from Tinne Holly and, of course, the cats.

She and her friends still had dinner together several nights and talked. That comforting habit got her through the days. Since she was concentrating on her relationship with Laev, she put her secret regarding *Lugh's Spear* and her heritage out of her mind.

She knew it was only a matter of time until Laev deduced who she was, but he was, manlike, concentrating on the sex and willfully ignoring clues. For her part, she was trying to avoid anything that might force him to confront the truth.

Laev drifted, then a wash of sensuality ruffled over his skin and his sex rose and he *knew* she was there.

He closed his eyes.

Then she was lying atop him, aligned. Her body on his . . . and clothed. He put his hands on her back, feeling the firm muscles that shivered under his touch, and he groaned. Her tongue swept into his mouth and he arched and his aching erection moved against the soft silkeen of her tunic.

But her taste was—almost—more important than his erection. Rich and flavorful with exotic spices he'd never tasted before.

Nothing was like he'd ever experienced before, not with any other woman. Only her, only in dreams.

With a thought, he banished her clothes, and soft breasts flattened against his chest. His hands curved over and squeezed the soft-over-firmness of her ass, trailed down her thighs. Perfect.

Her mouth worked his . . . dueling with his tongue, rough, then the sharp nip, laving, soothing, sweeping across his lips, nibbling.

He feathered his fingers down, between her thighs, into sweet dampness, played. She opened her thighs wider, breathed unsteadily. She arched, her upper body curving away from him.

Lifting her, angling her, he thrust into her, and what was left of his mind spun away. Only the physical was important. The scent of her arousal, the feel of her body around him, over him. The sweat between them as they moved.

His groan was matched by her panting whimpers. His thrusts complemented by the rotation of her hips.

Each twist in the rising spiral of passion was prime. He didn't want this pleasure to end. The slower they went, the more explosive the orgasm, and he wanted that, yearned for that—to give her that—more than anything in his entire life.

And one thought squeezed through his mounting passion. She'd leave him as soon as they shattered together.

He'd be left alone, holding nothing. Knowing that they'd only connected in their minds.

He was beginning to hate that.

She began to move faster.

No!

His hands clamped on her hips, forced her slower.

She mewled, but he paid no attention. Was ruthless in draining each drop of honeyed delight from their loving.

Slowly, slowly, the rub, the twist, the clamping of bodies together, straining, reaching, and *there*!

Orgasm shuddered through him. Pure bliss.

Vaguely he heard her high, piercing cry.

He'd been shattered and remade. He was whole. He was loved.

He opened his eyes, she vanished.

He was alone.

Laev awoke. As usual, they'd kept to the shadows, but he sensed his HeartMate knew who he was. And wasn't claiming him.

It hurt and relieved him at the same time. He'd heard tales of men and women hunting their HeartMates—usually the man, who was older and matured first, went through Passage first. Passages were when one linked with one's HeartMate, experienced those famous sexual dreams.

Much like the ones he'd been having lately.

So, yes, the woman who called him *lover* was his HeartMate. Whom he didn't want to claim, either.

He was putting his linens in his new suite cleansing unit, as he was doing every morning lately, when he was notified that Garrett Primross was at the gate.

"Please send a glider down the drive for him and invite him into the breakfast nook, offer him breakfast."

"Of course we will, T'Hawthorn."

Laev shrugged off the irritation of the Residence's tone and headed down to the nook. It was a chamber he and his FatherSire had begun sharing after the death of his father, more intimate than the formal dining rooms—even the smaller ones. The room was on the ground floor of the Residence, close to the kitchen, in a round tower with tall windows facing the courtyard and a sheltered and weathershielded herb garden that was green all year.

The table was small, seating no more than six, and a work of art in itself. Made of greeniron, the legs twisted upward looking like gnarly hawthorn wood, spreading up to hold a glass table insert. The rim showed hawthorn branches and blossoms.

Primross rose as Laev walked in. A large omelette and toast

were on his plate—one of the good china plates commissioned by Laev's FatherSire. Beside the plate was a tall glass of citrus juice in a rock crystal tumbler. Laev was pleased to see the man was being treated well, and even more pleased to see the investigator.

They clasped arms and Laev said, "Greetyou. Please finish your breakfast. It looks good." Before the words were out of his mouth, a server delivered his favorite omelette and he thanked her.

"Breakfast is great," Primross said, winding melty cheese around his fork.

It is. Brazos burped.

Yes. My FamMan is the best chef in Druida, Black Pierre said. He was lying in the sun on one of the window seats.

Primross smiled. He could obviously hear the Fams well, a good talent for a detective.

Brazos snickered. *You are too old and fat and always stay at home. All Fams know that Ash chef is the best.*

Black Pierre snored loudly.

Laev laughed. He and Primross ate in companionable silence, then Laev gestured for Primross to follow him and they left the Residence to walk across the great lawn down a path toward the ocean. Brazos remained sitting in the sun.

The investigator stopped just before the trail angled down to the beach and strode over to the bluff. "Don't want sand in my boots," he said.

"Ah," Laev said.

"I suppose you have a spell on your boots to keep sand out?" Primross asked.

"That's right."

Primross's mouth flattened, but he said nothing and looked out toward the endlessly rolling ocean. When he turned, his gaze was penetrating. "You aren't as focused on retrieving the lost Hawthorn objects as you were."

Blinking in surprise, Laev realized the man was right. "No."

"Nor your HeartGift, either," Primross shot out in a commanding tone.

"No," Laev answered quickly, then shook his head at the detective's technique. "No, I'm not."

Quietly, Primross asked, "When was the last time you used your Flair to probe for your HeartGift?"

Laev's brows rose. "It's been a while. You want me to try now?"

"That would be good."

Laev grimaced. "I haven't been able to find it for years."

"Try again."

Shrugging, Laev closed his eyes, thought of his HeartGift. For an instant he had the same feeling as all the other times, a dark, cramped place, a hint of scent—Nivea's scent, that had him instinctively pulling back.

Then his senses whirled and he almost *heard* the chatter of people, the warmth of a gathering, bustle. His HeartMate radiated contentment.

He jerked his mind away, opened his eyes, sank into his balance to keep his feet as the morning blue of the sky seemed to wheel around him. And he understood the point Primross had wanted to make. Any focus he might have for his HeartGift was being diverted by a true attachment to his HeartMate—whom he also *should* have wanted to find. His body and Flair yearned for her, wanted him to look for her, find *her*. His emotions didn't.

"So," the impassive detective said, "do you want me to continue to look for the lost Hawthorn objects and your HeartGift?"

With his own gaze steady, Laev met Primross's. "There was nothing new in my search for my HeartGift." He took a couple of sea-cleansed breaths.

"And?" Primross prompted.

"And none of my Family or the Residence is as upset as I was about the missing Hawthorn heirlooms.

"But, yes, I want you—Prime Investigations—to continue to look for my lost property." The quest had become less important since his nightly loving with his HeartMate. She'd begun to soothe Nivea's wounds, and he and his HeartMate seemed to have an unspoken understanding.

"Then the deal is still on." Primross relaxed beside Laev.

"Yes." Laev angled himself more to the ocean. "If you ever want an investor . . ."

Primross's fingers bunched into fists. "No."

"The offer stands," Laev said mildly. "Don't let your pride get in the way if you need help."

"I don't. I won't."

Laev sent him a half smile. "I'm good with gilt, but as you are no doubt thinking, I have much gilt to be good with. I've also had exceptional training."

Primross slid his gaze toward Laev, stretched out his fingers. "You're good at inves*ting* not at inves*tigat*ing."

"Not my specialty."

"And you're still beating yourself up about misjudging a woman when you were seventeen, though I bet you haven't misjudged a person with regard to that business of yours for years."

Laev said, "Is that all you want to say this morning?"

"Not hardly."

"All right, talk and walk, the breeze has become cold." Laev turned back toward the Residence.

After a couple of minutes Primross stopped again, this time staring at the castle, the long lawn and pretty paths up to it. "Makes a statement."

"That it does. I imagine the colonists were so relieved to find Celta and land here that they built the city in a fit of exuberance."

"All the FirstFamilies made good castles," Primross said grudgingly.

"Takes some gilt to run and maintain," Laev said.

"I'd guess a damn fortune."

"You'd guess right. Where do you live?" It was a question a friend would ask. Would Primross answer? Was Laev testing himself and his judgement of the man, whether Laev was right in thinking the detective was a friend?

"I don't have a house of my own," Primross said, but Laev heard the *yet*.

"But you get to choose where you live," Laev said lightly.

"Yes. I do." Primross sounded surprised at the thought. He grunted. "Right now I'm living in MidClass Lodge."

"Pretty place," Laev said. "I like the courtyard and the fountain."

That Laev was familiar with the property also seemed to take Primross off guard. "Yeah," he replied.

Once they reached one of the outlying gardens, Primross again angled off, gesturing to a greeniron bench. Since he didn't sit, Laev didn't, either, just lifted his brows.

"Since our deal is still on, I'll tell you that I took the initiative in buying this." Primross dipped his hand in his pocket. When he withdrew it, his forefinger had a large ring on the tip. "It has no Hawthorn mark, but I was assured it originally belonged to your late wife."

Laev recognized the light yellow of the square-cut topaz set in the rainbow-catching metal called glisten. Channel diamonds glittered on either side of the main stone. His gut clenched in surprise and pain, and the day seemed to dim.

Someday Nivea's actions would not surprise or pain him. His renewed anger split, also directed at himself that he was still affected by the past.

"That was Nivea's," he confirmed. "It was part of a set: necklace, two bracelets, and earrings." He'd commissioned T'Ash to create the jewels from the first good gilt Laev had made through investments, no more than six months after he'd married Nivea. His shock and disappointment at her not being his HeartMate had faded under her charm and sexual ministrations. She'd kept that up until they moved from Laev's small estate outside southern Gael City to T'Hawthorn Residence in Druida.

He supposed she'd considered she'd earned all the jewels and other expensive presents he'd gifted her throughout the years. Laev's FatherSire had not given her any of the Hawthorn ancestral jewelry.

"Nothing was said about a set." Primross studied the ring.

"I don't want it," Laev said. "But I will pay for it and any information regarding anything else that was Nivea's."

"Understood," Primross said. He flicked his fingers and the ring disappeared. "I've translocated it to the breakfast table. I'm sure one of your staff will take care of it."

"Yes."

Primross's gaze was cool. Obviously Laev hadn't hidden his reaction well enough.

The detective inclined his head. "Sorry for the news. I'll keep on looking."

"Fine," Laev answered, knowing he'd have to delve into the past and figure out what happened to Nivea's personal jewels. He'd thought they were in some Residence safe.

"Later." Primross teleported away.

There was a yowl and Brazos trotted up. *I wanted to talk to him.*

"Too bad. About what?"

The cat's tail flicked. *He smells of feral fox,* Brazos grumbled.

A chuckle escaped Laev and he was glad of it, glad Brazos was his. He picked the cat up, petted him, and looked into the yellow green eyes, answered his Fam mentally. *You wanted to rub against him so he smelled of you.*

Brazos didn't answer, but as Laev strode back to the gardens, he purred.

"So, Brazos, have you been up in the attics yet?"

The cat's eyes gleamed. *Everywhere, but I paid little attention to bad-smelling woman's stuff.*

"Um-hmm." Laev kept up his pace until they entered through a side door, then he addressed the house, "Residence, where are Nivea's clothes, jewels, and personal items stored?" He hadn't dealt with them himself.

Seventeen

The Residence answered Laev, "Many of the personal objects your late wife had when she came here and those that she purchased were given to her Family, as you wished."

"But not the jewels."

"Not the jewels, nor expensive gowns such as those you or she purchased from D'Thyme."

"Where are the jewels?"

There were a few seconds' silence from the Residence, then it said, "I sense jewelry cases in the MistrysSuite safe. I do not think that your FatherSire did anything with them."

"Thank you." Laev walked through the Residence to the wing that housed the MasterSuite and MistrysSuite. He hadn't moved into his FatherSire's rooms—the MasterSuite—yet. He liked his own suite that had been remodeled for him during the time he'd been courting Nivea at seventeen. A move on his FatherSire's to keep him happy.

When he and Nivea had returned to Druida, she had wanted the MistrysSuite and he and his FatherSire had agreed. The beginning of his and Nivea's estrangement.

He climbed to the third floor, and pushed through heavy spell-shielded security doors. Brazos leapt from his arms. *We are going into rooms forbidden to Me!*

Laev hadn't known that, but it sounded reasonable. "Yes." He opened the door to the MistrysSuite and stared.

It was completely empty. He blinked. The last time he'd been here, when he'd spent septhours by Nivea's bedside when she was sick and dying, the walls of all the rooms had been shades of sunny yellow, with dark brown and green accents, sunflower colors. The furniture had been curlicued iron, the carpet a medium beige.

Now the walls were a flat and expensive cream—indicating that they were ready for imprinting with complex Flaired murals. The floor was polished wood of red brown.

"Where is the furniture?" he asked.

The Residence answered, "We did not dispose of it, but it is stored in the last corner of the highest attic."

"Ah." Laev thought of the tall and fanciful lines of the wrought iron bedsponge platform and etagere. He looked down at Brazos. "You wouldn't want such furniture to climb on in your room?"

"Eeek-urk!" Brazos said, then made a strangling noise. *They are not good wood perches, they are slippery metal, could get neck caught in bad spots if fell.*

Laev supposed so. "All right."

I have seen a nice arrangement of wooden climbing posts and walkways and hoops and toys in the Fam store Mica told me of.

"Ah-ha. Already burnt through your allowance this month?"

Needed toys and pillows. Brazos lifted his nose. *My Sire has many toys and pillows and does not share.*

"Hmm." Laev knew for a fact that some members of the household had made toys and pillows for Brazos.

The cat coughed, a hair ball hit the floor, then vanished to the last drop of spit. Good housekeeping spells. *I think my catnip is inferior. I would like to go to the Ship and purchase more.*

Laev smiled. Bent down and stroked the cat. "Sure, go."

I would like you to come with me.

"Yes, definitely have burnt through your gilt."

Lots of things to do on Nuada's Sword.

"Very true." And Laev had decided that he wanted more plant life in the HouseHeart. "But right now we're investigating missing jewels."

Pretty, shiny rocks.

"Yes."

Lots of those around Druida.

"We do like our pretty baubles."

I do not need many pretty rocks on My collar.

"I understand that a FamPerson doesn't buy a collar for Fam until after six months have passed."

Buy! I am a Hawthorn cat. My Sire, Black Pierre, has a collar commissioned by your FatherSire from T'Ash himself.

"I think that's Black Pierre's third collar and he was Fam to my FatherSire for many years." Laev pretended to think. "Perhaps if you're an excellent cat, I will consider a collar in two months."

Brazos muttered a growl but said nothing more.

As Laev walked through the MistrysSuite sitting room to the bedroom, he asked, "Residence, why were these rooms refurbished and when?" He frowned. "I don't recall authorizing any major expenditures."

The window frames creaked a little as punctuation to the Residence's answer. "Your FatherSire informed me that upon his death I should remodel these rooms unless you specifically ordered me not to do so."

And Laev hadn't even known of that. "Any other requests that my FatherSire made that you haven't informed me of?"

"No."

But there was something in the Residence's tone that snagged Laev's attention. "Are there other secrets that my FatherSire and you had that you didn't inform me of?"

The floor groaned under his feet.

"Residence, I made a direct request for information. You are not allowed to refuse."

Brazos's ears pricked up. *What would you do if the Residence is bad?*

Over the months Laev had considered this. "As T'Hawthorn I can program certain matters—such as the Residence's personality. It's been a long time since the Residence had a female persona.

Perhaps, for instance, that I am tired of being a youngling and would like a less contrary Residence. I believe my twice G'Auntie Inanis's soft persona and voice are an option as a Residence for me."

"Eee!" Brazos rolled over and laughed and Laev stared at him. Cats were the ultimate anarchists, unless their own comfort was involved.

The air pressure around Laev changed, dropped until it was thin, then hurriedly increased to the perfect combination of humidity and warmth that he preferred—and kept in his rooms. From the exclamations he felt through his Family links, the whole castle had been changed—except for the kitchen, conservatory, and greenhouses.

In a low mental voice, nearly hesitant, the Residence answered Laev. *Your FatherSire consulted with T'Willow, the matchmaker, about your HeartMate.*

"What!"

I believe he—they—both T'Willow and your FatherSire discovered who your HeartMate was.

"Did either of the men tell you?"

A long second of silence. "No."

"Did they tell anyone in the Family?"

"No."

"But you, Residence, and perhaps some members of my Family know who she is?"

"Perhaps a few of us believe we know who she is," the Residence muttered.

Though Laev nearly thrummed with suppressed passions—anger, curiosity, wariness—Brazos was sniffing around the floor moldings of the room.

The Residence said, "Please, T'Hawthorn, Laev, do not ask me more questions. Your FatherSire cared for you greatly and for the Family, and did not believe you were ready to acknowledge your HeartMate."

Since Laev agreed, he shouldn't feel such anger, or taste the bitterness coating his tongue. And he'd known for years that if he'd truly put his mind to discovering his HeartMate, it wouldn't take long to learn who she was. "I don't care for secrets, Residence."

"No, T'Hawthorn."

"Good. You recognize that I am in charge, here?"

"Yes, T'Hawthorn."

A thudding came from the dressing room where the wall safe was, and Laev entered the space—which was larger than both his own dressing room and the MasterSuite's—to find Brazos leaping toward the safe set in a small alcove high in the wall. Laev returned to a previous topic. "So when were these rooms altered?"

He almost thought he heard the Residence sigh. "We did it the week after your FatherSire's death. You were grieving hard and did not notice. We used gilt from the petty cash fund."

Which meant the petty cash fund was a great deal larger than most commoner family fortunes. Laev hadn't scrutinized the housekeeper's fund, but recalled he'd thought it was healthy, enough to run the household for five years. He'd have thought that the staff would have come to him if they needed more gilt. "Does the petty cash need to be replenished?"

"No, T'Hawthorn."

"Very well. Open the safe."

The door swung wide and Laev looked inside. He remembered all the jewelry he'd given Nivea and there weren't nearly enough plush boxes. He pulled them out, found they were empty. There was a fine cloth jewelry storage roll with clear compartments. When he opened it up, he saw a few trinkets, but nothing of value.

"We didn't give any of her jewelry to her Family?" He wanted confirmation from the Residence.

"No, T'Hawthorn."

But Laev knew where they'd gone—probably where some of the Hawthorn items had gone, too. He kept his voice mild but inwardly seethed. "She was generous to her friends." Her lovers. She'd been generous to her lovers. "Send a copy of the inventory to Primross."

"Yes, T'Hawthorn."

Laev translocated the jewelry boxes with T'Ash's logo to T'Ash's

Residence package cache with a note that the contents were missing and the GreatLord could recycle the boxes. Then Laev rolled up the silkeen jewelry holder and sent that to the Sunflowers' house cache—they'd been too improvident to hang on to the Family home.

No use pretending to himself anymore that betrayal hadn't happened and hadn't stung. He'd known Nivea had had lovers, though he could never prove it.

"Residence, was my FatherSire ever contacted for gilt to redeem jewels that Nivea gave away?"

"No."

If T'Ash had seen anyone wearing jewels he'd crafted for Nivea, he would have told Laev's FatherSire or Laev.

Laev would have to tell Primross that someone was holding on to them. The same person who might have Laev's HeartGift.

He'd brought such a mean and petty woman into the Family. A woman who hadn't known the meaning of honor, who hadn't kept her marriage vows.

He needed a shower. Or sparring. Or good sweaty sparring, then a shower. "I'm going to the Green Knight. I'll be back whenever." He had no more work that had to be done that day. No heart to do it. He'd been working hard and even he needed a day off now and again.

I am going, too, Brazos said, trotting over to Laev. The cat had explored every corner, not that there was much to see. Laev paused, closed his eyes, expanded his senses to test every aspect of the room with his Flair.

No lingering resonance of Nivea at all. Everything was clean and fresh. These rooms had been cleansed, physically, by Flair, and spiritually after Nivea's death. The Residence itself had gone through many cleansings since then.

He strode back to the sitting room door, out into the corridor. "Laev?" the Residence whispered.

"Yes?"

"Would you care to inspect your FatherSire's rooms? You should have the MasterSuite."

His hands fisted. "The MasterSuite does not have a sparring salon."

"We need to remodel those rooms, too, then," the Residence said.

"This whole side is interconnecting rooms between the MasterSuite and the MistrysSuite. I want an additional room for the MasterSuite, but I do not wish to take one away from the MistrysSuite."

"We have a conundrum, then."

"Yes."

There was a very quiet noise that Laev couldn't quite place but recognized that the Residence made.

"Perhaps we could hire the architect, Antenn Moss-Blackthorn, to view the chambers and advise us."

Another of Laev's old friends. One he hadn't seen in a while, but who had never judged Laev, a reason he should have kept in touch with him, but . . . "Wasn't he off to the *Lugh's Spear* expedition?"

"He is returning. He stated that he is not interested in that Ship until it is ready to be excavated."

"Ah. Yes, bring him in." Laev looked at the sturdy door to the MasterSuite. Of course the rooms were the most shielded of those outside of the HouseHeart. "Open the door to the MasterSuite."

The Residence did and the scent of his FatherSire wafted from the dark rooms, making Laev's throat tighten. How he missed the man. Little light filtered through the heavy curtains on the western windows. Even as he squinted to make out the familiar room, the Residence flashed spellglobes into existence.

Laev's jaw flexed.

Brazos bolted through the doors to explore more forbidden territory, and Laev relaxed. Another being he loved. Not one who would ever replace his FatherSire, but the cat was his in a way no one and nothing had been. It was enough to remember that.

"Contact Antenn when possible for a consultation to reorder the suites." Thankfully, the work wouldn't be fast or easy. Laev was reconciling to the notion of relocating into the MasterSuite, but it would be a while until he was ready. "Move out all the furniture and the carpets. Have the walls tinted the same color as the MistrysSuite."

"There are masterpieces that have been in that suite for generations—holo paintings, other paintings, old-time books, rugs . . ." Even as the Residence recited, images of his FatherSire's favorites flashed through Laev's memory. All too painful. He wanted nothing in there. "We have no-time vaults where such masterpieces can be stored, don't we? If I want anything from the suite, I can always have it returned."

"The storage areas are full."

Laev couldn't tell whether the Residence was fibbing or not. "Then designate another room and have vaults put in—by D'Thyme."

A hesitation. This time Laev knew the Residence was scrying the home of D'Thyme. "She is booked for three months. Unless you want to pay a premium . . ."

"I don't mind staying in my own rooms."

Alma Hawthorn, the housekeeper, came up the stairs, a fixed smile on her face. Obviously the Residence had contacted her for reinforcements. He glanced at her. "I haven't reviewed household expenses to see if anything should be cut." He knew she purchased some favorite herbal tea from *Nuada's Sword* for herself from the funds and didn't share. Her eyes widened.

"Is Brazos in the MasterSuite?"

"He won't hurt anything." Laev hoped.

"Ah, Laev, T'Hawthorn," Alma said. He thought her tone was supposed to be light and firm, but it wobbled a bit and was higher than usual. She reached for his arm, then withdrew her hand. "I know you like the styles of a century and a half ago. Your Father-Sire didn't. You might want to peruse the objects in those no-time vaults and see if there's anything you'd prefer for the MasterSuite. Then furniture can be switched out."

Laev stared at her. "We'll be remodeling the entire Master- and MistrysSuites, perhaps changing the dimensions of the rooms to include a new sparring room." The more he thought of it, the more he liked the idea. A visual of Camellia Darjeeling fighting passed through his mind. "Put the sparring room between the suites. No one ever said a D'Hawthorn might not like to fight, or need to."

"Ah, Laev, the beds in the MasterSuite and MistrysSuite were made for them. Their veneers can, of course, be exchanged, we bought a full range when the beds were made . . ."

"I want reddwood. Make sure Antenn knows that moving them from the bedrooms will be problematic, but we might be able to angle them differently. I'll want to see Antenn as soon as he comes, clear my calendar for that, and I am available for him any time he is here. He's my friend, not just a consultant. Now I'm off to the Green Knight." He recalled something and smiled. "It's time for the Master Melee. A lot of my old friends will be there, maybe even Antenn. If he is, I'll let him know we want him as a consultant. I trust my wishes are understood?"

"Yes, T'Hawthorn."

Brazos trotted from the MasterSuite door, dropped a dead and bloody mouse at Laev's feet, sat, and preened. Laev bent down and rubbed the cat's head. "Excellent." He glanced at Alma. "Take care of the mouse, and you and Residence check the MasterSuite for any more." He turned and walked back to his rooms, donned his fighting clothes, and teleported away.

*F*eeling *warm and satisfied after a Master Melee session in the* Green Knight Fencing and Fighting Salon, Laev said "merry parts" to friends and began walking toward the teleportation pad in the atrium of the building. Antenn Moss-Blackthorn had not been at the fight, might not have arrived in the city yet.

Laev rolled his shoulders and congratulated himself that he felt fitter and wouldn't ache as much as he had before. His body had finally become accustomed to sparring and exercise again.

"T'Hawthorn?" A big man puffed out Laev's name as he hung a coat and scarf up on one of the pegs. He'd arrived by glider instead of teleporting.

"Yes?" Laev struggled to place him, then realized the GraceLord had lost weight and toned since Laev had seen him last. The man had about fifteen minutes before review drills started. This was Camellia Darjeeling's sparring partner. "T'Lemongrass?"

"Right. Honored you recalled my name. A moment of your time, please." His tone had a compressed intensity that caught Laev.

"Of course."

"Think I have something of yours—Hawthorn's," Lemongrass said.

Laev's blood chilled and chugged sluggishly through his veins. He forced himself to remain casual, though he wanted to roll his shoulders again to loosen muscles that had tightened into bands. "Yes?"

"Yah. Glad you're here. I was going to have Tinne lock them up until tonight. You usually attend melee and I can't tonight—our Family was one of the lucky ones invited to participate in the annual Great Labyrinth Weekend Celebration and Fair."

"Sounds fun." Laev hadn't attended that new fair. The celebration had started after he and Nivea had moved to Gael City, and bloomed in the years when they were gone. Nivea had never gone, either.

"Yes, the Family is very pleased our name was drawn, but it's a responsibility to show the best of who we are. Need to spruce up our Family shrine. The descent into the bowl of the crater and chant is tonight," Lemongrass enthused. He slanted a look at Laev. "You should come. You know all of the FirstFamilies are automatically invited."

Had Primross said that, it would have been a sneer at privilege. Lemongrass stated it as a fact of life he had no intention of arguing about.

Laev smiled. "Maybe I will."

A chime sounded and Lemongrass winced. "Running a little behind and I came early and all to have them stored proper." His face set into a weighty expression and a sigh rumbled deep from his belly. "Suppose it must be meant that I meet you here and now." He opened and closed his fingers. "M'Flair's telemetry—sensing an object's past—and I could tell that the things were stolen, but they are so damn beautiful." He rubbed his face. "But they gotta go back to you."

Lemongrass had said *they*. Disappointment twisted Laev's gut that it wasn't his HeartGift, and he flipped through his memory for a missing *they*. Only the desk set . . .

But Lemongrass was pulling a box half a meter square from a bag he'd kept under his coat. The dark wood gleamed richly. Fancy brass showed at all the corners and a brass catch was in the front to keep it closed. With a jerk of his head, Lemongrass gestured Laev to walk out of the path of the door and the teleportation pad to the far corner.

Breath caught in his throat, blood humming in his temples, Laev waited as Lemongrass balanced the box on his brawny arm, flipped the catch, and lifted the lid.

Nestled in purple quilted velvet were a pair of blazer pistols, black and sleek and deadly. Laev had never seen the things before in his life. Never even known the Family had had such treasures, but tiny T'Hawthorn leaves were engraved in the hilts. Definitely a Family thing. He reached out and touched one, felt an old Family connection. "These are more than a couple of centuries old."

Lemongrass nodded. "Beautiful antiques. They took their dueling seriously back then. Pistols still work well, too." He cleared his throat. "I tried them a couple of times."

"Anyone would," Laev said. How and where and when had Nivea found them? She must have been thrilled to take such a treasure from the Residence. Of course Laev had not been told. Fury spurted through him again that the Residence and his FatherSire had "shielded" him about Nivea's thefts until he'd discovered her depredations for himself. And here, this morning, he'd thought he was distancing himself from the wound. Fligger.

"Thought the blazers might be tricky for me to teleport with . . . antique and all, so came by glider." Lemongrass shut the box and handed it to Laev, who tucked it under his arm and hoped the bloused sleeve of his shirt disguised it. "Thank you. Where did you find them?"

"Bought them from a guy last year in Gael City. Knew at once they weren't his, of course. The blazers had had two, maybe three sets of past thieving vibrations." The teleportation pad bonged with a signal of an arrival and Lemongrass glanced at it, shifted his feet, waited until the new guy had left the atrium empty again. "And a very odd circumstance."

"What?"

"Guy I bought them from was T'Darjeeling, the GraceLord."

Eighteen

❦

*Grace*Lord *Darjeeling looks a little like me, in build anyway."* Lemongrass grimaced. "You know, that was the reason why I was assigned to practice with his daughter, Camellia. You were there." He coughed. "Odd, odd thing. The man is . . . not a good 'un . . . but his daughter, she's fine. Hardworking." His jaw jutted. "Don't like sparring with her, but figure since I was asked, and I want to exercise more, I should." His protuberant blue eyes cooled, his softish mouth hardened. "Must be a reason she needs to practice with a man like me. Can't bow out now."

"And *you're* a good one, too," Laev said.

"Thank you."

"Let me reimburse you for your purchase." Laev would have liked to add something more for the man's trouble and honesty, but deduced he would insult the GraceLord.

"No need." His gaze went past Laev's shoulder. "Thieving leaves smudges on the objects, and these were stolen and passed on through at least three people."

Which meant the lord had felt Nivea's residue. Raising a hand, Laev said, "Please. You know I can afford it." He'd just paid in humiliation once again, the gilt didn't count.

The man named a figure and Laev immediately had his Residence transfer the funds to Lemongrass's account.

GraceLord Lemongrass flushed and bowed, looked once more at

the teleportation pad. "Camellia's late, so she'll be irritated at herself. I'd better get ready." Now he loosened his limbs. "I've gotta chance at taking her if she's mad in practice session before we're judged on our progress."

Laev bowed. "Thank you again."

Lemongrass returned Laev's bow. "My pleasure." Then he trotted through the doors to the practice rooms.

Another bong announced an incoming person. Sweet frissons of anticipation flickered through Laev. Perhaps he'd stay long enough to meet Camellia . . . maybe ask to observe the bout.

It was she who arrived, and attraction surged through him at the sight of her flushed face, her hair haphazardly put up under random clips, and her new fighting garb a little askew.

Her eyes widened when she saw him, and he thought her breasts rose and fell a little faster. Her smile was as pleasant—and as wary—as always when they'd met the last few days. "Greetyou, Laev."

At least she'd begun calling him Laev and her curtsey was a mere bob of knees.

"Greetyou, Camellia."

Her eyes went to the box under his arm, but she didn't ask about it, just hopped from the teleportation pad and flipped the switch to show it was free. Then she pushed a straggle of hair from her face. "Gotta run. Late."

Laev nodded. "Lemongrass is already here."

Her smile turned into a baring of teeth. "Grrr." She rushed by him into the practice rooms, words spit out at him. "Schedule changed. Small time for practice, then quick progress review, then a damn—a melee bout for the best." Her face turned into a pout just before she disappeared through the doors to the private salons.

He was still watching her when the teleportation pad indicated that someone else had arrived. The person who appeared was Holm HollyHeir, Tinne Holly's elder brother.

Laev lifted his brows. "Since when do you arrive here in the atrium instead of the private areas?"

"Since the private teleportation pads are busy," Holm grumbled. He stared at the box under Laev's arm. "What do you have there?"

No use pretending it wasn't weapons. Holm had already recognized the shape of the box.

Laev opened it and showed Holm the slim black blazers.

Holm Holly's eyes widened, and he gave a long whistle. "Fine, fine implements. May I?"

"Sure."

Holm picked up one of the pistols, weighed it in his hand, sighted it at the opposite wall. "Very nice." He put it back in its nest, then flexed his fingers. "Energy isn't right for me, though. Bet it's been tuned only to your Family. You might want to check with the weapons maker T'Ash about this. I'm sure he'd be interested."

"I'm sure he would," Laev said.

"He'll be here shortly, maybe already is here."

Before Laev could respond, Holm continued, "So you heard that we're opening a better shooting gallery?"

Was that the occurrence that had prompted Lemongrass to bring the pistols to Laev? "No," he replied.

Holm studied him with a narrowed gaze. "You've trained with us for years. You know, you're not good in knife work." He paused and they both paled as they recalled that Laev had wounded Holm's mother with a knife as a boy. No, Laev never would be good at knife work.

Then Holm continued on. "And your unweaponed sparring is good." Which meant Laev was still in the master class. "But if I recall, your shooting was exceptional."

A surge of pride washed through Laev. "Yes?"

"Yes. You should buy a membership to the shooting gallery, come and practice your skills. You might even match me." Holm waved greetings at three more people who arrived together by teleportation pad. He smiled, teeth gleaming. "Now I'm going to beat my brother. Got to win my title of best fighter on Celta back."

From what Laev knew, that particular title fluctuated from brother to brother on a nearly weekly basis.

"I thought this time is for drill review."

Holm waved. "Tinne is cutting that short so we can attend the Great Labyrinth Fair as a Family outing." Holm grinned. "Parents and us and the kinder, too. Only those who want to stay will keep the Residence and the business going." He winked. "In truth, I think our cuz Nitida will be glad to have this place for her own a bit."

Again Holm studied Laev. "You're looking better."

"I'm feeling better," Laev said.

Holm nodded at the main sparring room, grinned. "I'm inviting you to the Best of the Best spree."

"Already been beat up once today."

Laughing, Holm clapped Laev on the back. "T'Ash is coming, too."

"Just what I've always wanted, to be smacked around by T'Ash. Will Cratag be here?"

"Yes, but not his son, Cal. We've all agreed that Cal needs to settle stronger into his new body."

The way Holm phrased it had chill grue sleeting through Laev.

Holm said, "And into his new life." Then Holm's expression was serious. "You can help with that."

"I consider Cal my nephew. He'll be spending plenty of time at T'Hawthorn Residence with me and mine."

"Good." Holm sighed, repeated, "Good." He tipped his head. "See you shortly." And walked through the swinging doors with the near swagger that said he knew he could fight any man in the world and win.

Laev's perscry hummed the low, nearly threatening bars he'd assigned to Primross. Laev went to a privacy booth, dug it from his trous pocket, and put it on an eye-high stand. "Here."

"Got some new information for you," Primross said.

"And I have some for you."

The man's dark brows rose and he grunted, waited a couple of seconds for Laev to speak, then began himself. "I traced the ring to a man, a GraceLord, of all people." There was a hint of satisfaction in Primross's tones, as if he was glad to catch the nobility in misdoings.

"GraceLord Darjeeling?"

Primross scowled. "You know?"

"Just heard about him and know he was selling Hawthorn items last year in—"

"—Gael City."

Laev shook his head ruefully. "Interesting how we got the same information at nearly the same time."

Shrugging, Primross said, "Happens that way sometimes. Things come together in a case. From what I understand, this Darjeeling has a lot of long-term connections in the underground markets."

"I'm certain my Family never dealt with him," Laev said.

"But you know his daughter. The Darjeeling of Darjeeling's Teahouse and Darjeeling's HouseHeart. You're both members of the Green Knight Fencing and Fighting Salon. She is a new member."

"That's right. I've met her several times." Laev was surprised to feel more than irritation at Primross's implications—the edge of anger along with strong protectiveness.

"You can play this two ways," Primross continued. "You can talk to her about her relatives and find out—"

"No."

"Or you could back off a little."

Laev hesitated, frowned as he looked inward, considered his gut feelings. He didn't want to back off, just the opposite. But it appeared as if Camellia might be involved in the thefts.

No. Just thinking that was wrong, he knew it. She hadn't liked Nivea. Had given him information about the Salvage Ball. Both Tinne and Lemongrass hinted that Camellia's father had abused her. "I won't be backing off."

"You might wish to consider that the very existence of that Salvage Ball is due to Camellia Darjeeling."

"What!"

Primross nodded. "During a lawsuit regarding the salvage of a ship—"

"I know all about that. I was at JudgementGrove observing that trial at the time. I saw Camellia prove that her Family lost a tea set when that ship went down and it wasn't insured. The judge awarded the set to Camellia if it could be found."

"Ah." Primross looked down at piece of papyrus on his desk; notes, Laev deduced. "Well, Camellia Darjeeling asked D'Kelp, who was the person salvaging the sunken ship, to look for this expensive tea set and Kelp found it. To present the salvage to the girl, D'Kelp staged a surprise party."

"I see," Laev said.

"That was the beginnings of the Salvage Ball, and the next year it took the format it has today." Primross frowned again, tapped his writestick on the papyrus. "Odd that SupremeJudge Elder awarded the set to the girl and not her father."

"Camellia offered the case and the documentation."

"Still odd."

"And you might want to consider that my source stated Grace-Lord Darjeeling wasn't a good man."

Primross shrugged. "Obvious."

"And that Tinne Holly has assigned a man who has much the same build to be Camellia Darjeeling's sparring partner. For her own good, I believe."

Fire lit in Primross's eyes. "Is that so?"

"Yes."

"The man abused her," Primross stated.

"So it seems. Not to mention that GraceLord Darjeeling insulted the Sheela Na Gig."

Primross leaned back, as if wanting to distance himself from such words, events, repercussions. "You don't say." His face hardened. "I didn't hear of any such thing. Why didn't I?"

"I would imagine that the GreatCircle Temple is keeping all mentions of the incident confidential."

Mouth turning down, Primross said, "It's damned—ah—really difficult to get information about the GreatCircle Temple and the priests and priestesses." Another couple of taps of his writestick. "All right. I accept your reading of Camellia's character, but I'll continue to research her father." He glanced up at Laev. "I suppose this means that you don't want me interviewing her at the moment."

"No. Not right now."

"Your gilt's paying for the investigation. I've got a lead or two to tug, might head down to Gael City."

"Good idea." The buzzer announcing ten minutes before the melee sounded. Laev winced. "I must go now. Keep me informed."

"Will do. Later." The scry pebble went dark.

Laev hurried to change.

Y ou're doing very well," Tinne Holly said to Camellia and Cymb Lemongrass. "Both progressing fine, better than expected, in fact. I anticipate in two eightdays you will be ready to test for the next level."

"Fab . . . fab . . . u . . . lous," Cymb Lemongrass panted from where he was collapsed on the floor beside her.

Camellia didn't bother trying to speak, but rubbed at her sweaty scalp.

"And since you've both been very understanding about cutting practice time and drill review short today, I'd like to invite you to take part in the Best of the Best melee." Tinne walked to the door of the practice room and stopped with his hand on the latch. "Neither of you would embarrass me now."

"Thanks," Camellia managed.

"Thanks," Lemongrass huffed. "But my Family's involved in the Great Labyrinth Fair this year. Gotta go." He heaved himself to his feet, offered a hand to Camellia, and she accepted it to roll to stand.

"Good, the Hollys will see you there," Tinne said. "We'll make sure to drop by your shrine and booth."

Lemongrass grinned and bowed. "My thanks. We're three-quarters up the bowl in the southwest."

"We'll look for you. What of you, Camellia, want to try the bout?"

She didn't but didn't think it was an offer she could really refuse. "Of course."

Tinne laughed as he left.

"Good job, partner." Cymb put an arm around her and hugged. Like always, he smelled of citrus. Camellia could only wish she smelled so good.

"We did it." She hugged him back.

"That we did, and I wouldn'ta made it without you, so thanks." He smiled and a crease showed in his face. "And I've got more stamina, so my wife says to thank you, too."

"Uh. Ah. 'Welcome," Camellia muttered. Usually he was teleporting home by now, instead he was walking to the door with her. "Not 'porting?"

"Not tonight. Not strong enough in Flair to 'port all the way to the Great Labyrinth, but m'Family and I can do it in three hops, don't want to use anymore Flair than I have to. Came by glider."

"Oh. Thanks again." Impulsively, she kissed his cheek.

"'Welcome, partner." He hurried off to the atrium, and after a big breath, Camellia straightened her shoulders and entered the main sparring room. She noted that the Best of the Best really was that. All the Hollys, even GreatLord T'Holly, were there. So was her teacher, Acacia Bluegum. Camellia walked to stand next to her.

Acacia scrutinized her. "You're looking good."

"Thank you. How's the building refurbishing coming along?"

Rolling her eyes, Acacia said, "Slowly, but I'll be able to get rid of a lot of frustration here."

The thirty-second bell rang and the gym fell silent. With a quick glance, Camellia saw that Laev Hawthorn was fighting . . . and there was a group of cats in a corner. Not many people of her own rank were there, and hers was the lowest rank.

A buzzer honked and all stepped past the lines and bowed. Then the fight was on. The melee scrum was rough and scary, exhilarating. All levels took part, though those who were higher—like Laev T'Hawthorn and the Hollys—tended to wipe the floor with anyone lower who strayed into their area. Camellia was watching Laev from the corner of her eyes until she was taken down by another woman and she had to concentrate on getting her own back.

Like most of her rank, she was ruled "dead" long before those at the higher levels were finished fighting. Instead of going to the waterfall rooms like a few others did, she sat on the sidelines and watched with most everyone else. She saw the great T'Holly himself was there, and a few more men well known as fighters, such as T'Ash and Cratag T'Marigold. More, in the far corner away from the humans, cats were tumbling and playing. Mica was wiped from the challenge even before Camellia, and when she sat on the rolled mat, Mica crawled into her lap with a whimpering, *Hurt.*

Danith D'Ash came up to them, said, "Let me look at you." She ran her hands over Mica and pronounced, "You're good enough. You need to eat better, though." Danith shot a look toward Camellia, who raised her hands.

"I can control what she eats at home. She begs at the teahouses, and my staff are soft touches. She goes to other places outside my control."

The animal Healer sighed and plopped down beside them, and said, "I understand that. I have a prime moocher in my household, T'Ash's FamCat, Zanth." She glanced over to the men still fighting and Camellia looked, too. Only men were on the floor, even Acacia Bluegum had been defeated.

"Oh, they've aligned according to generations." There weren't many men T'Holly's age, and just before he went down, his sons broke from their own generations—Holm with T'Ash's group and Tinne Holly with the younger Laev—and the Hollys took on all the rest.

Laev wasn't the first to fall and Camellia took secret pride in that, and, again, he'd lasted longer than his Fam. Brazos was at the line designating the fighting area as Laev rose, rubbing his shoulder. *Zanth cheated!* Brazos projected.

Camellia figured the black cat was lying. She was pretty sure that cats had few rules and none when fighting. Laev picked up Brazos and petted him. *You did very well.* And Camellia figured that was a lie, too. Laev wouldn't have had time to watch his cat. But it was a good idea. Still petting Mica, Camellia said, "You did well, too."

Thrashing her tail, Mica said, *Yes, but I do not like to fight, I like to eat better. I will not play again.*

A groan and a swear ripened the air and announced the downfall of two more fighters. One was the uncanny Vinni T'Vine, the other a member of the new noble Family, the Clovers. The only non-Hollys now were Cratag T'Marigold and T'Ash, and a few minutes later they went down under the onslaught of the three men.

The Hollys broke into identical grins, slapping each other, then bowed to each other.

Laev dropped down on the other side of Camellia.

She tensed only a little.

Here he comes, Brazos said. *The CHEAT.*

"Oh, dear," Danith D'Ash said.

A large cat splotched with black and white swaggered around the floor, a ribbon in his mouth. The infamous Zanth, T'Ash's Fam-Cat. He came up to Danith and dropped the ribbon on her feet, revved a purr that reverberated off the walls.

ME WIN! ME ALWAYS WIN! the cat shouted mentally, loudly enough that everyone in the room heard him. T'Ash joined his HeartMate. "Good job, Zanth."

"Yessss," Zanth vocalized, then moved to touch his nose to Mica's. *YOU ARE PRETTY.*

Mica purred. Brazos growled. Zanth looked at Brazos and said, *YOUR SIRE FAT, BLACK PIERRE.* He sniffed.

Danith hopped to her feet, hauled the large cat up in her arms. "Not another sinus infection, Zanth. Sorry, we need to leave. Playtime's over."

T'Ash laughed, put his arms around his woman and Fam, and they vanished.

Many smiled at that and headed toward the waterfalls.

Laev's arm wrapped around Camellia's shoulders and he squeezed. Glancing down at Brazos, he said, "There is usually someone better than you. Get used to it."

I am a wonderful YOUNG Cat, Brazos said.

"Yes," Camellia soothed.

Mica leapt from Camellia's lap, rubbed against Brazos. *I like you better. You have nice long fur.*

I do, Brazos preened. He stared at Laev. *You smell sweaty.*

Laev laughed. "I do, so does Camellia." His eyelids lowered. "Essence of woman."

"Which means I need to take a waterfall." She stood, shook her limbs out before they stiffened too much.

He stepped close to her. Then he captured her hand and brought it to his lips, bowed and kissed it, meeting her eyes, his own gaze fathomless. "Come with me."

"What?"

"I want to get to know you better. I'll buy you a drink—tea, caff, whiskey. We can talk."

Her mouth was hanging open, she knew. Surely one of the knocks on her head hadn't cause hallucinations, had they?

He flung out an arm as if encompassing the whole world. "I've the urge to see the Great Labyrinth Fair. I've never been and would like to experience it with you. Come with me."

So he was following urges—due to testosterone from fighting?—dangerous urges that might sweep them both up if she wasn't careful.

Nineteen

❤

Camellia's heart thumped fast and hard, near pain. He was getting far too close emotionally. He threatened her peace. This could be the start of him thinking about an affair with her, and the more she withdrew, the more he'd pursue.

As far as she could tell, he wasn't interested in anything long term. Flirting, bed games . . . and he didn't know they already had mental sex. . . . and he didn't know they were HeartMates, did he?

HeartMates, bonded mates so close that if one died the other followed within a year. That should scare him as much as it did her.

But she wasn't allowed to tell him that they were HeartMates. That was usually because a HeartMate wanted to claim the other, and to tell someone they were your HeartMate took away free will.

So even though she might use the fact to discourage Laev, if she told him, she'd still be breaking the law, and that didn't sit well with her.

Maybe there was another way.

She looked around, the space was still busy with people going to and from the waterfalls and the teleportation pad. The Hollys had gone into their private office. No one appeared as if they were watching Laev and her, not even their Fams, who were interacting with the remaining cats.

She wetted her lips and his stare dropped to them. With the hand he still held, she drew him to the wall, lowered her voice, though she didn't look at him. "You know those hot and sweaty dreams you've been having?"

He stiffened abruptly beside her, not looking at her.

"I've been having them, too."

Slowly his head turned. His eyes had widened, his beautiful lavender irises nearly lost by the dilation of his pupils.

He understood what she was saying. He dropped her hand, nodded to her, and walked away.

It hurt, a lot. More than she'd anticipated.

Stup! That was what she'd wanted, right? Despite all the progress she'd made in the last few weeks, she didn't want a real lover, true intimacy.

She'd given in to her fears.

But so had he.

Laev kept walking. The knowledge was too sudden and huge. The pain it could bring, also huge. He strode across the gym, into the men's rooms, and to the cubby that held his clothes and the pistols. He'd said the strongest protection charm on the small space, along with placing an alarm on it that would have been heard throughout the building. The weapons were safe. He flipped open the box to see them and double-checked, closed it. And stood, wondering what to do.

If he went home to the Residence in this stunned state, his Family and the house itself would fuss. But there was nowhere else he wanted to be. Despite his earlier set-down of Alma and the Residence, they would still be nosey.

As he would have been if any other of the Family looked as if they received a blow that made them look . . . he went to see himself in a mirror and found he appeared a little wild-eyed but collected.

Still, the Family would sense his upset, even if he stayed in his rooms.

He could go to the Great Labyrinth, walk the path. Since he'd never been, there might be a lot of welcoming and socializing expected. No. He also recalled that some of his cuzes would be manning the Hawthorn shrine and booth.

Where else? He belonged to a couple of social clubs but needed to be alone. In a cave perhaps. The image of Darjeeling's House-Heart flashed before his mind's eye and he knew that would be good—but impossible.

Which left his own Residence HouseHeart, a place he hadn't been in a while. *Brazos, teleporting in one minute.* There was a hiss in his mind from his cat, then he shot through the doors.

Too much hurry.

Laev shrugged, tucked the pistol box under his arm.

You did not waterfall and change.

No, come along. He'd only be in his bedroom long enough to dump his clothes in the cleanser and strip. Brazos hopped onto his shoulder.

On three. One, Laev T'Hawthorn, two, Brazos cat, three! They arrived in his bedroom, Brazos leapt from his shoulder, and Laev disposed of his clothes, picked up the pistol box again.

He padded to the corner and a hidden panel, Brazos twining around his calves, purring. Laev opened a piece of molding and pressed the fingertip indentations in the proper sequence. The panel slid aside and he stepped into an omnivator that would hold five. Brazos slipped in. His loud purr echoed in the space. The door slid shut and Laev opened a shallow hidden drawer, took out the petrified thorn, and pricked his finger, let three drops of blood drip to the floor.

Brazos stared at the red droplets that faded to brown and disappeared. The omnivator slanted down and southeast. When it stopped, Laev splayed his hand, blood welling again from his finger, against the door. It opened, they stepped into a space equal to that of the omnivator. When the doors closed behind them, Brazos gave a squeak. *Where are we going?*

HouseHeart, Laev replied.

Like Darjeeling's HouseHeart?

Laev snorted. *Not quite. This is a REAL HouseHeart, the core intelligence of the Residence.*

Brazos yawned, set his front paws on the ground, and did a whole-body stretch, tail up.

Once again Laev set his hand on a door—this one dark planks set between two small golden pillars that appeared like spiral-carved maypoles. He repeated a short, guttural sentence. The spell-words were a mixture of antique Celtan and ancient Earthan. With a long, low creak the door swung back.

Laev braced himself. He hadn't been here as often as he should have. Would the HouseHeart scold? He was never quite sure how much of the HouseHeart was in the main Residence awareness—probably all. But the place had a different voice.

"Greetings, Huathe Laev Oak Grove Hawthorn, GreatLord T'Hawthorn."

No sarcasm, good. Laev's shoulders eased.

Brazos bounded in. *Greetyou!* He skidded to a halt just before he fell into the bubbling turquoise hot pool, squealed as he tumbled backward.

"Greetings, Fam Brazos." The tones were rough, again the words oddly shaped. The resonant gruff voice old, old, not changed in centuries.

"Greetyou, HouseHeart." Laev bowed and stepped into the place, put the pistol box on a small table by the door. It fit well there. The door creaked shut behind him and the light that emanated from the pale marble walls brightened.

Not at all like Darjeeling's HouseHeart. Long ago the Hawthorns had smoothed the underground walls, facing them in sheets of light green marble. Once again, between the stone slabs were small moldings of gilded wood, carved in a spiral pattern. Above them was a faceted and domed ceiling of rock crystal, giving the impression of filtering light from a sunny day.

The room was more like a temple than a place deep beneath the soil of Celta, though the chamber was rectangular, not circular like Celtan temples.

Under his soles, the dark brown flagstones were gently warm. Laev sighed as he crossed to the pool and slipped into its steaming depths. Again, it was large enough to hold five and the mosaic on the bottom of the tub showed a pentacle of green set in white stone.

Brazos paced cautiously around the room, sniffing at the clumped Hawthorn bushes planted in one corner, scratched at the dirt . . .

"Don't you piss on those!" Laev cautioned. Good, his brain was still working even though it felt woolly.

His Fam lifted his head, moved on, just as if he hadn't considered that.

"It is good to have you here again, Laev," the HouseHeart said.

Again, no judgmental tone.

"I should have come sooner, and more often," Laev said.

"Why didn't you?" asked the HouseHeart.

"I'm sure you know." Laev sat on an underwater bench, let the herbal liquid swirl around him, leaned his head back against a soft neckroll. "I missed coming here with my FatherSire, and . . ."

"And?"

Easier to talk about old hurts than the new one he was still processing. "I felt bad about the mistake I made in wedding a woman who was not my HeartMate. Who wasn't worthy of being a Hawthorn." Here he could lay out a hard line of words like nowhere else in the world.

There was a deep gurgle of the pool as the HouseHeart answered. "You are, of course, the only T'Hawthorn or D'Hawthorn who has ever made a bad mistake."

Laev winced.

"Did not your FatherSire compete with the Hollys and hold a grudge so long that it became an obsession and a feud?"

Yes! Brazos hissed.

"Did not that feud cost several Hawthorn lives? Your own father's life?"

The water in the pool had heated and roiled enough that it threatened to drown him. Laev slipped out to move over to a towel-covered bedsponge.

"Well?" the HouseHeart prompted.

"Yes. But my wife stole from us."

"So did your FatherSire. He stole lives from the Family."

Laev swallowed.

"Nivea Hawthorn stole nothing from me," said the House-Heart.

"She wasn't often here." Hadn't liked visiting the HouseHeart with Laev. Because she knew she wasn't a good Family member?

"No favor tokens are gone. No ancient Family artifacts. All else is of no importance."

So his FatherSire had thought, too, protecting Laev. But he still felt he had to make right what was stolen from the Family due to his bad judgement. "I brought the pistols back."

"We are glad to note that; they were much loved and used by past Hawthorns. We have always been a Family of good shots."

A nice, distracting, thought. "Really?"

"Yes. You might want to reopen the shooting gallery."

"Didn't even know we had one," Laev said.

"I will inform the Residence."

"Good."

With another purr, Brazos leapt onto the bedsponge and curled up at the end. The air around them heated and drowsiness crept up on Laev.

"And you have brought a good Fam into the Family—"

"Yesss," Brazos articulated.

Laev was drifting into a doze.

"And will soon bring a good HeartMate."

That jolted him from lethargy. He'd learned of his HeartMate tonight, turned her down. Which, on the face of it, was stupid, but not something he wanted to remedy if his gut said to withdraw.

His gut said to run, his body whispered need.

Scented herbs swirled in the air. "Sleep, Laev," said the House-Heart.

So he did.

* * *

*F*or once Camellia didn't take the public carrier home. Her little house wasn't the sanctuary it had been. Nor did she want to speak of the fresh wound to her friends. She wanted to brood on it first. So she hopped on a transport and a few minutes later went through the back door of Darjeeling's HouseHeart and sat at a table in the middle of the room next to the gently chiming fountain.

The dark closed around her, cozy and comforting, with a few aromatic firefly glows of light from the incense sticks before the Lady and Lord.

The Lord statue that Laev had given her. She made out the vague shape of stone, then turned her back on it.

Her shoulders lowered and she propped her face in her hands. Tonight had brought forward all her fears for her to face, and she had failed. In one moment, one instant, she had failed.

And the thought of claiming a HeartMate still sent her into a downward spiral of disturbing emotions.

While the recollection of her dream lover's, Laev Hawthorn's, her *HeartMate's* hands on her body brought wild sensations of echoed ecstasy.

She rubbed her face and stood. Tea sounded excellent, a blend of hybrid Earthan chamomile and Celtan paleleaf. She brewed a cup and tidied up. Then returned to her seat to close her eyes and drink, and let the atmosphere of her place wash over her.

Quiet cheer, that was the feeling she got from her surroundings. Patrons happy to be here, servers happy with their work.

It was enough to have her relaxing further. This she'd built with her own hands. There was something to be said for being independent, not part of a couple, a HeartMated couple where one was bonded so close to the other.

The tea was good, just enough sweet on her tongue.

And she wasn't alone. She had Mica, who was exploring the room, staying away from the fountain and any stray droplets of water. Camellia had her close friends, Glyssa and Tiana.

She sat for a long while letting the peace and satisfaction of *her* place fill her with accomplishment, soothe her with the knowledge that she brought good food and good tea into others' lives.

A tapping came at her door and she froze, then sank into her balance, breathed deeply in and out, and prepared for fighting. Light-footed, she prowled to the peephole of the door. Sent out her senses to the person beyond . . .

It's Teacher! Mica said, prodding her forepaw against the door.

Acacia? Camellia asked telepathically.

Yes, it's me, Acacia said.

What are you doing here?

There was hesitation on her teacher's part, then a sigh. *It's so very female.*

What?

There's a piece of furniture in a shopwindow that I drop by to look at for my new social club. A humorously sly note came into her mind. *Why don't I show it to you?*

All right, Camellia answered.

And, um, do you have any strong caff?

Camellia unlocked and dropped the spellshields on the door, opened it for Acacia. "Just a minute and I'll bring you some."

It took no more than a couple of minutes before Camellia and Acacia were walking down the street, Mica trotting beside them.

"Nice night," Acacia said.

"It is, I think spring is finally here and summer's just ahead."

"Good night for the Great Labyrinth Fair."

"I suppose so," Camellia said. She really didn't want to think of it.

"I've never been," Acacia said. "Not much of one for walking around and meditating."

"Me, neither," Camellia agreed.

About a half block down, Acacia stopped at a bright window.

"Oh," Camellia breathed.

"Yup, thought you might like something in here, too."

"It's the wardrobe."

"Huh. I like the cupboard. The wardrobe looks a little fancy for you."

Camellia sipped her drink. "For the teahouses, sure. But for home . . ." She thought of the wall in her bedroom with her safe that her uncle had vandalized twice, willfully destroyed. If she moved the bed over a bit closer to the other wall, this beautiful piece would fit. She sidled closer to the window to check the price, sucked in a breath through her teeth. If she got the piece, she and Mica would be on a strict budget for months, emptying the no-time of food she'd already prepared. And that was counting on the Teahouse and HouseHeart continuing to do well.

I like it, Mica said. *Shelf on top behind fancy wood looks nice and wide. I could have a good sleep spot.*

Mentally, Camellia rearranged her ideas for the wardrobe, included Mica. It would work for both of them.

"So, you think the cupboard would fit in well with our plans for the social club?" Acacia said.

Tilting her head, Camellia visualized the space they'd planned. "I think it would be perfect."

Breath whooshed from Acacia, and she grinned. "I'm no good at these things, and I can't afford a decorator."

"Thanks a lot."

"You and me are doing a trade," Acacia reminded Camellia. "I got you into the Green Knight. You're doing well, by the way. Didn't embarrass me tonight. Should make the next level in a couple of weeks."

"That's what Tinne Holly said. Nearly word for word."

Acacia laughed, then stared at the clean lines of the cupboard and bumped Camellia with her shoulder. "Thanks again for indulging me." She sipped the last of her caff, tossed the container in the street deconstructor, glanced up at the shopwindow. "Clovers' Fine Furniture, good solid construction. The cupboard will last my lifetime, and that's all I ask."

"Yes," Camellia said, but her lips tightened. She didn't need to have furniture lasting longer than her lifetime, either. Once again

Laev's beautiful ResidenceDen flowed through her mind. She'd loved the style of that chamber.

Someday, she hoped, she would be courageous enough to go to Laev.

Her fearful behavior tonight still stung. What would she do when she saw him next?

Twenty

♥

She concentrated on the wardrobe. It represented something new in her life. Living with her Fam, another being. That was a start. Camellia would work on her emotional problems, maybe find a way to ban her father and uncle from her life—false hope, that. Still, in a couple of years, maybe she'd be mature enough to claim her Heart-Mate. If Laev could ever accept her.

A septhour later she and Mica were snuggled in bed. Mica at the foot on her blanket. Camellia was blocking thoughts and the self-inflicted pain of Laev leaving her. No dream sex tonight or in the nights to come, both she and Laev were strong enough in control to ensure that.

Tentatively she probed their link. He'd narrowed it to a thread. As narrow on his end as on hers.

Practicing some deep breathing exercises, she was drifting off to sleep when Mica said, *Zanth likes Me.*

Camellia found herself smiling. "Yes," she mumbled.

Brazos likes Me, too.

"Um-hmm."

Life is good.

Yes, life was still good.

After a couple of minutes, Mica said, *Black Pierre doesn't like Me.*

Making an effort, Camellia snagged a couple of thoughts to reply intelligently. *Life's like that.*

But Black Pierre is old and not fun, so I don't care and Life is still Good.

Laev was young and fun and Camellia cared too much, but sleep beckoned and she let herself slide into blessed surcease.

The next morning, Camellia gave in to her sore muscles and leaned back in her large square tub in the waterfall room, taking time for a luxury. Mica sat across the room on a folded towel, disapproving. Camellia's calendarsphere popped into existence, announcing, "The fee for salvaging your tea set, three one-thousand-gram tins of specially mixed tea, and three hundred ounces of pure Earthan green tea from the starship *Nuada's Sword*, is due to be delivered today."

"Ungh. Dismiss sphere." She'd already prepared the teas for the Kelps a week prior, but today was marked as the delivery day. And it had used most of the Earthan green tea that she'd had on hand, which meant another visit to, and skirmish with, the starship.

Head back on the cushiony rest, she breathed in steam. She'd hoped to wait and reveal her last secret to her friends later, but it appeared as if she'd need their help, again, since her father and uncle remained in her life. Time was passing, the window of opportunity closing.

Her peace sloughed away, she rose and ordered the bathing tub to empty then cleanse, and dressed in a good business tunic that included a shimmer of woven silver thread. Eyeing the wall where her safe was, she decided to just have the gouges fixed and not use the cache anymore. No reason to use it if her uncle could get into the safe at will and broke it just to be mean.

"Here, Mica," she called to the cat who was sulking over her smaller portion of clucker meat on her dish in the kitchen.

I am here. Mica walked in, tail held stiffly.

"Can you use your Flair with me to move the bed frame and bedsponge closer to the entry wall?"

Why?

"Because we decided to get the wardrobe, didn't we?" Camellia said with weighted politeness. "But if you've changed your mind . . ."

Mica sniffed. *No, I want My shelf.* She came and sat next to Camellia, leaned against her leg, and the bond between them strengthened with the touch. The cat's energy was odd, but they were Familiar companions so Camellia could use it.

"Ready? On three push with me. One, Camellia, two, Mica cat, *three.*"

The frame and sponge slid easily two-thirds of a meter, leaving a smaller walkway along the wall with the door, but more than enough space for the new wardrobe.

When do we get new wardrobe? Mica asked, following the line of dust where the edge of the bed had been. Camellia winced at the sight, sighed, walked into the hallway. "Come out of the room so I can do a whisk-and-vanish-dust spell." With the energy she was spending, she wouldn't be teleporting anywhere today.

When do we get My new sleep shelf space? Mica insisted but strolled over to Camellia.

"I'll have to study the business accounts. Probably not sooner than next month, so at least two weeks."

Mica sneezed, probably from the dust, and Camellia raised her arms and said the couplets and cleaned the room.

Then she scried Glyssa. "Come over for dinner tonight."

"Yum!" Glyssa said, moving restlessly. "I'm left watching the Library while the parents and my brother are at the Great Labyrinth Fair."

Camellia accepted the pain the mention of the fair and its association with Laev gave her, accepted that anything reminding her of him would twinge her heart.

"Isn't this the day you have to pay your fee to the Kelps?" Glyssa added.

"That's right. I'll contact them as soon as I call Tiana about tonight."

"Go ahead and call. I'll scry Tiana."

"Potluck tonight, bring a dish."

Glyssa's eyes widened at that. "What's going on?"

"I've got a new purchase in mind. If you and Ti have the time, take a look at the wardrobe in the window of Clovers' Fine Furniture."

"Oooh. I love that store." Glyssa frowned. "But you have a closet and a dresser."

"I'll donate the dresser to Ti's Temple charity."

"She'll like that. Later." Glyssa's face fell back into dissatisfaction. "Gotta hurry if I have to prepare a dish for dinner."

Camellia figured her friend would just take something from D'Licorice Residence's no-times. "Love you," she said.

Glyssa smiled and it was brilliant. "Love you, too."

"And I have a secret I need your help with."

Now Glyssa's eyes sparkled. "I'll tell Ti! Later!" The scry panel went dark.

Secrets. Mica's tail thrashed. *You didn't tell Me this new secret.*

Actually it's a very old secret. And because it was such a secret, Camellia replied mentally instead of aloud. *Over four centuries old.*

"Whee!" Mica said.

The wall timer dinged. "Time for work, tell you later."

"Yessss."

Just before Camellia left, she put in a call to D'Kelp, the daughter of the woman who'd found Camellia's tea set. The GrandLady appeared busy. "Here," she said.

"It's Camellia Darjeeling, I have your annual tea."

"Oh. Yes." D'Kelp sifted fingers through her prematurely silver hair. "It is that time of year, isn't it, dear?" She puffed a breath. "Why don't I send my brother, Feam, to fetch it?"

"That would be good."

D'Kelp smiled. "How about at Darjeeling's HouseHeart? Lovely place, dear, and I don't think he's been."

"Also good," Camellia said.

Nodding, D'Kelp said, "Farewell," then ended the scry.

Staying busy helped Camellia keep her mind off the disastrous night before. After all, she hadn't known Laev for that long. Hadn't acknowledged he was important to her. So she could go back to concentrating on the rest of her life and on what she liked best, business.

It was past MidMorningBell and Camellia was talking to patrons in the room when Feam Kelp and a trendy, younger man walked into Darjeeling's HouseHeart, stopped, and looked around.

Camellia finished up her conversation with a diner and moved toward them. "Good to see you again, Feam," Camellia fibbed. "Would you like a table by the fountain or the fire?"

"Oh, fire, I think," said the young man.

"This way." She led the men to a table for four and indicated the touch-menu.

"Thank you," the young man said, sliding gracefully into a seat.

"Thank you," Feam said, staring at the menu. He smiled at his companion. "I always eat free at Darjeeling's."

"Nice." The young man spared Camellia a smile as he lounged casually.

"I'll get your tea and bring your selections out when it's done." Camellia waved. "Enjoy." She had no doubt that she'd be feeding the men some of the most expensive items on her menu. After the men had ordered, she brought out their caff along with a bag that held the tea tins.

"Thank you," Feam said, this time looking up at her with a smile.

"You're very welcome. I remember your mother with great fondness."

"Of course," he said. "She was pleased that she could find the tea set for you. That ship was the discovery of her life and the salvage of it her best memories." He reached in and lifted a tin out to display to his friend.

"Gorgeous!" The other man beamed at Camellia.

Since people had turned to look at them, and Camellia carried the tins for sale, she wasn't as annoyed as she might have been.

Camellia, Kelp's order is ready, her manager told her telepathically.

So Camellia smiled at the men. "I'll be right back with your food." She got the plates of marinaded thin-sliced prime furrabeast steak sandwiches on ritual bread from the kitchen and returned to the men. Over the next septhour and a half, she waited on them, and allowed herself a sigh of relief when they finally left.

Her manager shook her head. "And all that was free. They didn't leave a tip, did they?"

"No, but they shouldn't." Camellia opened her arms wide to stretch them as much to make a point. "Everything you see here is because Feam Kelp's mother found my tea set." She glanced at the piece on display. Maybe it would be better to replace the ginger jar with a holographic rendition. Yes, a pretty painting . . . No. Not now. The wardrobe came first. A new goal to work toward, business as usual to focus on, no diverging into sexual relationships. She'd concentrate on not judging men with a narrowed gaze.

But her manager was still staring at the table Kelp and his companion had vacated, and shaking her head. "All this is because you were smart enough to realize your Family's property was on the ship that had sunk. Smart enough to put a good legal case together and present it to the SupremeJudge, then you worked your ass off."

"I had plenty of help. I'll go clean the table."

"No, you're still working your ass off. I'll do it," her manager said.

Camellia was grateful but wanted to keep busy. She spent the rest of the day checking her accounts, working on her budget, with Mica napping on her feet or playing with a piece of papyrus in her office. She'd been generally right with the figures, except the HouseHeart was doing better than expected and Darjeeling's Teahouse had gotten a bump with the opening of the new place.

She looked down at Mica. "If you want the wardrobe, furrabeast steaks of thirty gilt apiece are things of the past."

The cat opened an eye, mewed. *Can't have both?*

"Nope."

Maybe we shouldn't get the wardrobe. We will be moving into T'Hawthorn Residence and it has many furnitures.

With a jolt, all Camellia's disappointment in herself and Laev hit like a sleeting ice storm. Mica didn't realize that things had gone wrong the night before, and Camellia knew that if she told the cat now there would be a loud hissy fit. Later. She locked the records away. "Let's go start dinner."

Food! Cooks get tastes.

Camellia didn't want to argue about that, either. "That's right."

And secrets later, the cat ended gleefully.

*O*nce *again Camellia was pacing her small house because she was* nervous about revealing a secret to her friends. That's what she told herself. But she was also frantically trying to think of anything except Laev and how she'd been a coward.

Secrets. Yes, that's what was important at this moment. Like that time so long ago at thirteen, she needed her friends' help to claim something that was hers—or rather her Family's. But her father and uncle would ruin everything if they knew. And like that dim time, she must be more clever than they to keep irreplaceable treasure out of their hands.

Mica watched Camellia make a circuit from the rounded top of one of the furrabeast chairs, paws tucked under her and purring softly. The dinner-altar room was clean and ready, a pan of three large stuffed tubers and stew sent mouthwatering odors throughout the house from the kitchen.

Camellia couldn't settle. She found herself standing at the threshold of the bedroom, staring at the holes in the wall around her safe. The place where she'd put the wardrobe.

Glyssa arrived on the teleportation pad first from her job at the PublicLibrary, and Tiana a few seconds later from the Temple. Both were full of the news of the day. Having them here felt good, felt like Camellia's life hadn't just shot in the wrong direction.

They ate and drank and she let her friends talk of men first. Tiana was in a desultory affair with another Temple student. Glyssa stated that she was occasionally testing the small thread that ran between her and her HeartMate, but otherwise was unaccustomedly closemouthed.

Finally desserts had been consumed, Mica was snoozing with half-lidded eyes on her pillow, and Camellia cleared her throat.

She sat huddled in on herself, hands cradled around a mug, looked at her friends over the rim as she sipped the strengthening tea.

"First thing you should know is that Laev, um, discovered that we were HeartMates and he walked away from me and the problem."

"How did he—" Glyssa started.

"It was my fault. He asked me to accompany him to the Great Labyrinth Fair. I, ah, hinted that we'd been sharing sexual dreams." Camellia straightened, managed a casual shrug to try to hide her feelings. "He knew then we were HeartMates."

"You panicked," Tiana said matter-of-factly.

"Yes."

There was a hissing gasp from Mica. She stood arched, all fur sticking out. *What? No! Everything was planned and plan was working!*

"I wondered about that," Glyssa murmured.

"How was it planned?" Camellia asked, knowing she'd finally get answers.

Old man knew about you and talked to Black Pierre who told Brazos and Me. We DESERVE to live in Residence like Brazos.

"So you only wanted to be my Fam because you wanted to live in a Residence." That hurt, too.

No. I love you.

"I love you, too."

But you make Me angry! Mica hissed.

"Ditto."

Mica lifted her nose. *I will go talk to Brazos. He can make Fam-Man come back.*

"Good luck with that," Camellia said but didn't think that the young cat heard since she'd teleported away with a pop.

Tiana was there, patting Camellia. "There, there. It will all work out." And Camellia realized she was weeping, harsh, hurtful chest-sobs.

"The priestess is right. It will work out. You have all your lives." Glyssa took Camellia's teacup from her hands and substituted a wineglass. "Drink up. It just hurts, and Lady and Lord we've all been hurt by men and HeartMates. We'll get over it."

"*Through* the hurt to a brighter future," Tiana said.

"Yeah, of course," Glyssa said.

Camellia wept another couple of minutes until all her hurt was gone, then mopped up her face with a softleaf and drank the wine. "Enough of that," she said in a froggy voice. "Not what I really wanted to talk about tonight. Must get on with . . . stuff."

"Secrets," Glyssa said, toasted her with her own glass, sipped, then her face crinkled in a smile. "Mica will be peeved to miss it."

"Just as well," Camellia said, finishing the wine and going back to the tea. "I don't trust her to keep an important secret."

"Who knows with cats?" Glyssa shrugged but looked wistful.

"You'll get a Fam," Tiana assured.

"You are very optimistic and annoying tonight, Tiana. What was in your incense today?" Glyssa said.

That made them all laugh. As soon as they were back in their usual places and her friends were watching her expectantly, Camellia translocated a bundle of papyrus copies of ancient documents to the low table.

Glyssa blinked, sat up quickly, reaching for and thumbing through the sheets. "What do you have there? Lady and Lord, these are copies of *Earthan* documents! You have the originals?"

"Safely tucked away at T'Reed's."

Tiana frowned. "Where'd you get original Earthan documents?"

"I found them in a small box in the attic when our home was taken from Mother and me."

"Your father and uncle weren't around."

"Of course they weren't. Mother and I would have tried to make *them* deal with their creditors."

"The NobleCouncil stepped in to help you and so did the Temple," Tiana said.

"Enough to pay the bills and charge it against Father's and Takvar's accounts, and to find us a place to live." Camellia tried to keep her tone light. It had been a terrible time, and she'd hated leaving the Family house that was in poor shape.

She'd also hated the place that the Temple had put them into. For a building that had been constructed by the colonists themselves, it had had little charm. Everyone there had been beggars. She'd worked hard to get out of the place but hadn't made it until after her mother had died.

Glyssa scowled at the papyrus, choked, and with a wild movement knocked over her glass of wine. Camellia yanked the papyrus from the table while Tiana said a cleansing spell that sucked the liquid from the rug and dispersed it into the atmosphere of the house. The air suddenly smelled like good red wine.

Continuing to cough, Glyssa doubled over and Camellia and Tiana hovered, ready to teleport her to a HealingHall. Finally Glyssa gasped and waved a hand, croaked, "Water."

Camellia ran to the kitchen, came back with a tube of water for her friend. Glyssa drank it down, handed the tube back to Camellia, and wiped her eyes and nose with a softleaf, then collapsed back on her pillow.

Her gaze drilled Camellia. "Those are copies of a subscription to fund a starship to find and colonize a planet."

"Yes." Camellia tossed the tube into the deconstructor, sat up straight.

Another cough from Glyssa, who eyed the papyrus. "And," she whispered, transferring her awed glance from Camellia to Tiana, "the appointment of Netra Sunaya Hoku, a man who subscribed to the fund to colonize Celta, as Captain of the starship, *Lugh's Spear.*"

"Yes."

"Your Family is a FirstFamily, those who financed the colonization. Your ancestor *was the Captain of* Lugh's Spear*!*"

Twenty-one

$\mathcal{H}$*eat flooded Camellia, then faded, leaving her cold. She'd known* this would be difficult. "That's right. But *Lugh's Spear* crashed and he never got over that. Then he had to lead the remaining colonists from the crash site to here, where Druida was being built. Too much responsibility broke him. He didn't want to be of the First-Families, take a FirstFamily name. He wanted obscurity. So he didn't take a plant name at all, but one that reminded him of his roots on Earth."

"Darjeeling," Tiana breathed. She'd settled onto her pillow.

"That's right. And, like other things between then and now, his papers were misplaced and lost."

"What else do you have?" Glyssa asked sternly.

Camellia licked her lips. "His journals from when he was Awakened from the cryogenics tube to the landing and the trek to Druida."

"And?" Glyssa pressed.

Camellia didn't look at her friend, mumbled the last, the most important, find. "Maps and blueprints of *Lugh's Spear*, including his own notations of where the storage areas were, and his quarters."

"Cave of the Dark Goddess!" Tiana squeaked, put a hand to her temples as if to control the pounding of blood. "By Celtan salvage law, a Captain who has invested in a ship that is lost is entitled to a third of the amount of all retrieved salvage. He or his heirs," Tiana quoted. They'd all learned that at the time of the lawsuit of the sunken ship.

"Fortunes. Fortunes could be yours! Especially since they've found *Lugh's Spear* and are beginning to excavate!" Tiana said.

"No," Camellia said. "All these things could be my *father's* or my *uncle's*. They're first in line. Not me or Senchal. The only reason that I got the tea set is that I was the one who found the documents and pressed the case."

"Another Earthan name, all of the men's," Glyssa muttered.

"Yes."

"We can't let your father or uncle have any of the salvage. Ever." Glyssa was fierce.

"That's why I've kept the papers a secret, why the originals are with T'Reed. But the documents could help so much with the excavation. I know it's a dangerous undertaking. Maybe they could save lives if people knew where to work and such."

"This is like the tea set. We need to circumvent your elders so you can claim it," Tiana said.

They stared at the papyrus, then each other. "This isn't going to be easy," Tiana said.

"No," Camellia said. "I'd hoped to be able to present the documents to the proper authorities at this point. After the survey of *Lugh's Spear* was done and before the earth-moving began. The ground caved under the ship once, it could continue to do that under our machines. It's still dangerous. If the excavators had an exact map, they could go directly to the places most interesting to them."

She drew in a breath, "And, of course, I'm proud of my ancestry, of Captain Hoku. I wanted him to be honored more, his contribution to be more. I want him recognized as the great man he was. Providing his documents at this time would help the excavators and keep Hoku's name in the forefront of history."

"The Cherrys' play isn't enough?" asked Tiana.

Camellia waved a hand. "The Cherrys' play is about their ancestress. Captain Hoku is a remote figure."

"But heroic," Tiana pointed out.

"It's not *enough*. He was changed, nearly broken. No one knows the cost to him."

"All right," Tiana said.

There was a moment of silence. "I was hoping that my father and uncle would be out of the picture." Banished. Gone. Anywhere but alive and thriving in Druida City.

Glyssa hissed out a breath, then tucked her hands under her armpits and rocked herself, laughing humorlessly. "Such treasures and we can't claim them. I sat in on a consultation of an inheritance legal problem with my parents and a client and the SupremeJudge. It concerned a donation to the PublicLibrary. The end result was that the law doesn't care if the inheriting person is a bad person. As long as she or he doesn't do anything terrible to receive the inheritance, it is hers or his."

Camellia and Tiana stared at Glyssa, then Camellia flopped back onto her pillow, staring up at the mural of starry galaxies on the ceiling. "I thought so. If I put a case before the SupremeJudge again, the inheritance would come to my father and my uncle first."

"They'd do dreadful things with the huge amount of gilt they'd get from the artifacts," Tiana said.

"Or ruin the artifacts themselves," Glyssa said.

"If I ever truly own the documents, I'll give them to you, to the PublicLibrary," Camellia assured.

"The question is how do we get your father and uncle out of your life?" Tiana said calmly, surprising them all.

Camellia cracked a laugh. "Something I've been working on since I was fourteen and they showed up again."

"They're evil men," Tiana said. "Someday they'll go too far." Her forehead knit. "Your father's scorn of the Sheela Na Gig should adversely affect him."

"What kind of 'adverse affect'?" asked Glyssa.

Tiana leaned forward. "There's been some speculation by the FirstLevel Priestesses and Priests that his health would be affected. Not that I hope that happens, of course."

"Of course not," Camellia and Glyssa said at the same time.

"So Camellia's father might have serious health problems, and they both are criminals just waiting to be caught. You've been recording all their thefts from you?"

Camellia smiled brittlely. "Oh, yes. Down to the last steak."

"Sooner or later . . ." Glyssa said.

"Yes. Let's just hope it's sooner, for everyone's sakes."

"They can't press their luck forever. Someday their crimes will catch up with them," Tiana said.

Camellia shrugged. "It never has so far. I'm not counting on that. When Druida City becomes too rough on them, they move back to Gael, or wherever else they cycle through."

Still frowning, Tiana sipped her wine and said, "I really wouldn't want to be them when they pass on to the wheel of stars and reincarnate. Karma." A shiver went through her.

"By the way, Camellia," Glyssa said. "Could I, we, the Public-Library possibly have copies—"

Camellia translocated another batch, handed them to Glyssa. "Strictly confidential."

"Thanks!" Glyssa slipped the papyrus into her sleeve.

"It can't hurt to have your parents aware of the circumstances."

Glyssa nibbled her lips. "Worse comes to worse, we might be able to leak a little of the information to the *Lugh's Spear* expedition. Say we recently found old, original sources in our archives." She bent a stern look on Camellia. "You *will* provide the maps and blueprints, won't you?"

Sighing, Camellia said, "I suppose so. But the more people who have copies, the less likely my secrets will be kept."

"You know we can be trusted not to share anything you don't want us to."

"Yes." The Licorices had always been good to her.

"Anything else you want to talk about?" Tiana asked.

But Glyssa began humming absentmindedly, and Camellia shared a look with Tiana. They both knew to wait for Glyssa to think an issue through before commenting.

A distant look came to Glyssa's eyes, as if she were probing for her HeartMate. "He's east." She wobbled where she sat. "I think he might be with one of the Elecampane expeditions at *Lugh's Spear*."

Camellia caught a note of longing in her friend's voice. Again she looked at Tiana and knew they were both feeling anticipatory tendrils of dread. Glyssa would not stay in Druida forever. If her HeartMate didn't come to her, she'd go out looking. Her pride was enough to wonder *why* he wouldn't come to Druida City to claim her. She might track him down just to give him a piece of her mind.

Then Glyssa blinked, downed her drink, and said, "No, nothing more I want to say."

*T*he *weekend split between her two teahouses kept Camellia busy,* though her smile became tense when someone enthused about visiting the Great Labyrinth Fair.

She spent some time with her brother, Senchal, who was envious of Mica but cheerfully working on a project, a portion of a mural on a boy's center.

Mica was unusually loving, spending a lot of time with Camellia and purring—and dropping a few hints on what kind of collar she would like after six months.

After the weekend was over, on Mor morning, Camellia scried Cymb Lemongrass and got the blurry-eyed GraceLord. "Here? Hmm. Camellia? Wha'?"

She winced. She'd thought it was late enough that he'd be up, but she'd misjudged. "Sorry. If you can hook me into your calendarsphere—"

"Why?"

"I'd like to change our sparring schedule."

"Oh. Why?"

"I've found that before NoonBell is better for me." She'd be avoiding Laev and his usual time.

Lemongrass's eyes narrowed. "That boy say something about those pistols?"

"What boy?"

"Hawthorn."

"What pistols?"

"Never mind."

She felt in her bones that she should press, but didn't.

The next day the scry panel was flickering as she walked into the house after work. Her heart jumped at the light purple color. Over the last several days she'd repeated to herself often that she'd done the right thing. When, occasionally, she'd said it aloud, Mica had sniffed . . . then the small cat had grinned and started reporting what Brazos told him of Laev. That the man wasn't sleeping well. He was grumpy and very polite with the staff and his journeywoman.

Sounded like he was missing his dream sex—just as she was. It had been more than sex, had tipped perilously over into loving. She could still feel those soft strokes of his fingers on her back after they'd reached completion, the nuzzling and holding.

So she stared at the scry panel as it melded abstract patterns in Hawthorn purple. Mica hopped up to her favorite perch on the large, rounded chair back, glanced at the panel, and casually lifted a forepaw to lick. *That is from Laev T'Hawthorn.*

"Yes."

Mica slid her eyes toward Camellia. *Maybe Brazos wants to talk to you, too.*

Camellia raised her brows. "Brazos has never wanted to talk with me."

With an ingratiating smile, Mica said, *He is a good Cat.*

"I'm sure." Camellia went into the small kitchen and the no-time to get some mint tea. Her stomach was a little upset. Probably from clenching it so tight. Her hands trembled as she retrieved the tea, and she cupped her hands around the mug for its warmth. She shouldn't be so nervous.

She shouldn't want Laev so much.

She stood until her nerves settled, experimented with a few expressions before she went up to the panel. Impassive. No, she couldn't manage that. Her polite smile seemed more fearsome . . .

or maybe fearful. And each second wound the tension inside her so tight that every nerve in her body quivered and her hands began to shake. She put her mug down on a tile-topped side table, straightened her shoulders, and walked toward the panel, touched it.

The viz message began. Her heart stuttered as she saw Laev. In the few days that they'd been apart he looked thinner . . . or more refined, as if he was working as hard as she was . . . maybe sparring a lot, too. His eyes seemed set deeper.

"Lover," he said. And her knees simply gave out and she sat on the floor. His voice held a rough edge, like he was hurt and that hurt her. He leaned a little back in his chair and she realized he'd recorded this in his ResidenceDen. "Lover," he said again. His mouth twisted. "I need to speak with you." His gaze, which had been focused on the scry panel, now looked beyond it, and Camellia. "To discuss our . . . situation. Please scry as soon as possible."

Brazos leapt onto the desk, fur fluffy, stared at the panel, and yowled. Whatever the cat said made Laev smile. Then the stare came back, riveting her. "Viz me. Anytime."

Another grumbling comment by Brazos. "Or, if you recall the coordinates and light, teleport here."

Camellia couldn't chance that. She'd been hanging on to Laev when he'd teleported them to his Residence and had been focused on him. Now she recalled the feel of him, his scent, and she yearned so much for him she had to gulp back tears that had welled in her throat.

"Later," Laev said, and it was in that soft voice that echoed through her memories of their sex.

We should go right now. Mica leapt down to Camellia's lap.

"Have dinner first . . ." Camellia protested.

Mica raised her nose. Sniffed right in Camellia's face. *T'Hawthorn Residence has good food.*

That had Camellia raising her own nose. "Maybe for cats. *You* didn't eat bean curd sandwiches there."

Mica's tongue protruded from her muzzle and her ears slanted in disapproval.

"Yeah," Camellia confirmed.

Pig slop.

"Yeah."

I will tell Brazos that We must be fed well. Mica trotted to the corner teleportation pad. *Come ON!*

Camellia rose from the floor in one easy motion. Her matches with GraceLord Lemongrass had toned her more. "I need to dress."

The cat hesitated, paws lifted midstep, turned her head to look, then sat with a hiss. "Yesss."

Frowning, Camellia left her Fam lashing her tail in the mainspace, discarding clothes as she went.

If Camellia married her HeartMate, she'd be a FirstFamily GreatLady.

Her lungs seized. Moving in the highest of the stratospheric level of nobles. With a place at her HeartMate's side on the FirstFamilies Council!

She couldn't get her breath. Dots swam before her eyes. She let her legs fold and slid to her back on the carpet. Couldn't. Breathe.

Mica jumped on her chest; air wrenched from Camellia's chest. The little cat marched up Camellia's torso to touch noses with her. Mica's whiskers tickled. Camellia wheezed. Sucked in a breath. Out. Another in.

Raggedly she overcame her panic. What was *that*?

She'd known from seventeen that Laev T'Hawthorn was her fated mate. Known he would someday be *the* T'Hawthorn. Why was she laid low by that fact now?

Because she'd hidden her knowledge of him as her HeartMate for so long.

Because he'd been married and any status related to him did not affect her.

Because she'd disliked Nivea and didn't want to ever be like her. But Camellia was ambitious for her business, and it'd do so well if—when—she and Laev wed. And she couldn't help herself from thinking that, yet still despised the thought that she was thinking of her own gain.

Mica sat on her chest, staring at her. *We deserve to live in T'Hawthorn Residence.*

Trust a cat to think that. Camellia doubted. The price would be too steep.

Her Fam looked around. *This is a pretty place, but it is not T'Hawthorn Residence.*

Camellia couldn't argue with that.

And I want My own room, not a closet. Come on! They are waiting for Us!

"You have to get off me first."

Mica hopped onto the bed in her "supervise" mode. Camellia chose a dark brown raw silkeen tunic and trous set of the latest cut. The trous were more straight-legged, the hem on the tunic higher, with wide ribboned embroidery of silver on the seams. The colors, dark brown and silver, were her Family colors, and she hadn't realized the meaning of them until she'd found the box of documents.

She angled in the mirror.

You look good, Mica said, nearly pacing in anticipation.

And Camellia switched her frown from her reflection to her Fam. "Just how much time have you spent at T'Hawthorn Residence if you know it so well that you can teleport us both there?"

Mica ignored the question. *Brazos and Black Pierre will help us.*

"Oh."

Brazos and his FamMan waiting for Us.

Heat washed through Camellia. "You told them we are coming!"

We want food. Laev is getting Us good food. Planning well. Mica opened her mouth in a kitty grin and swiped her whiskers with her tongue.

Yes, Laev T'Hawthorn was a good planner. Camellia had always considered herself a good planner, too, but Laev had had the advantage of being trained by two of the best from a young age. Now that she thought on it, there had been something of the negotiator in that viz of his.

Hungggrrry!

"All right!" Camellia followed the small cat back to the main-space, stepped onto the pad, and held out her arms for Mica. Linking her mind with her Fam, Camellia saw the world in flattened shades of gray. Then they were gone from home and arrived in a castle courtyard.

Twenty-two

Two blinks of Camellia's eyes and she saw that the stone courtyard was surrounded by high walls, an inner courtyard of T'Hawthorn Residence.

Chef is waiting for Us, Mica! Brazos shouted mentally.

Mica hopped from her arms and took off after a streak of black.

Laev chuckled and her gaze swung to him and her breath stopped. He looked too good. She was in trouble.

His smile faded and his eyes held a wary melancholy. He came up to her and bowed, and she shivered. Though neither of them had said it aloud, they both knew, now, that they were HeartMates.

He bowed to her as a man would to a woman he cared for, even more, as a GreatLord bowed to his GreatLady. Oh, yes, her life was changing.

"Thank you for listening to my viz . . . and being willing to listen more to me." His smooth negotiator tones were back.

"I—" Her voice cracked. She flushed, cleared her throat, and opened her mouth, and realized she didn't know what to say.

He offered his arm. It was covered in butterscotch-colored leather, his full trous were leather and tucked into boots of the same color. An expensive outfit that he wore with ease, that had been tailored for him. He probably didn't give a thought to how much it had cost. "Camellia, I was truthful in saying that I want to speak to you about our circumstances."

That was the second time he'd danced around the word *Heart-Mate*. Rather like trying to ignore the looming presence of the star-ship *Nuada's Sword* in the city. But she approved.

She put her fingers lightly on his arm and the muscle tensed under them. With a wave of his other hand, a large picnic basket she hadn't noticed lifted. Just seeing the shape of it caused her mouth to water. She glanced up at Laev and managed a smile. "You do have dinner. Good, I didn't have much for breakfast or lunch and I'm starving."

His smile in return seemed warmer than her own—and was she going to measure every little item of interaction between them? She was irritated at herself and the way her mind worked.

"I promise, no antique sandwiches lurk in the basket." They walked through the courtyard, his stride matching hers.

"Where are we going?" She was very aware of his body moving beside hers, but the Residence itself filled her vision and bombarded her senses with sounds and smells of the Hawthorns.

"I thought we'd eat at a pavilion overlooking the ocean."

That caught her attention and she glanced up to find his intent gaze on her, his eyes dark with emotion she didn't want to analyze.

"That sounds wonderful." They came to a square wooden door that opened as they neared . . . and exited to a huge, smooth lawn of green. "How lovely."

"I'm glad you like it."

She tried to ignore all the implications firing in her mind about how all this could be hers. But she'd have to take the man. And his Family. And his Residence.

She didn't mind admitting to herself that she wanted the man as a man—as a lover for an affair, not so much as a GreatLord and certainly not as a husband or HeartMate.

They walked through gardens that had been tended for centuries, dream gardens with drifts of blossoming bushes, colors and arrangements that stopped her breath, and around the next curve was a panorama leading to a rise and a tiny jewel of a building at the top.

The octagonal pavilion was small and airy and built of white marble, with columns and a dome. There were lacily carved marble half walls. Inside was a table dressed in elegant pale lavender linens and the subtle gleam of china and silverware.

His arm was strong as they took the three steps up, then Camellia gasped at the view. Before her lay the Great Platte Ocean rolling in slate gray waves and tipped with white surf. To her right, closer to a direct path of the Residence itself, was a cut in the land that had been smoothed to a gentle declination down to a wide sandy beach.

Her toes curled. "I don't recall the last time I walked on the beach," she murmured.

"We can do that now, or after we eat or talk."

Since her stomach pitched acid like the waves, she glanced up at him. "Talk first."

He smiled. "Good. Do you want to walk on the beach and talk?"

She thought about how the wind would catch words and whisk them away, how her hair would blow into tangles, irritating her, distracting. How she'd be bombarded with scents and sights of the ocean and birds and shells and not able to focus on him in one of the most important discussions of her life. "I'd rather talk here."

"Good." He turned to her, smiled, took both of her hands. Then, to her surprise, he closed his eyes, making himself vulnerable to her, staggering her. When he opened his lashes, his gaze drilled into her. "I've missed you," he said.

Heat surged through her whole body in one great flush, bringing prickles of aching desire. She found herself leaning a little closer to him. She wanted to pull back, but he smelled so good and she could feel the warmth of him. Their auras impinged and merged, and she couldn't withdraw.

"It's good being with you again." He glanced around. "Being alone with you."

They hadn't been alone in anything but dreams since he'd first come to her office—and at that time she'd been hiding from herself, not able to enjoy his company. Now she could let herself feel the aura of him, breathe in his scent, stare at him all she wanted instead of sneaking glances.

As he stared at her.

"Come sit." He drew her to one of the window seats that ringed the pavilion, topped with plump pale lavender velvet cushions. Must have spells to stay so beautiful. The seat wasn't wide enough to lie down on comfortably, so sex might not be immediate.

Her heart pounded.

But the minute she sat, he loosed her hands and strode back to the basket and the table. "Wine? Ale? Whiskey? Brandy?"

She blinked. "You have all that in there?"

"What I don't have, I can translocate from the fully stocked bar in the ResidenceDen." His smile faded. "I've been having a drink or two before sleeping."

Clearing her throat, she glanced away. "Yes, so have I." Her mouth tipped wryly. "But mine's been sleepy-soothe tea."

His eyebrows rose. "That works for you?"

"Sometimes."

He opened the basket and pulled out a pretty bottle, smiled at her. "Springreen wine." She knew the special vintage by the curves of the engraved vines on the bottle. Very rare.

Laev said, "I noticed your wine menu at Darjeeling's House-Heart had several offerings of springreen wine, so I thought you enjoyed it."

Her mouth was dry, she licked her lips. "I do. And that vintage is unique. Tartness almost overwhelming the sweet."

"Almost, but not quite." He smiled, his wrist flexed as he removed the cork. Then he poured the wine and she heard the soft fizz of bubbles. When he handed her a glass—another crystal antique—he continued, "I like sweet and tart almost in balance."

"Me, too." She took a sip, let the wine lay on her tongue, nearly shuddered with how lovely it tasted. "Wonderful. Thank you."

He sat next to her, smiled. "You're welcome." With a tilt of his head, he indicated the view and they angled to watch the ocean and drink in silence.

Camellia became aware of a low and pulsing tone . . . then realized it wasn't something she heard, but that she *felt*. Very carefully she opened up her senses, her own Flair . . . and mentally saw a bond between herself and Laev.

It was golden, as HeartMate bonds were supposed to be, and larger than she'd have expected—nearly the circumference of a writestick. With her inner eye, she studied it. The cord also appeared to be stronger than she'd thought—and though the pulsing red of sex was certainly a component, there were other strands that signified mental and emotional links. Compatibilities? Or just connections? They shared more than she'd anticipated.

"I have a proposition for you," Laev said, causing her to jolt a little.

She savored more wine. He wasn't looking straight at her now, but she knew he was aware of her every expression, every movement. Their bond had begun to glow and throbbed faster, with tension on both sides.

When his words came, they were considered, measured. "It's no secret that I made a terrible mistake in my marriage." His throat worked, but he went on. "I am not ready for another . . . wife."

She found herself nodding, and narrowing her eyes to watch the bond between them. Their thoughts were matching. No surprise, amazement, nor disappointment flowed from her to him and his shoulders lowered, relaxed. His gaze glanced across hers, then back to the ocean, and she got the idea that he wanted a verbal response. The negotiator, planner, having terms stated aloud.

How much should she say? He probably already knew of her problems with her father and uncle. "I believe it's common knowledge among those who frequent the Green Knight Fencing and Fighting Salon that the reason I am training is because my male relatives are . . . abusive . . ."

Laev made a short growling noise that actually pleased her.

Then he cleared his throat as if he hadn't just displayed uncivilized, protective male behavior. "Tinne Holly might have mentioned the reason why he placed you with GraceLord Lemongrass. And Lemongrass and I have spoken a time or two, not much about you, though."

"Oh. Well." A notion formed. How much would he have looked into her background? He was cautious, so was she. She knew a lot about him, could find out more if she asked around. But she wouldn't, not right now.

What would he know about her? He was there the day she'd claimed her tea set at JudgementGrove—when this path unfurled for both of them and the trails split away, only recently coming back together. He knew of Darjeeling's Teahouse and Darjeeling's HouseHeart. He was a canny investor so he might even be able to gauge her business finances. She didn't doubt that he could find out all her personal finances to the last silver, but she didn't think he'd do that.

"Camellia, did you want to expand upon your male relatives?" Laev prompted.

Ah, yes, the terms. She looked into his eyes, discovered that she couldn't hold his gaze when speaking of her concerns, either. She drank a bit of wine to wet her lips, used his own words. "I am not ready for a husband."

They breathed quietly together. He reached out and brushed her hair from her shoulders, his thumb gliding along her cheek. She liked that, wanted more of his touch, leaned toward him.

"I enjoy just seeing you, meeting you, talking with you."

He was being so careful, they were being so careful of hurting themselves or each other. A good sign. She smiled, tried a bit of teasing. "You enjoy looking at my derriere."

He grinned, tipped his glass to her in a salute. "That I do."

She nodded, smiled around the rim of her glass. "It's mutual."

"Good."

This time the quiet buzzed with a hint of sexual attraction. Again she narrowed her eyes.

"Why are you doing that?" he asked.

Hesitating, she slid her gaze toward him, needed to wet her mouth again. So she drank another marvelous swallow of tart-sweetness wine. "I am looking at the bond between us with my Flair."

He stiffened. Calmly, she continued, "People attracted sexually have a bond." With her free hand, she waved. "Friends." She smiled. "I have deep bonds with my two good friends." Again she slipped a look at him. "I have a bond with my Fam. Even though it is newer, it is strong." She touched her chest. "Mica is close to my heart."

Millimeter by millimeter, his posture eased and his contemplation seemed to turn from her to himself, or what wove between them.

Golden! His mind whisper was harsh and Camellia didn't know if she was meant to hear it. So she ignored it, even as he gulped the last of his wine. Then his gaze sharpened, but his words, again, were measured. "A bond is not a terrible thing."

"No," she agreed.

"Within reason."

She wasn't sure whether either of them would be able to regulate their connection, whether the bond itself would fit into the outline of the terms, but wasn't going to say so. She didn't want to think of that, either. So she chose other words. "I enjoy being with you, too. I have my own problems . . . and secrets." She drank the last of the wine, rose, and went to the table for the bottle, returned, and poured a quarter glass in his goblet and her own, finally met his gaze squarely. "I prefer my relationships with men proceed extremely slowly."

Now he smiled and swirled his wine. "Slow is good." He held out a hand, more commanding than offering. She put hers in his and he drew her back to the seat.

Gazes matched, he said, "I want you back at night." His eyelids lowered until all she saw was a narrow, glinting gaze. "More. I want you in my bed for real."

Suddenly the wine wasn't cool liquid on her tongue, but fiery in her belly. She could match him. "Yes."

His fingers sifted through her hair, then his palm rested on her cheek. "How lovely you are."

The words came out of her mouth without thought. "My coloring isn't golden."

He flinched and pulled his fingers away.

Stup! She looked away, turned to stare determinedly at the ocean that roared in her ears. "Apologies." She shook her head, hard, so foolish tears should fly from them. "I should not have said that. I don't know why I did." She drank from her glass, didn't look at him as she continued, "With any bond will come . . . affection, I suppose. The ability to hurt and be hurt. Again, I'm sorry."

Breath huffed from between his teeth. "We have a past . . . moment."

Camellia figured they had more than one, but shut up and only said, "Yes."

"Nivea Sunflower was beautiful to me." It was a statement and Camellia frowned as she weighed it. No great emotion, no flatness, just a quiet statement of the past, as if he'd said, "The sky was pretty and blue."

He set his glass down on the windowsill, framed her face in his hands. "She was beautiful to me, but you are lovely, and that is so much more."

She blinked in confusion, and he smiled. "Hers was a breathtaking surface beauty. Your expressions, your character make you so much more. Lovely. Intriguing."

Camellia let out a breath at the bomb they'd managed to navigate around. "Oh. Good."

"And your coloring . . . I like it very much."

"Your eyes are fabulous," she offered. "Mmmm."

He laughed. "I think you're getting a little giddy. Let's see what kind of food we have in the picnic basket." He held up one hand, palm out. "I promise there are no antique sandwiches. I requested turkbird breast and spiced-yolk hard-boiled eggs."

"Oh, I love those but dislike making them."

"So I heard from Mica, who also seems to love them." His smile flashed. "But I have a chef, so I only have to request and it is mine."

Camellia lifted her nose. "I have *two* chefs."

"Yes, but I'm sure you wouldn't give them orders for your personal meal."

With a roll of the shoulder in agreement, Camellia said, "Maybe not."

They ate greedily with their fingers, laughing and getting to know each other. He told her stories of his apprentice, Jasmine Ash. Camellia responded with tales of getting the HouseHeart up and running. The talk segued to business, of upcoming technologies, as they walked on the beach. Camellia left her shoes and liners on a seatlike rock, unbuttoned the cuffs of her trous and rolled them up to her knee, said a "stay up" spell.

The ocean was wonderful, the sound of the surf thumping through her like a scour, rubbing away care.

She and Laev held hands and it was marvelous.

Later they returned to the pavilion, finishing up the last of the springreen wine and enjoying the atmosphere of the moment. All that they were to each other that they didn't want to admit enveloped them like a prickling mist.

Laev tipped his glass against hers and a crystal note sounded. A smile lurked on his lips. "Lovers."

"Lovers," she whispered. She drank, knew her emotions were churned up enough to affect her taste, and set her glass aside on the windowsill. She took one of his hands in her own and quivered inwardly. She wanted those hands skimming down her body, wanted her own on his. "I don't think I am brave enough to make love with you in a Residence."

He frowned.

She said, "So I'd like to invite you to my home tonight."

His eyes widened. His hand turned in hers and he lifted her palm to his lips, pressed a kiss in the hollow of her hand, a caress of tongue that went straight to her sex.

"Thank you."

He was good at the sophisticated moves. She let a sigh filter out as she looked at his face, thought that she would be watching that face and all Laev's expressions in bed tonight. A gift fate had given her that she would finally enjoy with a light heart because of the understanding between them. Easing forward, she kissed his mouth gently, felt the connection between them form deeper with the touch of lips.

"The cats can show you how to teleport to my home." Then she recalled the men of her Family. "Please promise me that you will always use the teleportation pad."

With a lift of his brows, he said, "Since you or Mica might be moving around the house, of course."

"Of course."

"What time?" he asked, voice husky.

A flush rose along her neck and face. "NightBell?"

Again he kissed her fingers. "NightBell it is."

"I have dinner with my friends several times a week," she said.

He nodded. "Understood. But we will also meet at the Green Knight some evenings for the open melees."

"That's right."

"We'll keep it slow and easy," he said.

"Yes. One more thing." She didn't look at him. "During Second and Third Passages . . ." They were being so delicate, and she liked that, didn't want to confront any inescapable knowledge head-on. But it made choosing words difficult. She sipped in a breath and continued, "It's a time when some people make a HeartGift."

His hand tightened hard on her fingers. Everyone knew that Laev had given his HeartGift to Nivea. Everyone.

No one but Laev and Nivea knew what had happened during their wedding night when they tried to HeartBond, and Camellia shoved the thought aside. She didn't want him to give her his Heart-Gift. "I've heard that such objects have peculiar properties."

Like igniting such lust in the HeartMates that they had sex right then and there, HeartBonded then and there. She didn't want that happening to her—to them. Was it wrong to be thinking of mostly herself, even now? She didn't know. Didn't know too much. She'd have to come to understand him and herself and this relationship better before she moved forward with her heart instead of listening to her head. "I'm not sure I would care to receive such a gift," she said.

Twenty-three

$\mathcal{N}$*o." Just one word, but stilted. He obviously didn't want to talk about* the HeartGift. He dropped her hand. Despair curled in her, she'd insulted and offended him. She still didn't want to be less than obscure, so she met his eyes, and slowly, carefully, bit by tiny bit, she opened the bond between them to the widest. He would feel, then, that she didn't mean any offense.

She met his eyes.

He was frowning, then staring, and he angled his head as if listening.

Then he touched her again, easily, as if he had the right—as if she'd granted him the right simply by opening the bond. His forefinger traced between her eyes. "You have a line, here. Don't be so concerned." He smiled and it seemed as if she'd never seen such a smile from him before. A special smile for her? Her alone? Her chest tightened and the backs of her eyes stung at the very thought that she'd receive a smile shaped for her alone.

His lips turned down. "And that's worse." He shook his head. "I can feel your worry." His hand went to her chin now, made sure her gaze matched with his. "I don't think there's anything we can say or do that would be wrong between us."

She stared at him. She hadn't heard anything so stupid in her life. Of course he could hurt her more than anyone. But she said nothing, just wrenched her gaze away from the depths of his eyes

and scrambled for more indirect words. "My—our—my circumstances . . . that is, when I had my Second and Third Passages, I
didn't feel, I mean I didn't *act* on the urge to, um, work with my
creative Flair."

Again his face went immobile, but she felt the spurt of disap-
pointment from him. He'd understood that she'd made no Heart-
Gift to give to him, would never be claiming him by giving him a
HeartGift.

He leaned away. "What is your creative Flair?"

"Flair manifests the gifts of a person, the personality, the interests," she babbled, covering renewed disappointment.

Waving that away, he said, "I know."

She shrugged. "I don't have a separate creative Flair. I mix teas,
blend different herbs and spices and tea and caff or whatever—"
Her gesture wasn't nearly as graceful as his had been, nor did she
think her smile was as pleasing. "I'm also good with cooking recipes."

"Mmmm. One of my favorite pleasures."

He stood and drew her to him, into his space, close enough that
his chest was just brushing her breasts, and the slight pressure had
her sex clenching. He knew her reaction to him because his eye-
lashes lowered and his smile turned dangerous. Spiraling sparks of
desire came from him to her through their bond.

He bent his head and their breaths mingled and his lips glided
against hers, once, twice, teasing her before his mouth settled on
hers and his tongue probed.

She let him in, more, she closed her eyes and savored his mouth,
his taste, and leaned against him.

Why hadn't she done this before? The feel of his body against
hers was superb. Taller than she, broader, stronger. His muscles
long and lean, virile, male. Then one of his arms was behind her
back, arching her toward him and she strained to match her body
with his. He was hard and desire bloomed and she was needy.

The fingers of his other hand slid along the back of her neck and
more nerves blossomed with desire. She whimpered and rubbed

against him, glorying in the rising passion. Knowing he could fulfill her.

And it wouldn't be only in dreams.

The notion was so delicious that she let all thought fall away. Her hands went to the tabs of his shirt at the shoulders and she peeled it down, letting her fingers roam on his back, enjoying the flex of muscle under skin.

Then air came between them and his lips were ruddy and he was panting, as she was. He lifted his hands and snapped a Word of command and they were nude.

He was the most beautiful man she'd ever seen. Nothing mattered but staring at him, at the lines of his shoulders, his waist, his thighs, at his need for her. Her knees went weak, wobbled.

With that devilish smile, he swung her into his arms. "Wha—" she managed, too many things making her dizzy, but mostly sheer, winding passion. Skin against skin was almost more than she could bear. Mind sex with him had been fabulous, but she hadn't known what she was missing. Small details like the rub of his chest hair against her, his soft breath on her cheek. Details that she might have imagined, but were true physical sensation now.

She was awash in pleasure. Every whisk of his fingertips was delight.

One fluid turn and she was lowered to the window seat, felt the sun-warmed cushions against her back. She grabbed the edge for balance and found that both seat and cushion had extended.

Plenty of room for sex now.

Her mind spun and her head was weak and the spring light coming through the wide and fancy windows dazzled. She shut her eyes, but then she couldn't see him and she needed to see him, the colors of him.

The ruddy sexual flush on lips and cheeks, the rise and fall of his chest with the swirl of black hair, the controlled wildness in his eyes darkened to purple. Yes, she needed to see all that, to feel this joining was right in her entire being.

She lifted her arms and he smiled and she saw white teeth and yearned to feel them on her, shocking her.

He stood over her, then sat next to her, both of his hands reaching for her chest, then his hands were on her breasts, her nipples caught between his fingers as he shaped her, and the slight sensations combined into an increasing coil of desire, winding her tight. He bent down and once again she arched, aching for his mouth on her.

And again he surprised her, kissing her lips, opening her mouth with his as his fingers stroked and rubbed and she went hot and wet with passion and yearning.

He moved, angled his body, and thrust into her, and she cried out, her arms clamping around his back. So good!

Together. They were truly together and the slide of him, inside and out, was so much more intense in reality. Their hearts pounded, but began to beat in the same rhythm. Her moans matched his groans. And the scent of him and the sound of him and the taste of him . . . Laev filled her world until they exploded with ecstasy.

Slowly her wits coalesced, as if they'd been spread through the atmosphere and sank back into a ball in her head.

He was heavy on her, and she didn't mind that, much, but though the benches beneath the windows of the pavilion were wide, they weren't at all like a bed. Odd that in their shared fantasies they'd always made love—had sex—on a bed.

"Ummm," she murmured, words still locked in her brain and not falling to her lips.

He pushed her hair back, smiled with a tenderness that made her uncomfortable, then held her tight. Seconds later she was being teleported and found herself on a soft blanket on the beach.

Gasping, she thumped him on the back and he rolled off her, laughing. Before she could catch her breath, he picked her up again, then ran across the sand to the ocean. She screamed as the cold water hit her, fought to escape his hold, and swallowed salt water as she slipped from his grip.

"You. Are. Crazy!" she panted, bare feet striving for purchase.

"Just getting us clean." He held her tightly enough that she knew he'd keep her safe, but let her find her feet. He seemed at ease in the water. With a quick spell couplet, he'd created a bubble of warm air around them and they walked out, his arm around her waist.

As soon as they reached the beach, he translocated not only their clothes but some huge, thick towels. She'd been planning to do an air-dry spell, but liked it when he picked up the soft cloth and wrapped it around her, pulling her to him and nibbling her lips with little kisses.

"I hadn't planned on our discussion reaching this conclusion, so soon," he murmured. "I'm hungry again." His smile flashed. "For food."

Once again he gestured, muttered a phrase or two, and the basket appeared on the equally large blanket. He began patting her dry with the towel, but now she was a little shy and took the task over. "You need to dry yourself before you take a chill."

He laughed. "FatherSire and Father and I did sea plunges weekly from the beginning of spring to midautumn."

"Tough men, the Hawthorns." She took advantage of him briskly drying his head and hair to slip into her clothes. After that, she felt more at ease with him. She wouldn't pretend that sex between them hadn't happened, exactly, but was content to keep the mood light, as if this were a passing affair.

He'd wanted to treat it as a passing affair, hadn't he?

She was fine with that.

"No food that I don't like," Laev said. He'd dressed, too, and was spreading wonderful-looking stuff out on the blanket, all with a small spell to keep dirt and bugs out. Such Flair, and used so casually. She wasn't used to it.

"One thing we didn't discuss." Laev sat beside her, picked up a piece of cheese on a cracker, and offered it to her. The touch of his fingers against hers felt sweet.

"A lot of things we haven't discussed," Camellia said, then

popped the food into her mouth. She recognized the nutty-tasting cheese, wonderful and too expensive for her personal budget.

"How serious do you want this affair to be?"

Camellia choked, forced the now tasteless cheese down her throat.

Laev thumped her back until she was breathing easily. Then he put his hand on her chin and turned her head to meet his amused gaze. "Yes, me, too. Not serious."

Breath whooshed from her. "No, not serious."

"But if we're seen a lot together, particularly by people who know our circumstances . . ."

"From the way I was treated at tea, I think some of your Family and Residence might have guessed," she said.

"There will be considerable pressure for us to formalize our connection."

The very thought of watching eyes, gossip, rumors, made her want to leap to her feet and run. Since the link between them was wide open and the flow of emotion back and forth told her that he was in agreement with her, she stayed where she was. "No," she said. "We've . . . just met. I'm not ready for more."

"No," he agreed. "I want to be private with you. Not ready for more." He kissed her temple. "My Family and Residence would have huge expectations, what of your friends?"

"They might tease. Tiana—the priestess—might push a little. Glyssa—the librarian—will be curious, but on the whole they would leave us to be ourselves."

"Nice."

"They are. Very." She thought of something else, smiled wryly. "I'll be changing my sparring schedule with Lemongrass back to what it was."

"He's an amiable man," Laev said.

"Yes."

There were yowls, then two cats were there, nosing around their plates and the basket. Mica hopped onto Camellia's lap. *When do We move into Brazos's Residence?* demanded Mica.

When will the architect come to remodel Our rooms? I want a bigger room! stated Brazos.

I want a room bigger than Brazos's.

You can't have that. MY FamMan is GREATLORD! Brazos said.

I can! Mica insisted.

"However," Camellia said drily, "our Fams may be a problem."

"Quiet!" Laev commanded.

The cats sat and stared at him. He'd taken on the manner of the highest Nobleman. A tingle of wariness slid over Camellia's skin. Definitely not ready to give up her independence. Only ready to explore sex with Laev, and some time out of bed with him.

Laev continued, "Camellia and Mica will be staying in her house. Brazos and I will be at T'Hawthorn Residence. We will take this association very slowly."

But you are HeartMates! Mica complained.

Laev's jaw went hard. "We will *not* be using that word." With a gesture, Mica vanished with a screech.

Brazos growled, then he, too, vanished.

"Sent them outside the estate pigsty," Laev said, then, "I apologize. I should not have teleported your Fam away."

"Apology accepted," Camellia said. "It's a lot quieter without them." She added thoughtfully, "And I think only a demonstration would have shut them up."

"And keep them in line," Laev said.

"I suppose so."

He rolled until they were face-to-face. "This is new to me."

"Me, too."

Inclining his head, he smiled, then said, "Slow."

"Slow," she agreed.

"Private."

"Private," she repeated. Again with the terms, but since they were in accord, she didn't mind.

"Which means discreet." He pushed hair away from her face. "And that means a little planning if we want to be together but keep gossip and expectations at a minimum. Open your mouth." Again he held cheese on a tiny cracker. This time the wafer had poppy seeds and the cheese had streaks of wine.

She ate the bite and chewed slowly, humming with pleasure. He offered her more wine and the clash and complementary tastes made her close her eyes to savor. She sighed at the pleasure of the moment.

When she lifted her lashes, she saw his intent gaze focused on her. And a blush heated her cheeks as she noticed a flush of desire along his cheekbones.

He leaned toward her and kissed her, and they were falling over on the blanket and the scent of herbs from the soft cloth and the ocean and the summer flowers made her dizzy.

Or maybe it was just Laev.

He rolled back and took her with him, and she could feel that his body wasn't exactly in "planning an affair" mode. More like acting.

"Plenty of time and ways to figure out being discreet," she murmured, kissing him on the mouth, sliding along him so their sexes met.

He groaned. "Plenty of times and ways to have sex."

And that was the last time they spoke.

Later, they sat and fed each other and it was easy and so lovely her heart hurt. A good beginning to an affair.

*T*he rest of the week, they met every night, usually made love in her house, though once it was at the pavilion and once on the beach itself. She was achingly happy at the newness of an attentive lover.

On the morning of Playday, when she was talking to customers in Darjeeling's Teahouse, her perscry in her sleeve pocket jingled the small lilting tune she'd assigned to Laev. She excused herself to return to her office, closed her door, and sat behind her desk.

She knew she was wearing a silly smile when she answered, "Here."

"Greetyou, dearest."

The affectionate term warmed. No one had ever called her one with true affection.

"Greetyou."

"I called to ask you to the Birches' party tonight."

A FirstFamily party. That stopped her lungs. But she pushed enough breath out to say, "Discreet?"

He smiled and his eyes sparkled. "That's the fun of it. A masquerade party."

All the romantic images such words conjured tumbled through her head. Scented gardens under a sky of glowing twinmoons and blazing stars. Laev as a handsome stranger who made the blood pulse hot in her veins . . . her lover masked and dangerously seductive.

Fun, eating, dancing, and more. It was the *more* as well as the mystery that appealed the most.

He looked so pleased! Was being around people as a couple important to him? She wasn't even used to being a couple. That would take a few months. Sadly she realized she'd never been a couple with anyone, only a part of a good-friends trio.

Even as she watched, the pleasure was dimming from his eyes, the lines in his face getting more serious. Had he offered amusements to Nivea and she'd turned them down? Of course.

Hurt slithered through Camellia that he'd been with another woman. That Camellia kept thinking of Nivea. That Nivea had hurt Laev.

Camellia had just better get used to accepting there would be twinges of pain as they tried things as a couple for the first time. Did things they might have with other lovers.

"You surprised me. Thanks for the invitation," she said, beginning to think of what she could wear.

"But?"

"But nothing. I want to go."

Delight flashed in his eyes, but his smile was slower, approving, lingering. "Wear something sexy."

She raised her brows. "You, too."

"I'll come by with a glider—"

"No, I'll meet you there. I'd like to arrive separately . . . your mysterious date." She bobbed her eyebrows but was thinking rapidly. Noble Country. The public carriers didn't go through that part of town very often.

His smile moved into a grin. "I'll send a glider for you."

"What?" She stared.

He shrugged. "I bought a couple of new ones. No coat of arms on the doors. Smallish, two seaters. Pretty much fully automated." He lowered his lids and smoldered. "I am at the Birches on the portico when a masked, beautiful woman steps from the glider . . ."

Oh, they were into the game of the masquerade already.

". . . I am dazzled. For the night. Forever."

He was moving pretty damn fast, being swept up in the romance of dreams. He'd had such dreams once, she knew, had tried to fulfill them. For her, relationship dreams had always been illusions and fantasies.

"All right," she whispered. "What time?"

"The glider should reach your house by DinnerBell. The ride to the Birches will take twenty minutes."

"Where you'll be waiting."

"Oh, yeah." He picked up a piece of papyrus. "I have the invitation." His lips pursed in a small kiss. "Later."

"Later."

Ooooh, the Birches. Mica grinned wide and slicked a paw over her ear. *Brazos is going, too. Invitation only for Fams.* She flexed her whiskers, groomed them. *We don't often get to explore Birches. They have spellshields against Fams.*

"Is that so?"

Yes. There was an unfortunate incident with a dog.

"Ah. Want me to make sure Laev knows that you'll be coming?"

Brazos will tell him.

"All right."

I think there is a fishpond.

"High excitement."

"Yesss."

Throughout the rest of the day, Camellia had to forcibly wrench her mind back to her tasks—and she had a conference with her managers telling them that she was working on a new project and would be in the teahouses less.

Aquilaria retorted that she hoped the project was male, it was about time. And her other manager stated that having a gallant looked good on Camellia. She flushed but said nothing more, just smiled through the rest of the discussion about scheduling. Then, her worries eased about the functioning of her business, and on a surge of exuberance, she and Mica teleported to Clovers' Fine Furniture.

Once there, they swept into the shop and over to the wardrobes, and stopped. The one Camellia had liked in the window was still there, but it had an additional box attachment specifically for Fams along with a quilted pillow on the top. She and Mica oohed and aahed together, and a salesman convinced them to special-order one. They settled on a different piece with a bit more fancy carving. Out of Mica's hearing, Camellia ordered special knobs that stymied FamCats. She had no intention of coming home one day and finding Mica settled on an inner shelf where she intended to keep her silkeen shawls.

That evening she ate sparsely, wanting nothing too heavy in her stomach, her excitement was so great. She'd considered various different costumes and finally decided to wear an outfit that she'd purchased for a Bright Brigid's Day fair a couple of years ago. It was a long dress with no trous and no long sleeve pockets. Instead, the sleeves were slightly bloused with tight wrists. Over the dress, she wore a traditional cook's apron that was rarely seen outside any kitchen. It had a large bib, was tied in the back with strings, and had a series of different-sized pockets around the waist. The dress itself was a light beige, the apron a darker brown. She also had an ancient chef's hat in dark brown.

At the fair, she'd brought packets of blended teas and various flatsweets that would complement the drinks. It had been a month after she'd opened up Darjeeling's Teahouse, and giving away the tea and flatsweets had been extremely good advertising.

From a drawer, she'd riffled through the few masks she had and found a simple black one that covered her upper face and molded over her nose. Perfect.

She was bathed and dressed and sitting in her mainspace waiting for the glider to come when Mica gave a little cough.

Camellia looked down at her Fam. "Yes."

I have no costume.

Twenty-four

❦

"Y ou're a calico cat," Camellia said to Mica. "You always look like you have a costume on."

Mica sniffed and Camellia knew that her answer had not been sufficient. She could be dramatic, too. She let her breath out in a long-suffering sigh. "What do you think would be a costume for you? Especially if you consider that you might be fishing in a pond?" Camellia narrowed her eyes. "I've seen some really cute little Fam-Cat hats."

No. Collar.

Camellia indulged in another sigh. "We've had this conversation. No Fam collar yet."

I would like a collar with a feather.

A small sense of warning had Camellia's neck tingling. "Have you already found this collar?"

It's almost made. With a whistling breath, Mica translocated a glittery gold garter and a fat blue feather. She'd been observant when Camellia had opened her small costume chest. The garter would never grace Camellia's thigh over leggings again. She glanced at the timer. "We might just get this done for you before the glider comes." Working fast, she measured the gold sequined garter around Mica's neck, attached the blue feather that curled over the cat's head, and mended the edges with Flair.

Then Camellia referred to D'Ash's instruction holosphere, met

Mica's gleaming eyes, and said, "If the collar gets caught on any-thing, it will fall off and you will lose it."

Mica smiled wide, showing pointy teeth. *You are the BEST FamWoman EVER.*

"Thank you."

A few loud notes sounded from outside the front door and Camellia picked her cat up, opened and closed the door with a few Words, and set the spellshields. The glider gleamed an elegant dark blue and the door lifted at the touch of Camellia's fingers. There was only one cushiony bench, and she put Mica in first, slid in, and pulled the door closed.

The glider smoothly accelerated and they were off to adventure and romance!

Dark fell as they rode to T'Birch's estate. Camellia had second thoughts about her costume. It wasn't sexy . . . unless she took off the dress and only wore the apron, and that would be scandalous. But once they were alone after the party, that might be an option. She had the feeling that Laev might think so.

When they arrived, the greeniron gates were open and the glider continued to the front portico of the Residence. Camellia got more nervous. She definitely was dressed as a middle-class or lower noble would be. Which she essentially was. She had no idea how richly others would be dressed, except she knew that appearances were always important to the Birches.

Then the glider pulled up to the front of the Residence, directly behind a huge old Family vehicle that sat rocking gently on its land-ing stands. Five men and women dressed in Birch livery a century out of date—Birch Family and staff members—helped the occupants of the first vehicle out. Both wore long, enveloping thin scarlet robes over their clothes in lieu of a costume and large feathered masks.

Ooooh, Mica said. *I would like a feather or two from those.*

"I thought you were more interested in collecting fish," Camellia said.

Mica ignored her and leapt out the moment the door raised, slinking with cat sinuosity, and sped away into the night.

"Invitation," grated a large man who appeared more guardsman than greeter, holding out his hand.

"Let me help you, lady," said Laev, and handed the Birch guard the heavy piece of papyrus. "For the lady and the FamCat. Also my FamCat and myself." His intonation was slightly archaic.

"As you say, sir." The man bowed himself away.

"And what have we here, a maiden?" Laev asked, offering his own hand. "Perhaps in need of a gallant escort?"

He'd dressed sexy. Camellia's breath caught. Light gleamed dully on his narrow-legged black leather trous and black leather vest, his hair slicked back in a style she vaguely recalled seeing in history vizes. He wore no shirt underneath the vest. The lack of it only emphasized the beauty of the body she'd seen naked. He wore a black half mask, too. On each hip were blazers in functional holsters. Something about the practical grips sent a chill down her. They weren't toys.

Camellia extended her own hand to Laev, and he took her fingertips and placed them on his arm. A jolt of sensuality rushed straight to her core, and she suppressed a gasp.

He smiled as if he'd felt and welcomed the same sensation. When she got out, he didn't move aside, so she brushed against him. His teeth showed white and even as his smile widened. She stepped away and he followed, still within millimeters of her body. With an arrogant jerk of his head, he signaled to one of the greeters to tend to the glider.

His aura surrounded her. He'd used a different fragrance, one with more musk, and she became aware that her clothes smelled of the honey she'd used when baking the flatsweets. Though only the tips of her fingers on his arm connected them, they moved up the stairs in step.

Once they were in the great hall of the Residence, the muscles under his arm shifted, and he took the lead, always keeping pace with her. He guided her down the hallway toward double doors, where two more members of the Family stood in Birch livery of white and vibrant spring green. Voices and the sound of musicians tuning their instruments floated from the room.

All the nerves Camellia had had about a FirstFamily ball vanished, muffled under the pure sensuality of being with Laev. Only he mattered, his closeness, his scent, the shadow of his body slanting over hers.

She tried to pull her mind from the daze, but being with Laev, in public, at a ball given by the highest sticklers of the FirstFamilies was a fantasy.

Then he was bowing before the Birches, and Camellia was sinking into a curtsey . . . one not so low as to give away her own meager rank. She was on Laev's arm, after all.

D'Birch's gaze was locked on the delineation of Laev's chest. "What kind of costume is that?" She didn't seem to hear her own rude words.

"Shooting costume," T'Birch said, eyeing the blazers. No doubt he could tell they were real, too. "Two centuries ago, FirstFamily bucks liked to show off their muscles." He flexed his arm and his wife, who had her hand tucked into his elbow, glanced from under her lashes to him. "I'd love to see you in something like that."

T'Birch reddened a little but smiled. When his wife turned back to them, her gaze cooled as she looked at Camellia. "A . . . cook? How quaint."

Camellia smiled mysteriously and responded, "Everyone knows that the original D'Cherry was a baker." The Cherrys were prominent in the news because they and the Elecampanes were excavating the lost starship, *Lugh's Spear*. And Camellia hadn't actually claimed she was a Cherry, just stated a fact.

Laev's hard arm went around her waist and she swallowed, focused again on him.

"The next dance is a waltz, I believe. I'd like to waltz with my prize."

The GreatLord snorted and waved them away. The music changed, and within two strides she was in Laev's arms, her body whirling as much as her mind. He held her close and felt incredible against her. "Ah, lady," he whispered huskily in her ear. "I don't want to spend much time in the light with you."

Her pulse quickened and her heart thumped hard.

"Say you will walk in the gardens with me. Find a sacred grove, look at the stars."

Around and around they went, entwined like dancers atop a music box. She couldn't miss a step in this perfect dream.

"It's warm in here, don't you think?" Laev said.

She'd never really concentrated on the shape and fullness of his lips, but now that they were accented by the half mask, they beckoned. She wanted to nibble on them, test their texture, and pull the taste of his mouth, his taste at that particular point, deep inside herself. Learn all his tastes.

The taste of him would change through the seasons. The thought jangled distant warning, which she ignored as he danced her out the door and onto the terrace.

There were a few other people there—a clump of men talking, a couple swaying and whispering to the music instead of dancing, an older couple matching steps and swirling faster even than Laev and herself—Cratag and Signet Marigold.

Laev and she reached steep stairs. One minute they were at the top, then, with a small flex of Flair, they were at the bottom, still in step. The music faded from her hearing, replaced by the sway of top branches in a breeze, the rustle of leaves, and the distant song of a trickling stream, only faintly accented by the murmur of voices from the Residence.

One last turn and their arms were linked and they were walking down a path of crushed stone. The scent of cleansing herbs came from it and the gardens beyond the hedges. Fluting, haunting music wafted in the air. Camellia glanced at Laev, saw the small muscles around his mouth relax in surprise. He looked at her, tugged on her hand, and a few steps later, they strode into an open garden with other couples listening to the music. Again there was dancing, this mostly free-form by individuals. Around the circular space were rustic stone benches. Laev picked up his pace and ran his palm warm against her own and she followed. They slipped onto a bench just before another couple. Laughter erupted, and that was the best sound of all.

After a tapping toe and pouting lip from the younger lady of the couple, the older one drew her partner into the center of the circle to dance.

Laev brought Camellia's and his linked hands to his lips, brushed light kisses over hers. "And so I have procured a seat for my lady, and not just any seat." His free hand lifted and swept the horizon, and Camellia looked at something other than he. Her breath caught in her throat. Atop a low rise ahead of them was a sacred stone circle, large gray vertical plinths linked with horizontal slabs in sets of three.

Black against the night sky, the stars in the spaces between seemed to beckon as portals to other worlds. The twinmoons showed bright and waning silver crescents above them.

The hidden flautist wove eerie beats, the dancers blurred, becoming colorful sweeps of cloth and feathered masks.

She leaned against Laev and didn't think a moment had ever been so perfect.

Finally, the last note sounded and the dancers collapsed in giggling heaps on the ground. Laev turned to her and kissed her lips, softly, gently, tenderly.

The taste of his mouth was more heady than the moons and stars, whirled her senses more than watching the dancers. Drew her into lands more tempting and mysterious than the starry portals embraced by stone.

His fingers brushed her jaw and his mouth opened and darkness seemed to envelop her until there was only the taste of his tongue sweeping into her mouth and the throbbing need of her sex.

As he withdrew, she sucked on his tongue and tasted wine.

Meeting her eyes, he said, "Lady, you undo me. Unravel my control." His breathing was ragged. "I cannot do what I want with you here and now."

She smiled as if she were primal woman herself, seducing a man.

With a hitched breath, he dropped her hands and shifted away, angling his body to the front.

A fiddler stepped into the circle and the dancers rose from the ground, shaking their costumes out, turning to face the sweet song of bow across strings.

Laev swallowed, then deliberately relaxed beside her, though a glance from under her lashes showed her that he was still aroused. Camellia smiled.

The tune became lively and couples on the bench flung themselves into the dance circle, trading places with those who wanted to sit and watch.

Linking fingers with her again, Laev smiled, and she knew that deliberately charming smile, but it still stirred her heart in her chest. "I have brought my lady pleasure?"

A twinge of sheer desire speared through her at the edgy rumble of his voice.

When she didn't answer, he kissed their twined fingers again, murmured, "I danced with her, and walked with her, and led her to this magic place to experience many things." His eyes showed the amusement of his smile.

She cleared her throat. "Yes," she whispered.

He leaned close, until she felt the warmth of his body deliciously slide all along her torso.

"Then please tell me," he whispered, paused.

"Yes?" She was dazzled by him.

"That you have flatsweets in your pockets."

She jerked back, and only his grip on her hand kept her from falling off the bench.

His head tilted as laughter roared from his throat, and he was beautiful. She could only laugh, too, and use the Flair of her shooting pulse, his surging delight, the ambient Flair of the dancers, and the amusement of the fiddler to translocate a box of two dozen flatsweets from her home pantry.

When he stopped laughing, she said. "No."

He gasped, frowning.

She took the box from the far side of the bench and placed it on her lap, opened it, and the scent of sweet and flour and honey and cocoa rose.

The fiddle stopped on a long sweep and the man was the first in line.

Laev dug into the box and took out a handful of thin flatsweets, stuffed half a one in his mouth.

With a charming smile, the fiddler asked, "Any with cocoa bits in there?"

Camellia turned the box around for the man to peruse. He took two flatsweets with dark cocoa bits, stuffed one in his trous pocket. "Hungry work, fiddling," he said.

She laughed.

The next in line was a middle-aged woman with purple hair and a plump stomach. She chose a curved and powdered almond crescent, popped it into her mouth, closed her eyes, and hummed with pleasure. The tall man behind her drew her close to him and smiled at Camellia. "Anything in there with raisins?"

"Maybe," Camellia said, held out the box.

Sniffing, the woman finished chewing, then announced in a carrying voice, "I know these flatsweets. They come from Darjeeling's Teahouse." She narrowed her eyes at Camellia.

"Maybe," Camellia repeated.

"Or maybe Darjeeling's HouseHeart," Laev said. "Plenty of good food"—he glanced at the fiddler—"and good ambience at both."

Golden. The moment was golden. Her lover praising her craft. Camellia blinked back tears.

"We'll have to go there"—the tall man drew the woman away—"but now more . . . dancing." He nodded at the fiddler, who grinned and returned to the middle of the circle, where someone had placed a carved and polished tree stump with a thick green pillow on top.

Soon the flatsweets were gone. Laev translocated the box and whirled her into the dance. Then the tune became a circle dance and all linked hands and they spun faster and faster, until the music abruptly ended and Laev pulled her into the darkness of trees. He pushed her against a thick-boled oak and she scented summer growth. His mouth took hers and his hands went behind her to curve over her butt and they were center to center and she used her breath to moan.

He grasped her wrists to link them behind his neck, wrapped his arms tight around her back. An instant later they weren't in a grove on the Birches' estate, but encircled by rocks on a beach. Spume broke around them, and it seemed the surf beat against the rocks in the same pulses as her heartbeat—hers and Laev's heartbeats.

Then they were on the damp sand and their clothes were gone and he gleamed pale and was in her and all the stars in the universe danced around them as they shattered together into space.

And when a wave broke over them and cleansed them and brought the scent and the salty taste of the sea, Camellia used the dazzling Flair all around them to teleport them to her bed.

Laev woke just before dawn, snuggled with Camellia. She felt very good in his arms, against his body. Of course his shaft rose, but he treasured these rare moments of stillness with her. He liked her vulnerability now, the softness of her with no edges, no haunted wariness in her eyes.

This was very good. He tried not to think that it would have been better if they'd found each other earlier.

The past was past and it seemed to him that the greeniron gates that had locked the future away had opened a crack.

Cherish the present and the warm woman, the loving they shared, the laughter. Lady and Lord knew she challenged him. He'd spent a day with her at her tearooms and was amazed at her energy, how her sharp eyes and even sharper mind noted and fixed problems while he was still soaking in the atmosphere.

Her office in Darjeeling's Teahouse had been retinted, the furniture replaced.

He had invested in a restaurant and a social club before and knew how hard it was for the businesses to survive. Camellia made it look easy. Of course, her food was great, and it was obvious that she loved her work.

His mind drifted to the night before, when joy had pulsed through her—through them both—cycling through their link. She'd been a different woman, open and flirting. The connection with her had been amazing, the largest expansion of the golden cord between them. Even now, in sleep, the bond had contracted from what it had been in the night under the stars.

And he was fighting the urge to push. Who knew that he'd want more intimacy so soon? He'd like to spend more time with her. At odd moments, he'd considered mentioning the second office next to his ResidenceDen. She needed a place outside her businesses to work—for her next expansion idea. Drawings and holos that were neatly stacked in piles on the small table in a corner of her mainspace.

But she wasn't progressing in this relationship as fast as he was.

She stretched and her body rubbed against his and his lust spiked. Then she rolled over and angled her head back and smiled up at him. He realized it was just light enough to see her rosy cheeks and her eyes that were the gray of a depthless ocean. She had mysteries enough for him to explore for a lifetime or several. He wanted that.

"Mmmm." She kissed his chin.

Pleased satisfaction throbbed through Camellia. She'd given and taken ecstasy from this man last night, then provided him with a good place to sleep.

She could give more.

The thought surprised her. With her father and uncle, she supposed it was natural for her to think *give* and *take* between herself and men, and maybe keep a tally. She'd have to work on that. But she'd never felt so generous.

Laev yawned and made a morning grunt and she smiled. Her man. Her lover. Her—no, man and lover were quite enough for now. His lavender eyes stared into hers and her heart seemed to expand and envelope her in dangerous love.

She swallowed, would have drawn away, but his fingers wrapped around her wrist and she couldn't stuff the love back into herself or behind a door. Not ever again, and she was afraid.

He had her now, but didn't know it yet. She couldn't allow him to discover that.

"Good morning." He smiled.

"Good morning," she croaked. He shifted and the scent of him, man with an elusive floral fragrance—and wouldn't he be embarrassed by that?—slid around her. She was torn between two primal impulses. To withdraw, run away. Or to open to the love, be generous to him, and to herself.

Twenty-five

$\mathcal{L}$aev lifted her hand to his mouth and kissed her fingertips. "Pretty Camellia."

"Thank you." Yes, all her feelings were expanding like their bond and she *needed* to give with an open heart. "Laev, what are your favorite foods?"

Blinking, she saw his mind engage. "Why?"

She leaned over and kissed him on the mouth, swept her tongue over his lips. "Because I want you to come to dinner. Because I want to cook for you."

Now his eyes were wide, he grabbed a large pillow from the floor and shoved it behind his back. His gaze gleamed. "You're going to cook for me?"

"Yes."

"Not just pull something from the no-time."

She just shook her head. "How do you think the no-times get stocked? *Someone* has to cook and put the meals inside the food storage at the proper temperature, hot or cold."

He laughed. "Sounds like you've said those words before."

"I have." She moved to sit cross-legged. "I make dinners for my friends, and the Licorice Family, and occasionally send dishes home with Tiana to the Mugworts."

"The FirstFamilies have chefs," Laev said, as if that was news. "So we usually eat fresh. But I'm sure they stock the no-time food

255

storage units, too. I think a couple of my older female cuzes make some of the ritual foods so that offerings to the Lady and Lord are done by Family hands." His brows drew together. "But I think they consider that more of a duty than a pleasure."

"Um-hmm," Camellia said. "Back to my original question. What's your favorite food?"

He licked his lips. "What if it's fancy?"

"I can do fancy."

"Sure." He stacked his hands behind his head, considered, slid his gaze to her. "Whatever I like the best?"

"That's right, though if it's overly fancy, I'll have to shop and cook, it won't be dinner tonight."

"Hmm. A trade-off between time and quality," he said. "Or, um, time and extra effort." He closed his eyes again. After a moment he opened his lashes and his purple gaze met hers. "Spring greens salad, traditional Beltane clucker stew, and strawberry wine–infused strawberries with white cocoa mousse."

The menu made her own mouth water. "I have some Beltane stew broth left from the holiday," she said. "The other items are available. But I like to cook my stew all day, and it's best if the strawberries soak up the wine for a couple of septhours, too. Why don't we say dinner here tomorrow night?"

"Why don't we?" He rolled over and took her into his arms. "And an appetizer this morning."

She pushed against him, and with a puzzled look, he let her go. Kneeling beside him, she slid his black hair back from his face. "Let me give to you." There, the words were out of her mouth. Though Laev might not know how momentous they were, she did.

Framing his face with both hands, enjoying the prickle of beard stubble on her palms, Camellia kissed him again on the lips, watching his eyes the whole time. They darkened, blurred.

And as she drew her mouth away, she knew that she'd made a promise. Perhaps only for the next few minutes, perhaps only for the morning, but she was completely open to him. *Giving* to him.

She slid her hands along the column of his neck, saw the hollow between his collarbones, and knew the essence of his flavor might be found at that point. It was. She flicked her tongue there, he shuddered, and she wanted to be atop him, but not yet. Again she dipped her tongue to taste. She cooked, she knew flavors, and now she knew his. She would never forget it. Man, of course, but *Laev*, with his touch of oak heritage, the very slight undertone of wild hawthorn flowers that no one but a lover would notice. She closed her eyes, feathered her mouth in small kisses along his right collarbone.

She didn't feel like herself, felt more like primal woman enjoying her man, the throb of life, of sexuality hummed through her veins. She skimmed her hands down his chest, through his light chest hair, stopping to experience the thud of his heart on her palm. A vibration that ran through him, through her, connecting them both. Now the golden bond between them had no limits, was only a golden glow in her mind, enveloping them both.

Her hands went to his sides, down the frame of his chest, his flanks, tested his muscular thighs and legs and folded around his feet. She set her thumbs in his arches and he twisted on the bed. His own hands gripped the linens, white-knuckled. Groans poured from his mouth, making her smile with satisfaction that her torment was so fine and lovely.

Moving between his legs, she noticed his scent had become nothing but the sexual musk of a man in need.

As she needed.

So she trailed her hands up his thighs, which rippled with tension, let the panting of his breaths speed her own, let her mind dim with the passion sizzling in her and demanding a release. Only his body was important, how she could make him tremble, how she could tremble in response.

She put her mouth on him, and was lifted and tossed to her back and he was in her and plunging and she was screaming as all the stars in the universe gathered inside her and broke her apart into glittering sparks.

Later, she wasn't sure how long, he was leaning over her and kissing her. "Lover." It was nearly a chant from him. "Dearest.

Lover. Camellia." His mouth formed "HeartMate" and a jab of fear that he might say the word had her getting out of bed quicker than she'd anticipated.

Still, she bent and kissed him. "Laev, dearest *lover.*"

She heard the tuneful chiming of a calendarsphere. More than one. Two were in the corner of the room pulsing and sounding in harmony. Staring at him, she asked, "Did you reprogram the sound after meeting me?"

With a smile, he shook his head. "No. Did you?"

"No."

"Guess we're naturally compatible," he said lightly. He stood at the closed door. "May I use your waterfall?"

"Of course." Her hair was flopping in her face and she slicked it back. "I won't join you."

His jaw flexed and he shook his head. "No. Not a good idea if we both are expected anywhere else today." Then his eyes widened and he grinned. "Tomorrow night, my favorite foods. What time?"

She jerked her head at his calendarsphere. "Consult that."

"Calendarsphere, display tomorrow evening," Laev ordered. The face of the silver globe faded from the morning appointment it had been flashing. "Late afternoon sparring with Tinne Holly."

"Good," Laev said. "Continue."

"Tentative melee sparring," the calendar said.

Looking at her, he said, "Cancel."

"Evening month of Holly Dark Moons ritual at GreatCircle Temple."

"Cancel."

"Late-night consultation—" the sphere began.

"Cancel everything tomorrow night and the next morning—"

"Item marked important on Mor. Trip to see property in Rushes Vale for purchase."

"Hmm." Laev raised his brows at her. "Care for a short trip with me to the northeast on Mor?"

She did a rapid mental review of any appointments: nothing. "Yes. I'd like that."

"Good." He opened the bedroom door, glanced out and around. "No Fams." With a last look at her from over his shoulder, he said, "Favorite meal tomorrow evening." Then he walked with a jaunty step toward her waterfall room.

His ass was even better naked.

*L*aev whistled as he left Camellia's house. His glider had been instructed to return to Camellia's after the ball. She and Mica and Brazos had already teleported to Darjeeling's Teahouse.

He looked up and down the street. It was quiet. Pretty with small homes in big grassyards and large trees. Upper middle class, he judged, and most folk at work. At the end of the block, he saw a full public carrier trundle pass. Running a hand over the sleek and shining dark blue glider, he smiled as he recalled the night before and all the joy of being together and loving.

A twist of papyrus on the street near his glider door caught his eye. Odd because it was heavier than the few bits of other detritus in the street.

He picked it up, feeling slick Flair, unrolled it. Hand-printed words said:

You tortured and killed my lady. I will torture and kill yours, and that will torture you. I will let you live.

His whole body jolted. Was this a joke? Again he looked around, thought he saw a shadow or two standing at the windows—nosey neighbors or threats—or witnesses?

He didn't even know if the note was for him. Why in the street and not attached to his glider? He turned the papyrus over, saw one word on the back. *Vengeance.* Then the thing burst into small flames in his hands. He swore, watched the ash lifted away.

Gliding home, he considered the note. He had never tortured or killed a woman. He couldn't imagine that anyone else on that pretty block would have either. If *his* lady, Camellia, was in danger, he should hire a bodyguard for her. The best bodyguard in the business was his brother-in-heart, Cratag T'Marigold. He could just imagine what Camellia would say if Cratag followed her around.

Instead, when he got home, he scried Primross, who was still in Gael City, and told him about the piece of papyrus. "How seriously should I take it?"

Primross hesitated. "Anyone could do that little fire trick, either with spells or stage magic."

"You said the Sunflowers made ludicrous charges against me. You interviewed them, do you think any of them would do something like that?"

"No," Primross replied. He grimaced, shrugged. "You married into a lazy Family, Laev."

"That's my opinion, too. Anyone else you've spoken with who might feel this way? Perhaps an ex-lover of Nivea's? That's the only thing I can think of, but you're the professional."

"In my investigation, I haven't run across any past lover of your wife."

"Odd in itself, as she had them."

Primross shrugged. "They might be dead, too. Or just out of the picture for some reason or another. Your wife has been dead for two years. If a man or a woman was obsessed with her, why wait until now? *Are* you seeing a lady?"

"Yes. That might be the reason, if the person was obsessed," Laev said.

"If the person was obsessed. But we don't know that the note was aimed at you or not." Primross lifted a hand. "People don't usually threaten FirstFamily Heads of Households. It's bad for the health. But we'll take this seriously enough. I'll contact Guardsman Winterberry, who liaises with the FirstFamilies, and talk to him about the case."

Laev winced, so much for keeping the investigation quiet.

"Winterberry is a good man, and can be damned closemouthed. I'll also hire someone to keep watch over your lady when you're not with her until I've returned."

"A bodyguard?"

"Not exactly, an observer, who would call the guards if there were problems." After a beat, Primross said, "A bodyguard might irritate your lady, but she might not notice an observer."

"All right."

"Would you recognize the printing if I brought you samples?"

"Maybe."

"Later. I'll be back in Druida in four days."

"Later."

Occasionally Laev thought of the note, but another matter preoccupied his mind. He hadn't anticipated anything so much in a long time as the dinner at Camellia's. His favorite meal, but sure to have different spices. The very thought made his mouth water.

He was aware that the Family was watching him closely. They'd have sensed whenever he'd brought Camellia to the estate. But though he was sure they were all raging with curiosity, including the Residence, no one spoke to him about her. Finally they were allowing him to conduct his wooing of Camellia in his own fashion, without meddling.

He'd flexed his GreatLord muscle again. One more time and he thought that everyone might accept that he was in charge. He wondered how his FatherSire had demonstrated to the Residence and the Family that he'd become the GreatLord, but would never know. He and his FatherSire had never spoken of when Huathe Hawthorn had been a young man. Had his FatherSire forgotten that time? Had Laev been too interested in his own concerns to have asked? As he'd often done in the last few months, he wished he'd had more time with his FatherSire. Laev had never quite made it to equal adult status with the older man. Another casualty of his mistake in choosing Nivea.

The thought of his late wife didn't hurt. Not even a sting, since he was so involved with Camellia. It was as if Nivea was in his far past.

His courtship was more important than any recollection of the remnants of his marriage. And he was wooing Camellia. He knew his emotions were growing too rapidly, he was tempted to move too fast with her.

Brazos and Mica had been more discreet, too. Or perhaps it was their belief that now Laev and Camellia were together, nothing could go wrong.

Laev felt unexpectedly exuberant himself. By the time Evening-Bell rolled around on the day of the dinner, he was seething with impatience and his stomach was rumbling. He took the bouquet of summer flowers he'd set in a special holder from the glider. No one else in this area had a glider, so it was conspicuous on the street, but he didn't care.

The flowers were for Camellia's dining room table. He'd noticed that she was fond of roses, and the brighter, the better.

As he strode up her front sidewalk, the smells coming from her house were more delicious than he'd imagined. Before he knocked, she opened the door and greeted him with a kiss. He liked that she did that in semipublic. The cats squealed and stropped his ankles. Naturally they were where the food was.

Sire Black Pierre is jealous, Brazos said. *He says not, but he is.* Brazos opened his mouth in a cat laugh.

Chef in T'Hawthorn is old. Like Black Pierre, Mica said. *He does not do new foods. MY FamWoman does new foods all the time.*

Camellia laughed and took Laev's flowers and turned back to the kitchen. Laev's mouth watered and it wasn't just from the food. He hadn't gotten her to wear only her apron . . . yet. Maybe tonight.

"Every chef has their own recipes they like." She slid a glance toward Laev. "And usually become complacent or not, depending upon whom they serve."

He nodded. "Ours knows that as Black Pierre's FamMan, I wouldn't cross him, unless he makes an egregious mistake."

Brazos sniffed, but his stomach made noises, too, so his dignity was impaired.

Mica trotted into the kitchen. *We will have some clucker bits and nice broth from stew made for humans.*

"And a few greens for your health," Camellia said austerely as she arranged the flowers in a large crystal vase.

When she stepped back to admire the bouquet, Laev couldn't wait and pulled her into his arms, against his body, so he felt her and smelled the fragrance of the cooking herbs that lingered on her skin and in her hair.

"It's been too long since yesterday morning."

She blushed and he liked that, then she pushed him away with a stern look. "We'll eat first."

"Somehow I don't think that stew that's been simmering all day and strawberries that have been marinating will lose too much flavor if we postpone dinner."

"Then you don't know much." She smiled, waved a spoon—was it made of wood? something so antique and odd?—at him. "I just put some leafy vegetables into the stew and the dish should be served just after they wilt."

"Um-hmm. If you insist." They had all night.

"I do. Go take your place at the table."

It was tucked into another corner of her mainspace, close to the kitchen, and round. So there was no head of the table and no foot. Laev sensed that she was satisfied with that. He quashed the small notions drifting into his mind about investing in her business. That would be the last way she'd ever trust a man. With his brain, he understood, but his emotions wanted to be close to her in every way that mattered. And business mattered greatly to both of them.

When could he broach the matter? Impatience was prodding him.

He'd no sooner put a prettily patterned softleaf on his lap when his attention was drawn to the fine shape of her bottom as she ladled stew into bowls for the Fams.

She was wonderful. The thought surfaced that Nivea would never have expended so much effort to please him. Probably not so much to please anyone. And she'd taken any such effort to please *her* as her due.

Nivea had never been interested in having a Fam, taking care of another being.

He could pity her now. The person she'd been.

Camellia turned to him, chin tilted, that look in her eyes that she had when she was checking their bond. What had she felt?

A smile curved her lips and her gaze softened. "I'm experimenting with a new salad glaze on the greens." Her smile widened. "I've been with you often enough to understand which greens you prefer." She took a bowl from the no-time. It was deep red showing sprigs of his favorite leafy vegetables. When she placed it before him, he saw seeds and a bit of egg, and knew that the salad was just for him. She put down another bowl and sat across the table from him. Her salad wasn't the same as his.

Personal salads. Why didn't he have such a thing at home? Because the cook was old and set in his ways? He was still eating the same nutritionally balanced diet he'd had as a child.

"Thank you," he said.

She nodded. "We thank the Lady and Lord for blessing us with this good food."

"We thank the Lady and Lord for blessing us with this good food," Laev echoed. Then he added, "We thank the Lady and Lord for blessing us with excellent company."

The FamCats slurped loudly.

He and Camellia laughed and ate their salads.

"So," he asked, "is this salad nutritionally balanced?"

She chuckled in her throat. "No, but the meal is."

"Yes?"

"Yes. And I made the strawberries especially for you. Another new recipe."

He couldn't stop the words. "Could you keep one recipe private, just for me, and not used in the tearooms?" Then he felt stupid.

"Of course. Which one, the salad glaze, the stew, or the wined strawberries?"

"All are different?"

"I experiment with herbs, spices, and foods a lot." Her brows dipped as she chewed. "I think this glaze would be better heated."

The idea would never have occurred to him. She was a wonder. And he wanted exclusivity. He was sure she had no other lover, but that wasn't enough. She wasn't the kind of woman who would have more than one lover at a time.

Cooking and business were important to her, and cooking had just become important to him. Which made him recall that he hadn't shown her his sculpture studio.

Nor had he given her a gift that showed he cared for her, like she was doing now. That lack struck him with the force of a blow.

She looked up. "What?"

He'd stilled. He didn't want to explain whatever she'd felt through their bond, so he cast his mind back to her question.

"What's different about the Beltane clucker stew?"

Her eyes gleamed. "It's not the usual clucker and grain. I used a spring chicken and some Earthan sorrel from my herb garden on *Nuada's Sword.*" Her expression changed to uncertainty. "I think you will like it."

"I'm sure I will. I've never had anything I didn't like from you," he said. She'd been feeding him well whenever he'd come over.

She stood, then, with a bright smile. "Well, shall we try it?"

"You didn't taste as you cooked?"

"Yes."

"Then you know it's good." Before he could rise to take his salad bowl to the cleanser, she whisked it away from him, put it in the cleanser herself.

Brazos sauntered over to Laev's chair and burped. *You will like the clucker stew.*

Of course he will, Mica said. Her left ear rotated. *I am going to nap on My big pillow in the mainspace.*

Laev petted Brazos as the cat wanted, scratched him under the chin before he turned, waved his tail, and walked to the opposite corner. *That is OUR pillow.*

Mine, Mica said telepathically, but it was soft and sleepy.

Brazos grunted, hopped on the pillow, and curled up next to the calico cat.

A bowl was placed in front of Laev and steam teased his nose. He glanced up at Camellia. She didn't look anxious, but there was a slight tremble in her fingers that the hot-gloves didn't quite mask as she brought her own bowl to the table.

She was a professional. She *must* have confidence in her work. He'd seen that when he'd visited her teahouses.

Which meant he, and his opinion, was important to her, and not just because he was a FirstFamily GreatLord. She didn't think of his status anymore, especially when it was simply the two of them and the Fams together.

"This has smelled great since I got into the house," he said. He noted she was watching him from lowered lashes as he dipped a spoon into the bowl, tasted. Lemony flavor sank into his tongue, he swallowed and tasted herbs he couldn't name. He had to have another bite, and another. The clucker was delicious. He didn't realize that he'd ignored Camellia until half his stew was gone. When he glanced up, he saw her smiling at him, and she gestured to a piece of toasted bread with a thin crust of melted cheese on the top. "Wonderful," he said, wanted to praise it more. "Fabulous." That still wasn't enough. "Best—" Words failed him. He shrugged, smiled lopsidedly. "Best."

And she gave him that smile he hoped she saved only for him. The one of pleasure, with a hint of anticipation of other delights than food.

They finished their stew in silent harmony. When Camellia stood, he did, too, and took his bowl, handed it to her as she walked into the narrow kitchen. He shook his head. "I would have thought you'd have liked a larger kitchen."

She glanced over her shoulder. "If I need to, I can use the tearoom kitchens at any time. Having a large kitchen in the house wasn't as important as other things. I like the neighborhood a lot."

He nodded, though he didn't really know what she was talking about. Noble Country, which held the huge estates of the FirstFamilies, wasn't exactly a neighborhood, and that was all he knew.

"I love it here."

Tension slipped along his nerves. She loved it here in this small and cozy house. How would she take to a great Residence?

"You like cocoa, don't you?" she asked.

"Yes."

She moved aside and took the front off what looked like a solid wall in the corner, revealing a no-time. Laev stared, checked the standard two no-time cabinets. "You have three no-times in this kitchen?"

"That's right. I didn't use this one much until lately." She shrugged. "No one thinks to look for a third no-time."

Something in her voice told him not to press further.

She flashed him a smile. "And if I do want to cook a lot in the tearoom kitchens for myself and my friends, I need the storage space here."

He leaned against a cabinet, essentially blocking the exit, raised his eyebrows. "And you've been cooking more lately."

"Yes. I have a new Fam," she said.

He laughed.

She drew out a tray of cocoa-covered strawberries and his mouth began to water.

"You didn't say you'd like the strawberry wine–infused strawberries dipped in cocoa, but I thought you wouldn't mind."

He couldn't stop from moving in, grabbing a small one, and popping it into his mouth. It was not quite room temperature, not quite cool. The cocoa shell crunched and broke and the sweet fruit soaked with wine spurted nicely in his mouth. "Mmmphrr." He nodded vigorously.

Laughing more—and had she ever laughed so much in his company before?—she shook her head at him, pulled out a bowl of brown-flecked white mousse and a tube with a bulb on the end to fill the hollow berries. He gulped down his treat, moved closer. She smelled better than dessert. "I think that might be almost too much."

"The white mousse? You said you wanted it." She was still smiling as she filled the tube with mousse.

"Almost too much, but I'm up to the challenge," he said. "What are those brown bits?"

"Very fine nuts. You like nuts, too."

"Yes."

"Just wait."

"I think I've become an impatient man. And not only for dessert." And not only for just sex.

But lust dominated now, and he slid in behind her. There was barely enough room for both of them, and that was delicious, too. He nibbled at her neck and she sighed.

"Just make three for me. Put the rest back in the no-time for later," he said. His body had roused and decided on a different after-dinner activity than dessert.

"Sounds good to me." She took two for herself, put them all on a white plate, then led him to bed.

Twenty-six

I am ready for the trip to Rushes Vale! Mica yowled in Camellia's ear, shattering her sleep with the telepathic shout. Camellia jerked awake, sat straight up.

We are ready, too! Brazos exclaimed.

That was when Camellia realized that she was alone in the bed except for Mica. Laev was already up, and if her ears weren't betraying her, he was in the kitchen. Probably raiding the strawberries for breakfast.

Camellia had overslept, no doubt due to the several bouts of sex she and Laev had had during the night. She needed to scramble to get ready.

There was a slurp and a nude Laev stood in the doorway, tilting his head and dropping a cocoa-covered and white mousse–dipped strawberry in his mouth. He mumbled something.

"What?" Camellia asked blearily. The bed linens were tossed and tangled, half on the floor. Even the tapestry covering the wall safe and the gouges around it was hanging crookedly. Hadn't they rolled off the bedsponge onto the floor and . . . Oh, yeah. They had. She flushed and yanked the coverlet up over her bare torso.

Laev sighed. His tongue came out to sweep a dab of white mousse from the corner of his mouth. "You should dress warmly. It will be cold in Rushes Vale."

"Um," she said.

"We'll leave in half a septhour," he said. His smile was dangerous. "We have time for a waterfall before then." He marched over,
whipped the cover from her, lifted her in his arms, and strode to the
tiled room and the steamy waterfall and steamier sex.

A dazed Camellia thought that someday their lust for each other
should ease to a slow simmer, but right now it only took one glance
to heat to a rolling boil.

The cats ate heartily of furrabeast bites and greens, but that
didn't stop Mica from scolding Camellia.

You are not ready. You didn't plan what to wear.

"No, I cooked all day."

"And I am thankful for that." Laev grinned.

*You did not put out what you should wear last night on the
clothes chair,* Mica continued.

Camellia remembered having sex on the chair, too, after a late-
night snack. "Just as well, my clothes would have ended up on the
floor, too," she said blankly.

Laev snorted, coughed. "You're not as sharp as usual this
morning."

She pointed at him. "*You* are a detriment."

And he was. He insisted on milk and more wine strawberries for
breakfast, and he'd "helped" clean up the kitchen. That only took
several minutes longer than if she'd done it herself. He did do a
good job of attaching the false front to the extra no-time. Until
she'd started cooking for him and Mica, she hadn't used it. Now it
occurred to her that if her uncle didn't deliberately do a scan for it,
he might not remember it. Unlike the safe, she'd rarely kept anything in the no-time. Food, at least, could be hidden there. Her
uncle would *always* scan a house for jewels and find any hidden
caches.

A few days ago a guard had dropped by to set an alarm on her
house. She didn't bother to tell the woman that would be useless.
Her uncle always scanned for alarms, and never triggered them.
Though the guardswoman was earnest in explaining the spell would
notify both Camellia and the guard station, Camellia just smiled

and discounted the assurance. The alarm might take Takvar a while to get around, but when he'd finally broken into the house, he'd be furious enough to destroy the place.

Two calendarspheres appeared, chiming that it was time to leave. Fam telepathic voices added to the confusion. Finally Camellia just grabbed the first tunic trous suit she found—a soft gray wool that would be warm in the cool weather of the northern hills—and dressed. She added a paisley scarf in primary colors.

Laev handed her a heavy cloak, hustled her to the teleportation pad, and the next thing she knew, all four of them were in a luxury airship ready to fly to the valley.

The three-septhour trip itself was uneventful. As soon as they exited the vehicle, the Fams spotted some small fluff-tailed rodents and took off chasing them.

She and Laev stood on a ridge looking down into a green valley, holding hands.

"Yes," Laev said. "I think I'll take it." His shoulders shifted and a half smile curved his lips. "I got a buzz about this place. The company that wants to farm and settle the land is right. It will draw people."

"Why?" Camellia asked.

"First, the land and weather are perfect for growing NewBalm, the recently developed hybrid Earthan-Celtan herb."

Camellia stared at the slopes of the valley. "I've heard of that. It's a derivative of the herb that was used to mitigate the sickness two years ago. The medicine stopped the epidemic."

"That's right. The FirstFamilies Council has allocated a great deal of gilt to studying the plant and its properties. We have the science and Flair to begin exploring the DNA of plants that the starship, *Nuada's Sword*, still has locked within itself. Celta is a harsh planet, and modifying plants from our home planet to grow with flora here could help our numbers."

"Everyone agrees with that," Camellia said.

Laev nodded and his smile faded. "Yes, we all agree that Celtans must multiply. Deciding on the means to ensure that are hard-fought battles." Camellia suddenly knew that he and his FatherSire must have worked hard in the FirstFamilies Council to make sure the gilt was available for the development of the herb. She squeezed his hand.

He smiled again, tugged on her hand, and they walked along a path toward the river that flowed into the valley from the northern mountains. "Not only that, but in the next couple of generations, as the general Flair of our populace rises, this valley will be within teleportation range of the Great Labyrinth, and the town that is growing there."

"The north wasn't hit as hard by the sickness as Druida and Gael City in the south."

"No. And we've funded studies to learn about that, too." He stopped and scanned the land again. "I think we'll buy the eastern side of the valley. That way the project can go forward even if no one else invests." He shrugged. "We may take a loss, but it's important research that must be done." Eyes narrowed, he continued, "I'll have Vinni T'Vine, the prophet, evaluate the options. But I do feel that buzz of success." He slid a glance to her. "Even a small plot here might bring a good amount of gilt in the future. Or an investment in Medica, the company developing the herb."

Her heart fluttered as she understood that he was sharing confidential information with her, that he trusted her, that he cared enough to give her financial tips to make her life easier. She stood and kissed him on the mouth. "Thank you." Kissed him again. "I think that I'll stick with my tearooms."

He drew her close and the next kiss was a full-body experience— a tasting and cherishing of each other, the bond between them throbbing with . . . affection. Laev withdrew first, and as she caught her breath, she saw that he was shaking his head at her, but smiling again. "You're a very independent lady."

"Thank you."

"I'm not sure that was a compliment."

She chuckled. "That's all right."

He dropped her hand and focused on the valley. His back stiffened. "I hope you know that if you ever . . ." He stopped. Probably because she'd moved away and the bond between them was now flowing with irritation from her.

"I won't ever need gilt." She tried to keep her breath even. "I have a tea set worth a fortune."

Turning, he stepped close again and framed her face with his hands. "And I know you love that tea set." His eyes were dark, intense, and demanded she meet them. "I don't ever want you to feel desperate. Never. Anything that is in my power, I will give you."

She swallowed hard. He was moving faster than she in this relationship. He wanted more from her, from them.

A burden seemed to settle on her shoulders. How had she missed that? Words hammered in her brain, scared words, defensive words, angry words. She should say none of them and for once she was smart. "Thank you."

Laev jerked a nod, stepped away, but she thought he was disappointed in them both—himself for pushing her, and her for her fear. He turned and led the way back to the waiting airship.

Fams, we are returning to Druida City! he shouted mentally.

You woke us, Brazos grumbled. *We finished our hunt,* there was a small catch in his telepathic stream that seemed like a burp. *And returned to the airship. This place is not as good as alleys.*

"Oh," Laev said. With a laugh, he reached for Camellia's hand and she let him take it.

They walked into the airship and saw the cats tangled in a large, cushioned saucer-seat with a security field over it. Mica opened an eye and smiled at Camellia but said nothing.

Once she and Laev were seated again and the ship was on the way back to the city, his jaw flexed and he stared out the window and said, "I spoke out of turn, but you must know that you can call on me if you need." He cleared his throat. "You must know that I am not the only one who would . . . ah . . . help. There is D'Ash. She is interested in tea, and her daughter is my journeywoman, always interested in new ventures."

"Thank you." This time she summoned a sincere smile.

He turned his head to look at her and she saw vulnerability. That made her more wary than his financial offer. Too much was happening in too short of a time. The sex had been wonderful, the time with him so comfortable that she hadn't noticed how truly strong the bond was between them.

"I care for you," he said, his head angled, awaiting her response.

But she could give him that. "I care for you, too."

"Good."

But the word *HeartMate*, and all the binding ties that concept brought with it, echoed in the quiet.

They watched the scenery pass under them. Then the airship drink no-time pinged and a tray protruded holding two mugs, one of black caff for Laev, the other sweetened tea for her. Laev took the mugs and passed hers to her. "Your calendarsphere showed dinner with your brother tonight?"

"Yes, every first Mor evening."

"Ah. Do you cook for him, too?"

"Yes. He has a fondness for thin-sliced furrabeast sandwiches and rice. Some are in the no-time." The hidden one.

Mica yawned, added, *It is the only time he gets to eat furrabeast, with us.*

"Oh." Laev grimaced. "I have no siblings. My closest relative is my aunt Lark, married to Holm Holly. I go eat with them once a month. She insists. We usually dine with the rest of the Hollys. They are a loud Family." He shifted in his seat. "Before dinner there is sparring, and T'Holly usually pummels me." Now Laev smiled. "But I've been practicing and I have a new strategy for getting Holm and Tinne on my side that I'll try out next time." Laev rolled his shoulders. "T'Holly may have been the premiere fighter of Celta, but for pure strategy, no one can beat the Hawthorns," Laev ended with satisfaction.

Which only made Camellia wonder how much he was steering and planning this affair. Not much, she thought. But the longer it went on, the more he'd consider how to control the relationship, wouldn't he?

* * *

*A*s soon as Camellia and Mica walked into the house, she knew her father and uncle had been there. Of course the alarm spell had not notified her, nor had the guards contacted her by perscry, so the alarm hadn't contacted them, either. When she tried, she found no trace of it with her Flair

Horrible smell!

"Rotten meat," Camellia said, going immediately to the kitchen. Low-grade ground furrabeast was smeared on the floor and counters. She stopped just outside the small room. Keeping her mouth shut and blocking her nostrils, she pressed a spot on the kitchen wall and a deep-cleaning spell rippled through the area. Mica sat and watched with round eyes. In under a quarter septhour, the place sparkled.

That was the new spell you bought earlier this week.

"Yes. It wasn't cheap, but it's good value, and I didn't have to spend my own Flair and energy."

Bad men were here.

"Yes."

I'd better check all my toys. And my fish. Mica trotted away.

Feeling a small trickle of satisfaction, Camellia went to the concealed no-time, slid off the panel that made it look like part of the wall, and checked it. Full of good food. The other two had been raided, but she hadn't kept anything but the furrabeast in there.

Hopefully her father and uncle were thinking they continued to win the nasty game they played, that they were depressing her spirits so she didn't keep food or valuables around.

And in one way they had won. She'd packed her treasures away and given them to Tiana to store. She'd replaced the knickknacks with minor objects that she'd only feel a twinge or two if they were broken. Still, she thought of that as fighting back.

She went to the bedroom and saw that the tapestry had been ripped down and the wall safe opened. She and Tiana and Glyssa had put some trinkets they'd wanted to get rid of in there. Camellia had recorded them all in a sphere and would send it to the guard-house. Maybe that would help trace her relatives, certainly it would add to the evidence against them.

At least the wall wasn't damaged any more than it had been. The gouges around the lockbox were still ugly, but they'd be hidden by her new wardrobe, which was scheduled to be delivered the night after next.

Camellia sat down on her bedsponge and Mica settled into her lap. *My fish is safe.* Mica purred. *And all My catnip toys. And Brazos's toys, too,* Mica said.

Stroking the cat, Camellia said, "That's very good."

"Yessss," Mica said, then added telepathically, *They did not break anything.*

"Not this time."

Maybe they were in a hurry.

"That could be," Camellia agreed.

But they did what we thought they would! They found the furrabeast-for-Fams and threw it around, and took the bits of jewels.

"That's right."

We can strategize, too.

"Yes, we can." Gratification unfurled inside Camellia. This time she'd lost nothing that she'd miss, hadn't spent energy or Flair in cleaning up or in worry. It wasn't much, but it still felt like a small triumph.

Her brother knocked on the door and Mica hopped to her feet and ran to the mainspace. Senchal had begun bringing string toys to the Fam. It was always good to please a female FamCat who might someday have kittens.

Camellia followed and opened the door.

Senchal seemed to glow with pleasure.

"Work went well today?" Camellia asked.

"Yeah, very well. Finished the mural project. And you'll never guess who gave me a commission!"

"Who?"

"That Feam Kelp, the son of the lady who found your tea set in that sunken ship. He wants a wall holo of his mother working underwater on that ship." Senchal rubbed his hands. "A real challenge."

"Great!"

"Yeah." Senchal smiled and was charming. Then he unrolled a string and added a little Flair and the scraps on the end became a dancing spider for Mica to play with. She squeed and pounced and he left her to it to hug Camellia.

"What did you do today?"

We went to Rushes Vale, Mica said, rolling on her back and all four paws tangled in the string. *You should buy land there!*

Camellia simply froze, along with the smile on her face. How much had Mica overheard, how much would she reveal of Laev's plans? Of the confidential information.

Quiet! she snapped mentally to her FamCat. *He talks to the bad men, remember!*

But Senchal shivered. "Up north? No. If I move anywhere it will be to an artist's colony. Mona Island or or Toono Town in the south."

Mica abandoned the string and sat, head tilted, looking at him. *You smell like the bad men.*

"Bad men?"

The ones who come in here and break things.

"What have you been telling the cat?" Senchal said to Camellia, flushing. From the sibling bond between them, she felt more anger than embarrassment from him.

"I don't have to tell her anything," Camellia said. "She lives here and sees what happens."

They take things and break things, Mica said. *They took My furrabeast steaks.* She picked up the string and dropped it on Senchal's shoes. *I do not want toys from you.*

Senchal's mouth dropped open, he jerked a shrug. "They aren't bad men."

Yes, they are, Mica said.

"Yes, they are," Camellia said.

We go to the guardhouse all the time.

"You're reporting them!" Senchal gasped.

"Every time," Camellia replied. "They'll never change. They'll always be vicious."

"Maybe a little selfish . . ."

Camellia stared at him, knew he still wanted to please the older men. She turned on her heel and went to the kitchen, gesturing to him to sit. "Your dinner's ready."

"Cammi—"

"We're not going to agree on this, Senchal," she said.

"I hate that we can't all love each other," he said. "Thank you for the meal."

She served herself a bowl of clucker stew. Just inhaling the scent of it steadied her. "There was precious little love in our Family."

Senchal's eyes dampened. He sent the warmth of love to her through their bond, said quietly, "Don't ask me to choose between you, please, Camellia."

"When have I ever?" She ate quickly, not savoring her food. "But I can't go on like this forever. If they don't leave Druida City soon, I'll sell this place and move into D'Licorice Residence." The words sprang from her lips, that option sudden and fully formed.

"Father isn't looking well."

She met Senchal's eyes with a hard gaze. "That might be because he blasphemed the Sheela Na Gig."

"No!"

"Yes."

Senchal choked, put his sandwich on his plate, stared at Camellia. "If what you say is true, father and uncle will pay someday."

"That's right, and the sooner the better."

*L*aev finished his notes on Rushes Vale and authorized the purchase of the property. Jasmine bought a small parcel on the western slope. It was all she could afford since T'Ash and D'Ash hadn't made the final decision to give her a quarter of their funds to handle. Grumbling to herself, she waved good-bye to Laev as she left for home.

He checked his message cache and heard from Primross that the investigation was proceeding well—but no details. The man had spoken to Winterberry about the odd note, and his observer had reported no unusual threat to Camellia from an unknown person.

Laev's housekeeper had left two-dimensional blueprints of the MasterSuite and MistrysSuite on his desk, along with notations of all the ways they'd been configured in the past. At one point, there had been a kitchen in the present MasterSuite. He didn't think that floor plan would work when Camellia moved in.

A hole opened up inside him and all the bad memories of being wed to Nivea bombarded him. Watching their marriage deteriorate as the illusion she'd woven around him peeled away. The discovery that she'd wed him for status and wealth only the first betrayal.

But Camellia wasn't Nivea. What would have happened this morning if Nivea had been standing on the ridge looking down at Rushes Vale? He wouldn't have told her of his plans, not even in the beginning. Nivea was bored with business.

And when he'd offered her the financial advice, Nivea would have cooed that he should put some of the property in her name, linked arms with him, rubbed her head against his shoulder. She'd always expected to get something for nothing—or for nothing more than sex.

Never would she have been irritated or angry, staunchly independent, insisting on making her own way.

Camellia, his HeartMate, was not anything like the woman he'd married.

It was time to accept that Camellia was his HeartMate, the woman he should bond with this lifetime, so closely that they would die within a year of each other.

Time to push her a little. No more being indirect, dancing around the subject of HeartMates. Camellia had shown him how constricted he had been, living with Nivea. How his love hadn't been true, but infatuation and sex that might have been a fleeting but wholesome part of his life if circumstances had been different, if Nivea had been more honorable.

But first, a gift. Not the HeartGift; he still couldn't find it by himself, and Primross wasn't back from Gael City.

Camellia had shared her talent with him, had spent hours preparing food for him, had created special recipes for him . . . none of which would be used in her tearooms. Nivea never would have done something like that.

For the first time in weeks, he went into his studio with the intention of working. There was a heated pressure infusing his body, not sexual but creative. He *needed* to sculpt. He wanted to give Camellia something of himself. The statue of the Lord had been a standard image, and part of a trade.

Last night she had made special Beltane stew for him. Tonight he'd sculpt for her.

Twenty-seven

His lost HeartGift ghosted through Laev's mind. *No, he didn't want* to give Camellia something that important. He couldn't duplicate those circumstances of creation anyway. Deep in Passage, hardly knowing what he did, he'd carved the Lady and Lord from marble. Through the hours that he'd suffered and sweated, every stroke of his chisel reflected who he was. Flair had created it, was bound up in it.

He prowled his studio, went to the worktable that held the rough bust of his FatherSire. The man had posed for studies for septhours, and Laev was glad of that. The time they'd spent together was a treasured memory now. He still hadn't quite gotten the angle of GreatLord Hawthorn's jaw right. Someday he would. There would be less grief mixed with his love when he worked on the piece again. For now he shrouded it and thought of Camellia.

A statue of the Lady, a goddess, would please him. Standing before shelves of ristal, he selected a jagged block about a meter high and half a meter wide. Ristal was wonderful to work with. Just by using Flair and his hands, he could create a sculpture. This piece was a rosy pink, and he liked it for Camellia. His hands curved on the stone, an image arose, and he began.

Two septhours later he stepped back and studied his creation. He had an image of the Lady, all right. He also had a nude model of Camellia herself. If he knew his lover—and he did—she'd be uncomfortable with the sculpture. It pleased him very much, the line of her thigh, buttocks, spine. No, he couldn't give this to her, but he wanted something special. What?

Taking a dinner and some caff from the no-time, he ate and let his gaze wander over the room. He wanted to give her something *now.* Tomorrow at the latest. He was willing to work all night if he found the right idea.

Think. A sculpture that was just right. Not too intimate like the one he'd just finished of her. Nothing standard. Something that showed he cared, that he appreciated her. That she was unique.

Absently he wiped his mouth on a softleaf, sent the dish and cutlery and mug to the cleanser, and walked over to view the slight gleam of jade that had caught his eye. That thing.

One of the final assignments the master sculptor had given him years ago. Which he'd never finished, never had the urge to finish, until now. Mentally he called up the objects Camellia had decorated her house with and knew that this would be a cherished objet d'art.

He lifted the fussy sphere of jade down. The bottom fit in the curve of his fingers. Then he went to a different corner of the room and called up the brightest spellglobes, opened the drawer of his small worktable for equally small tools. Now was finally the time to finish the puzzle ball—a series of balls carved within each other that moved freely. He had six layers. The outer ball was to be ornately carved with sinuous mythical creatures, and needed to be finished. The second, third, and fourth balls were done, also carved with creatures as well as fancy latticework. He'd never figured out a pattern for the innermost balls, the fifth and sixth, but now he knew. They would be the twinmoons, first Cymru, then the tiniest, innermost would be Eire.

"ResidenceLibrary, project three-dimensional models of the twinmoons on the wall before me."

"Yes, Laev."

Once again he got to work, manipulating tiny tools to chip away stone, smooth it, whispered words to polish as he went along. Now and then he glanced up at the models, grunted, ordered them to be rotated.

Finally as dawn was breaking, he laid down his tools and examined the carved spheres. Satisfaction surged through him. He'd done it! Always before he'd been too impatient to work on the puzzle ball, not interested in the thing for himself.

But for Camellia . . . yes, she'd love this. Instead of mythical beasts on the outer sphere, there was a carving of cats chasing fishes, full of a graceful limb here, a flowing tail there. Mica would like it, too.

His gift was finished, and he'd used plenty of Flair in getting it done.

"Residence, please cancel any appointments this morning and request a luncheon date with GraceMistrys Darjeeling at the Acorn Cup, the café near the Green Knight, at NoonBell."

"Done, Laev. Camellia confirms."

"Right." Laev stood and stretched, cracked his back, looked around for a proper box for the puzzle ball, found one of the right size though it was Yule red. He wrapped the puzzle ball and its pedestal in softleaves, placed them into the box.

A good gift, although not his HeartGift. He needed to tell her what happened to that gift, too.

*L*aev had always liked the Acorn Cup. It catered to the business crowd who worked in CityCenter and to those who trained at the Green Knight Fencing and Fighting Salon. The dark brown furrabeast-leather booths were all deeply cushioned, easy on strained muscles. The wooden tables were functional and showed carved initials of important patrons.

Due to the feud between his Family and the Hollys, he'd started training at the Green Knight late, a few months before his Passage at seventeen. He hadn't come to this eatery until then, either, and had been too self-conscious to carve his initials in a table.

Impulsively, he took out a folding knife and whisked it around in a few deft motions. A heart, and inside it L.T'H. + C.D. It was foolish, and heat wrapped around his neck, rushed up into his face, but it was done.

Since the carving looked too new and raw—as raw as his feelings—he rubbed a thumb over it and drew tint from the whole surface of the table to darken it until it appeared to be a couple of months old. Still new, but getting accustomed to the fact. Like he was.

But this restaurant no longer pleased him as much as before. It lacked the atmosphere so carefully tended in Camellia's teahouses— the casual cheer of Darjeeling's Teahouse and the serene but mysterious Darjeeling's HouseHeart. He realized that the ambience fluctuated here. Testing his Flair, he sent his senses out around him, found the common problems of working folk, stains of ambition, failure, distress. He shut down his psi but could now smell an undertone of mostly masculine sweat, spilt ale, and whiskey. The Acorn Cup was clean, but the smells still lingered.

Then the door opened and there came a feminine fragrance— fresh water and herbal cleansers, and the scent of his woman. Camellia had arrived.

She nearly bounced toward him, running on endorphins from her session. Laev heard heavier steps approach the bar, Lemongrass order a steak sandwich.

And Camellia was there. Dazzling. More beautiful than Nivea had ever been, the glow of her aura, her natural honest vibrancy filling the booth as she slid in opposite him.

"Greetyou, Laev."

"Blessings, Camellia."

She grinned at that.

"Good workout?" he asked.

"Oh, yes. I took Lemongrass down, and in the melee I got a blow in on Tinne!"

"Excellent progress."

"We all think so."

She wrinkled her nose, a common habit of hers that he'd noticed here, when they'd been here before with other fighters. Now he knew why. She said nothing about the atmosphere, though. The Acorn Cup had its menu against the wall and she ordered a cup of vegetable noodle soup and tea.

Laev was pretty sure that the tea here wasn't up to her standards, either. He wished he'd asked her to a more elegant dining room.

"I need to tell you about my HeartGift." He put the box containing the puzzle sphere, the token that was so much less than what he wanted to give her—everything, all—on the table.

She flinched back, withdrew even her hands from the table. "I don't want your HeartGift." Words coming from her so fast that he could barely understand them. She stared at the gaily wrapped box as if it carried the plague. "I don't want—" She stopped, horror in her eyes, but he'd felt all the repudiation of him as the bond between them narrowed to a thread.

"You don't want me." After a knife-thrust of hurt to the chest, he was stunned, numb, but knew that was just a receding wave. Agony would flow back.

"I—yes!"

"Not enough to be public with me. To show all that we are a couple . . . a progression of our relationship."

She opened her mouth, shut it, swallowed, looked aside.

"You won't take my gift?"

Biting her lips, she shook her head.

He slid from the booth. Stood. He didn't want the puzzle balls, either. How many times would he be giving gifts that weren't valued?

It fliggering hurt.

She didn't trust him. She didn't think that he was any better than her thieving father or her evil uncle or her worthless brother or any other man close to her that abandoned her.

She believed he was undependable, too. Dishonorable.

He felt the ice of generations of pride slide through his veins, coat his skin, cover his outer expression.

Her eyes went wide, dilated, as if she were surprised at his reaction, might be hurting, too. Tough. He could be tough. Easily. An ancestor didn't scrape and fight to fund a starship if he wasn't tough. A GreatLord didn't remain part of the FirstFamilies if he wasn't tough.

The ice was flexible enough for him to bow most formally. He wanted to curse—her, life, the Lady and Lord. Instead he said, "Bless you on your journey. Now and on the wheel of stars between lives, your next life and forever."

She paled. Yes, this was definitely the end of things between them; how could she believe it would not be?

He pivoted and walked away, and as he did so, the last whiff of her came to his nostrils and everything inside him clenched, ached, scraped with every breath.

He *hurt*. Nothing in his life hurt as much as this. Not the fear he'd felt as a teen that he'd be executed for killing a GreatLady. Not his father's death, or his FatherSire's. Not even understanding he'd been played a fool by Nivea, that she wasn't his HeartMate. He'd still had illusions then, about love.

Now he had none.

Once again, he had nothing but pride, and honor and duty.

"Laev . . ." He thought he heard her whisper in a clogged voice. He ignored it. Even in the depths of this agony, he knew he had his Family, and his Residence, and his friends. He strode into the future, unpaired but not alone.

*C*amellia was doubled over the table when her order came. The scent of vegetable soup made bile pool in her mouth. She knew she'd been foolish, but she couldn't call him back. Couldn't take back the words that had revealed her fear even though the pain of hurting him, hurting herself, was more than the fear, now.

"What's wrong?" asked a light and lilting voice of a female server.

"I'll take care'a her," said Lemongrass, and his shadow fell over her, no longer as bulky as her father's would be, and she'd never been so glad to see him.

"So which'a you ended it this time?" he asked.

She just mewled.

"Eat your soup."

"Can't."

"All right." There was the noise of Lemongrass paying, then his big hand wrapped around her arm and she noted dimly that she had no reaction to him.

No, she'd saved all her fear for emotional threat this time.

"Come on. We'll walk to the teleportation pad and I'll take you somewhere. Where do you want to go?"

Somewhere to die. No. Of course she wouldn't die. A few ideas lightninged through her mind, blazing bright and fading fast as she discarded them. Not her house. It didn't seem like home anymore. Not to Tiana's Temple or Glyssa's Library. They would yammer at her or try and make her talk and she didn't want to.

"Darjeeling's Teahouse, can you do that?"

"Of course." He was calming. He pulled on her and she walked blindly with him, smears of color blurring in her sight. She wasn't sure why she couldn't see, except she felt as if she'd fallen into a pit and been impaled on a stake of her own making.

Then there was some blackness and the beloved scent of the teahouse.

"What's happened?" Aquilaria's voice was concerned, and Camellia knew she was scaring this friend, too, and Lemongrass, and her heart ripped a little more.

"Where do you want to go?" Lemongrass asked.

"Office," Camellia whispered at the same time that Aquilaria said it.

Then they were there and her good chair cradled her and she scrabbled for the books. Doing the books would keep her from feeling, would keep her mind going and not thinking. She hoped.

"What happened?" Aquilaria demanded again.

"HeartMate breakage." Lemongrass sighed. Camellia knew him well enough to know he was shaking his head. "Don't know if she or Laev sundered the relationship."

"She did." Aquilaria was definite, her voice holding an edge of scorn that almost cut through the rest of Camellia's pain. Then her manager was there, shaking her, and Camellia flopped like a raggedy doll. "Stop this. Go after him."

"Ouch," Lemongrass said and Camellia didn't know whether it was in response to the shake or Aquilaria's tone. He continued, "Man's got pride. That boy has pride. No man has more pride than a Hawthorn. And that boy's already been savaged by one woman. Won't be easy to get him back."

Another shade to the painful gloom descending through Camellia. "I'm going to do the books now," Camellia said thinly. She blinked and blinked again; the office came into painful focus. "Keep me occupied."

"All right." Aquilaria huffed an exasperated breath. "Shall I get the books from Darjeeling's HouseHeart?"

"Please," Camellia said.

Aquilaria clumped to the corner teleportation pad and vanished with a deliberate pop.

Camellia pulled out the recording sphere that held the figures for the teahouse and attached a link to a special writestick that would enter data into the sphere. With a husky spell couplet, the file for the last two eightdays opened.

Citrus scent wrapped around her and she felt the brush of a kiss disturb the hair at her temple. "I'll go get that gift—not a HeartGift since I could see it—that the boy gave you, send it to your house cache. Take care. We'll move our schedule back to before NoonBell. Keep the schedule. It'll help." Lemongrass vanished, too.

She lost herself in figures. Sometimes she drowned in them, having to fight her way back to find sense in them. When she was done, her hand was cramped and she sagged in the chair. Eventually the recording sphere blinked off.

Then Tiana and Glyssa came into the office and whisked her away, and she rambled and wept and slept with them and Mica close all night. None of that was a comfort.

* * *

Laev went straight to the Green Knight's shooting range. With a surfeit of rage and pain, he had the energy to translocate his pistols. He spent hours practicing, until he "killed" all the stationary targets, then all the simulacra one-on-one, one-on-two, one-on-three. The Hollys didn't run to four simulacra. Maybe he should donate one.

Holm Holly dragged him back to the main salon and the melee. Cratag was there, and others that didn't often come, so a grand fight was on. That helped.

Finally Laev teleported directly to the HouseHeart, let Brazos in, who hissed and stomped and railed against females.

Laev wasn't too proud to drink a soothing potion from the HouseHeart no-time. It distanced his emotions and let pain trickle in slowly, as he was able to deal with it. Laev thought that he was becoming an expert at surviving a long bitterness. His marriage with Nivea, his grief at his FatherSire's death, now this. He had much in his life to be grateful for. None of his past mistakes had been fatal, or so dire that he'd been unable to recover from them.

Tomorrow was another day, and he'd make sure he didn't see Camellia.

Twenty-eight

❧

*E*arly the next morning, Camellia walked back and forth on the sidewalk outside the stoop of the Green Knight, not quite sure what she was doing here. It wasn't open yet and usually didn't have people waiting to enter. Like all Holly properties, it was canny in defense. The stairs were steepish and the stoop itself could hold one big man, which meant the door could be defended by one man.

To her horror, she saw a small figure materialize on the porch. Little Cal Marigold, age four. She jumped up the stairs to take his hand, hopefully to keep him safe from walking into the street or teleporting anywhere else.

He looked up at her and offered a sweet smile. "Do you want in?"

That might be the safest place for him until she could scry someone. "Uh, yeah."

He put his palm on the door and said a few words and the shields dropped. Camellia didn't know how those particular shields worked, by aura-lifeforce or spellwords or a combination of both, but decided she'd better mention the situation to the Hollys.

She opened the door, felt a ruffling as if Laev was in there . . . even if he was, she couldn't leave now, not with Cal. Letting a quiet breath out, she made sure the boy was in—and kept a solid grip on his fingers—closed the door, and physically locked it.

Spell-lights were on. "I think someone's here," she said.

Cal nodded solemnly. "Oh, yes. Dey are all here talking about

me. Neutwal gwound for Papa and Laev." He smiled deeply and she
noticed he had two killer dimples. "Not Hawthown or Holly Wesi-
dences."

He'd mentioned the Hawthorn family first, did he now consider
himself more Hawthorn than the epitome of Holly-ness, Tab Holly?
The questions buzzed in her mind, scarily unaskable and unanswer-
able.

"It was fun living in dis place, above de salon, but now I live in
de most beautiful house on Celta." Another smile.

"Uh-huh." She'd never been to D'Marigold's Residence but had
seen holos.

Cal was tugging on her hand and she took small steps to match
his and they went through the atrium—she noted that the empty
teleportation pad showed it was in use. To prevent Cal from teleporting to it? She didn't know. But the feeling of impending doom
seemed to rush toward her, then the swinging doors opened and
Vinni T'Vine, the prophet, stepped out from the main gym.

"Greetyou, Cal. Ah, GraceMistrys Darjeeling, good to see you."
He looked at her hand holding Cal's and seemed relieved. A smile
flashed across his face as he bowed to her. But when he straightened, she felt his fearsome attention focused on her.

"I don't meddle much in others' affairs without asking . . ."

"Dat's not twue," Cal said loudly, clearly.

Vinni winced and glanced over his shoulder.

"And I tink if people are talking about me, I should be dere."

"I was speaking to GraceMistrys Darjeeling, Cal, of *her* life.
Mind your manners."

"Sowwy, Vinni. Sowwy, Camellia." Cal squeezed her fingers,
then went on, "*Her* life?" Now Cal, too, was completely concentrating on her.

Camellia stiffened her spine. "I don't—" Her words and mouth
dried as she met Vinni's eyes that held a great sadness. Her heart
thumped hard.

"I did promise Laev that I wouldn't interfere more in his life
some years ago," Vinni said softly.

"Dat's twue, I heard it," Cal said.

"But I wish to tell you to be careful, and that I am sorry you chose the path you did."

Oh. Yeah. *That* was helpful. Camellia dropped Cal's hand and the boy marched past them, pushing hard at one of the doors.

She managed to swallow, nod. "Thank you, GreatLord T'Vine. I hear you."

"Yes, you heard and you listened." Another quick smile. "It might be enough. Thank you for the courtesy." He pivoted, stretched out an arm, and shoved the door open, holding it for her after Cal bulleted through. So, of course, she couldn't do what she really wanted to do and run.

She entered to see all the Hollys, Cratag, and Laev, and T'Ash, engaged in a melee.

"Huh," Cal said.

"Not everything is about you, young Cal." This time Vinni's smile was without shadow and he winked at Camellia.

Cal walked onto the floor. The room quieted. Obviously everyone had heard that the boy was the reincarnation of Tab Holly. The child set his hands on his hips, looked at the Holly men. Before he could say anything, Vinni T'Vine swooped down on him, picked him up, and whirled him around. Cal laughed.

In the still silent room, Vinni said, "Didn't we agree that it was wrong to mix lives?"

Cal looked at him solemnly. "Maybe dere's a weason I wemember."

"Maybe," Vinni said, but handed the boy over to Cratag, who'd strode up.

"The Cherry theater is advertising a role for a child in their new play. What say you and your mother and I go down there and see how you'll do?"

"Weally? Weally!" Now Cal was all child, wriggling in his father's arms. "Yes! Let's 'port *now*."

"I can't teleport," said his father.

"I will—" Cal started.

"No. The glider awaits and we will drive home. But we can take a fast, luxury airship in a septhour. Your mother mentioned that auditions run today and tomorrow."

Cal began chattering excitedly.

Vinni T'Vine nodded at Cratag. "Well done."

Cratag nodded back, nodded toward the other men. "Had help." Then carried his son from the room.

She looked at Laev, who had retreated from the cluster of fighters and was across the room, dressed in the black leathers he used to shoot in.

For the first time since she'd met him again, Laev looked tough . . . and mean. He was wiping blood from the corner of his mouth with an expensive white softleaf.

And she knew why she'd been compelled to come to the Green Knight. Deep within, where their bond lurked, she'd known he was here.

Now she knew that she had to follow her heart. She had hurt him, and that was wrong. She would be brave now, and vulnerable. That was right.

So she strode over to him, saw the haughty mask of a GreatLord descend upon him . . . not only his face, but his whole manner stiffened.

After one huge breath and putting some stiffening of her own in her knees, she said, "I'm sorry I hurt you. I was wrong and fearful and I apologize."

He flicked a hand as if wanting her to go away. His gaze burnt into her own. "Do you trust me?"

"Yes." She swallowed. "With everything I have. I want to get back together."

"No." He pivoted.

"I love you," she said, and his shoulders tensed and she knew it was too little, too late. Nivea had probably told him she loved him. He wouldn't know that this was the first time Camellia had ever said the words to any man other than her brother.

Oh, she hurt! As much as he must have. She pushed that away—

she'd been in the wrong, was still in the wrong. Both she and Nivea had abused his feelings and she loathed that she was in the same category as the woman.

She turned and Vinni T'Vine was there, looking sympathetic. "What do you think I should do?"

He stilled, surprised. "You're actually asking me?"

"Yes." She wouldn't have second thoughts.

"People don't usually do that outside of formal consultations. Thanks." He studied her thoughtfully, glanced at Laev disappearing into the men's room. "Fight."

Camellia blinked. "Fight?"

"Everything you do today, fight. Don't give up."

She took a step in Laev's direction but couldn't face him again.

"Leaving him for now is also good. I didn't mean him, now," Vinni said.

"All right, you're confusing me."

Vinni shrugged a shoulder. "He's your HeartMate, he'll come around. Eventually. Just as you did."

She and Laev had been doing a back-and-forth dance. She let a breath sift out. He *would* be back, or she would say the hard but lovely words to him again. In a while. A couple of months, maybe.

She turned aside, noted that all the men seemed to be studiously avoiding looking at her. Fine. Nodding to Vinni, she said, "See you later."

"I hope so. Remember, fight."

And that just terrified her, so she stuck their conversation into the back of her mind and teleported away.

*I*t was one of those days when everything went wrong—in both of her teahouses—and kept her scrying back and forth, with the occasional teleportation.

Mica had been whiney and underfoot so much that Camellia had banished her from the businesses. Camellia had had to call and cancel her morning training with Cymb Lemongrass and teleport home to change into a different set of clothes. A large urn had broken and poured tea all over her trous suit, which, of course, had been cream colored.

She'd taken a quick waterfall and wanted to sink into one of her chairs for just a few minutes to gather her thoughts when a knock came at her door.

Extending her senses, she knew it wasn't anyone she knew. Walking silently to the door, she looked out of the peephole and saw a large, ruggedly featured man looking back at her. Something was familiar about him, and she realized she'd seen him before, watching her home.

"Who are you?" she projected through the door.

"Garrett Primross, private investigator." He held up a card and she stared at it.

"Why are you here?"

"I want to talk to you about your father and uncle. You want me to shout my questions through the door so the whole neighborhood can hear?"

"Most of the neighborhood already knows what's going on with my father and uncle," she retorted.

Let him in, Mica said, trotting up to the door. *I seen him.*

Camellia switched her stare down toward her cat. *You've seen him!*

He is at Brazos's house sometimes. She sat and licked a forepaw. *Laev's friend.*

Ideas whirled and clicked into place. Laev had come to her office and she and her friends had deduced that Nivea had stolen from him.

At least Camellia had never done that.

But that was why this Garrett Primross was here. And how did her father and uncle feature into the whole business?

She laughed in a broken voice, shook her head. Of course her father and uncle would feature into FirstFamily thefts if at all possible. And . . . could this have been another fateful thread to bind her and Laev together? Maybe.

It was all too sad, though.

"GraceMistrys?" the investigator prompted.

She opened the door. "Come in." Gesturing to the mainspace, she said, "Sit down, do you want anything to drink?"

Primross's brows rose, then he smiled, and Camellia noted it was a good one, something that might stir a heart. But not hers. "I like smoky tea," he said.

Camellia suppressed a sigh. That could mean at least three packets of leaves that she had on hand. She went to the tins lining the kitchen counter and chose the blandest.

"Sweet or milk?" she projected her voice.

"No, thanks," Primross said.

She boiled water in two sturdy mugs with a Word—since she did that all the time it took little energy. She brewed the tea, knowing that as the minutes passed, the investigator was in her largest chair and studying her space. He murmured to Mica and rubbed her.

When Camellia exited the kitchen and gave him the mug, he said, "I'm here on behalf of Laev T'Hawthorn."

Her heart jumped in her chest, even as she knew that Laev wouldn't have sent him for any personal reason. Then she noticed the card he was holding out.

"Prime Investigations," she read aloud after she took it.

"I'm a private detective searching for certain items that became missing from T'Hawthorn Residence."

She put into words her own previous deduction. "Nivea Sunflower Hawthorn took Hawthorn heirlooms."

The large man shrugged. "That's right."

"I told Laev all I knew about the Salvage Ball."

"I've read the file on your recent complaints against your father and your uncle."

Heat flooded her, then chill. "You haven't reported that to Laev, have you?" The day before yesterday, Laev would have used all his considerable resources to find and bring her male relatives to justice. Now she didn't know.

He raised his brows in a cool manner. "No."

Her muscles remained tense, the knowledge hadn't eased her.

Primross continued, "Some artifacts belonging to Hawthorn Residence passed through your father's hands, particularly when he was in Gael City. I've just returned from there."

She wanted to close her eyes, but even that minuscule comfort was beyond her, she was wound up. "When you report to Laev, can you not mention my complaints?"

The detective considered her, then inclined his head. She responded. They both knew that the items just being in her father's possession would be enough for Laev to act against him and her uncle. They'd made an enemy of a FirstFamily GreatLord, and no one did that and prospered. Their rampage would come to an end, sooner rather than later, just as she'd hoped.

It gave her no joy. Her being seemed hollow.

"What puzzles me," Primross was saying, "was how your father and uncle continue to enter this place easily."

She blinked. "Isn't that in my report? There's no alarm my uncle can't disarm. There's no door he can't open, no hidden safe he can't find and open."

Primross jackknifed up. "What?"

"My uncle can get through anything."

The detective plunked his mug down hard enough that the bottom thunked against the wood of the table. His eyes gleamed as he got to his feet. "Now I know them. They've been implicated in robberies in Gael City, were part of a gang operating here some years ago."

None of that surprised Camellia.

"I can't believe it wasn't in your complaint."

Camellia shrugged. "I'm sure I told the guards. One of the men never approved of me filing complaints."

"Fligger," Primross said. "I need to look at all the files again, but this is the last bit of information I need to close some cases. May I teleport away?"

"Sure."

He stepped onto her teleportation pad, his face hard. "Laev told me that he couldn't find his HeartGift." Not looking at her, he added, "Seems to me that the other party might be able to do that. Might be a nice gesture."

She shook her head violently. "No, it would only remind him . . ." But the man was gone. Still she finished the sentence. "Of us both." She didn't want to, daren't.

All she could manage to do today was get through it the best she could.

"Let's go back to the teahouse," she said to Mica. "It's time for me to make a round with my customers." Since pretending good cheer was exquisitely painful, Aquilaria had her doing it more often today. Almost every septhour.

You are a stup, Mica repeated, something *she* said almost every septhour.

"I know."

Laev is a stup, too.

"He's a proud man."

Stup. Even Brazos is a stup. I am the only Smart One in the Family.

Camellia winced.

Twenty-nine

*A*fter *his morning session with Jasmine, Laev contacted Cratag* T'Marigold by scry since the man was in Gael City. He and his HeartMate, Signet, and Cal all beamed out at him on the large panel. "I suppose I must congratulate you on getting the part, Cal?" he asked.

"Yes!" The boy hopped up and down.

"That's wonderful," Laev said.

"What's wrong?" Cratag asked.

Laev hesitated. The Family and Residence knew that his wooing had crumbled into splinters, but Laev hadn't said it aloud and didn't intend to now.

"HeartMate problems. I know that look," Signet said. Her pleasure dimmed a little as she grimaced. She punched Cratag in the biceps. "I saw it often enough on my face for some weeks, years ago."

Cratag looked away—from his wife's pain and from Laev's. Memories of how Cratag had been the only one from the Family at Laev's wedding shot through Laev.

"Not again!" Cal said.

Laev cleared his throat. "Cal's . . . recollection is why I scried."

All three stared at him curiously.

"What?" asked Cratag.

"I want to make Cal my heir. I need to designate one . . . just in case."

Cal scowled, thrust out his tiny chest. "I am Mawigold. I am not Hawthown."

Laev raised his brows. "The closest young relatives I have are my cuzes, who are Holm and Lark Holly's children. I cannot, in good conscience, let the Hawthorn holdings go to a Family with whom we feuded. I am closer to Cratag than anyone else in the Family. He's a good man and like a brother to me. Cal, you are his son, younger than he and me, and most likely to survive us both. I want you as my heir. The Hawthorn House Heart approves."

Signet's brow creased, her eyes looked troubled. "We understand. But we'll discuss this as a Family."

"For now, can I record my choice with the FirstFamilies Council clerk?"

"For now," she agreed reluctantly.

"Good. Thank you. When you return, I'd like you all to spend the day here. I don't think Cal's toured the whole grounds or Residence."

Cratag inclined his head. "We can do that."

"Good." Laev waited a beat. "I am hiring Antenn Moss-Blackthorn to redesign the MasterSuite." He dredged up a smile. "The Marigolds are famous for their good taste, I could use your input."

"Done." Signet's smile was a whole lot nicer than his. Then she said softy, "It *does* get better, Laev. Every day. And HeartMates are forever."

He felt his face get stony. "Blessed be."

"Love ya, Laev!" Cal piped.

Now Laev's smile was almost real. "Love you, too. And you, Signet and Cratag."

"Love you," Cratag said gruffly, and Signet in that same soft tone that made his insides ache.

Laev cut the scry and another one came in immediately from the Green Knight. "Here," he said.

"My brother told me you were incredible at the shooting range yesterday," Tinne said. His teeth showed in a slightly predatory smile. "Perhaps even better than me."

"I wouldn't say—"

"Shut up, Laev. Don't you know a challenge when you hear it? Pistols at the range, EveningBell. Be here. Dress the part. The prize is teaching youngsters shooting, consider that. Later."

Laev actually found his lips curved slightly. He liked teaching Jasmine, he might like teaching others.

Signet was right. It got easier. She'd gotten the culprit wrong, though. He was the one sticking now. He wasn't sure how long it would take him before the pain diminished enough for him to trust life and destiny and his HeartMate again. A year. A season. A month.

Not today. Meanwhile, he needed an heir who was *not* a Holly. So he drafted the formal paper and got on with his life as a Great-Lord.

Tiana scried as soon as Camellia arrived at home at WorkEndBell. "A colleague has requested me to officiate at his wedding tonight in GreatCircle Temple! You're invited! Can you come?" she panted.

"Congratulations."

"For all of us. The marriage is an impulse, but we all think it's a good match. Say you'll come! The Licorices are all coming!"

Camellia frowned. "I have the delivery of the wardrobe shortly, but as soon as Clover puts it in place, I'll be there."

"Thanks! Later!"

No use telling Tiana she should relax, or reminding her that she'd done half a dozen other ceremonies and been an excellent priestess. Camellia shook her head. Then sagged a bit. She dreaded going to Temple. A wedding. How hard.

Loud knocking came at her door and she pushed her hair away from her face. She didn't want to answer it.

"Clovers' Fine Furniture!" a man shouted.

Her wardrobe! Her spirits lifted a little. She'd been living moment by moment, and this particular moment felt better than the rest that day. She hurried over to the door, opened it. A brawny man stood on the threshold, balancing the wardrobe with a glider spell. "Where do you want it?" he asked.

"The bedroom. East wall where the tapestry is. You can take the cloth down." She gestured to the hallway. "First right."

He scanned her mainspace. "Can I push this through or will I have to translocate it?"

"You can glide it through." She waved a hand.

The scry panel sounded.

"Go ahead and take that." Clover smiled cheerfully, walking slowly by her, pulling the wardrobe.

She answered the scry panel; her stomach knotted when she saw her father's face. "I'm sorry, Father, I have someone—"

"Stop. If you want to see your brother again, listen carefully."

"What!"

Her father smiled. "You like Senchal. You can keep him alive, for a price."

The words made no sense. "He's your son!"

"I doubt that."

Realization was beginning to set in. Nausea splashed through her, settled in her throat. "You have no reason to doubt that. He looks like you."

Her father just shrugged.

The Clover in the bedroom called, "You've got a mangled wall here. I can patch these gouges around the safe. Will cost extra. You sure you want the wardrobe in front of the safe?"

"Yes. Go ahead and patch and deduct the cost from my account," she yelled back, choosing to deal with the easy problem first.

"Pay attention!" snapped her father.

"Listening," she said.

"The boy means nothing to me." Her father smiled. "Little to me, or rather not as much to me as to you and the gilt you can bring me."

It felt like she stood in winter snow, she was so cold, her mind frozen. "What do you want?" she asked, but she knew. Tears were frozen deep within her, too. She was going to lose the possession she prized the most.

"The tea set. It belongs to me and your uncle. Never should have come to you."

No reason to tell them again that they never would have found it or been able to claim it on their own. That didn't matter. And no tea set, as much as she loved it and however incredible its value, was worth a life.

The Clover walked out of her bedroom, dusting his hands. "You're good." With a last nod, he left.

"We have a buyer for the set," her father said. "You can translocate it and your brother will remain fine."

"You'll kill him anyway," she said listlessly.

"Why should we do that? And we aren't going to kill him. If you don't comply, he'll just have an unfortunate accident."

"How much hard gilt would you take for Senchal, for the tea set instead?" Finally her brain was working. If she raided all her accounts, sold everything she could . . .

Her father named a figure.

She gasped. Hard, hard, hard, but doable.

"I can get that."

Her father's eyes widened. "My, my, my, you have been busy, haven't you?" His face twisted. "I see we've been too easy on you."

Camellia thought her heart might shrivel hard in her chest, it hurt so much.

"You have a septhour and a half to give us the gilt, otherwise you'll have a dead brother and more consequences."

"I can't get it by then. I need to sell . . ."

He shrugged. "Borrow the gilt. Or you can get the tea set from T'Reed's Residence vault by then. He and his Family are out of town, but the Residence will let you in. I have it on good authority that it doesn't *care for any matters save the Reeds'* so it won't help you or report us."

Unfortunately that was true, not that she wanted to be indebted to the Reeds, which she would be if she asked for help—for her brother, she would, but impossible now. "Give me the address where he is, first."

Her father laughed in her face. "So you can muster the guards-men? After all those times you threatened me—threatened us—with them? No." When he finished laughing his smile was sharp. "I'll scry you in a septhour and three-quarters and give you the address where we'll meet. Bring along a noncancellable gilt scrip from the NobleCouncil for the gilt."

They'd planned well. All her accounts with a—she figured num-bers in her head—a nontransferable assignment of her annual NobleGilt and most of the profits from the teahouses for seven years, and she'd have enough to ransom her brother.

"And just understand, if anything happens to us, your brother is in a place where he won't survive the night."

Camellia shuddered. "Use my perscry."

"Sure. Better hurry." He laughed again, tapped his wrist timer. "Minutes are counting down."

She hurried into the bedroom, flung off her clothes, and yelled, "Whirlwind spell, max professional!" She spun and her clothes stripped from her, her body was scoured with a hot wind and herbs to cleanse her, her hair tugged into a fashionable style, and clothes wrapped around her, tabs fastened. By the time the spell was fin-ished, she was panting with stinging eyes. She glanced in the mirror. Looked good enough to convince anyone, including the Noble-Council evening clerk, that she wanted to assign all her gilt to her father. An acid hole gnawed the pit of her stomach.

She ignored it, shook her sleeves to check her pockets, and sent a mental sensing to determine she had everything she needed. Then she walked to her teleportation pad and scanned the signal of one of the pads outside the NobleCouncil office at the Guildhall. Free.

Camellia visualized the pad and the coordinates and the light and was there. She'd be using a lot of energy this evening, probably would exhaust herself and all her Flair, but her lips began moving in a silent prayer that she'd say every minute she was alone.

She couldn't call Tiana or the Licorices at GreatCircle Temple. She couldn't endanger them.

The next septhour passed in the agonizing slowness of bureau-

cracy, covering Camellia's skin with a thin layer of the cool perspiration of fear. The NobleCouncil clerk consolidated all of Camellia's
accounts at various banks to one the Council would monitor.
Camellia didn't like all of her gilt in one place, another price she
would pay for her brother. She signed papers to send the flow of her
NobleGilt and most of her profits to her father.

Of course the clerk asked if anything was wrong, and of course
Camellia denied it. Then, pleading the fact that she was overdue at
a ceremony at GreatCircle Temple, she hurried from the Guildhall.
The precious scrip was in the hidden pocket of her sleeve seam.
CityCenter was quiet and Camellia crossed to the round park and
sat tensely on a bench, her perscry orb cupped in her palm. She
wished she could return home and change, her tunic and trous felt
like a burden instead of clothing.

Her perscry pinged. "Here," she said as her father's face curved
weirdly in the glass.

He grinned and she flinched.

"You got the scrip?"

"I do. All the papyrus are in order at the NobleCouncil."

"Good. Meet me at SouthGate Temple transnow."

"I don't know the coordinates."

"I'll only wait five minutes, then your brother will suffer. More
than he is now." Her father shook his head. "Such a weak son. No
use to me at all."

Unlike her. She'd paid and paid and paid again. "You do know
that you have most of my gilt and future income." She couldn't keep
the bitterness out of her voice.

"For now," her father said, cheerfully, expansively. Shook his
head. "Damn shame your HeartMate T'Hawthorn dumped you,
otherwise you'd have a lot more." He shrugged. "But the Hawthorns can be stubborn. He'll be back, and Takvar and I will have
plenty of gilt to live on until then." He rubbed his hands.

Camellia sat in shock. "How did you know?" Her voice was
nearly a whisper and she glanced around the park, no one was
there.

Her father snorted. "You're my daughter, linked to me. Didn't you think I could tell you'd forged a newer, larger link with a HeartMate? Didn't take much watching or listening to know who he is." He rubbed his hands again.

"Besides, you always keep your eye on the main chance," Camellia said bitterly.

He nodded. "Always." Again he tapped his wrist timer. "South-Gate Temple."

"I don't know the coordinates!"

"Teleport to South Park pad and run, then. I'll meet you in ten. Wait for me."

"The address where Senchal is——"

But the orb went dark.

Camellia dropped the perscry into her sleeve. Her face was wet. Tears, and she hadn't even known she was weeping. Dammit! She would never be free of them, and they'd bleed her and Laev dry, too. Take more pride from her than Nivea had stolen from Laev, more gilt from him than his ex-wife had dreamt. Her relatives would brew up more scandal, keep them in a tempest.

Somehow she'd stop them, but there was no time to think of that now. Survive this latest contretemps and figure out what to do later. Tomorrow.

A thought occurred to her. Why wasn't her uncle with her father? It took only a second to know. Her uncle would be at her house, stripping it of anything of value.

Shock, anger ran through her. But her father had said ten minutes and to wait. Oh, that man had other plans, too. She didn't know what, but he'd make her wait while he finished carrying out his plans, and her uncle raided her house.

Oh, no, they wouldn't!

She hurried to the CityCenter park teleportation pad and went *home*.

And saw her uncle stuffing Laev's gift into a large furrabeast satchel. Probably had been a couple of other items she'd ordered in the house cache, too. He must have sensed the most valuable pieces were there and raided that first.

"Fligger," he growled. "Guri was supposed to keep you busy." His eyes narrowed, using his Flair, scanning her. He leapt for her and she whirled away, but he caught the sleeve of her gown that held the scrip, yanked, and the folded papyrus fell to the floor. He pounced on it.

She yelled and surged forward, but he fended her off with hard blows from his feet and elbows as he flipped open the papyrus and read it. Then he swung out an arm, and she had to duck before it connected with enough force to put her down and out.

Angry blood suffused his face. "Fligger, you made it out to your *father*. I told him it should have been me."

"No, your name isn't on it," she gasped, stripped off her tunic to stand in her undershirt, ready to fight. Waiting, watching him. "Maybe he doesn't trust you as much as you think he does."

"He loves me more than anyone else in the world," her uncle said matter-of-factly. "Certainly better than you or your brother." He plucked a small piece of paper from his trous pocket. "Don't you want to save your brother? This is the address. You love him." Her uncle shrugged. "The stup."

"And you only love yourself," she said.

"I'm the center of the universe."

"You're a warped criminal."

The musical note of the teleportation signal sounded and Mica was there, all her fur on end. *FamWoman needs Me!*

Her uncle jolted. His gaze fastened on the scrip with her father's name. "You fliggering flitch . . ." Evil lit within him and glowed from his eyes. He lunged.

He wasn't the size and shape of her father, of Lemongrass, but her body reacted as it had been trained. She knocked his arms aside with a blow of her own, spun, and bumped his body until he was off balance and down. He was stronger, his muscles leaner and tougher than her father's.

I will get him! Mica screeched. But she miscalculated her pounce and he struck her and she went limp. Takvar laughed, raised his foot to kick.

"Mica!" Camellia screamed. She'd been pushed too far. Now she would push back. "I will *kill* you for that." She rushed him and time slowed. She was aware of her balance, of her trajectory. Of the amount of force she'd hit him with, how they would fall.

The jolt of surprise formed on his face in slow motion. As if he finally saw in *her* something of himself and her father. His head turned back and forth as if searching for a way to evade her. Then he vanished and a hideous scream was cut short. She hit the floor.

Panting, Camellia rose and strode over to Mica, gently checked the cat's head. No terrible dents. Mica whimpered and Camellia thought that was a good sign. She picked up the cat—who wasn't quite limp, a tensile energy in her body that Camellia also thought was good—and put her in the corner of the sofa. Then Camellia limped into the bedroom where the shriek came from. There was a terrible smell and she stopped, stunned, on the threshold, her hand over her mouth in horror.

Thirty

*H*er uncle had teleported to the wall in front of her safe. Into *the* wardrobe the Clover had set there. After one shocked glimpse, she just stood stunned. She'd never seen anything like it—a mixture of splintered wood and shredded flesh and bone. Another brief glance and she knew her uncle was dead. Half of his bloody face was inset in the wardrobe door. One hand, too. Neither moved.

She gulped and ran back to the mainspace. Mica was stirring, softly moaning, tilting her head back and forth. "Be careful! Don't hurt yourself more. I think we need to take you to the animal Healer, D'Ash." Better to concentrate on her live and beloved Fam than her hated and very dead uncle. Camellia was cold and tugged on her tunic.

Nooo. An ear twitch, then a pink tongue sticking out. *Don' want to go nowhere. 'Specially don' wanna 'port.*

"All right, rest a little. I can call a glider and you'll go."

Very slow glider.

"All right." Camellia scooped up the scrip, ran to the hidden no-time—which was standing open, stuck it inside under *refreshing potion*, and locked it. She saw the papyrus with the address, one in the warehouse district, where Senchal was kept.

FamWoman?

"Sorry, scrying a glider now. You'll have to go alone. I have to save Senchal, he's in danger. I have to report my uncle's death."

FamWoman!

In an explosion of static and sound and more screams, her scry panel came on, her father's face red and contorted. "What did you do, you flitch! My brother is *dead*!"

He knew.

"I did nothing!" Camellia protested. "It was an acci—"

"You don't think I knew you'd 'ported home?" Spittle hit the scry screen. "Him there, for your personal gilt. Me here, for the gilt in the tearoom. Then we'd meet and get your scrip."

"What!" She'd been so focused on her father that she hadn't checked the small bit of surroundings behind him. Darjeeling's Teahouse. More screams.

"With the amount of this gilt, we'd live easy for the rest of our lives. I will kill you for this." Her own words, back at her.

"An accident!" she shouted.

"No! My brother is dead!" he raged. More horror as he grabbed a candle, flung it at a lace curtain, and flamed it into a streak of burning fire with a Word. When he turned back to her, she saw his fists clenched around gilt. Good, Aquilaria hadn't fought. He bared his teeth at her. "I'll kill you, for sure, but I'll kill that brother of yours first."

Sounds of breaking china, destruction—he'd enjoy that. Much as she hated hearing it, his rampage could slow him down. She saw the broad back of him as he upended the closest table, went on to another.

Aquilaria came into view. "Camellia, we need you."

Aquilaria's face was pale. Disaster had struck again.

For a few seconds, Camellia hesitated. Her teahouse or her brother? Her beloved business or a man who had always disappointed her like every other man in her life before Laev?

No question.

"Take care of the teahouse, Aquilaria, I can't handle it right now. Call the fire mages and the guardsmen. Report everything. Assure the customers that—I don't know, that we'll pay or compensate, or give them free—I trust you. I *must* go."

"Camellia, let me help you. Talk to me!"

"No time!" Camellia swallowed. "Call the guard for my place, here, too. My uncle teleported into a wardrobe." She forced down her gag instinct. "It's terrible. Contact Death Grove."

"What!"

Mica mewed.

"And send someone over here to take Mica to D'Ash's. Please, Aquilaria. That's how you can help!"

From the chaos on the scry panel came an authoritative man's voice, vaguely familiar. "What's going on here!"

Camellia recognized the profile. "Trust that guy, Primross! Gotta go!" She used the fear pumping through her to teleport away to the closest public pad that she knew of in the warehouse district.

It was dark with only a few spellglobes in occasional brackets in the buildings. The area was mostly populated by day. Camellia shivered, pulled the crumpled piece of papyrus from her sleeve pocket to check the address. Two streets north, then angle west. Hurry!

She ran, glad of her recent physical training, though her energy was draining. Maybe she had enough strength to teleport herself and Senchal . . . where? His place, maybe. Worry about that later.

Then she was there, standing before the hole of a door in a crumbling brick warehouse. The place was more than damp, it was at the edge of an old dock and she could see that the ocean had made inroads and was claiming the building.

With a whispered word, she lit a spellglobe that would precede her, saw a slight path through rubble. It looked like something had been dragged, like her brother's body.

Beyond the darkness of the door came the splash of water, the tide was rising.

"Senchal?" she called. Nothing. Taking step by cautious step, she followed the bobbing light into the building, and the blackness was even more complete.

Harsh breathing sounded counterpoint to water lapping. "More light!" she commanded, spending energy recklessly. The whole room brightened with a multitude of miniature suns. There was a drop-off in the floor, then it angled down to an open wall that faced the sea. Senchal was propped in a corner of the lower level, his face splattered with blood and a wound on his head. His legs were underwater, his torso shuddered with cold.

He wasn't conscious enough to save himself. She jumped down into the water; it splashed up to her knees, soaking her trous.

Then an emotional blow flattened her and she fell face-first into the chill water.

Her father was dead? Had she felt the violent snuffing of his life?

She rocked to her hands and knees, panting. Again she tested the bond, but it had been so tiny that she couldn't tell whether it really was gone.

Senchal thrashed and groaned. Grabbing her brother, she used more Flair to lift them to dry ground. She banished all but one faint light, regretting the energy she'd spent.

"Safe, you're safe," she sobbed as she held Senchal. They trembled and she thought the shudders came from them both. Swallowing hard, she reached into her trous pocket and brought out a softleaf, wiped his bloody face enough to see the purpling bruises underneath. He was holding his arm oddly and Camellia thought it might be broken.

"Can't . . ." His whisper sounded scraped from his throat. "Can't . . ."

"We'll 'port to AllClass HealingHall." She scrambled for the coordinates, the image and light of AllClass HealingHall, trying to set them in her mind so they could 'port successfully.

I can take him. The telepathic voice was low and growly, heavy. Camellia's visualization wisped away as if torn by the wind. She turned her head slowly. "Who're you?"

A large, old, and ponderously moving dog nudged them. Senchal struggled against Camellia's grip and she let him wrap his arms around the dog, who looked at her with calm eyes. *I am his Fam, Cherripunji. We found each other just today. Took me a long time to get here from his rooms.*

"They didn't hurt you. They didn't!" Senchal cried.

No. Cherripunji turned and licked Senchal's face. *They hurt YOU.* He looked at Camellia again. *I told him not to trust Father and Uncle, but he is not smart. I know AllClass HealingHall well and can take him there, but not you. We will go there. You will follow?*

"Yes." She wiped her arm across her face, uncaring that she smeared sweat and tears on her arm.

Again she tried to sense her father. Again she failed.

Finally, finally it was all over.

Her gilt and business were safe. She and her brother were safe from the two men who should have protected them, yet abused them all their lives. "We're safe."

She took a pace back, watched, sniffling, as the big dog and her brother vanished.

Before her breathing had time to steady, she heard footsteps and whirled.

"They may be safe, but you aren't." Feam Kelp stepped from the shadows, a shine highlighting the edge of his long, sharp dagger. "I'm glad I didn't have to kill the dog. It would have been a pity."

Cold spread within her, grabbed her breath. She was in more danger now than when she'd faced her uncle. She *forced* her lungs to move in and out.

"I don't understand." She lifted her hands to tuck them into her sleeves.

"Hands out where I can see them," Feam snapped. His face twisted into rage.

"Why do you hate me so?" she whispered.

He jerked a shoulder. "I don't. I hate *him.*"

"My brother? Senchal is harmless."

A rasping laugh. "Not *him.* You're as much of a stup as he is, though." Feam turned the long knife back and forth so it caught the light.

"My father, my uncle." She lifted her hands. "Whatever they did to you, they harmed us, too. They were bad men." Her mind felt dizzy at the thought of both of them being dead. Focus! This was *not* the time to lose concentration. "We're as much victims as you."

"Victim." Feam smiled and it wasn't nice. "You, my victim. I like the sound of that."

She was in trouble. She sent her mind questing to all the teleportation pads she knew—her own, the Licorices', the teahouses'. All in use. She couldn't just teleport to her house, there were bound to be people in it.

Feam's arm swept out and something flew to her, struck her in her chest. She stumbled back and hit her head against the wall of the building. Pain exploded and slid wetly down her head. Blood. A fighting baton she hadn't noticed fell to her feet and rolled.

Bad enough head injury that she couldn't 'port at all now. Her spell-light had vanished. His was bright white.

Feam laughed. He could afford to. She could barely move, barely blink.

"Look at *me*!" Feam demanded and Camellia slowly turned her aching head to face him.

He flipped the knife, again seeming fascinated with the blade.

"Why?" she formed the word with her lips, but the sound faded as soon as she said it. Feam seemed to understand, though. He gave her one of those enraged smiles.

"Why? Because I loathe him and he loves you."

Comprehension snuck through her pain-dimmed thoughts. "Laev."

"Ha!" Feam shook his head theatrically. "At last she understands. Yes," he hissed. "Because of Laev." Feam's mouth curled cruel. "He hurt her so much. *Tortured* her. Neglected her in her final sickness." His brows lowered. "He killed her, you know, hid the act and pretended that the sickness had carried her off. But it was him. Always him."

"Always him she stayed with, never you," whispered Camellia, deducing the path of Feam's fantasy.

His free hand fisted, he prowled forward. "She loved *me*. He only caused her pain. He tortured her," Feam repeated. "Like I will torture you."

Camellia didn't think so.

"She knew he had a HeartMate. That hurt *her* so much. She wept in my arms." His face turned fierce. "But we had some revenge. We hid his HeartGift. She took prizes from T'Hawthorn Residence, some we left on tables at the Salvage Ball." He grinned. "Some we gave to thieves to sell."

"So you knew my father and uncle. And recently you found out about me."

"It didn't take much"—Feam shrugged negligently—"just keeping track of your so-noble Sire and uncle." His lip curled. "They're lazy men, and once I found their lair, it was easy to listen in on them and their plans. I let them torment you a little, but it wasn't enough."

Strength was soaking from her into the cold wall, the cold ground, and she didn't like the way Feam carved the air. One. Last. Chance.

She gathered her energy, her Flair, surged toward him.

He yelled. The knife slid into her like ice. She flung up her fist, broke his nose. But didn't send the shards of bone into his brain. She hadn't had the power. He fell and didn't move.

She fell, too, limply. Pain gnashed on her with jagged teeth and dimness threatened.

She was dead and nothing mattered but her mistakes. She loved Laev but had sent him away.

But she could call him. That was truly her last chance. Trust that he wouldn't abandon her. That he would come when she needed him. That he wouldn't ignore her because she'd caused him so much pain. She'd treated him, her HeartMate, worse than she'd ever treated anyone in her life. Dared to hurt him more than she'd ever dream of hurting her friends.

Because *she'd* been afraid.

And it didn't matter if he saved her, though she wanted that. The yearning filled her until it overwhelmed all other pain. All that mattered was that he knew she loved him, respected him, honored him. She flung the bonds between them, bonds she'd kept narrow for most of her life, wide, wide, wide.

Found that his side was not as threadlike as she'd imagined. Not huge, but solid.

Laev! she shrieked mentally, with all of her strength. *Laev! Love you. Lov . . . lo . . . y.*

Camellia! What! Camellia!

Dy-in' . . .

No! His anger, fear, blasted her senses.

Where! he roared. But the angle of her vision changed and she knew he could see through her eyes . . . feel the draining of her blood sinking into the ground.

And he was there.

"Hold on. Hold on. We'll get you—"

"Love," she managed on her last breath before darkness bit into her and rended her and swallowed her.

$\mathcal{F}$*ear spurted through* $\mathcal{L}$*aev. Camellia lay crumpled at his feet, a* blacker shadow in the darkness. He'd focused on her, teleported a half meter from her. Risky, but it had paid off.

"Finally, the hero arrives." The sarcastic tones came with a voice that was thick and cracked and cackling. It echoed off walls of a damp and dark building. Wetness, the sound of the ocean. A warehouse at the docks. Didn't matter.

"I got her, just like I said I would. She didn't suffer as much as my Nivea, but I killed her the way you killed my woman."

Cold chilled Laev from the inside out. The note hadn't been a mistake or simple mischief. All Laev wanted was to grab Camellia and leave. The fligger was wrong, life still trickled through her, but that trickle was sluggish.

"And now I have *you!*" Wild triumph lifted the voice to a scream.

Movement. From behind him and to his right. Body acting as trained, Laev drew and fired. A painful shot. In the quick stream of the blazer, Laev saw swollen features of a vaguely familiar man.

The guy clapped his hands to his head, leapt, and rolled. Made noise as he staggered from the building.

No time to hunt and kill him. Camellia was dying.

He picked her up, made things worse. His mind scrambled for images of Primary HealingHall, bright lights . . . no dimness . . . autumn sun . . . No!

He had to be a rock, concentrate, push all fear away . . . . ignore how his heart pounded nearly out of his chest.

Here, here, here! yelled Brazos. Literally hopping up and down on his four paws. Mica was doing the same, her wild screeches echoing in Laev's mind.

Brazos jumped onto Laev's left shoulder, Mica his right, then the next thing he knew, they were all standing in front of a door in a wall.

Open, open, open! shouted Brazos.

Laev fumbled at the latch. *Where?*

Mica whined. *FamWoman dying!*

Desperation washed through Laev. *Quiet, let me think of the HealingHall* . . . But the wooden door swung open and he stood on a threshold with thick spellshields tingling his skin, probing him for—who cared?

Then two women were there—one resembled Tiana Mugwort. Her sister Artemisia. Artemisia was a Healer! Yes!

The women surrounded them, wrapped arms around him. "'Porting on three," said the older one calmly. "Let us do it, Great-Lord. One, and Cammi, two, and GreatLord, *three!*"

A hint of movement, then he was in a chamber that looked like a hospital room.

"She's dying."

"I won't let her!" said Artemisia.

"Give her to us," said the women and tried to pull Camellia from his arms.

"Mine!"

"Yes, yours. *Let go!*" A sharp command.

Reflexively, he loosened his grip. Camellia was placed on the bed. She looked terrible. Dark blood against her tunic. How had that happened? Didn't matter. He lunged toward her, but Artemisia fended him back with an arm. "Let us work on her!"

"She needs blood?" He flung out his arm. Looked solid to him. Fisted his hand to show the veins.

"Very brawny," the older woman said.

"Take my blood. Anything. I'm her HeartMate!"

Two gazes focused on him.

"HeartMate?" the older woman questioned. She looked like her daughters, except her hair was lighter, blondish. She pointed to a bedside chair. "Hold her hand. Connect with her. Keep her soul in this world!"

Fear throttled him. He nodded, took Camellia's cold fingers in his own, and opened himself to her.

Then he was with her in a different space. A space dim with shadows. A shining ahead of him. The shining moved and he saw it was a wheel. The wheel of stars! For the next life. He didn't want her to leave!

But if she did, he would, too.

Thirty-one

Camellia, he whispered softly. *Drew her close. He couldn't see her, but* he could feel her body. It seemed limp in his arms. He would command. *Camellia!*

Ouch! Her head rolled back and forth on his chest. Good. He let a breath filter out. Maybe they would get through this thing. They *would* get through this thing. What was important, he kept.

Stay with me. In that space, he held her.

Laev? Her attention was turning to him, though he was aware of a steady pull of the wheel of stars to her.

Yes, stay with me.

I love you, she said and he felt it, the warmth of her love enveloping him, infusing him. She slipped from his arms as if that was the last thing she needed to say before she moved on.

No! He reached, clawed at her essence, caged it, brought it back. *Would you abandon me?*

That seemed to shock her into physicality again . . . she was no longer spirit, but woman-shaped.

I . . . do . . . not . . . abandon. She put her arms around him and his breath stopped. He had her.

Of course you don't.

You do not abandon, either. Her tone was tentative.

I'm here, aren't I? I came when you needed me? He waited, on edge now. If she didn't trust him, she could go away again. They

319

weren't HeartBonded, but he would be hard-pressed not to follow. Let the Family and the Residence take care of themselves. They could. They didn't need him. He'd follow Camellia to the wheel of stars.

You came when I needed you, she agreed.

His arms tightened around her. *I will always be here.*

Yes. Her breath was a whisper and she relaxed against him.

Stay with me? he asked.

Yes. She was linked to him, their bond strong and thick as a chain, open both ways, but her consciousness was fading, steady and grounded with him, but . . .

Sleep now, he said. *I'll be here when you awake.*

Yesh.

"She'll be fine." The audible voice was stringent against his physical ears after the low, caressing tones of inner communication.

He straightened and saw Artemisia Mugwort. Suddenly he knew where he was. The legendary First Grove, the original colonial Healing Grove that now only admitted the desperate.

"Yes, she will. When can I take her home?"

A rustle from the door attracted him, and he saw the older woman standing there, hands in opposite sleeves, wariness emanating from her. He didn't think that she would introduce herself. "We have been so careful to keep this place secret from the First-Families," she said.

"I can't thank you enough for the help you've given us and the sanctuary." He breathed deeply and met her eyes, then Artemisia's. "And like the other desperate people who have been graced with the power of this place, I promise never to speak of it." He smiled wryly. "Our Fams teleported us to the door, so I have no idea of the location. No doubt I won't recall how to find it again in any event."

"It's rare for a great noble to find himself or herself desperate. Not even T'Ash found this place as a boy."

"We think he ran the wrong way, and couldn't run very far. Soon afterward he had Zanth as a FamCat," Artemisia murmured.

"No one could argue that a boy with Zanth would ever be desperate," Artemisia's mother ended.

"It may be rare for a FirstFamily GreatLord to find himself here, but as you can see, not impossible." Laev gave a half bow, still holding on to Camellia's hand. "Again, you have my word that I will tell no one . . ." He frowned. "Unless someone I know has need." He shrugged. If someone he knew had need, Laev would help them himself, but no use binding himself too much.

"We accept your word," Artemisia said.

If Camellia was all right, he wanted to leave, and fast. To find Feam before the fligger's trail went cold, hunt the man down as soon as Camellia woke. "I have some business I need to take care of."

"Business?" asked Artemisia sharply.

"FirstFamily business." The older woman snorted.

Laev smiled mildly. "That's right."

"You're going after the man who wounded your HeartMate," said a deep voice from the doorway. Laev looked up to see an older man standing there. His finger was marking the page of an antique book. "Take some advice from a former judge," the man continued.

The older woman sucked in a quick breath. The man waved her concern away with a hand and a half smile. "One can always count on the honor of a Hawthorn, especially this one, my dears. He conducted himself with great character during the Hawthorn-Holly feud."

"The advice?" Laev fought to keep from shifting with impatience.

"Think about what you intend to do, the consequences to yourself and"—the man nodded at Camellia—"your relationship with her. You are not HeartBound yet, and murder could break that fate. And . . ."

"And?" Laev replied promptly, no time to play games.

"Your FatherSire and father, indeed, the whole FirstFamilies Council, learned that no one is above the law."

Laev inclined his head. The only thing the man had said that had given him hesitation was the warning about his bond with Camellia. They'd already had too many highs and lows, and each low had been terrible and had intensified. "Thank you for your advice, GraceLord Mugwort."

The man smiled again with a sincerity that was disarming. "Just Sinjin Mugwort now." He switched his attention to his wife, obviously a HeartMate, gazing down into her eyes. "Can we release these youngsters?"

Be glad to see them go, growled a mental voice that Laev realized was the Residence.

Artemisia sighed. "Always so courteous."

Apologies, Artemisia, now the tone was almost fawning. Then a defensive note, *He is too powerful. He could destroy us.*

"I wouldn't, and you have helped others who are powerful, Captain Ruis Elder, for instance. Tinne Holly."

That is true. Pride infused the telepathic communication.

Laev continued, "And you helped my relative, Cratag Maytree, now Cratag T'Marigold. I owe you for that, too."

"The boy's right. And none of them have betrayed us. In fact, Residence, they banded together to bring us as a Family to care for you," Sinjin Mugwort said.

Also true, but he is still powerful and has business elsewhere so he should go, the Residence ended.

Laev bowed, though he didn't know if the Residence could see him.

"May I take Camellia home?"

"Her wounds are Healed," the older woman said. "Her Flair is good, her energy is reviving. But it was a dreadful wound and she will be physically weak for a while. And her blood will take time to rebuild."

"I understand."

The woman looked at Artemisia. "I would appreciate it if you would recall that my daughter helped save your HeartMate's life."

"Mother!" Artemisia protested the hint for reward.

The former GraceLady Mugwort lifted her chin. "The old scandal surrounding our Family still lives. Artemisia uses a different surname because she might be discriminated against in her career in the HealingHalls."

"I am grateful and will . . . ah . . . watch her career?" Laev asked.

"Yes. We would appreciate it," the man said.

"Father!" Artemisia appealed to the scholarly-looking man.

"Influence is influence," said her father. "And you are my child, I want you to prosper. If there comes a time when T'Hawthorn can help you, I want to be able to count on him to do so."

"Done," Laev said. "And in addition, I will give your daughter Tiana a golden favor token. So your Family can call upon the Hawthorns up to the death of anyone save the Head of Household. A life for a life."

"We do not feud. The Mugworts have never feuded," the man said. "We doubt we would demand a life." He sounded appalled.

From what Laev had heard of the ex-lord and lady, they hadn't fought when they should have, hadn't stood up to the rumors surrounding them. He shrugged. Their past was not his concern. They'd helped him now and deserved the gold token.

The woman curtsied deeply. "We thank you, GreatLord T'Hawthorn."

He nodded, gently slid his arms under Camellia, and lifted her. "Teleporting on three," he said. Artemisia moved to join her parents. Each put a hand on her shoulder.

Envy twinged through him. They were a close and loving Family, and he knew that had Camellia shown up at that door by herself, she'd have been considered part of that Family.

But she was his now, and he would protect her. Feam Kelp would never have a chance to hurt her again.

And someday they would have children of their own, perhaps someday stand like that, a Family.

"My thanks again," he said.

Wait for Us! screeched Brazos. *Stup Residence didn't let Us in!*

The people at the door parted and once again the two Fams

leapt onto Laev's shoulders. He smiled. He had his own Family with him now. "Teleporting on three," he repeated, then counted down. "One, Camellia, two, Laev T'Hawthorn, *three*!"

And they were gone from the lost grove. The familiar comfort of T'Hawthorn Residence surrounded him and he cherished the feeling. They stood on his teleportation pad in his sitting room.

"Residence audio to the entire castle, all the Family within!" Laev snapped.

"Yes, T'Hawthorn. Audio ready."

"My HeartMate was injured and has been Healed. I want servers standing by."

"It will be done," T'Hawthorn Residence whispered. "She is well?"

"She is well and will be staying here. Contact—"

"*You* are well?"

"I'm fine. Contact guardsman Winterberry—"

"He has already been here," the Residence said.

"Our lady's uncle had a disastrous accident teleporting into a wardrobe in her bedroom," the Residence said.

"What!"

I was there. Mica growled. *Serves him right. He hurt Fam-Woman. He hurt Me! Had to go to D'Ash's!* She wrinkled her nose. *Nasty look and smell, though.*

Brazos licked her ear.

The Residence said, "And our lady's father set fire to Darjeeling's Teahouse. He was killed by blazer fire by Garrett Primross."

Laev should have put Camellia down on his bed immediately. He staggered from his sitting room to his bedroom and laid her tenderly on his bed. It was not a bed he'd ever shared with Nivea, and he was glad of that.

Camellia looked perfect there. He thought she might also look perfect in the generational bed in the MasterSuite. Both Mica and Brazos hopped onto the bedsponge.

Knocking came at his sitting room door and he reluctantly left his HeartMate to answer it. As soon as he did, his housekeeper and several of his female relatives who worked as maids bustled in. They brought basins of warm herbed water and towels.

He held the door for them, and by the time the last was through, his housekeeper, Alma, was exclaiming at Camellia's state. Laev's jaw flexed. He strode into his bedroom to see it lit by several spell-globes and the women bathing a nude Camellia. There was a dark red scar where the knife wound had been, but that would fade.

The cats sat, watching every movement.

"Laev, you should go and let us take care of her."

"No. Wash her and leave her be."

His housekeeper sniffed. "I'm sure she would be more comfortable in a nightgown." As soon as she said it, a delicate pale green gown covered her arms in soft folds. It looked long. Laev had never seen Camellia wear a long nightgown.

"She prefers a sleep shirt of antique fashion," he said.

"Hmm." Alma frowned, then the gown vanished and a bright red silkeen sleep shirt appeared with rounded hems in the front and back.

"Dress her and go away."

"You should go—"

"No. If Winterberry shows up, I'll talk to him here. I promised I'd be here when she woke, and I don't want you around."

"Manners," Alma said.

"I have them. Not using them. Go. Away."

"Oh, very well."

The women dressed Camellia, tucked her between the clean linens, and drew up the comforter. Then they left. Laev set a chair by the bed and reached for Camellia's hand and held it. He wished he'd asked the Mugwort Healers how long she would sleep. He worried.

And he itched to find Feam Kelp.

Brazos, do you think you could track Feam Kelp for me?

Laev's Fam sat straight and proud. *So We can hunt him?*

"Yes." A little of the cat's energy and lust for the hunt infused Laev. He wanted to hurt Kelp.

I can find him. I am a very gifted Cat. I will go now.

Now Mica rose to lick his ear. *I will stay here with my Fam-Woman.*

I will go back to warehouse. Brazos 'ported away.

Laev's scry panel sounded. "T'Hawthorn here," he said.

Guardsman Winterberry, the guard assigned to the First-Families, appeared on the screen. "Greetyou, T'Hawthorn."

"Greetyou. Tell me of the damage to Darjeeling's Teahouse first."

"The only casualty was GraceLord T'Darjeeling. There were a few injuries, quite a few scared patrons."

Laev winced.

The white-haired guard said, "I believe that if D'Darjeeling is generous, she will not lose any patronage, but will gain in publicity."

"Residence?" Laev asked.

"Here, T'Hawthorn."

"Contact the managers of Darjeeling's Teahouse and Darjeeling's HouseHeart. Have them do whatever they believe is necessary to handle any expenses or complaints with regard to the problems at Darjeeling's Teahouse tonight. If Antenn Moss-Blackthorn has arrived in Druida, please request he go to the location of Darjeeling's Teahouse and give me an estimate as to the damage and any construction costs. We will guarantee all payment by Darjeeling."

"Yes, T'Hawthorn," the Residence said.

"Also contact Garrett Primross and have him report."

"I have a formal report from him, T'Hawthorn, that I can forward," said Winterberry.

"Thank you."

"Primross stated he'd been retained by you to investigate the elder male Darjeelings."

"That is correct," Laev said.

"GraceLord T'Darjeeling's death has been ruled accidental."

"How?" Laev asked.

"All the patrons fled the premises. Garrett Primross fired a low-stun warning blazer stream at the man, but it hit a Flaired mirror that freakily magnified the blazer power. T'Darjeeling stepped right in front of the ricocheted stream."

Laev stared at the man. "You're sure that's what happened?"

Winterberry's lips curved in a cool smile. "There were staff witnesses, and we are sure the hit was accidental. I believe scientists and priestesses are already arguing about Flair, mirrors, and trajectories. As well as curses."

"Very odd," was all Laev found to say.

The guard's expression turned serious. "Both bodies are in Death Grove." Winterberry cleared his throat. "Along with a wardrobe from Clovers' Fine Furniture."

Laev winced. He didn't recall such a wardrobe in Camellia's house, obviously her uncle hadn't known it was there, either.

"Several cases of theft seem to be solved by Primross," Winterberry said.

"That's good. Is there anything else you need of me? My Heart-Mate is injured."

Winterberry gazed at him with steady eyes. "Not at the moment. Her brother is being treated at AllClass HealingHall. His Fam is with him."

Laev didn't know much of what had happened, but that could wait. Camellia was stirring.

"I must go. Please send me complete reports on tonight's events."

"I will. When will your lady be available for interviewing?"

"Not tonight. I don't know when she'll be able to talk to you."

"I understand," Winterberry said. His tone was matter-of-fact, but the set of his shoulders showed that he would not be deterred from discovering the entire story.

"Later," Laev said and ended the scry.

Camellia opened her eyes, put her free hand to her head, and moaned, then her gaze fastened on Laev. She sighed, frowned. "I thought I heard . . . How is Senchal?" she asked. Again she touched her head. "It hurts to project telepathically."

Laev could have just relied on Winterberry's report, but instead sent a tendril of a thought toward Senchal, who was now linked to him through Camellia. "Well enough." Laev shrugged. "Not at the HealingHall anymore. I think he's back home."

"And . . ." She licked her lips. "And my father?"

Gently, Laev said, "You know he's in Death Grove."

To his surprise a tear slid down her cheek. Laev moved from the chair to sit on the bed next to her.

"I didn't love him. I didn't even like him," she said.

He was MEAN, good riddance, Mica said.

"Yes, but I wish it would have been different."

You are softheaded from lack of blood. Mica said what Laev hesitated to put into words. Camellia was *not* her usual self if she spared an iota of pity for her father.

The calico cat circled the area near Camellia's feet and curled up.

"Your father's gone onto the wheel of stars," Laev said. He looked into her eyes, nearly silver with the gleam of wetness, and saw his memory of the wheel reflected in her eyes. They'd shared that.

"He wasn't there to meet me or walk with me to the wheel," she said. "Only you were there in the soft dark."

Laev hugged her. "Yes."

One side of her mouth turned down. "I wouldn't have wanted him to be there anyway."

Mica said, *I hope he comes back as a mouse.* The claws in one forepaw flexed.

"I'm not sure it works that way," Camellia said on a quiet breath and wiggled a little in Laev's grasp, so he straightened the pillow under her, smoothed the bedclothes. Her lashes half covered her eyes. But their gazes met. And he knew they contemplated the fate of her father—not one, he, Laev, would care to experience, that was for sure.

At that moment Brazos teleported in, looking bushy from his hair standing on end. His eyes were wild. *I found him. Found the bad man. Let's go chomp him!*

The scent of night, of prey, swirled in the room. Laev's pulse surged, picked up a beat. He rolled his shoulders, shook out his limbs, became aware again of the leather on his body . . . felt fine. And the holsters with pistols on his thighs felt excellent.

"You can't just hunt him down!" Camellia protested.

"He won't ever hurt you again," Laev said.

Thirty-two

Camellia lay there in his bed, in his home where she belonged. She appeared unusually frail, her eyes large in her pale face, lines of strain in her forehead, around her mouth. Oh, he wanted to kill.

He grinned, knowing he showed teeth. "Let's do this thing right, then. Scry panel on." It flickered to life. He strode over to fill the screen. "Contact GrandLady Kelp and the Guildhall."

"Guildhall, here," said a sharp-nosed clerk. He bowed. "Great-Lord T'Hawthorn."

Laev nodded. "Stand by."

A few seconds more passed before a middle-aged woman's face appeared. She was dressed in bedclothes. He didn't care. "I, Huathe Laev T'Hawthorn, cry feud on you, the Kelps, for attempted murder of my HeartMate."

"Wha—?"

"Prepare your warriors."

"Wha—?"

"Cut scry."

"Laev—" Camellia protested.

His grin widened. He pulled his blazer pistols from his holsters, spun them in his hands. "There, nice and tidy." He slanted a wolfish look at her. "Following tradition, here. The feud has begun."

She struggled upward and he placed his blazers on a table, was there with her, his arm under her back—she felt so small and fragile for the first time since their acquaintance—and he translocated pillows to prop behind her.

Mica was dozing near her feet and Laev poked her. "Go get Tiana Mugwort and Glyssa Licorice and bring them here."

Opening a bleary eye, Mica said, *I am helping My FamWoman by staying with her.*

"All right," he said aloud, then snapped, "Brazos, bring Tiana Mugwort and Glyssa Licorice here to watch my lady."

"Yesss!" Brazos grinned and his was full of teeth, too. He vanished.

Laev kissed Camellia's forehead. "You wait here." He checked his blazers. With the excess of adrenaline energy, the anticipation of the hunt to come, he charged them fully. Though he yearned to dial the power up to max force, he set them to medium stun.

"You can't—"

His jaw clenched as he looked at her. "Feam Kelp tried to kill you. Nothing will stop me."

"The other Kelps—"

Laev waved. "The women will be fine unless they get in my way. They're only stupid."

"What!"

"They didn't notice their brother, their cuz was murdering?"

"Maybe they couldn't do anything to stop him."

And Laev knew she was thinking of her father and uncle. "Not the same," he said, feeling his face harden. "You tried. You filed complaints. You let others know they were dangerous. Cave of the Dark Goddess, *the* primary priest and priestess of the Lord and Lady knew your kin were . . . not good men. The Kelps didn't know their relative was bad."

"Maybe they're just gentler than we are."

"Had it easier?" Laev snorted, settled the pistols in his holsters. "Maybe they just didn't want to see what was there."

"Maybe he hid it."

Laev made a chopping motion. "Enough. Now he'll pay. They'll pay."

"Don't kill him."

He gave her a cool stare. "I'll do what needs to be done."

"For your own sake, don't kill him." A pulse of love came from her to him, and he knew that cost her energy, and that she had so little, had come so close to death, made the red mist rising in his mind seethe.

There was the soft sound of air being dislocated, and Laev went to the door between the sitting room and his bedroom. Tiana and Glyssa appeared on the teleportation pad. They both wore identical ritual tunic and trous in shades of blue. Laev figured that Camellia might have one, too. The simple thought grounded him, erased some of the anger. Glyssa's red orange hair seemed as wild as Brazos's.

The cat was prancing around the room, waving his tail. *I found them. I brought them. They can stay with FamWoman while we go. Hunt. Kill.*

"—and that's what happened," Tiana said on a rush of breath.

The women moved to the bed and Camellia.

Glyssa ordered a brighter light and Camellia winced. "Sorry, Cammi. You're sure she's all right?" choked Glyssa.

"Yes, both mother and Artemisia Healed her wounds." Tiana frowned. "She looks a little wan. Loss of blood, perhaps."

We will go. Hunt and kill! Brazos chanted, walking across Laev's feet.

Tiana glanced at Laev. Flinched. He didn't care.

"Perhaps we should take her to Primary HealingHall. Just in case," the priestess offered weakly.

"Residence?" Laev asked.

"Yes, Laev."

"Request T'Heather come here."

"Contacting T'Heather Residence. Done."

"Thank you." Laev considered whether to take a sword or long knife with the pistols. Decided that he was better off with just blazers. He knew he was also better than Kelp in hand-to-hand combat.

"What is going on here?" demanded the retired FirstLevel Healer of Celta.

Laev spared him a glance. "My HeartMate's been wounded." He bowed to the man his FatherSire's age. "I would greatly appreciate if you would examine her."

"My mother and sister are good Healers!" Tiana said.

"I'll just take a look," the Healer, who appeared more like a farmer, soothed. But T'Heather's glance nailed Laev. "Shouldn't be dressed for battle, young Huathe."

"The Kelps have called on their allies," the Residence said. "They have warned Feam."

Laev swore.

"Promise you won't kill him!" Camellia said, but she groaned as T'Heather lifted her.

"You're in good hands," Laev said. "I'll be back soon."

I know where he is. He will not escape us, Brazos said. *We will go and hunt and kill!*

T'Heather sent a fulminating glance at the cat, then switched it to Laev. "Bad as the Hollys."

Laev just grinned again, opened his arms wide for Brazos to jump into, and teleported with him.

They arrived on a quiet street between empty warehouses. Since there was no slap of water against piers, no scent of the ocean, they were in northeastern Druida and not by the docks.

A caged spell-light illuminated a small area and he cursed it under his breath. It would ruin his night vision. Brazos jumped down and slunk to the shadows of the opposite building.

He was here. Let Me look. Do not move, you are too noisy.

Laev stood still, drew his pistols from the holsters. Better he take Feam down at a distance. He could control his anger that much, if the man was a shadow in front of him like a target. If Laev got his hands on the guy, anger, the remnants of fear, might push him too far. He strained his ears, heard nothing.

The leather on his body was beginning to cool as a breeze wrapped around him. He was all too aware that the spring night had slid back to winter instead of forward into summer. His chest was cold. Soon, soon he'd be active.

There was a short yowl of warning, then a hint of rushed air, and he pivoted, got hit by a solid blow to the ribs from a foot, grabbed the ankle, and continued to turn. Man was a terrible fighter.

Feam fell under him. Laev heard the crack of a breaking limb and Feam shouted in pain. Laev smiled. "Got you. You'll never hurt my HeartMate again, you fligger."

Kelp's eyes were wild with pain and fury. Blood showed black on his mouth. He'd bitten his lip through and through. Fury was rising in Laev and he hung on to his temper by threads. This had been too easy. He longed to pound Feam.

Licking a trace of the blood away, Feam grinned up at Laev. "But I will," he rasped. "I will win and I will hurt you and her both. Make you suffer as you made my beautiful Nivea suffer. You have no HeartGift to give that girl." He laughed.

Yes, this man had been Nivea's lover. "Where's my HeartGift?" Laev growled, grabbing hold of Feam's hair, ready to lift his head and slam it into the ground.

"Guardsman Winterberry here," said a cool voice. "I had a trace on you, T'Hawthorn, and was notified the moment you cried feud on the Kelps."

Feam smiled into Laev's eyes. "I don't know. Nivea never gave it to me."

He lied. Laev knew it, but also knew that the man would never tell. That would be Feam's—and Nivea's—last revenge.

Four days later, Camellia sat quietly on a chair in Laev's sacred grove at T'Hawthorn Residence. She lifted her face to the spring sun, welcoming the warmth that would sink into her chilled bones.

She should have been rested and serene. Instead she was on tenterhooks.

A Hawthorn had brought Senchal to a cottage on the estate where he could practice his art without care for gilt for the rest of his life. He'd fallen in clover.

So had she.

The day after her father died, she'd given the Licorices Captain Hoku's documents. His maps of the landing of *Lugh's Spear* and the blueprints of the ship had been sped to the expeditions. Hoku was a hero again. She and Senchal had been confirmed as the Captain's ultimate heirs. Gilt would flow their way, but that was in the future. Now she understood that she had needed to bring solid proof of worth to her marriage.

That didn't change her current circumstances. The way the Family and Residence were treating her made it evident that they had great expectations of her if . . . when she became D'Hawthorn. Enough expectations that would interfere with running her tearooms and business.

Since the horrible night her father and uncle had died, Laev had handled the payoff of her patrons, the reconstruction of her tearoom. She should have fought him but was still recovering from shock.

Psychic shock that her father and uncle had died, violently, both hating her, had pummeled her more than expected. The complete strangeness of living in T'Hawthorn Residence, along with the knowledge that she'd never return to the house that had been her home and sanctuary. If she closed her eyes, she could still see her uncle intermingled with the wardrobe.

Not to mention that her body was still recovering from blood loss. All the Healers from T'Heather down had recommended that transfusions be minimized, so she hadn't had any. Apparently it would take a month to get back to normal.

Laev was treating her like the finest crystal. When she was asked her opinion, he didn't argue, even though she could see from a line or two in his forehead that he didn't agree. They'd had a very polite discussion where he offered to buy into her business and she'd refused. She hadn't been able to read him or sense through their bond whether he'd been disappointed.

All was smooth and surface emotions between them. They'd had no sex—made no love.

She couldn't live like this.

He had given her more than she had him, and it was stupid to think that way, but she couldn't help it. She *must* stop thinking that way.

And she would, when she accomplished one more thing.

Primross had said Laev couldn't find his HeartGift. She could.

Subliminally, she'd felt the emanations from the object from the moment Laev had begun to create it. Like everything else with regard to him, she'd denied, denied, denied—locked it behind that door in her being.

Now it was time to be truly free, to acknowledge her love and move on with her life. So she relaxed deeply, leaning back in the chair and letting the bond to the gift unfurl as a small gilt thread. Her link with Laev was large and strong and golden, more a bridge-cable than a rope.

She waited, tested, considered. Better not to teleport.

A lot of people were being more careful about teleporting.

So she made sure she knew the direction, held it in her mind as she walked back through the beautiful grounds to the awesome Residence. As she passed by the ResidenceDen, she heard Laev lecturing Jasmine Ash, and the girl's light laughter, and smiled. Laev had more friends, more people who respected him than he knew.

If—when—she stayed, she'd live in fabulous rooms surrounded by luxury. He was sharing that.

She was sharing nothing but her problems. Oh, she knew she loved him, that she gave him support and love through their bond, so she was contributing equally in that way to their relationship. But she *needed* to show her love.

She changed clothes from a loose houserobe and into one of her favorite tunic and trous sets of a celadon green that she wore so much it was shabby around the edges despite physical and spell mending.

Do you go out, Camellia? the Residence asked, a hint of worry in its tone.

"That's right."

"Alone? Let me call a guard to accompany—"

"Not this time, Residence, I'm not going anywhere I would need a guard. The feud with the Kelps is over." The women had paid Camellia's Healing bills and Camellia's debt had been cancelled. The Kelps' humiliation had been deep and public.

They were relieved that Laev was satisfied with the criminal mark magically tattooed on Feam, the tracker spell laid on him, and his banishment from Druida and Gael City. Camellia had the idea that Feam would have to work hard in the future. No more support from his Family.

"It's dangerous outside my walls," Residence stated. Camellia stopped and considered that. The Residence beings would be the ultimate agoraphobics, worried about everything outside. How would that affect their personalities? Would they be obsessed about keeping their Family indoors? Right now the Residence was mildly concerned about Camellia's safety. What would happen four hundred years in the future? Had anyone thought of this before? Were people studying it? She should speak to Tiana about it. Residence personality disorders. Huh.

Mica popped through the cat door set in the thick wooden one to Camellia's room. *Are we going somewhere?*

The Residence must have called her.

A surprise, Camellia whispered through the bond that only she and Mica shared.

Goodie! Then the cat looked at the scry panel. *Residence, I will go with My FamWoman. We will be fine.*

They left Camellia's room and walked through the castle.

"Please take one of the gliders," the Residence said.

If she'd been in her own home, she could have walked out and caught a public carrier, but they ran much less here in Noble Country. "All right, one of the new smaller ones." Without Laev's arms or colors.

"It will be in the front. I will notify—"

"I'm on an errand for a surprise *gift* for Laev," Camellia said.

"A *gift* for Laev?" The Residence sounded thrilled. They were in the oldest part of the Residence with small chandeliers. Crystal tinkled.

Camellia was sure that the Residence didn't know she hadn't made a HeartGift for Laev, so that's what it was thinking of.

I am here to accompany you. Brazos swaggered into the hall.

Camellia hadn't really expected that she and Mica could leave without him. She fumbled for the mental connection that she shared with only him. *We are going to get a surprise for Laev.*

Brazos ran around the room in excitement, long hair flowing. Camellia wondered if he was naturally that fast or was using Flair.

She timed her steps to the door to miss him, then opened it. Mica paraded out, tail high and tip gently waving, dignified. Brazos shot out the huge double front doors, yowled at the glider under the portico, and zoomed into the vehicle through the crack as its door rose.

By the time Camellia reached the glider, both cats were sitting in the driver's seat. Even though she didn't actually know how to steer or maneuver the vehicle, Camellia thought she should be there. So she stood with the door open until they noticed.

Let's GO! Brazos insisted, turning his head and nearly glowing yellow green eyes at her.

Ready! Mica wiggled her butt a little as if settling.

"I don't think Fams are allowed in the driver's seat," Camellia said.

Two astonished cat faces, whiskers twitching, eyes round, stared at her.

What! Brazos said.

No! Mica said.

"We can, of course, go back inside and ask the ResidenceLibrary. It would know," Camellia said.

Mica hissed. *I want to go NOW.* She hopped into the passenger seat and lifted her nose to see out the front window, as if she was ready to be chauffeured.

With cat grumbles, Brazos moved to sit beside Mica. Camellia shut the door, circled the glider, opened her door, and slid onto the furrabeast-leather seat. She closed the door. "Webbing on all," she said, and they were encased in physical and spellshield safety webs. She didn't touch the steering bar to pull it out of the console.

"Nav on," she said, blessing the few times she'd ridden to rituals with the Licorices. She was sure she knew enough to get where she was going. She wanted no other witnesses than the FamCats. A square three-dimensional projection appeared. Camellia licked her lips. "Follow voice instruction." She'd just lean back in the comfortable seat and trace the gilt thread to Laev's HeartGift. "Down the gliderway to the gates of T'Hawthorn estate and turn north."

The glider eased forward with little motion.

How fast does it go? asked Brazos.

"I don't know, and we aren't going to find out. You'll have to ride with Laev for that," Camellia said, murmured to herself, "Not through CityCenter, good." She looked at the expectant cats. "This is a treasure hunt."

I can find anything, Brazos boasted.

I can find anything, Mica said at the same time.

"I think I'll be able to find this by myself, but thank you for your help." A few minutes later they were out of the estate and cruising north. "This may take a little while," Camellia warned. The Fams didn't answer; they were busy looking out the window.

Goes faster than feet, Brazos said.

And see more than teleporting, can only teleport to where we've been. Mica rotated her ears. *Seeing lots of new places!*

Camellia figured they were good to ride without complaining for a few more minutes at least.

The city itself was beautiful. Flowers were in full bloom, and there were plenty of parks and groves and Temple grounds that showed furled leaves ready to open. Spring was like a goddess in a green petticoat trailing through Druida.

Some minutes later, the glider wove down one last narrow alley and stopped. The stands descended and they rocked to a halt. Camellia stared at the gray stone building.

What is this? asked Mica.

"I think it's a multiple-living-unit building. Apartments."

Brazos grunted. *Like MidClass Lodge?*

"That's the most well-known place of this type, yes," Camellia said. If she hadn't wanted her own grassyard and garden, she'd have lived in MidClass Lodge.

Not as nice as MidClass Lodge, Mica said, and Camellia realized the cats had explored more of the city than she'd thought.

Door open! commanded Brazos and his door lifted. Camellia pushed hers up, too, stepped out. Silence lived in the alley. She said a couplet that encased the glider in a spellshield, then walked up to the building, up the stairs, to see a stone lintel with a Hawthorn branch above it. A sudden premonition shivered through her. She would bet that Laev owned this building.

And she would bet that Nivea had known that.

During his short trial, Feam Kelp had made wild accusations against Laev . . . that he had neglected his wife, had let her die alone. The Residence had sent holospheres of the last illness of Nivea Sunflower Hawthorn that contradicted this, but Feam hadn't believed them. He accepted nothing but his own views as the truth. The fact that Feam had been Nivea's lover had not been openly stated, but it was obvious.

Now Camellia was going to find the secret meeting place between Feam and Nivea, a lover's bower, and it filled her with dread.

She didn't want to see a place where infidelity had flourished. Where two people amused themselves at Laev's, and the Hawthorns', expense.

But she wanted Laev's HeartGift and there was only one way to get it.

Thirty-three

The cats had already mewed the standard spellshield down, the door open, and were standing in the small atrium sniffing lustily.

Mice! said Brazos, and he took off.

Mica glanced at Camellia, down the hallway where Brazos had disappeared. Camellia understood, if given a choice of hunting mice or a treasure, the cats would choose mice. "Go."

Mica projected, *Wait for Me!* to Brazos.

The gilded cord led up the stairs. At the top there were only two doors, so the apartments were large. Her senses tugged her to the left. The hallway was tinted a dark gold with brown trim, Nivea's colors.

When she reached the sturdy oak door, she laid her fingertips on the wood, *knew* Laev's HeartGift was beyond. No fancy spells shielded the door. She opened it to a sunny yellow room furnished with luxurious pieces that she would never have been able to afford. Neither would have Feam. Furrabeast leather of the finest grain. Carpets straight from Chinju, and not one, but stacked atop each other for the softest of cushions for the feet. The art on the walls had Camellia's eyebrows raising . . . holographic sex-party scenes.

She slipped inside, pulled the door shut after her. How much would seeing this hurt Laev? She didn't know. Her first impulse was to take care of clearing the whole place out without telling him. Would that be sparing him or not?

The bedroom was tinted peach that would have complemented
Nivea. The bed was elegant cherry and draped with gauze. Very
pretty, but Camellia's nostrils pinched at the thought of what must
have occurred there. The breaking of marriage vows.

Yes, she was judgmental, so what? She firmly believed that if
vows were made, they should not be broken, otherwise why make
them in the first place?

She could call the Clovers and have them dismantle the apart-
ment. Marching to the right corner, she threw open the door and
breath stopped in her throat. This room was a shrine to Nivea.

In each corner were holos projection of Nivea in a specific
costume . . . summer, autumn, winter, spring, smiling and waving.

Camellia shuddered. Each wall held a holo painting of the dead
woman, and as Camellia narrowed her eyes, she saw the sheen of
tiny glass bubbles in the wall that meant at least one mural was
programmed into it. "Show mural."

A naked Nivea plunged up and down on an equally bare Feam.
"Stop! Erase!" The action halted and sickness swirled up Camellia's
throat. "Erase!" Nothing happened. "E-rase!" There came a hum
and the mural faded. Camellia found herself panting and leaning
against the doorjamb. No one should have seen that. She did a little
cleansing spell for the room, a calming spell for herself.

She felt a throbbing from Laev's HeartGift. It was near.

Jewelry was set out on an altar . . . cuff bracelets rather like
marriage bands, long dangling earrings of golden topaz or yellow
diamonds, an amber drop necklace. Again, because of the quality
and value, Camellia was pretty sure that Laev had given the gems to
Nivea. What should Camellia do with them?

Her mouth dried.

There was a tall, narrow, triangular cupboard in the corner for
ritual tools and holiday altar dressings. The piece was dusty, the
wood dry and slightly warped. Near the top, she sensed Laev's
HeartGift.

Everything else in the room and all other thoughts faded. The
HeartGift itself was shielded. If not, the pure sensuality imbued in

the piece when it was made would draw Camellia—as Laev's HeartMate—into mind sex with him.

She tried not to think about when it was made . . . the night after they'd met in JudgementGrove when he was seventeen.

Laev's Passage had sparked that day, Camellia's triumph at winning the case had spiraled wide to snare him, to ignite HeartMate vibrations between them . . . which he'd attributed to coming from Nivea.

Camellia brushed the air before her face as if waving away bitemites. No more thinking of that. No more regrets. The past was now and ever would be in the past. She had a strong hold on the future if she had the courage to grab it. And, finally, she'd summoned that courage.

She focused on the door to the cabinet, placed her fingers against it, and felt shielding Flair. Frowned. Was the door trapped to explode or destroy if she tampered with it? She should call in an expert. Or contact Laev through their link.

But that wasn't the way she wanted to do this. She wanted to bring his HeartGift to him as . . . proof that she loved him? As price of forgiveness? Neither of which he demanded. Both of which were self-serving. She put a hand between her breasts. Self-serving or not, this action was something she needed to do to be right with herself, and that was enough damn analysis.

She closed her eyes and felt the HeartGift. It warmed her with sexy desire for Laev, but she ignored that. She felt the mass of it, the general shape, the subtle throb of *its* shielding. A headache began to gnaw, but she pressed on. Yes, she knew the shape, knew the shield, knew the mass. It was tilted, jammed on the smallest top shelf near the ceiling. She . . . could . . . shift . . . it.

The cupboard door buzzed ominously just under her physical hearing. She leapt across the room. The door exploded out.

Camellia dived for the floor, but no splinters hit her. After a few gasping breaths, she tilted her head so an eye was above her protective arm. Pieces of the wooden door were slowly drifting to the floor. Objects on the shelves rocked but did not fall.

Nothing in the room was harmed.

She caught her breath. Of course. Feam Kelp would not have wanted anything in the room to be harmed. If a person—

What happened! both Mica and Brazos screeched mentally.

Camellia amended her thought. If a being, person or Fam, had tried to physically open the door, or was close, within about sixty centimeters, the blast would have been fatal. But she'd survived.

Two cat bodies hopped on her heavily. Mica ran along her legs and over her butt to sit beside Camellia's head, touch noses, and lick her face.

Brazos, heavier, bounded along her until he sat in front of the corner cupboard staring up at it and curling his tongue in that extra sense cats had. *Thing at top smells very strongly of Laev.* He turned an approving gaze on Camellia, still stretched out on the floor. *You found it!* Then the cat squinted his eyes at her. Glanced around and seemed to notice the shards of the door. *Messy about it.*

Mica glared at Brazos. *My FamWoman is wonderful.*

With a grunt, Camellia levered herself up. The door fragments hadn't harmed her, but she'd felt a concussion of Flair and would have bruises from her dive.

Mica yowled, staring at the hologram of Nivea as the Queen of the May. *What is SHE doing here? Don't like, don't like, no!*

Brazos was at the altar, nosing the jewelry. *This smells of Laev, too, but mostly of bad-smell woman and scary madman.*

"Nivea and Feam, right," Camellia said, shaking out her limbs and saying a small spell to clean grimy smudges off her clothes. Tilting her head, she extended her senses to see if anyone in the area was interested in what had just happened. She felt only a few people, went to the window, pushed aside the drape, and looked out and saw no one. "It would have been a long time before this place was found."

No reason for Laev to see these rooms.

This place is BAD, Brazos said, and the cats trotted away. Then shredding noises came from the direction of the bedroom. Linens and the bedsponge.

Camellia found an old-fashioned scrybowl and called T'Hawthorn Residence. It confirmed that the Hawthorns owned the building and was outraged that Nivea and Feam had been using the place as a clandestine assignation hideaway. Camellia insisted on handling the refurbishing of the place herself, and won her first argument with the entity.

She translocated the jewelry to the T'Hawthorn Residence cache and was informed that Laev *had* purchased it for Nivea. The Residence ended the scry by informing her that Laev was concerned she wasn't there.

She'd delayed as much as she could. Now she had to face the HeartGift. She walked slowly to the cupboard and looked up at the top shelf, just within reach.

Swallowing hard, she just stared at the sculpture. She had no idea Laev was so talented from the small cat he'd done as a youngster and the image of the Lord he'd given her. Irritation flushed through her. The man *must* have a studio, and had he shown it to her? No, in that way he hadn't revealed all of his secrets, either.

Time for them to get over their problems. They were both mature adults. So they'd been hurt. Everyone in the world had been hurt. That was the past, and before them was the unlimited future. She would take that first step, but she'd make sure that he was with her. She felt a little weak, the future before them was so grand and dizzying.

The first step, though, was to take his HeartGift to him. The last time she'd glimpsed it had been at the Salvage Ball years ago. She reached up and lifted it down with both hands. Despite the spellshield on it, sizzles of lust ignited within her. She put that aside to concentrate on the beauty of the statue. The Lady and Lord had arms around each other's waists and were stepping forward as if about to tread a dance pattern. In his free hand, the Lord carried panpipes. The arm of the Lady that was not clasping the Lord was flung out as if in joy, there were tiny cymbals on each of her fingers. Her filmy-appearing skirt whirled around her. The Lord was bare-chested and dressed in tight trous. He gazed down at his consort and partner with tenderness and love. The Lady's expression was mischievous, but her arm was tight around his waist and they would have to step together to the measures of the music or fall.

Camellia had been out of step with Laev from her thirteenth year. Now was the time to remedy it. She'd give him the statue, and hope . . . that she and he would step forward into the future together. And if they stumbled, they would depend on each other.

She could do that now.

Recalling that there were lovely padded boxes sold at Darjeeling's HouseHeart, she translocated one and put the sculpture inside. A perfect gift for Laev.

A septhour later she walked into T'Hawthorn Residence with Mica and Brazos.

The glider ride had given her time to fret about offering the gift to Laev. She didn't think that he would reject her, not after all the care he'd taken with her . . . but they hadn't made love, not even had telepathic sex, since her injury.

But she didn't know for sure whether he'd spurn her. Her nerves felt like ants crawling over her skin.

Brazos and Mica left to have a snack and tell Black Pierre all about their adventure. Camellia climbed the steps to the wing that held the Master- and MistrysSuite, then pushed through the heavy security doors.

The door of the MasterSuite opened and she heard male voices. Just like when she'd first met him when this whole thing started. A frisson of Flair twined up and down her spine.

She knew Laev's voice now, so well, the other man she didn't recognize.

Then Laev was coming toward her, as he always came toward her.

So was a man who appeared slightly younger than he, shorter and leaner, with serious eyes but a quick and charming smile. Camellia noted that though the man was dressed as a noble, he didn't seem to have FirstFamily features and she felt less wary of him.

As they walked through a shaft of sunlight slanting in from windows, she stopped, speechless, as Laev strode toward her. Somehow, when she hadn't noticed, he'd come into his own. No one looking at him would believe he'd ever been less than a self-assured, never-suffering FirstFamilies noble. His aura was one of supreme confidence.

Laev's smile was only a twitch of the lips. "You've returned. I wish you wouldn't do too much." He kissed her gently on the mouth.

"I'm not doing too much." She tried to keep her tones even. "I'm not doing much at all."

Laev's brows rose and he gestured to the man walking with him. "Antenn, my lady, Camellia D'Darjeeling. Camellia, my friend, Antenn Moss-Blackthorn. He's been helping me with the design of the new MasterSuite and MistrysSuite." Another smile from Laev. "You don't have to make any decisions right now, dearest."

She didn't look at Laev. It was true she'd been skittish about planning what would become her suite. But that was over. "Greetyou," she said politely to Antenn.

Antenn bowed. "Greetyou."

Laev shifted, seemed to notice the box she carried for the first time. "What's that?"

"A gift for you."

His eyes widened. He took a long pace back. A line of red edged his cheekbones. "I don't think we—you—I don't think—"

She turned to stare at Antenn. "Can you consult with Laev some other time?"

He grinned. "Oh, yeah. I'll be happy to go away." He showed her a large record sphere. "I'll just take this down to your Residence-Den, Laev."

"Lock and shield the doors behind you," she said.

Antenn clapped Laev on the shoulder, nodded at her, and was out of the doors in two seconds.

"Now, Laev."

He raised his hands, but his pupil-dilated stare was on the box. "You found my HeartGift."

"Yes."

"I don't want to hurt you." He was beginning to pant. He didn't seem to notice that he'd run his fingers down the front tab of his shirt, opening it.

The bond between them was wide and his lust began to affect her. Heat pooled inside, her thighs loosened, she was flushing, too, as her body began to ready itself for him. Need, *craving*, slid into her blood.

She wanted his arms around her, his weight atop her. Wanted their breaths and heartbeats and emotions to mingle. Their bodies to rub together, to plunge together, to soar together.

Laev wasn't backing away now, appeared to be stuck to the floor, was watching her every move, and she realized she'd opened her tunic, too. She only wore a breastband beneath.

What had he said? Oh, he was afraid he'd hurt her.

"You could never hurt me," she replied, her tongue thick. Her mouth, too, needed his taste.

She walked toward him, holding out the gift.

"Bigger'n you," he rasped.

"Mmmm." She shivered with anticipation.

He groaned.

She panted, then the hint of an idea surfaced in her mind. The HeartGift! She was holding it, and it was working on them. That was good.

But she had to give it to him, had to appreciate his talent—his sculpting Flair—with him. Had to tell him how beautiful the statue was.

She fumbled for the box opening, pulled up the latch. The box fell away and she was left holding the sculpture. But she didn't look at it, was more focused on Laev, the man who'd made it, than the lovely piece. He'd begun to perspire and there was a sheen on his firm chest. She knew what he'd taste like if she kissed him there, licked him there, and she swallowed. Yes, she needed that.

There was a half-round table against the wall. Blindly she set the HeartGift on the table and walked up to Laev, skimmed her fingers up his chest. She kissed his beaded nipple, and he groaned, "Camellia!"

His control broke and he spun her against the wall. He ripped off her trous and pantlettes and plunged into her.

She screamed with the pleasure of it.

Then their bodies moved together and ecstasy surged from him to her, through her and back to him. Flair sparked around them, enfolding them. Infusing them.

Before her mind's eye, Camellia saw the coiled, pulsing golden cable of the HeartBond.

She didn't know which of them touched it, sent it to the other. Both. At the same time. Maybe.

The HeartBond wrapped around them, merging them, and their emotions, their love blew open all the connections between them.

Love.

Even more fabulous than the quaking orgasm that rocked them and whirled them together through galaxies.

When she came to her senses again, her mouth was against Laev's neck and the taste of him sank into her very bones, never to be forgotten. Always to be cherished.

Her hands were on his damp back, and she stroked him. He shuddered again, pushed, and aftershocks went through her, her legs tightened around his lean hips. Thought vanished again.

A few minutes later she became aware that their ragged breathing sounded loud in the empty corridor. Their hearts beat together. The wall was hard behind her.

She'd never had such sex. Never had such *loving.* It had been hot and fast and violent. She thought she got a couple more bruises. Wonderful.

"Fabulous," she whispered.

"Gimme minute," Laev said. Then his hands went to her rump, he angled away from the wall. "Bed. Need bed. Def'nitely bed!"

"Privacy shields!" She frowned in concentration as she set them around the entire floor, especially the doors.

By the time she was done, they *were* in bed. Under the linens even, with Laev on his back and her on her side, her head against his chest.

His heart still raced in the same time as her own.

He breathed heavily a few times, then said, "That wasn't the way I'd planned on initiating the HeartBond."

She laughed. "It worked. And I thought I'd init-initiated the Bond."

"We're together now. It's done."

"That's right." She propped herself up to look at him. "Do you think I regret being HeartBound to you? I don't." She swallowed, got enough spit in her mouth and courage to say the words. "I love you, Laev Hawthorn."

His smile was the best she'd ever seen from him. "I love you, Camellia Darjeeling Hawthorn."

She chuckled and subsided back onto his chest.

Let Us IN! The cats yowled together, mentally and physically.

Laev drew the covers over them. A wave of his hand and she saw a flash of her clothes zooming into the cleanser.

"Are you ready for them?" his voice rumbled under her ear.

She heaved a sigh, but smiled. "If we must."

"I think so." The cat screeching had become near unbearable.

"All right."

Laev dropped the shields and suddenly there were cats flying through the room, as if they'd been battering the shield physically and with Flair. He lifted a hand and caught Brazos. Camellia used her Flair to snatch Mica close.

"Eeeeee!" Mica panted as she set her claws into the comforter.

Brazos was wheezing as if he couldn't catch his breath, tail whipping.

"I expect you two to respect all privacy shields when they are in place," Laev said.

Neither of the cats said anything.

"Or there will be consequences," Laev continued. He raised his brows at Camellia.

She cleared her throat. "Your own private spaces will be down-sized. Closets are excellent for cats—"

I promise to respect the privacy shields! Mica said, giving in first.

"Collars might also be affected," Laev said.

I promise to respect privacy shields, Brazos rumbled mentally along with a purr, smiling ingratiatingly.

Mica purred, too. *I have My FamWoman and My Brazos.*

I have My FamMan and My Mica, Brazos agreed.

"I have my Brazos and my beloved HeartMate Camellia." Laev's arm tightened around her.

Camellia laughed, rubbed her cheek against Laev's chest, and completed the round. "I have my Mica and my beloved HeartMate Laev." She drew in a breath. "And we have the Family and the Residence. We all belong to each other."

"Yes." Laev kissed her.